Ben Watkins

Complete Choctaw Definer

English with Choctaw Definition

Ben Watkins

Complete Choctaw Definer
English with Choctaw Definition

ISBN/EAN: 9783337401160

Printed in Europe, USA, Canada, Australia, Japan

Cover: Foto ©Andreas Hilbeck / pixelio.de

More available books at **www.hansebooks.com**

COMPLETE

CHOCTAW  DEFINER,

ENGLISH WITH CHOCTAW DEFINITION.

————BY————

BEN WATKINS.

FIRST EDITION 5,000 COPIES.

VAN BUREN, ARK.:
J. W. BALDWIN, PRINTER & PUBLISHER
1892.

PREFACE.

THE purpose of this volume is to supply the great demand for a complete Choctaw definer. We have given the subject our undivided attention for many years, and when completed, submitted it to the best experts of the Choctaw Nation, who pronounce it as nearly perfect as the different idioms of the two languages will permit.

There has been no effort to make a literary display—the object being to make the English as simple as possible.

Very Respectfully,

THE AUTHOR.

CHOCTAW ALPHABET.

LETTERS.	NAMES.	SOUNDS.
A, a	ah.	as a in father.
Ai, ai	i.	a dipthong, as i in pine.
Au, au	ow.	a dipthong, as ow in now.
B, b	be.	
Ch, ch	che.	
E, e	a	as a in made; as e in they.
F, f	fe	
H, h	he.	
Hl, hl	thle	{ aspirated before a consonant; written lh, thle also.
I, i.	e.	as i in pique and in pit.
K, k.	ke.	
L, l.	le.	
M, m.	me.	
N, n.	ne.	
O, o.	o.	as o in note..
P, p.	pe.	
S, s	se.	
Sh, sh.	she.	
T, t.	te.	
U, u.	oo.	as oo in wool, or u in full.
U, u.	uh.	as u in tub.
W, w.	we.	
Y. y.	ye.	

NASALS:

A a   I i   O o   U u

A COMPLETE

CHOCTAW DEFINER.

A—ho—ha, an indefinite article after a noun in the objective case, with h and y, according to the ending of the preceding word. Sometimes o is used: Wako pisali, I see a cow; ohoyo ho pisali, I see a woman; ulla yo pisali, I see a child.

Abandoned. *a.* Akshoh; abandonment, *n.* aksho; to abandon, . ., akshochih.

Abase. *v. .* Akkulusichih, kalaksichih, makalichih; abased, makali; abasement, makali.

Abash. *v.* Hofahyalih; abashed, hofahya.

Abate. *v.* Halatah shiollih, habollih, habofah; to cause to abate. habohlichih, habofcchih; abated, shiotah habofah; as water, shippah; one that causes the abatement, habohlichi.

Abate, *v.* Habofah; plural haboblih, abatement, habohlib; to cause to abate, *v.* habohlich, one that causes the abatement, habolich.

Abdomen, . Ikfoka, iffoka, takoba; a large abdomen, or belly, behenna; to extend the abdomen, behenuechih; my abdomen, sekfoka.

Abet, *v.* Apela, apelcchi; to continue to help or abet, apela hanchi.

Abhor, *v.* Inukkillih, ik ahnincho.

Abide, *v.* Ai anta; plural aiasha, antah, ahantah.

Abode, *n.* Ai anta, aiahanta; an abode, chukka.

Abolish, *v. t.* Issechih, akshuchih; abolished, akshot taha.

Abominable, . Ik achukmo, okpulo fehna.

Abominate, *.* Inukkillih, ikahnincho

Aboriginal, . Tikba, ummona.

Aborigines, *n. pl.,* Okla ai uttahpi.

Abortion, . Ushi im okpulo.

About, *prep.* Beljka; . to turn about, folotoah. filimoah turn about, folotoah; to turn about, (plural,) fitimosh; about this time, himak foka.

Above, *p. .* Pakna, paknaka; just above, paknaka uba; high above, uba chaha, uba pillah: land above, uba yakni.

Abroad, *ad .* Hainaka; gone abroad, iksho, kunia.

Absent, *v.* Kunia, iksho, ikhaiako.

Absorb, *v.* Ishko kunia; absorbed at, akcuiah.

Abstain, *v.* Issa; to abstain from, hullochih one who abstains, hullochi.

Abuse, *. .* Amihae hih; abusing cruelly, ilbeshechi-ilbushachih; to abuse, okpunih nukhaklochih, ilbeshallih; abused, okpulo ilbushah, nukhakloh.

Abyss, *n.* ahofobi ahofobika, ahofombika.

Academy, *n.* holisso ai ithana chito.

Accept, *v. t* Ishih, ai okpechih. habenah.

Accident, *n* Nabueli; to have an accident happen to, ishkunnapa; to cause to meet with an accident, ishkunnapu chi; accidental, ishkunnapa.

Accommodate, *v. t* Im atahli; accommodated, im ulhtaha.

Accompany, *. .* Auant aya, iba takla; to keep company with, ahinnah; to put another one as company, ahinnochih.

Account, *v. t* Ahpinchih, hotinah, anolih; accounted, holhtina annu; on account of, hokak ocha. hokak oua, houa, hocha.

Accuse, *v. t* Anumpah onochih achokushpalih; accused, anumpa ouutulah achokushpah; to falsely accuse, aholabi.

Accustom, *v. t.* Abychih; to cause an animal to be accustomed to a place, achayuchi; to be accustomed to, ai imomachih.

Ache, *v.* Hotupah, kommichih; to cause to ache, hottupachih, hottuplih; I am aching, sakommichih, settopah, sahottupah.

Acid, *.* Hawushko, hominchi; to become acid, homi; to cause to acidity, hawushkochih.

Acquaintance, *v.* Itikbana, hatak ikbana.

Acquire, *v. t* Ahauchi, ishi, ahayuchi.

Across, *prep.* Tunnep; to lay across, ai okhannilli; laid across, ai okhannayah; being across, ai okhauah.

Act, *v. t* Akaniohmi, akaniobmichi; to act with, ibacheffah ibainchuffah; to act wickedly or dishonest, isht akanohmi; to act with close intimacy, ittachukolbih; an act passed. ulhpisah.

Acting, *un* Yummohmi; acting together, ittibahfokah.

Action, *n.* Akaniohmi.

Acute, *v.* Chasah, haluppa.

Add, *v. t* Achakalichi iba foki, *yl.* iba kahli; added, ibulhkaha, iba foka, ulhchaka; to add more to, ibahkahli, ibani; more added to, ibalhkaha, ibani.

Adder, *n.* Hahta, hahwush.

Address, *v.* Anumpa isht hika; a short address, anumpa kolofa, anumpa tillofah, anumpa tillofasih.

Adequate, Alauih, alauichih.

Adhere, Ulbo, hahanli asitia ai ulboh; to adhere to, alapah alapalinchi; to cause to adhere, ai ulbuchih, ittai akmochi, ittakmochi, ittihalullih, ai ulbuchi; adhered to, ittulboh; adhereing, shinushbi.

Adjourn, Ubanublichi, tisholih, tisholichi; adjourned, ubanopa tisholi.

Adjournment, . Tisholi.

Administer, Nan im apesa. (More properly to administer justice.)

Admire, anuksitah, unuksita; to admire intensely, annuksittiah.

Adoption, Ulla toba, ushi isht atoba, atapshon.

Adorable, Ai okpcchi ulhpesa.

Adore, *v t* Ai okpuchih.

Adorn, *v t* Aiuklichi, aiuklichichi, shemuchi; adorned, Shema ai okli.

Adult, Asonn, hatak asunochi.

Adulteress, Hatak i haklo.

Adultery, Hatak i haklo, itin lumaka; femgon haniu, hanlu toba; to commit adultery, itin lumaka.

Advance, *n.* Achakalichi; to advance in file, baiuliit maya; advancing, i hiyah, .. i shalichi, ishali maya, i shaht ia.

Advertise, *t.* Otunuchi; advertised, otuni, haklochi haklo; advertised.

Advise, *v i.* Nan i miha, im anumpuli, alumih, alumichi.

Advocate, Isht anumpulih.

Adz, Peni isht chaya, peni isht kula.

Affection, Im anukfila achukma, chukush achukma.

Affirm, *v.* Anoli; affirmed, annoa.

Afflict, *v.* Ibushah; afflicted, ilbusha, nan ikauihmi; I am afflicted unto death, siaiokpuloh, siaiokpulokah, siabckah; affliction, ai ilbusha.

Affright, Nukshobli, nukhlakushli; affrighted, nukshopa nukhlakancha.

Affront, Chukush hotupah; affronted, chukush hotopa.

Aforesaid, Chash, chash inli, chash akinli, ash, kash, yash, chash kint; this refers to remote time, yummuk o achili chashkint; that is what I said loug ago, the aforesaid, chash o, implying remote past time which is already known or seen; hatak oh chash o miha li; the aforesaid man I mean; it is the aforesaid, chash oka, chash ocha, chash ona, chash okak osh, chash akuto, chash oke, chash osh, chash okut, chash okhuno; even the aforesaid, chash oh kia; aforesaid, hash, some definite action recent and known, the aforesaid, hash ona, hash o, hash kia, hash ocha, hash oka, hash okak o, hash okak ocha, hash okak anto, hash okak osh, hash oke, hash oh kia, hash okuno, hash okuto hash okut, hash osh, hash uto.

Afraid, Nukshopa, nukwia, anukwia; to be afraid of me, gnukwiah; to be afraid of, innkwiah; I am afraid, sanukshopah sanukwiah.

African, Hatak lusa, nipi lusa, Afilka hatak.

After, Hayo, haya, himmak; after all, polaka.

Afternoon, *n.* Tabokoli ontia, okuttaha.

Afterward, *a v.* I himmak, i bimmaka, haya hayo.

Again, *a ..* Anonti; *in j.* Again! What! Again; unnonti, psbaw: to set or act against, ichapolih; to cause to act against, ichapolichi.

Age, Afumi kanohmi; middle or passed middle age, kawashuchi; aged or old, kamussull. sipukni; to make old, sipuknichi; I am old, susipokni.

Agent, Isht im utta.

Aggravate, *v. t.* Aiyabachi; aggravated, ai yebbih.

Agree, Ai ibachofa anumpa ittim apesah; shall or will agree, ai okpancha hinla; agreed, anumpa itim apesah; an agreement, anumpa ittim ulhpisa; agreeable, ulhpesa yukpa.

Ague, Yunha hochukwa, hochukwa yanha; aguish, hochukwachi.

Ah, *interj.* Anne, ikkike.

Aid, *v t* Apela, ap luchi; his aid, anumpa im eshi; nid de camp, anumpeshi.

Aim, *v.* Anumpisachi (i. e. to take aim) *v. t.* atokoli; aimed, atokon.

Air, Mahli fiopa, ea. atmosfia; to air, hufkah; aired, holufkah; not aired, ikhofkoh.

Alarm *v.* Anukhlakushli, nukshobli; alarmed, anukhlakancha nukshopa.

Alas, Okokko! yakoke! (fem. gen. aiena!) bush, hushba! chcha huk or hok.

Albumen, Akak ushi i tohbc, akak ushi i wulaha, akak ushi i wulukuchi.

Alder *n* Itukawiloha.

Alight, *v.* Fobopah.

Alike *adv* Iti holiba, ittiobah.

Alive, *a.* Okehuya: I am alive, saiokebaya.

All, Bano, illa, beka, bicka, moma, uha okluha, ai okluha, puttn. moyuma; pro lst. per. plu. cho, e, mouinchit momiut; to make all, banochi; all together, ittai oklubut; all entirely, kummohmi; after all, polaka.

Allay, *v.* Nuktalali, hopohluchi, hopohlcli; allayed, nuktola; hopohla; to allay, chulosuchi; allayed, chulosah.

Allege, *v.* Miha.

Alligator, Hachunchuba.

Allot, *v.* Ima, apesa.

Allow, *v.* Ima yohmi ahni.

Allspice, Tishi homi lusa holba, nau uni balama.

Allure, *v.* Apakummi; allured, apakuma.

Ally, Apela.

Almanac, Hushi nittak isbt ikhunna.

Almost, *v.* Ahe, ghesi, ngha; almost happen, ahetoh.

Alms, Naholhpila, na hulbina; to give alms, na habenuchi.

Aloes, Ishkot hlopulli, alos.

Alone, *n.* Akbano, akbat, bano, beka, bicka, kakbano, yakbano, hakbano; I am alone, salapuchuffah; he is gone alone, ilup akbat ia.

Alphabet, Unmoua, holisso ai isht ia, alfibit.

Already, *v.* Mashko.

Also, *v.* Akinli, akkia, hokak kia, aiena. anonti, mak kia, yak kia, hinla, mut.

Altar, Aholuknil, uba topa holba, uba tola alta.

Alter, *v.* Ai inluchi inla, ai inla, inla tobu:

altered, ai inlah.
Altercate, Anumpa itti launchi; altercation anumpa itti lawa.
Alternate, . Ittelhtoboah, ulhtobah.
Although, . Atuk kia, kia, ak kia, hokak osh, hokak ot, hohkia.
Altitude, v. Chaha.
Altogether, v. Bano.
Alum, . Tuli holuya.
Always, . Billa, beka, bieka, chatuk, chukumo, chokosh; always so, aiemoma; to be always, billiah; it is, or always was, so, chokumo.
Amaze, v. . Nukhlakushli; amazed, nukhlakancha.
Amen, v. Ikabli, ik yohmi, ik yumohmi.
American, . Miliki hatak, miliki okla.
Amiable, a. Hulhpashi.
Among, in Takla.
Amorous, Ai yushkummi.
Amputate, v. Bushlit tuplih.
Amuse, v. . Yukpali, haksichi; amused, yakpa haksi.
An, Ho; (see A)
Ancestor, . Hatak in tikba, hatak in tikba.
Ancient, a. Tikba, tikba, chashpo.
And, j. Ahma, aiena, anonti, cha, micha, mihma, mikma, mihmet, mikmut t.
And-i-ron, . Luak in tikeli, luak ituksita.
Angel, v. Uba, hatak, enchil.
Anger, v. Hushaya, nukhobila; angry, nuk hobilah; to cause anger, nukhobiluchi.
Animal, v. Nampoa, nau ulhpoa.
Animate, v. . Yinintuchi, okchali, chilituchi; animated, yiminta, okcha, chilitah; animation, isht awiha.
Ankle, v. Iyi imoksak, iyimosak.
Annex, v. . Uchakuli; annexed, uchaka.
Annoy, v. Ataklumnichi, atcklumnii, anumpulichi; annoyed, ataklama.
Annuity, v. Afemmikma ilhpita, ilhpita.
Annul, v. . Issuchi, akshuchi; annulled, issa, aksho.
Anodyne, . Nusechi, ishkot nusi.
Anoint, v. . Ahammih, bila, ahammichi fokkichih; anointed, ahama bila ahama; to anoint frequently, fokkihinchi; to anoint at last, fokki chi.
Anonymous, . Hohchifo iksho.
Another, . Inla, (more properly another one,) to take the place of another, ulhtobah.
Answer, v. f. Anumpa i falummichi, afulummichi; answered, anumpa i falama, afutoma; it will answer, ulhpesa; an answer, anumpa falama; answering, anumpa falummihinchi; answers, anumpa falumoa; to answer, falummichit anumpuli.
Ant, . Shukuni.
Anthem, n. Ataloa, uba isht talon, holisso ataloa.
Antiquity, n. Hatak tikba.
Antler, n. Issi lupish.
Anvil, n. Tulaboa, tuli chito.
Anxious, a. Komunta, bunna, ahni fehna.
Any, . Kia; any how, akinli; have you not any, ikchim iksho ho? not given you any, ikchemo.
Apart, Ittifalummi; to tear apart, ittahlilafah, ittahliluffih, ittahlilalih; to come apart, itahakofah; too far apart, yauahah to make a distance, a distance apart, yan-

ahuchi.
Ape. Hatak shaui, hatak shaui chito; to ape, hobachi.
Apoplexy, . Haiochi.
Apostasy, . Uba anumpa i filemmi.
Apostatize, v. Uba anumpa issa.
Apostle. . Ubanumpeshi, ubanumpeshi ummoma, apostil; the Apostle of Jesus, Chisos im ubanumpeshi.
Apparently, . Chinih.
Apparition, . Chukkishikanchik, kahshi kanchak.
Appeal, v. Kanullichi, uchakuli, im issa.
Appear, v. Haiyakah; to appear this way, et haiyakah; to appear to be so, chinih; appears to be, ai ahoba; appearance, hainkah; the place of appearing, akuchaka.
Appease. v. Nuktalali, nanaiyuchi, chulosuchi, chulosali, hopohluchi; appeased, nuktula, nanaiya, chulosah hopoblah.
Applaud, v. Ai okpuchi, ahuinchi.
Apple . Takou chito, takon misufa; thorn apple or Jameson weed, hlachowaikhish, ikhish kosoma; custard apple, umbi.
Appoint, v. Atokoli, apesa; appointed ulhtokh ulhpisa.
Appointee, . Hatak ulhtoka; appointment, ulhtoka.
Apprentice; v. Toksuli ithana im ulhpisa.
Approach. v. Bilinchi, minti, ula hosi, i bilinchi, im ula, im ona, okanalih, bilinkuchi; to cause to approach, akanulichi.
Approve, v. Ome achi, ulhpesa ahni, ai okpuchi ahuinchi; may or can approve, ai okpuchu hinla; does not approve, ai okpuchi keyu; will not approve, ai okpuchu ho keyu.
Approximate, v. Akanuli; to cause to approximate, akanullichi.
April . Eplil.
Apron . Tikba takali.
Arbiter . Hatak nan olubichi.
Arbor, . Hoshontika.
Arch angel . Enchil i miko, enchil puta i miko.
Ardent, . Achunnachi, chilita, homi, yiminta achilita; arduous, ahcbiba, kullo, palummi.
Argument; . Anumpa isht ittichapa.
Arise, v. Wakaya, tani; to arise or increase from, isht achaka.
Arithmetic. . Na holhtina holisso.
Arithmetician, n. Na holhtina holisso impunna.
Ark, . Peni itombi.
Arm, . Shakba; to arm, na nalupa atahli; armed, na halupa im ulhtaha; arm between the wrist and elbow, ibbak usto; to hold me in arms, sasholih; my arm, sashakba; arm pit, hatampi.
Around, . Folota; to turn around, folullichi afulota.
Arrange, v. Apoksiachi; arranged, apoksia; to arrange in order, hiohlichi.
Array, v. Shemuchi, atahli; arrayed, shema, ulhtaha.
Arrearage, v. Ahoka takali.
Arrest, v. Takchi, yukachi; arrested, yuka.
Arrive, v. Haiyaka minti ona; to arrive with, ibai onah; to arrive in a row or line, baiullit ula; not arrived, ik aionah ik haiyako.
Arrogant, . Ilefenuchi.

Arrow, *n.* Nakfohko, shumo, shomotti.
Artery, *n.* Chukush issish į hina, akshish chito iniskola.
Articles, *n.* Nana, nana puta, ulhpoyak.
Artificer, *n.* Nan ikbi.
Ascend, *v.* Oia, uba ia.
Ash, *n.* Shinup; prickly ash, iti kaposa, iti hachunchuba.
Ashamed, *.* Ilofahya; not ashamed, hofayа iksho; I am ashamed, sahofahya; to be ashamed of, įhofahyah.
Ashes, *.* Hituk chubi; to burn to ashes, tubilah; ash leach or hopper, hituk chubi uhoyo.
Aside, *a.* Naksika.
Ask, *r.* Panaklo, asilhha; asking, po nahaklo; to ask for me, saponaklo.
Asp, *r.* Sinti okpulo; asp.
Asparagus, *r.* Koni holba.
Ass, *n.* Isuba haksobish falaia.
Assassinate, *v.* Haksint ubi, haksiuchit ubi.
Assemble, *v.* Itunnaha, itahoba.
Assent, *r.* Ome ahui, ome achi.
Assert, *v.* Miha, achi.
Assimilate, *v.* Ilobachi.
Assist, *v.* Apela, apelcchi.
Associate, *r.* Ai ittupihah
Assuage, *r.* Chulosah, halatah, shiollih; assuaged, habofah.
Assume, *r.* Isht ilonochi.
Assure, *r.* Anumpa kullochit miha; assuredly, pulla.
Asthma, *n.* Nukshinjfa.
Astound, *v* Anukhlakauchali, anukhlakashli.
Astringent, *n* Homi.

Asylum, *n* Hatak tasimbo aiasha.
At, *n. r.* Kuno, hokuno; to be at, ai antah.
Atheist, *n* Chihowa į yimmi keyu.
Athirst, *a.* Itukshila, nukshila.
Athletic, *a.* Illampko.
Atmosphere, *r* Mahliñopa, atmosfia.
Atonement, Isht ai iti nan aiya, isht iti nan aiya, isht iti kunа.
Attach, *r.* Yukachi; to be attached to, anuksita, įhulloh.
Attack, *r.* Amokufah.
Attend, *r.* Haponakloh; good attention, haponaklo achukma.
Attest, *r.* Ahlichi.
Auctioneer, *n.* Isht tahpula hatak.
Auditor, *n.* Haklo, hapouaklo.
Auger, *n.* Isht fotoha, iti isht fotoha; auger hole, afotoma.
August, *n.* Akes.
August, *r.* Chito, holitopah.
Autumn, *n.* Hushtolahpi, onafahpi.
Avenue, *n.* Anowa, hina.
Avoid, *r.* Apakfopah.
Awake, *r.* Okchali, okcha; awoke, okcha: to awake, falamot okcha, falummintokchulli, hapuunayoh; to be awake, okchah; I awake, saiokchah.
Away, *.* Kunia; away off or yonder, illupa pilla, yumma pilla, pillah.
Awful, *.* Okpullo, ikachukmo.
Awkward, *a.* Ik į mako, ik ithano.
Awl, *n.* Chufak; scribing awl, isht hlafa chufak, an awl handle, chufak aieshi.
Ax, *n.* Iskifa, iskifa; grub-ax or hoe, itakshish isht ulmo, itakshish isht kuchi; broad ax, iskifa putha; hatchet, iskifushi.

B

Babble, *v.* Anumpulli illahobbi; babbler, anumpulli illahobi, himak fokalit anumpulli.
Babe, *n.* Ullosi; baby, pushkush.
Baboon, *n.* Hatak shaui chito.
Bachelor, *r.* Tekchiksho.
Back, *n.* Nuli; upper bark of the back, shanukha; lower part, hotip; backbone, nahchuba nulbuchcha; back of the neck, iyuchuna; back of the head, chushak, back of the hand, ibbak paknaka; to come back, falumminchi, falummint; to answer back, falumminchit anumpulli, to send or throw back, falumminchit pila falamint pila; to give back, falummint ibbak fohki; to sell back, falamint į kunchi; to take back, falumuint eshi; to carry back, falummint isht ia.
Back-bite, *v.* Anumpa chukushpa ikbi, anumpa chukushpali, hatak nanumachi; back-biter, hatak nanumochi.
Backslide, *r.* Ubanumpa issa falamut yoshoba.
Backward, *adv.* Obulhpilla ulbul pilla; to cause to go backward, obulhpiluchi, ulbul pellachih.
Bacon, *.* shukba nipi shila.
Bad, *.* Okpullo, haksi, ikachukmo; a bad place, ai okpullo; going into a bad place,

ai okpulloka chukkon; to put in a bad place, ai okpulo fohki; put into a bad place, ai okpullo fohka; to be bad, haksi, okpuloh; badness, okpuloka; being bad, okpuloh; I am bad, siokpuloh, acting badly, tasimbo; to cause to be bad, tasimbochi.
Badge, *n.* (of mourning) Tabashi isht atuni.
Baffle, *r.* Ilaksichi.
Bag, *.* Bahta, shukcha; work-bag, shukchusbi, huchik; a cow's bag, ipishik; bagging, bahta toba; a letter bag, holisso į shukcha; a'small bag, huchik.
Bail, *.* Isht talakchi, ahalulli.
Bait, *r.* Im ashachi, nan upa in takalichi.
Bake, *r.* Puska, puluska; a baker, hattak puskikbi; a bakery, puluska ai ikbi, hatak puska champuli kunchi.
Balance, *n.* Aheka takali, isht weki, isht weki chi.
Bald, *.* Yushmilali, yushkilali; slightly bald, okmilanii, okmilonli; to make bald, okmila lichi; bald headed, okmilashli.
Ball, *.* Towa; to play ball, tolih; a ball play, tolih; to cause to play ball, tolichi; ball play conjurer, tol apoluma; ball sticks, kapucha; ball of the foot, iyi isht hapli; a round ball, lumbo; to make a ball round, lombochi.

Ballot, n. Fot holisso bohli, holisso isht atokoli.

Balm, n. Na balama, bam, shinuk tihleli.

Bambo, n, Iti okehcmali

Bamboozle, v. Haksichi.

Band, n. Afohowa; belly band, ikfoka issita, ikfoka isht tellokchi; head band, bitilih, ish bitilih; buck band, nel abana.

Bank, n. Sakti, iskoli acheli.

Banter, v. Isht yopula, i pafi, kinilichi; bantering, kinnihan.

Baptism, n. Baptismo; to baptize, baptismochi; baptized, baptismo; one who baptizes, baptis mochi.

Bars, n. Ai oksbillihta; (bar, i. e., a bank of sand, akehenak); the bars or bar hole in the post, holihta ai achushkcchi; a sand bar, okehowaha.

Barbecue, v. Abani cbeni; barbecued, ulbcui.

Barber, n. Hatak nuktakhish umo, yusk abalichi; barbered. yuskabali; to shave and cut the hair, yuskabulichi.

Bare, a, Nipi bano; barely, peh.

Bargain, v, Itin apesa, anumpa ittin apesa; bargained, itin ulhpisa.

Bark, n. Hakshup, akehulhpi, hakehulhpi, iti hakshup; hickory bark, used in making rope, balnhehi; dry, or tan bark. chulhpi, hakehulhpi shila; the bark of a dead tree being cracked open, katenli.

Barque, n, Peni chito.

Barrel, n, Itelhfoa.

Barren, n, Ik cheloh-ushi iksho; barrens, ompela.

Barter, v, Itatoba, itatobcchi.

Barrow, n. Shukha hobak.

Bashful, a. Takshi, nukwia, hofahya; to produce bashfulness, hofahycehi, hofnhyalichi; to be bashful, takshi; being bashful, takshi; bashfulness, takshi.

Basin, n. Isht ishko mahala, kolukbi, oka-talaiya.

Basket, n. Kishi, tepushik; work basket, tulbel; square basket used for sifting, tepak.

Basswood, n, Pishunnuk.

Bat, n, Halambisha.

Bath, n, Aiyupi, ycpi; to bathe, yupechi; vapor bath, ahobcchi.

Bay, n. Homma; a bay of water, okhuta telemmi chito.

Bayou, n. Bok.

Bead, n. Shikulla; long white bead, oksup.

Beach, n. Boksakti iti takla, yakni-akheta sakti iti takla yakni.

Beak, n. Ibichilu, ibishakni, ibicholo.

Beam, n. Itibuchaya; beams, itibachoha; the beam of a loom: Pauola apakfopa.

Bean, n. Bela, tobi; bush bean, tobi hikint uni; pole bean, tobi uski atoya; bean pod, bula hakshup; bean porridge, bela okchi; butter beans, bela putessa, tobi tekessa; boiled beans, bela labuna; white beans, tobi tohbi.

Bear, v. Chelih, cshih, shuli; to cause to bear, chelichi; to bear up, halanli; to bear in arms, sholi; bear (n. an animal), nita, bear meat, nita nipi; bear's fat, nita nia; bear's oil, nita biha.

Beard, a Nutakhish.

Beast n. Napoa; tame beast, nan ulhpoa.

Beat, v Isso, lulli, neakulllchi,. bohli hopiysa; beaten, boa, i shallichi, lulla, i shalli imaiya, timikli, timikrchi: to beat at, ai ixso: to beat fine at, alelli, alullichi; a place for beating fine, alula; to beat in a mortar, bahli, hussih; beating with a stick, bukkaha, bakalichi; to beat frequently, bohunli: to beat fine, botohli, botullichi; beaten, holussin: beaten down, (as grass), blohama; to beat one's self, ilclohlih; several beating one. itti bakahah; to beat with something. kabbahah; to beat with the fist, sakkyhah; to beat one on the nose, wokkahah, woblohah.

Beautiful, a. Aiokli, pisa achukma, ayumba; to beautify, ai oklichi; to cause to beautify, ai oklichichi; beauty, aiukli, pisa achukma.

Beaver, n. Kinta; beaver skin, kinta hakshup.

Because, conj. Hakta, akta, hoka, hokamc, hokamba. hokuto, hatnkosh, hatokocha. hatok oka, hatuk okc, hatck ona, hatokot, ka, ba, kambn, ki, pe, ta; because it is, ak oka, ak ocha, ak okut, akta, kakta.

Beckon, r. Fahli.

Become, v. Isht imaka, isht impunna.

Bed, v. Topa, ai onusha; bedding, patulhpo, ai onusha; bed clothes, anchi; bed cord, topa impanola; bed curtain: topn i holmo; bed quilt, nan itclhkcta; bedstead, topu; feather bed, hushi, hishi patelhpox bed hug, topa i shushi, chuka i shushi; bel chamber, anusi; to go to the bed, anusi ona; bed time, anusi onah, to bed up, bunai yuchih; to make, making, or one who makes up a bed or pallet, patahiih.

Bee, n. Foishke, foi, foi bilishke, tobil: ishke; bees-wax, foi akmo, foi uin drones. foi bila ishke hochito; the king bee, foi bila ishke i miko; the queen bee, foi bila ishke cpokni; bee bread, foi i lakna; bee hive, foi i chuka.

Beech, n. Hatombelahu.

Beef, n. Wak nipi.

Beet n. Bet, akehish homma.

Beetle, n. Shakshampi.

Befall, v. Im akaniohmi.

Before prn. Tikba, tikba, tikbanli, chgshpo, kush; go before, mia; before me, satikba; beforehand, tikbanli.

Befriend, v. I kana.

Beg, v. Asilhha.

Beget, v. Tobachi.

Beggar, n. Asilhha shahli; beggar lice, Bissa hlukko.

Begin, v. Isht ia; beginning, aiamonah, ai isht ai ummona; the beginning, um-mona.

Beguile, v. Apakemmi, haksichi; beguiled. haksi.

Behave, v. Hapoyuksa. achukma; behave badly, isht atapa; well behaved; hopoy-uksia.

Behold, v. Hopompoyoh, hopokoyo'yakeh.

Belch, v. Akelanachi, belched; akelaua; to cause to belch, akelauachichi.

Believe, v. Yimmi; believe, nayimmi; I believe, sayimmi.

Bell, n. Tulula, suba innuchi; bell collar, issuba innuchi isht talakchi; bell clapper, tel ola unukaka takahli; bell rope, tulola isht halulli.

apufuchi.

Belly, *n.* Ikfoka, takobba; my belly, sukfoka; big belly, shittina, lower part of the belly, ikfeksa.

Belong, *r.* Ai ahalaya, immi; belonging to, ai immi.

Beloved, *a.* Holitopa; most beloved, helitohompa, holitoyimpa.

Below, *p.* Nuta

Belt, *c.* Uskafachi, ikfoka isht tellakchi.

Bench, *n.* Abinili, ai ominilli,ai obinili falaia, iti wayn; work bench, atoksvli.

Bend, *r.* Bikulli, bichulli, bikota; bent, bekota, b chota; bend in a stream. bokfolota, bok pohloma; bent down by being broken, akochofah; to bend down, akochulli, akochullichi; to cause to bend, bicholichi, bekullichi; while bending, bekunlih; to bend down, chusselah, chusselohah, kochutti; to cause to bend down, chusselachi; bent down, kochufah; to bend the sharp edge, paiatti, paiollih; bending edge, paiofah, paiota, paiokachi; to cause to bend, palolichi.

Beneath, *i.* Akka, nuta.

Benefactor, *c.* Nan achukma imatahli, habenechi hattak yukpali.

Benefit, *v.* Im achukmali, achukmalichi, im atahli; benefitted, im clhtaha; benefitted with, nan ishtil aiyukpa, isht il aiyukpa.

Benevolence, *n.* Inla yukpali ahni.

Bereave, *r.* Clhtaklvchi, im ishi; bereaved, clhtakla, nan ikanihmi.

Berry, *n.* Uni, anih.

Besmear, *r.* Ahaminih, akasholichi, akasholfi, alepvli, aleprlichi.

Best, *a.* Achukma, achuyukma, achukma, moma ishahli.

Bet, *r.* Kahli, ittesiah; *p. p.* kaha; to bet at, ai ittesitch, one that bets, na kahli, ittesita; betting, ittesitch; let us bet, ke kahli.

Betray, *r.* Haksichi.

Betroth, *v.* Abohlih, ittebahll.

Better, *a.* Achukma i shali; to make better, ai iskinchi, achukmalichi, apoksiachi, hochukmalichi, hvchukmali.

Between, *pr.* Iti takla, itintekla, littvkla, takla.

Bewail, *r.* Isht tabashi, isht nukhaklo, isht yaiya.

Bewitch, *v.* Haksichi, yushpakemmi; to continue to bewitch, haksihinchi; bewitched, haksi, pakamah, yushpakama; being bewitched, pakamoah; bewitching them, pakamoli; to bewitch them, yushpakummolichi.

Beyond, *pr.* Misha, misha pilla, mishihma.

Bias, *n.* Hanaiyah.

Bible, *n.* Holisso holitopa.

Bid, *v.* Atohnochi, isht tahpela, i niha, imunali; one who bids, isht tahpela, chumpa.

Bier, *v.* Hatak illi ashali, ai onutula.

Big, *a.* Chitoh, hochetoh.

Bile, *n.* Lakna, basunlesh.

Bill. *n.* Ibichilu, ibishakui.

Billow, *n.* Baucthuchi poakchanchi; a billow, banctha.

Bin, *n.* Aiclhto chito, itombi chito, aiashachi.

Bind, *r.* Takchi, seteli; *pl.* sitohli; bound, talakchi, sita, sitoha; to bind, afohlih, af-

ohlichi; bound, afohoma; one that binds. atohomm; binding, sita; to bind the hair with binding, siteli; to bind. sitohlih; bound, sitoha.

Birch, *n.* Opa haksun.

Bird, *n.* Hushi, cba hushi; a winter bird, hlafintini; a bee martin or king bird, hush pettak; black bird, okchchla; large black bird, hahlon; blue bird, okchglush; jaybird, tishkila; brant, shilaklak; buzzard, sheki, sheki falaia; crane, wahtonlak; sand hill crane, wahtonlak oshi; white crane, oskup tohbi, hush tohbi; currion crow, sheki kolofa, sheki tullo; dove, puchiyoshoba; duck, okfochush; drake, okfochush nakni; wild duck, (with green head,) hakhoba; wood duck, hinluk; a diver, oklubbi, kabaku; muscovy duck, muskoki, okfochuch; eagle, osi; bald eagle, ibahlumpa; grey eagle, tahlako; geese (wild) shilaklak, hakha; geese, (tame) shilaklak clhpoa; goose, shilaklak; gander, shilaklak nakni; gosling, shilaklak ushi; guinea, kofi clhpoa; hen hawk, hatak hlipush; fish hawk, chukcho; squirrel hawk, hasimbish homma, hasimbish hommak; large hen-hawk, blakak; prairie hawk, iba fokchi, hvtaba fakchi; pigeon hawk, hchcb, hanvn; forked-tail hawk, pash falakto; blue pigeon hawk, tysobi; small hen hawk, aiyichi fichi; sparrow hawk, shikkiliklik; night hawk, oksup afohli, oksup iba fohli; night heron, iti keshayaiya; humming bird, hlikyhlo; lark, shonolo; kingfisher, teshalali; loon, okchchla chito; martin, chuki; mocking bird, hushbelbaha; owl, opa; horn owl, iskitini; prairie owl, opa shilup; screech owl, ofunlo; paroquet, kiliki; parrot, kiliki chito, kiliki clhpoa; peacock, okchanlush chito; pelican, chilantakoba, pigeon, pcchi; prairie hen, shunlolo chito; quail, kofi; raven, fula chito; crow, tula; red bird, bishkomak, hushi homma; rice bird, konabancli; robin, bishkukuk, bishkonlak; snipe, lopina; snow bird, aksakinu; sparrow, chusa, hushi iskitini; sparrows, hushi chipunta; cock sparrow, hlefintini; swallow, chukoba; chimney swallow, chupihlah; swan, okak; turkey, fakit; thrush, taluktak; whippoorwill, wahwull, chukkilkblla; woodcock. isi nia pichechi tikti; woodpecker, bakbak, sap-sucker, oktik, chukchuk, biskinik chito, biskinik iskitini; wren, okchiloha, chikchik; a bird cage, hushiai clhpitta, hushi i chuka; bird's feather, hushi hishi; a bird's nest, hushi im clhpichik; a bird trap, hushi i chuka, hushi isht hokli, hushi isht clbi; a bird's claw, hushi iyakchush; a young bird, hush ushi; to kill birds, hushi ubi.

Birth-day, *n.* Ai etta nitak.

Bishop, *n.* Cbannumpa isht etta, apesvchi, nan im atahli, bishop.

Bison, *n.* Yanush.

Bite, *v.* Kapoli, haksichi kislich; *pl.* kobli; to bite at, akopullh akopulichi; biting, as fleas, kislih; bites of insects, shushi kopoli; bites of snakes, sinti kopoli; bites of mad dogs, ofi tasimbo kopoli.

Bitter, *a.* Homi; to make bitter, homlchi;

bitterness, homi nghomi; somewhat bitter, homi chohmi; very bitter, homi fehna; to become bitter, homi; to become somewhat bitter, homi chohmi.

Black, *v.* Lusa; to blacken, lusachi; to blacken at, alusachi; a place at which to blacken, alusa; to mix with black, alusbichi alusvchi; to color black, lusachi I am black, salusah; blacking, isht lusachi, shulush isht lusachi; blacking to make a line with, nan isht lusachi.

Blackberry, *n.* Bissa; blackberry root, bissvpi akshish; blackberry briers, bissvpi.

Blackboard, . Itibusha lusa aholisochi aholi sochi lusa.

Blackgaurd, *n.* Chakapa; blackgaurding, chakaha pa: a blackguard, hattak chakapa.

Blacksmith, *n.* Teli boli.

Blackroot, Ikhish nowa.

Bladder, . . Ishowokchi.

Blame, *v.* Ik ahuincho anumpa onochi.

Blanket, . Shukbo anchi; bed blankets, topa i shukbo.

Blaspheme, *v.* Ikhobaloh anumpuli; blasphemy, ikahobalo anumpa.

Blast, *v.* Bushshi; to cause to wither or blast, bush shichi.

Blaze, *v.* Libbi; to make a blaze, libbichi tohwikelichi; a blaze, libbika; to blaze a tree, iti tihli; blazed, tihla.

Bleed, *v.* Issish kuchi, issish kucha issish mint! hlunipli: bled, issish kucha hlumpa; bleeding at the nose, ibi koa.

Bless, *v.* Yukpali na yukpali holitobli aiokpcchi isht ai achukma he abnit anumpuli; bless you, yakoke; blessed, nayukpa holitopa; blessdness, isht ai yukpa, nan isht il, ai yukpa.

Blight, *v.* Bushshi; blighted, bushih.

Blind, . Lvpa, ikhoponyog; partially blind telhbah; blindness, ikhopopoyo.

Blister, *v.* Wulhkochi; blistered, wulhkoh; a blister, wulhko: continually blistering, wulhkohonchi.

Bloated, . Shatahli; I am bloated, seshatvplichi.

Block, *k.* Bakapa. to split into blocks, bakali bakli: to cause to split into large blocks, bakuhlichi

Blockhead. *n.* Hatak im anukfila iksho.

Blood, *n* Issish; blood letting, issish kuchi: blood sucker, (leech) hallus lessus yallus.

Bloom, . Pakanli, na pakanli.

Blossom, *i.* Pakanli.

Blot, *v.* Lusachi; blotted, lusa.

Blow, *v.* Mahlichi, mahli pufah; to blow atamahli amahlichi; to blow the nose, hlinka; blowing, mahli; to blow gently, mahlichi; blow with the nose, as a horse, pihlokah plotokah; to cause to blow, pofcchi to blow upon, pufa.

Blue, *v.* Okchamali (deep); okchakko (pale).

Bluff, *n.* Sakti.

Blunder, *v.* Ashechi, ibetobli; blunderhead, hatak nusilhha shahli.

Blunt, *a.* Ikhalupo.

Blush, *v.* Takshi hosh nashuka homina hommochi.

Boar, *n.* Shukha nakni.

Board, *n.* Iti bosha, iti shima.

Boast, *v.* Isht ilawata; a boaster, hattak ilawata.

Boat, *n.* Peni; boutman, peni isht ayn, hattak peni fohkot gya; flat-boat or ferryboat, peni putha.

Bodkin, *n.* Chufak chito; botkin.

Body, *n.* Haknip; of an animal, nipi; of a tree or plant, vpi.

Bog, *n.* Hlabeta, hlafchn, hlafeta, hai iko haiyiko; to make boggy, haijkochi hlabetcchi, hlafchvchi, hlafetcchi.

Boil, *v.* Wahlelli, wahlelichi, tobulli, honi; to boil done together, ahlabocha; a vessel in which to boil (boiler) ahobi; to boil down, ashipprchi; boiled down, ashippa; to boil up this way, et tobollih; boiled until soft, hlacopa; boiled to or by itself, ilahonni; various food boiled, nghonni; to boil up or out, (as a spring,) tobullih; pounded meat boiled in or together, obahachi; boils, huchi.

Bois-de-Are, *n.* Kutli lakna; iti kullo.

Boisterous, *a.* Shakapah.

Bold, *a.* Iknukwiyo, nukwia iksho, boldness, chukosh nakni.

Boll, *n.* Nan vui.

Bolster, *n.* Ulhpishi,falnia.

Bolt, *n.* Isht afacha.

Bone, *n.* Foni; backbone, nahchuba nalapissa; pain in the bones (rheumatism) foni hatupa; bone joints, foni itta chu kuli; bone ache, foni konmichi; cortex bones, foni tushbi; to set or re-set bones, foni falvimmiht itti fohki; collar bone, imiskowata; a bone, ng foni.

Bonnet, *n.* Iahlipa, ohoyo i shapo; to wear a bonnet, inhlipili; wearing, or one that wears a bonnet, iahlipili.

Book, *n.* Holisso; a pocket book, holisso nan aholisso, holisso i shukcha; a register book, holisso anumpa atakahli; hymn book, holisso ataloa; a blank book, holisso ik aholisso, holisso tohbi haksbup asha; small book, holisso iskitini; a book shelf, (sing.) holisso uhckia; (plu.) holisso ahlohli, holisso alasha; a book store, holisso akvnchi; a book case, holisso ai vlhto; to make a book, holisso ikbi; book worm, holisso i shushi; to talk about a book, holisso isht anumpuli; account book, ahek a holisso.

Boot, *n.* Shulush chaha; to give boot in a trade, alapanli, alapalinchi; a boot tree, shulush chaha atoba.

Borax, *n.* Isht ainkmo.

Border, *n.* Ai vlhli, nlaka, takcha, takchaka.

Bore, *v.* Fatohli; bored, fatoha; not bored, ikfotohoh; an instrument to bore holes, isht hlumpli, isht hlumpa.

Born, *v.* Utta; first born, vttahpi; to have first born, ishahpi; not having a young one born, ikchelo, ushi iksho.

Borrow, *v.* Pota; borrower, na pota, na pota shahli.

Both, *a.* Bika, ittatyklo, ittaninchit; both going, or both gone, ittiachi.

Bottle, *n.* Katoba.

Bottom, *n.* Lyssah, lyssa anyka, bok anyka yaknl; oka abachaya; to search for the bottom, akka hoyo; bottomless, akka iksho.

Bound, *v.* Tulli, tolupli; bound on (as an arrow,) hollotti; bounds or boundary, ai vhli; to make a boundary, ai vlhlichi.

Bow, *v.* Bikulli; bowed, bikota; to bow the head, akahchunnoli, chunulli; bowing the head, akachunni, yushcnonali; to bow down on the face, akkahlipkuchi, akkahlipiah; both bowed down on the face, akkahlipkaivachi; head bowed and back up, like a poor hog, chunmulli; to bow down, hlipkuchi; not to bow the head, ikakahchunalo; not to cause to bow the head, ikakahchunolicho.

Bow, *n.* Iti tanampo: ox bow, wak tokselli, ikoula afoka; wak tokselli, ikonla atohoma,

Bowels, *n.* Takobba, ikfoka; to run off from the bowels, ikfiah.

Bower. *n.* Hoshontika:*to make a bower, hoshonti kachi; to embower, hoshontika ashahchi.

Bowl, *n.* Ampo; ampo al ishko chito; wooden bowl, iti ampo, iti kula; tamfula or dirt bowl, lukfi ampo; a wash bowl, ampo al okami, am o ul achifa.

Box, *n.* Itombi, itombushi, ai ulhto; ash box, hituk chubi ni ulhto.

Boy, *n.* Olla nakni; boyish, olla holba, kostini keyu.

Brace, *v.* Hlampkochi; braced, hlampko; brace and bits, isht fotoha tonoli.

Brackish. *a.* Homi, takba.

Brads, *n.* Chufak chipinta.

Brag, *v.* Isht ilauata; a bragger, hatak ilauata, hatak nan isht ilauata.

Braid, *n.* Situ; to braid, tanoffo, paanih; braided, tonncffo punah.

Brain, *n.* Nishkobo lupi, lupi.

Brake, *n.* Abohli.

Bramble, *n.* Bisokchakini, bisokchunnakko.

Bran, *n.* Hakhlopish, hoshunlok.

Branch, *n.* Nakshish (of a tree;) bokushi (of a stream;) to branch off, felcommih, felommnchi; to branch out wide with limbs, shauialoha; to cause to branch wide, shaawalohuchi; branching out wide, shnuwala; branchy, washalali, washalohah.

Brand, *n.* I chywa, ishtinchywa, teli isht in chywa; one who brands, i chyli.

Brandish, *v.* Fahfolih.

Brave, *v.* Chilita; bravery, chukcsh nakni.

Bray, *v.* Hopush.

Braze, *v.* Akmochi; brazed, akmo.

Breach, *n.* Akobofa.

Bread. *a.* Puska; flour bread, bota tobbi paluska; corn bread, tanchi paluska; to make bread, puskah; thin bread, (butter cakes,) puska, tupuski; crackers, puska, tupuski shila.

Breadth, *n.* Hopclhkn.

Break, *v.* Kobudi, litoffi, pakulli, koli haui; broken, kobafa litafa, pakota, koa, kaui; to break to or with, akahlali; broken to or with, akahla; to break and bend down, akanwi, akanwichi, broken and bent, akauwa; to break in or at, akobofil; broken in or at, akobafa; the place where it is broken off, akobofa; to bend down by being broken, akochulh; bent down by being broken, akochofa; to break and bend down, akushii akushlichi; bent down by breaking, akoshalu; to break up, at or on, allshowa; to break open, wuhli, mitoili, mitahli, mitahlichi, bakufil fakopa, fakowa; broken open, bokafa, fahoja, wuhla; to break open by bursting, bokahlichi; broken open, bokahli, mi-

tofah: to break in pieces, bushulli; to break off, fakolichi; to break, (as eggs,) kahloli, kokoa: breaking several, kokolih; many being broken, kokoah; breaking down from stalks, kotahli; to cause to break down, kotahlichi; to break a joint or neck, koludi; break fine (as powder,) lishoif; broken up (as a rope,) litahli; broken pieces, litahlih; to break into short pieces, litahlichi; to break into, litoifi: broken into, litafah: continually breaking open, mitrhafah; to break off, (its limbs) nachohli; broken off, nachufa; being broken off, nachohah; to break off from, nachuffi; broken off from, nepofa: broken off, tilofah, tilohli; to break off, tilohli, pe, tiletfi, tusha, tushafa; broken pieces, toshali; being continually broken off teptyhowa.

Breast, *n.* Ikishi, hakship ipishik, akchaya hrshship: my breast, sahushship.

Breath, *n.* Fiopa, ilhfiopak; to breathe, fiopah; shor: breath, fiopa ikfulaio; last breath, fiopa ishtaiyopi; breathless, fiopa telia, fiopa tepa; to cause to breathe, fiopuchi: breathing, fiopa.

Breed, *v.* Chelih: to cause to breed, chelichih; a breeder, cheli.

Breeze, *a.* Mahli; to blow a breeze, malichih.

Brew, *v.* Honnichth; brewed, honuih.

Bribe, *v.* Launakfila chumpah, chumpah.

Brick, *n.* Lukfi nuna; brick kiln, lukfi nuna nikbi.

Bridge, *n.* Iti pat'lhpo, iti patupo; a foot bridge, ahcho,a.

Bridle, *n.* Isuba kapali; bridle reins, issuba isht folullichi, kapali isht talakchi.

Brier, *n.* Bissupi; a bamboo brier, kentek: low briers, having red berries, yacho, chakfih i yacho.

Bright, *a.* Halnlakcchi, hauta; to brighten, shohmalalin; to cause to brighten, shohmalalichi.

Brimstone, *n.* Hittuk lakna.

Brindle, *n.* Basou.

Brine, *n.* Hupi okchi.

Bring, *v.* Isht ula, isht minti; to bring out of, akuchichi; brought out, akucha; to bring forth, eshi.

Brisket, *n.* Imbichuko, bichuko, i bichuko.

Bristle, *n.* Shukha, chushuk hishi, chushak hishi kullo.

Broach, *v.* Isht ahlopulli, teli kucha.

Broad, *a.* Putha, hoputka; to broaden, puthchi.

Broadcloth, *n.* Chukfi hishi tunna lapushki.

Brogan, *n.* Shulush kullo.

Broil, *v.* Apushli; broiled, ulhpusha.

Broken, *v.* Kobafa, koa, litafa, pakota, akahlah.

Brood, *n.* Akuk ushi pehlichi.

Brook, *n.* Bok ushi, okhinushi.

Broom, *n.* Isht bushpoa, isht pashpoa; a broom handle, isht bushpoa cpi

Broth, *n.* Okchi.

Brother, *n.* Ittibapishi; my brother, (used only by females,) a-nakfi; her brother, i nakfi: brother-in-law, (one who married another's sister,) imaluk; a wife's brother, imalakusi; an elder brother, imonni; a wife's husband's brother, umbalaha, im umbalaha.

Brown, *n.* Lusbi, haton lakna, holussi, homakbi; to color brown, haton laknuchi, lusbichi; dark brown, lusakbi: to color a dark brown, lusakbichi; baked brown, tubelhko, tuwelhko; to roast brown, tubelhkochi, tuwelhkochih.

Bruin, *n.* Nita.

Bruise, *r.* Litoli, lullichi; bruised, litowa lulla.

Brush, *r.* Kasholichi; clothes brush, ilefoka isht kasholichi; a brush, bush or thicket, bafaha, shanwa; a shaving brush isht pokpokechi; brush broom, small, isht bushpoa iskitini.

Bubble, *v.* Honi; to cause to bubble, honichi.

Buck, *n.* Issi nakni, lapittah.

Bucket, *r.* Ishtochi.

Buckle, *n.* Teli takahli; *pl.* teli takohli; to buckle, takalichi; buckled, takahli.

Buckskin, *.* Telhko.

Bud, *n.* Bokopli, bikopli; to bud, bokapli, bikopli; budding, bikopli; to cause to bud, bikopllehih.

Badget, *n.* Bahta, shukcha.

Buffalo, *n.* Yanush; buffalo meat, yanush nipi.

Buffet, *v.* Temauchi.

Bug, *n.* Shushi; a water bug, hasun, a bed bug, topa i shushi; a lightning bug, helba; red bugs, shukoma shushumma.

Build, *r.* Ikbi, itabeni; built, toba, itabana.

Bulbous, *a.* Babeki.

Bull, *n.* Wak nakni; bull dog, ofi nakoa; bull freg, halonlebi.

Bullet, *n.* Naki lumbo.

Bullrush, *n.* Kashahechi.

Bulwark, *n.* Hohlita kullo.

Bumble-bee, *n.* Osihi.

Bump, *n.* Wokkola; many bumps, wokokowa; bumpy, bomboki, bombaki.

Bunch, *n.* Lokussa, pokussa; in buches, lukluki, luklukit.

Bundle, *n.* Lona; to bundle up, bonui, bonullichi.

Bung, *n.* Akameli, elhkamoah.

Bar, *n.* Hakshup.

Burden, *n.* Shapoh; to bear a burden, shapole; to cause to bear a burden, shapolichi.

Burial, *n.* Hoppi, hattek hoppi; burial place or cemetery, a hollopi: buried, hollopi; burial service, a hopi ka ebanumpa, isht ai etta he elhpesa.

Burn, *r.* Luachi, hokmih, hushmih; burned or burnt, lua, holukmi, hollushmi, a burn, holukmi, holhpa; to continually burn, luahauchi; continually burning, luhowah; burning, hollushmi.

Burst, *r.* Bokeili; bursted, bokafa.

Bury, *r.* Hopi; buried, holopi, hollupi; unburied, ikhollurpo.

Bush, *n.* Bafaha, shanwa; a clump of bushes, bafelli talaia; small bushes or underbrush, bafelli.

Bushel, *n.* Bushil; half-bushel, bushil isht uehpesa; bushil iklunna, peck; bushil iklcuna ya iklcuna.

Busy, *a.* Isht etta; isht eshwauchi.

But, *prep.* Ak mako kia, amba, hakakano; but not, hatok kia, as ia la chi hatokkia; akiyo, was to have gone but I have not.

Butcher, *n.* Nipi beshli.

Butt, *n.* Atakali, teli atakali; *pl.* teli atakohli.

Butter, *n.* Pishukchi nia.

Butterfly, *n.* Hetapushik.

Buttermilk, *n.* Psihuhchi nia okchi.

Butternut, *n.* Habe heta.

Button, *n.* Teli haksi, isht akonessa, isht atapechi; to button, takai'echi, aka maseli; buttoned, akamessa.

Buy, *r.* Chumpa; bought, chumpa. to cause to buy, chumpechichi; can be bought, chumpa hinla; cannot be bought, chumpa he keyu: not bought, ik chumpo; to buy with, isht chumpa: a buyer, chumpa na chumpa.

Buzzard, *n.* Sheki.

By, *prep.* Bilinka; by and by, hopukikmako, hopukikma.

C

Cabbage, *n.* Hishi hoputka, tuhi, kabich.

Cage, *n.* Afoka, i chuka.

Cake, *n.* Paluska champulli, kek; batter cake, puska tapeski.

Calamus, *n.* Akshish balama.

Calculate, *v.* Hotinu; calculated, holhtina; continually calculating, holhtihina.

Calendar, *n.* Heshi nitak isht ikhunna.

Calf, *n.* Wak ushi; cow and calf, wak ushi lauinli; calf of the leg, iyi holbki iyi ishitukwa.

Calico, *n.* Kaliko; nantapuski, nafoka toba; blue calico, nantapuski okchako; dark calico, nantapuski lusbi; green calico, nantapuski okchamali; light calico, nantapuski heta; pink calico, nantapuski tishepa; red calico, nantapuski homa; yellow calico, nantapuski lakna.

Call, *v.* I hoa, im paya, tehpela-paya, hochifo; called, hohchifo; to call out toward this way, ettehpala; an instrument to call with, isht i howa; repeatedly calling, paya.

Callous, *a.* Selbo; to cause callousness, sulbochi.

Calm, *a.* Cholusa; to calm, cholushechi; calmness, chulosa.

Calomel, *n.* Ikhish kullo.

Calumniate, *v.* Anumpa okpullo onochih, calumny, anumpa okpullo; calumniator; anumpa okpullo onochi; calumniated, anumpa okpullo onotulah.

Camp, *n.* Bina, binut asha, binut aiasha; to encamp, binanchi elbinanchi; continually camping, binahchi; to camp at, abinechi; to camp with each other, itibinauchi; to camp on, ebinechi.

Camphor, *n.* Haiochi ikhish, kafa.

Can, *v.* Ahinla, hinla. chike; cannot or never can, hatoshba, yatoshba; cannot

be, hatoshke; cannot, ahetoh, he keyu.
Canal, *n*. Yakni kula okhina.
Cancel, *v*. Kashofi; uncancelled, takali.
Cancer, *n*. Shalukwa okpullo.
Candid, *a*. Ai ulhpiesa, apisanli.
Candle, *n*. Pela.
Cane. *n*. Oski; switch cane, oskish.
Canister, *n*. Itombushi, ai ulhto.
Cannibal, *n*. Hatak upa; cannibalism, hattak upa.
Cannot, *v*. He keyu, aheto; cannot be, ak ut; cannot be so, chint, chihchint; cannot but hokakguo.
Canopy, *n*. Hoshontika.
Canter, *v*. Abatullih, babatakli, hatulli hatonli; to cause to canter, hatullichi.
Cap, *v*. Hituk lakna atukafa.
Capacious, *a*. Chito.
Cape. *n*. Shokulbi.
Capitol, *n*. Chukka henta.
Captain. *n*. Kapitoni.
Captivate. *v*. Yukachi, chukush yakachi, yukpalit kanchi, chukush eshi; captivated, yuka.
Captive, *n*. Yuka, hattak yuka.
Carcass, *n*. Nan illi.
Card. *v*. Shelichi; cards, isht shiahchi cards, (to game with) buskah; to play with cards, buska, busto; not playing, ikbusto.
Care. *n*. Aha, ahni; be careful, ahah! carefully, aha ahnit; careless, aha ikahno; carelessness, aha ahni iksho; carelessly, aha ahni keyu; to take care of, ilanclih; to care for us, pieshi; caring for us, pieshit.
Caress, *v*. Pushohli; to caress me, sapushohli.
Carpenter, *n*. Chuk ita bunni, chukikbi.
Carrier, *n*. Na shali; one that carries on the head, intalali; a wood carrier, hatak iti sholi.
Carry, *v*. Isht ia, isht aya, sholi shali; to carry in, isht chukowa; to carry back, falummint isht ia; to carry on the shoulder, ia banali; to carry through with, isht hlopulli; to carry water, ochih.
Cart, *n*. Iti chanulli; cart body, iti chanulli, talaiya; cart tongue, iti chanulli tikba hikia; cart wheel, chanaba.
Carve, *v*. Bushli; curved, busha.
Cascade, *v*. Oka chopa.
Caxe, *n*. Afohka.
Cast, *v*. Pila; to cast down, akkapilah; to cast or count, hotina; casted or counted, holhtina.
Castor Oil, *n*. Ikhish bila.
Castrate, *v*. Hobuk ikbi, hobuk tobachi; castrated, hobuk.
Cat, *n*. Kuto, ketus; wild cat, shakba tina; Small wild cat, koinchush.
Cataract, *n*. Oka chopa.
Catarrh, *n*. Hotilhko.
Catch, *v*. Hokli, ishi yukachi; caught, yuka; not caught, ikhoklo; to catch one by several, itti hokli; to catch with claws, yichiff; caught with claws, yichifa; to catch a disease, ulmoli, haleli; I have caught the disease. halelih; catching or contagious, ulmoli.
Catechism, *n*. Katiki-ma.
Caterpillar, *n*. Hatak holhpa, hatak halhpali haiowene.

Cattle. *n*. Wak, wak laua; young cattle. wak himitta.
Caution. *n*. Ahah ahnih; cautions, ila nuktahla.
Cave. *n*. Yakni in chiluk chito, hochukbi; caved in, lobahll, oka lobali; to cause to cave in, lobalichi; cavern, yakni chiluk; cavity, choluk
Cease. *v*. Issa. anola; ceaselessness. ahokofa iksho; ceasing, anuktupa; ceased, yokopa; cessation, yokopa.
Cedar. *n*. Chuahla.
Cede. *v*. Ima, kanchi; ceded, kenia.
Cebebrate. *v*. Holitublit isht anumpull, celebrated, holitoput isht anumpa.
Cellar. *n*. Chuka, nutaka yakni kula, aboha nutayakni kula.
Cement. *v*. Ittelbochi, ittai okmochi, ittakmochi; cemented, ittelbo.
Cemetery. *n*. Hattak aholopi.
Census *v*. Hatak holhtina, hattak putto holh,tina.
Cent. *n* Sint.
Center. *n*. Ai iklunna, chukush.
Century *n*. Atemmi tohlcpa achoffa.
Certain. *a*. Ahli, pulla; to make certain, ahlich i; certainly, ahli tokba, akut, akta, ba; it is certain. ahlishke; certainly it is. akta, hakta.
Certify, *v*. Hohssochit anoli;; certified. ulhtokowa.
Chafe. *v*. Oshenachi. pihloffi, pikofli; chafed, pihlofa, pikofu; chaff. hakhlopish.
Chain. *n*. Teli, iti takeli, teli chusopa; chain hook. uli chanakbi; chain link or ring, toli chtanaha; chain swivel. teli chunaha fatokuchiace chains, telilili schuopa; log or ox chain, teli iti takeli chito; chaining, halan to chain, teli iti takeli isht takehi.
Chair. *n*. Aiobinili, aiominili ai o asha; chair bottom. ai obinili o hlipa, chair leg, ai obinili iyi; rocking chair, aiobinili faiokuchi.
Chalk. *n*. Lukfeta. lukfatah, talhpa; red chalk, talhpa homma; chalk-ine, ponola isht apissali.
Challenge. *v*. Pafi, i pafi.
Chamber. *n*. Uba patalhpo; chamber stairs, uba patalhpo atuya.
Chameleon. *n*. Funi imalukosi.
Champ. *v*. Noti kiselichi, hogsa, hopasa.
Chance. *n*. Nahueli.
Change. *v*. Iti tobechi, iti toba, inlchi, ai in lochi; changed it, ulhtoba, inla, ai inla, small change (money) bushulli; not changed, ikbushullo.
Channel. *n*. Oka ayanulli.
Chap. *n*. Kichanli; chapped, kichanlich.
Chapel. *n*. Uba anumpa ai atoshowa chuka.
Chaplain. *n*. Ubanumpa isht etta ulhtoka.
Chapter. *n*. Anumpa nishkobo, chapta.
Char. *v*. Akabushlih.
Character, *n*. Holisso.
Charge. *v*. I miha, apitta; charged, ulhpitta; to charge with, onochi; charger, hittuk isht ulhpisa.
Charcoal, *n*; Tobaksi; charcoal powder, tobaksi bota; stone coal, teli tabaksi.
Charity, *n*. Nan i hullo.
Charm. *v*. Yukpuchi. yukpalit, chukush ishi; charmed. yakpa; to charm. fappo—

chi, afoppolichi, fappo onochi; charmed, fappo onuttula; a charmer, foppo onuchi.

Chase. *v.* Hliohli; chased, hlioha.

Chasm. *n.* Itapahlata, chulok.

Chastity. *n.* Hapoyuksa, ghli, baui anukfila iksho.

Chatter. *v.* Himak fokalichit anumpuli; chatter box, anumpuli shali.

Cheap. *a.* Ikholitopo, ielli ikchito.

Cheat. *v.* Haksichih; to cheat with, isht haksichih; cheated, haksichih; to cheat frequently, haksihinchih.

Check. *n.* Bakowa; *v.* to check or stop, hilichi.

Cheek. *n.* Ittisupi, itti sukpi; cheek bone, itti supi foni; cheeks enlarged by wind, itakpofoli; my cheek, satisukpi.

Cheer. *v.* Yukpali, yukpa, yimintechi, naknichi; cheered, yukpa yiminta; cheering, naknichi, yimintahanchi; cheerfulness, chukesh yukpa.

Cheerish. *v.* Holitoblichit hofantichi; cherished, holitipa hofanti.

Cherrytree. *n.* Itellikchi.

Chest. *n.* Itombi itombi chito, haknip ikkishi, hushship; my chest or breast, saheship.

Chestnut. *n.* Oti, uti; chestnut color, lakna.

Chew. *v.* Hoasa, hopasa; a chaw, hopasa; to chew with, isht hopasa.

Chicanery. *v.* Haksichi.

Chicken. *n.* Akaka; young chickens, akak ushi; a brood of chickens, akak ushi pehlichi; a chicken house, akak in chuka; a stealer of chickens, akak hukopa; a spur of a chicken, akakichahe; chicken feather, akakhishi; a prairie chicken, kofichito; chicken roost, akaka anusi; a hen, akakishki; rooster, akak nakni; a guinea chicken, kofi chipoa.

Chicke t-pox. *n.* Akak in chiliswa; chicken snake, abeksha.

Chide. *v.* Nan i miha, i uukoa.

Chief. *n.* Miko, hatak i miko; a war chief, hopaii.

Child. *n.* Ulla; I am a child, si ulla; I am still a child, si ulla moma; when I was a child, si ulla moma met; childless, ulla ikimiksho; children, ulla ushi chipota.

Chill. *n.* Hochukwa; chills and fever, yanba hochukwa, hochukwa yanba; to chill, hochukwchi, kapessoli; to be chilly, hochukwochi.

Chimese. *n.* Eskuffa yoskoloii.

Chimney. *n.* Ashobohli, luak ashobohli.

Chin. *n.* Nuktakfa wishakchi, nutakfa.

China. *n.* Itolhpoa.

Chinch. *n.* Tupa i shushi.

Chip. *n.* Shukolli; chipped, shukafa, shukali; chipping, shukahlichi.

Chisel. *n.* Iti isht kula; cold chisel, tule ishit tuptuli; to chisel, kulli; chiseled, kula.

Choice. *n.* Holitopa.

Choke. *v.* Nuktakali nuktihliffi; to choke with, nuktakalih; choking, nuktihlolih; choked, nuktihlifa; I am choking, sanukshifa, satohno.

Cholera. *n.* Abika kullochi, kalili; cholera morbus, itahlakla ontia.

Choose. *v.* Atokoli; chosen, atokoa, ulhtoka.

Chop. *v.* Chanli, chant, chahanlit; chopped, chaya; to cause to chop, chanlichi; to chop down, chant, kinulli, akcchi; to

chop and score, chant bekli; to chop a notch, chant lampli; to chop down into water, chant okcechchi; to chop into small pieces, chant tushtuli; to chop off, chantupli, a chop or gash made with an ax, chayot pachafa; not chopping, ikchanlo; to chop wood, iti chali.

Christ. *n.* Klaist.

Christian. *n.* Cbanumpuli, cba anumpa yimmi.

Chronometer. *n.* Heshi kanolli isht clhpisa.

Chub. *n.* Nuni teli heta.

Church. *n.* Ai ittcnaha chukka, cba anumpuliiksa, chuch, aboha heuta; church member, iksa iba foka; church yard, ahollopi cba isht ai anumpa chuka i bilika.

Churlishness. *a.* Hatak nakoa, shahli.

Churn. *n.* Pishukchi a niachi; churn dasher, pishukchi isht niachi; churn top, opoholmo.

Cider. *n.* Oka hanashko, saita.

Cigar. *n.* Hakchuma shoma, sika.

Cinnamon. *n.* Iti hakshup balama, sinimon.

Cion. *n.* Nakshish iskitini.

Cipher. *v.* Holhtina isht etta.

Circle. *v.* Boluktu, chunaha, kulaha; to lay circularly, chanahochi.

Circuit. *n.* Afolota.

Circuitous. *a.* Tolotah.

Cistern. *n.* Yakni kula oka ai clhto.

Citation. *n.* Imanowa; cited, imannowa.

Citizen. *n.* Yakni uchefa hattak, temaha hattak.

City. *n.* Temaha chito; town, temaha; village, temchushi.

Civil. *a.* Hopoyuksa, kostini, clhpesa; uncivil, hopoyuksa he keyu.

Civilize. *v.* Hopoyuksechi, hopoyuksali; civilized; hopoyuksa; not civilized, ikhopoyukso.

Clad. *v.* Fohka; to clothe, illefoka, fohka.

Claim. *v.* Halelli a claimant, halelli.

Clam. *a.* Oka folush.

Clamp. *n.* Isht kiseli.

Clan. *n.* Iksa.

Clang. *v.* Chemakchi.

Clank. *v.* Chemakchi.

Clap. *n.* Yukbebi.

Clasp. *n.* Ittakamessoli; clasped, Ittakamussah.

Class. *n.* Ai itapiha, ai italukoli.

Clatter. *v.* Chemakuchi, chemplichi.

Claw. *n.* Iyakchush; to claw, yichiffe; to catch with claws, yichiflih; caught with claws, yichiflia.

Clay. *n.* Lukfi; pipe clay, palosak.

Clean. *a.* Kashofa; to clean, kashofii; cleaned, kashofa; not clean, litiha.

Cleanse. *v.* Kashofii, kashofichi; cleansed, kashofa

Clear. *a.* Oksha uanli, kashofa, masheli, bafta; to explain or make clear, imottuni, lhaiyaka; to make clear, mashilichi; to clear up, shohmalali.

Cleave. *v.* Alapalih, alapalichi; to cleave or split, bakahli; cloven, cholakto; to cleve, cholaktochi; to cleve together, ittihgiulli.

Clemency. *n.* Chukush yubi, element, chukosh yubbi.

Clergy. *n.* Cba anumpo isht etta clhtoka uhliba; clergyman, cbanumpa, isht etta clhtoka hattak.

Clerk *n*, I hallisochi. hattak hallissochi..
Clever, *a*. Chukosh yuhbi, yukpa, impunna.
Cliff, *n*. Sakti; cliffy, sakti lana.
Climb, *v*. Oia, apakchulli.
Cling, *v*. Kullot hokli, kullot isht; to cling at, aiasitiah; to cling to, halulli.
Clink, *v*. Chamakchi, chamak; clinking. chamukahanchi; to make jingle or clink, chamalichi.
Clip, *v*. Tupli amo; to clip off once, himona topli.
Cloak, *n*. Anchi. il foka anchi; to put a cloak on another, auchichi.
Clock, *n*. Hushi kanulli isht ikbana chito, hushi isht ik huna
Clog, *v*. Ataklommi; clogged, ataklama.
Close, *v*. Okshita, akamih, okhishta, akumi, hakoflih, yakopli; closed, yokopah, hokofa, ahshilita, akama, ulbkama; *fl*. close by, bilika; to be close or covetous, ihullo.
Closet, *n*. Abohushi; put into a closet, abohushi fohka; to put into a closet, abohushi fohki.
Cloth, *n*. Nantunna; woollen cloths, chukti hishi tuna.
Clothe, *v*. Fokichi, tohkuchi, ilafohka; clothes brush, ilefoka isht kasholichi; clothes line, ilefohka aholufka.
Cloud *n*. Hoshonti; to becloud, hoshontichi; cloudy, hoshonti; to reach the clouds, hoshonti pit tikeli; cloud capped, honshonti pit bekeli; to be cloudy, hoshonti toba; thin clouds, hoshonti tapuski; flying clouds, hoshonti heli yiblipa
Cloy, *v*, Yummichi; cloyed, yummi; to cloy me, sayummichi
Club, *n*. Bonuta. tobi.
Cluck, *v*. Tuktuah.
Coal, *n*. Tobaksi, teli tobaksi; coal mine, tobaksi akula.
Coast, *n*. Okhuta lapalika, Ontolaka.
Coat, *n*. Na foka, kot.
Cobble, *v*. Akulli; cobbled, ulhkuta; a cobbler, akulli. shulush akulli.
Cobweb, *n*. Chukhlampuli hachnkhlampuli
Cock, *n*. Akaknaknt. abichili; cock crowing, akak ola, to cock, (as a gun), hilechi; cocked, hikin. hikah; uncocked, ikheko.
Cocklebur, *n*. Pashtahli.
Cockroach, *n*. Nia chupka, bila chupka, nuni chuka.
Cocoon, *n*. Upanukfila silik toba.
Coffee, *v*. Kafi.
Coffin, *n*. Hattak illi im atombi.
Cog, *n*. Achushua, afuskuchi.
Cohabit, *v*. Aiinah, ittaiinah.
Coil, *v*. Chanabuchi; coiled chanaba.
Colander, *n*. Bila isht hoya.
Cold, *v*. Kapussa, hush tnla chohmi; to be cold with, abochukwah, nkapusscchi, akapussali; a cold place, climate or region, akapussaka; to be cold, hochukwa; very cold, hochukwa fehna kapussa fehna, hochukwa illi; to have a bad cold, ibishuno, nukshummi; to cause a bad cold, nukshummichi, to cool, kapussili; to cause to cool, kapussullichi; I have a bad cold, sabishshuno; I am cold; sakapussa.
Colic, *n*. Ikfoka katapa, ikfoka hutupa.
Collar, *n*. Afohoma ikonla foka; horse

collar, issuba ikonla afohoma, issuba ikonla fohka; collar bone, immoskawata foni
Collect, *v*. Ittunahli; collected, ittunaha; collector, nan attobichi.
College, *n*. Hollisso ai ithhana chito.
Colloquny, *a*. Itlimanumpuli.
Colonel, *n*. Kancl.
Colonize, *v*. Linohlichi.
Colt, *n*. Issubushi.
Colter, *n*. Yakni isht patafa tikba hikia; rolling colter, yakni isht patafa tikba bikiachanaha.
Column, *n*. Anumpa bachohu; a column, anumpa bachaya.
Comb, *v*. Shilli; *n*. a comb, shalintak hashhintak: side combs, nasika lapoli shalintak; the comb of a chicken, akakunpusha: an ivory comb, hashintak tohbi; coarse comb, hashintak shachaba; a fine comb, shalitak issop isht ubi, hashintak issop ishtulbi.
Combine, *v*. Iitibafohki; combined, ittibafohka.
Come, *v*. Minti, ula, toba, ai,ulah, ta: come and (as ant anta), come and stay; to come out of, akncha, shufah; coming out, shohufa; the place of coming out, akuchaka; to come out from, akuchawiha; to come at last, ai yuvalo, polgka minti; to come down, akowa; to come in file, baiullit minti; to come to want, as food or water, baiyunnat; we come, ela; we all come, iloh ula, iloh ai ula; to cause to come off, fokolichi; to start to come back- falamut minti; to come out, haiyuka: not come, ikhaiyako; to come to, faluminot okcha, okcha ihaiyaka: Coming, minti; come along, minti chu; to come up, (as plants) offo, okpichillit; to come out of me, siakucha; coming to pieces, tiapah.
Comfort, *v*. Nuktalali, hopohluchi yukpali; comforted, Nnktxia, hopohla, yukpaia comforter, hopohluchi, ngunktalali, na hapuhlachi, to cause to comfort, nuktulalichi; to make all comfortable, nuktullohli; I am comforted, sahopohlah.
Command, *v*. Pelichi i miha, anumpa apesa; commander, pelichi; commandment, anumpa ulhpisa, nan ulhpisa; the ten commandments, Chihowa im anumpa ulhpisa pokolo.
Commence, *v*. Isht ia; commencement, holisso apisa kucha; the commencement, ai isht ia ummona.
Commend, *v*. Aiokpanchi, ahniuchi. ·
Commonly, *a*. Bieka, chatuk, atak, beka.
Compare, *v*. Ishtapesa; compared together, ittupisu; compared to. ittulhpisa; Comparison, holba.
Compass, *n*. Falommi isht ikhuna; compasses, isht hlafi. isht ulhpisa.
Commune, *v*. Ittimanumpuli.
Complete, *v*. Tabli, isht ahlopulli, loshumi aiahlichi, aiahli; completed, taha loshuma, ai im ulhtaha, ulhtaha, aiulhtaha, taha; completion, ai ulhtaha; completely, huba.
Complexion, *n*. A light complexion, okshanali; light complexions, okshanashli; to produce a light complexion, okshangshlichi.
Comply, *v*. Haklo; complied, hakloh.

Compose, r. Hollissochi; composed, holisso; composition, holisso; composer, hollissochi.

Comprehend. r. Akostininchi; not comprehending, ikakostinincho, akostinincha he keya.

Compute, r. Hotina; computed, holhtina; computation, holhtena.

Concave, r. Bochussachi, bochopli; concaved, bochussa.

Conceal. r. Aluhmi, aluhmichi; concealed, ikhuiyako, aluhma.

Conceive, v Chakali; to cause to conceive, chakalichi; to be conceived with, ai isht i chakali.

Concern, r. Ahalaiyah; concerned, ahalaya.

Conciliate, o Hopohlvchi; conciliated, hopohlah.

Concubine, n. Alina, ittalina.

Condemn, v. Nan im apesa, poslihvchi; condemned, posilhah: condemnation, nan isht ilbusha ulhpisa.

Condition, r. (As a condition(akta, hakta.

Conduct, r. Pchlichi, apesachi, halulli.

Conference, n. Ittimanumpuli.

Confess, r. Il anoli anumpa il onochi; confessed, il anuoa; confession, ai otonichi, ai il anoli, ai aotkowa; confession of faith, ubanumpa yimma he nauulhpisa holisso.

Confidence n. Ainuukchito, anukchita.

Confluence, w. Ai ittafama, ai ittusiteli.

Confusion, r. Haksuba; to confuse, haksubachi.

Congeal, r. Akglepechi, akmochi, kalampichi; congealed, akaleplh, akg lepil taha, akmi, akino, kalampi.

Conjecture, r- Himak fokalechit miha.

Conjure, r. Isht uhullo. hottusichi. hottosi; conjurer, hattak yushpakumi, haitak fepo.

Conjure, r. Asilha

Connect, r. It afvmmi, itiba foki, ita fama, connected, itafama, itaba foka. it uchaka, ahalaya; not connected, ik ittachoko; connection, ikonomi.

Conquer, r. Im aiyvchi, i shahlichi; conquered, im aiya, i shallli; conquerer, imaiyvchi.

Conscience, n. Chukush im anukfiilla, nan isht akostluinchi.

Consecrate, r. Ilin issa.

Consequently, ad. Kama, kamba, chomba.

Consider, r. Anukfilla. achukmalit anukfilli. not considered, ikanukfillo; considered, anukfilli taha.

Console, v. Hopohlvchi; consoled, hopohla; unconsoled, ik hopohlo.

Conspicuous, n. Haiyaka.

Constable, n. Hatak yukachi, isuba o binili.

Constantly, acc. Beka.

Constellation, n. Fichik lokoli.

Constitution, n Anumpa nushkoba, kenstitushon.

Construct. r. Ikbi.

Construe, r. Anumpa tushali; construed, anumpa tushowa.

Consume, r. Hokini okpuni, bukustoli, lua; consumed, holukini opullo taba okpolo, bckusto, tomafa,; consumption, hatlihko shila, nakshummi isht abeka; I am consumptive, sanukshummi.

Contagion, n. Haleli; contagious, ulmolli

Contemn, r. Shitilema, kanimanchi.

Contemptious, a. Okpullo, iknchukmo.

Contend. v. Itim afoa, ittichapa i itibi; to contend for. afoa, ittimofou; to contend against, mokafa.

Contiguous, a. Belika.

Continent, n. Yakni talaiya.

Continual, a. Bilia; continue, biliah.

Contradict, r. I sanali, ichapa, it achowa.

Controversy. n. anumpa itti laua.

Convalescent, a. Illakofit isht in..

Conversation, n. Anumpulih asha.

Converse, v. Itim anumpulli.

Conversion, n. Ubanumpuli toba, inlet toba.

Convey, r. Shali, isht aya, kanchi, ima.

Convulsion, n. Haiochi, Haiochichi.

Cook, n. Hoponi honi, hlabushli; cooked, holhponi, honi; to cook by boiling, hlaboshli, hlabohlichi; a cook, hlaboshli, uahoponni; to cause one to boil food, hlaboshlechichi, honnichi; to par boil, houi umona; par boiled, honeminona: boiled food, hahonni; to cook done, nun a chi; cooked, nuna.

Cool, a. Kapessei, shippeti; I am cooling off from fever, sashippah; cooled or cooling, shippa; to cause to cool, shippulichi.

Coop, n. Akak in chukka.

Copper. n. Asonak lakna, lakna cholmi; copper mine, asonak lakna akuli; copperhead snake, chahlakwa, chihlakwa; copperas, nau isht lakuuchi.

Copy. n. Hobachi holissochi, kapi; to copy from or after, hlafithobachi.

Cord, n. Ponola honula, akshish..

Cork, n. Kotoba isht ulhkema; to cork, akamuli, ulhkamoah.

Corn, n. Tanchi: corn tassel, hinak; corn laid by, holhpechi; to lay by corn, hopochi, to hill up corn for the first time, hopolhchi, the last time hopohchi: pounded corn boiled, tgfula, (Tom Fuller), bulhponi; a corn crib, tanchi i chuka, kanchak, pichu; corn row, tanchiHlina; corn silk, tanchi okshuli; fodder, tanchi hishi; corn bran, tanchi hak hlopush, tash hakblopish; yellow corn, lanchi lakna, flint corn, tanchi hlunishko; gourd seed corn, tauchi nihi fulaia; white corn. tauchi tohbi; early or small corn, tanchushi: cern stalk or corn cob, tanchvpi; pop corn, tash bokali; corn meal, tash fotoba, tashpushi, tanch bota.

Corner, n. Chukbi, chukbika.

Corpse. n. Hatak illi, haknip illi.

Correct. r. Apoksiachi, femmi; corrected, foma; verp correct, alahli fehna, al ghli achukma; to correct al isklah; incorrect, ikghlo; correctness, alhli.

Correspond. r. Ittinholissochi.

Corroborate, r. Klampkochi.

Corrupt. v. Okpuni; corrupted, okpullo, haksit okpullot taba.

Costly. a. Iulli chito, iclli chaha.

Cottage. n. Aboha shikkia; cottager, abohushi vtta.

Cotton. n. Ponola, pokpo; cottonwood. shombela.

Cough. n. Hotilhko.

Could. *v.* Ahetuk, chintok, chin tuk, fehna hinla; could have, hetuk, hiula tok, hinla tuk.

Council. *n.* Nan apesa; clerk of the council, nan apesa i hollissochi; Sergeant at Arms for council, Nan apesa i holisso shahli: door keeper of the council, Nan ai apesa okhisa atonl.

Counsel. *v.* Nan i miha; counselor, nan i miha, Hatak anumpouli.

Count. *v.* Hotina, hopena; counted, holhtina holhpena; a place to count from, aholhtina; countless, holhtena atopa; continually counting; holhtihehna; to count together, ittibahotina; to count each other, ittihotena.

Countenance. *n.* Nashukha.

Counterfeit. *n.* Holabi.

Country. *n.* Yakni, haiyaka.

Course. *n.* Anowa, bachaya.

Court. *n.* Aiapesa, koat.

Courteous. *a.* Aiokpanchi.

Covenant. *n* Ittim apesa; covenanted, ittim ulhpisa; a covenant, nan ittim ulhpisa, nan ulhpisa.

Cover. *v.* Opohomo, holmo; covered, opoholmo; covering, holmo; (roof), a cover, ishtopoholmo; to cover over, qholmochi qhlippilli; covered over, qholmo, qhlipia; covering, holmo.

Covet. *v.* Anushkanna, impotenno; covetous, benna, nana ahauachi, benna atampa, ihullo.

Cow. *n.* Wak, wak tek; cow and calf, wak ushi lauinli; miich cow, wak bisachi; cow pox, wak in chalakwa.

Coward. *n.* Hobak.

Cower, *v.* Bikottokochi.

Coxcomb, *n.* Hattak ilak shema shahli.

Crab. *n.* Shakchi chito.

Crack. *v.* Bisgli bisinli, bisalichi; a crack, bisgli, wakla, bisanli, kobafa; to make a small crack or crevice, besin waklachilichi; cracked, bisinli bisali, wohlopa; to crack open, hokufii, fachanli, betaseli; to cause to crack open, bitanlichi, bokanlichi, fachanlechi wohlolichi; cracked open, bokanli; to crack a whip, hlukalichi, hlukata olachi; the sound produced by cracking a whip, hlukata ola.

Cracker. *n.* Puska kello, pesktupuski shila.

Cracking. *n.* Hlukahachi, basahuchi basahlichi, basakuchi: basahahanchi, basahkahanchi.

Cradle. *n.* Onush isht busha, onush isht umo, isht umo.

Crag. *n.* Okfa.

Cramp. *n.* Hlifa; a cramp in the leg, hauoli hlifa; I am cramped, sahlifa.

Crane. *n.* Wahtonlak, wahtonlak oshi, oskup tohbi, hushtohbi, wahtonla, wahtonla tohbi.

Crape. *n.* Nantonna lusa isht tabashi.

Crave. *v.* Benna, itukchuba.

Craw. *v.* Impafakchi.

Crawl. *v.* Shalall, balali, yalolli; crawling, shalali; continually crawling, shalalgli.

Crazy. *v.* Holillubi, tasimbo; to make crazy, tasimbochi.

Creaking. *n.* Kuchukuchi.

Cream. *n.* Pishukchi pakna nia; cream cup, pishukchi pakna aiolhto.

Create. *v.* Ikbi; creation, nana moma toba,

ikbi, nana moma ikbi, nana oklyhu ikbi.

Creator, *n.* Ikbi; the Creator. Chitokaka.

Credit, *v.* Ahekuchi, iyimmi, aheku; to get on credit; ahekah; a creditor, ahekuchi: a debtor, aheka im asha, aheket ishi; to sell on credit, ahekachi; amount not paid, aheka takgli: to let me have on credit, si ahekuchi, stahekuchi, ak chim aheka.

Creek, *v.* Bok, bokushi, okhinushi oka ayanoli, oka abachaya: junction of creeks, bok ai ittoseli; the channel, bok ayanolli, swamp or creek bottom, lyssa, bok anuka; mouth, bok asetili; the branches of a creek, bok chuhbli, bok chuhlahli: a branch of a creek, bok chuhlofli; long creek, bok falaia; the fork, bok falakto; the side, bok i tunnup; the other side, bok mishtunnup; this side, bok ola tunnup; main creek, bok upinli; head, bok wishakebi; a bridged creek, bok iti patelhpo.

Creep, *v.* Balali, baloli; to creep up slyly, apuhli.

Crevice, *e.* Bisinlichi, bitanlichi; a crevice: bitanli, wakla; crevices, waklali; to make a crevice, waklachi.

Crew, *n.* Hatak kanohmona, hattak kanohmi ona.

Crib, *n.* Kanchak, picha, tanchi i chuka.

Cricket, *n.* Shalontaki.

Criminal, *n.* Anumpa kobufli; criminate, onochi.

Crimson, *n.* Tishepa, natishepa, homma.

Cripple, *v.* Chahlklichi, tabiklichi; a cripple, hattak imokpulo.

Crockery, *n.* Amp heta, ampushi; broken crockery, amp kokoa.

Crook, *v.* Tanakbichi, shanaiyuchi; crooked, chassullah fulumoa; tanakbi, chanakbi pe tauantobi; a crook, chasala; to cause to crook, chassalichi; crooked, (as legs), ikchisimo.

Crop, *v.* Bushli, topli; cropped, busha, topa.

Cross, *v.* Taiyukhunoll, atak lumni; crossed, taiyukhuna; to go across, atampichi; a crossing, atanapa; cross, indisposition, bashka iksho, holhpgsi, iksho, okpolo; to cross at, akuchi; to cross, hlupulli; across, hlopulli; to cause to go across, hlopullechi; to be cross or ill, hushaya; to make another cross, hushayuchi; to lay wood across, iti abunscali iti abenna; cross, (an obstruction), katapa; lying across, nan aiyukhuna; a crossing or ford ahlupulli; crosswise; hanaiuchi.

Crotch, *n.* Iti falakto, falakto.

Crouch, *n.* Bikuttokuchi.

Croup, *v.* Fiopa tahli.

Crow, *v.* Ola, ilawata; a crow, fula, a raven, fula chito; carrion crow, sheki kulofa, sheiki tullo; a scare crow, fula atoni; to watch crows, fula atoni, tuli isht afenna.

Crowd, *n.* Hatak laua; to crowd, lokoli.

Crown, *v.* Mikochi; a crown, ia chuka; to wear a crown, ia chukoli; the crown of the head, nushkobo, iafufo.

Cruel, *a.* Kullo, nan okponui kot im achukma.

Crumb, *n.* Puska, bushulli.

Crumble, *v.* Boshullichi, boshulli, fakolichi; crumbled, bushulli, fakoha.

Crumple, *v.* Shekufli; crumpled, shikofa,

Crush, v. Pichifli; crushed, pichefa; to crush any hollow thing, wohlopli; crushed, wohlopa.

Crust, n. Hakshup, puska hakshup.

Cry, v. Yaiya, payya; crying, pahaya; a crier, tahpela; to make cry, yayechi.

Cub, n. Nitushi. na poa ushi.

Cubit, n. Kubit, man tenna ish clhpisa iklena foka

Cucumber, n. Okchak holba.

Cud, n. Hopasa.

Cull, v. v. Aiyua; to cull, aiyuachi.

Cultivate, v. Apoksiachi, achukmalichi; cultivator yakni isht lapushkichi, yakni isht patafa lana tauchi isht luli.

Cumin, n. Kummiu.

Cunning, n. Haksi.

Cup, n. Isht ishko; cupping, lepish takalichi; cupboard, uba tula ampo aiasha, uba tula; cream cup, peshukchi pakna aichto.

Cupidity, n. Holitopa bonna.

Curable, a. Hlakofa hlulu; to cure, hlakofichi ulluchi, masalichi.

Cured, v. Hlakofli, utta; will be cured, hlakofachi; incurable, hlakofa he keyu; to commence to cure, hlakofit isht ia; to cause to cure at, ahlakofichi; cure at, ahlakofi; to cure self, ileblakofich I.

Curd, n. Walaha; to curdle; welakuchi; curlled, wnlahah.

Curl, n. Yikyua, yushbouli; to curl up, bochussalih, bochussachi.

Current, n. A yauelli.

Curse, v. Chakapa, issikopali, annumpa okpullo isht miha.

Curtain, n. l helmo nan tenna toba.

Cutlele, v. Hakshup.

Carve n. Chussula' to make curl, chessulachi.

Custom, n. Ayohmi, nan clhpisa, uan aka niohini chatuk, customarily, ke, kanche ke.

Cut, v. Chruli, chuhli, bushli; to cut, chaya chubla. besha; to cut off, chanut tepli; to cut from or at, abesha, akolufli; cut at or upon, abushli; the part cut off, ahokofa;

the place where cut off, ahokofa, ahokoufa; to cut off together, ahokolichi, abokohli, ahokoflichi; to cut off with knife or saw, bushlit tepli; cut off, bushut upa; to cut a piece, bushlit tushufli; cutting a piece, bushlit teshafa; cut in, chokoah; to cause to cut in, chakolichi; to cut meat for drying, chakolib;cut up into small pieces, chanut teshtuli, chakowah; to cause to cut or chop, chanlichi; to cut down, chant kincffli. akuchi; to cut a notch, chant lampli; to cut down into water, chant okuchchi; a cut or gush make by an ax, chayot pachafa; a cut; chaya; cut lengthwise; chuhlata; to cut in narrow strips, chublulli; to cut to a point, halupuchi; to cut off once; himona tepli; cut off, hokofli; cut pieces, hokohli, to cut piec. hokolichi; not cut, ik basho; not cutting, ik chanlo; to cut one's self with a knife, ile bushli; with an ax, ile chanli; to cut each other, itti chanli; to cut with scissors, kacheh: cut with scissors, kalasha; to cut down kinufli; to cut trees down, kinahlichi. to cut off.kalufli, nachohlichi tebli; cut off. kolofa, tepa: to cut several pieces. kololichi; cut in many pieces, kolohli; to cut up many, ketulhhli; many cut up, ketohli; to cut open, mitahuchi, mitahli, mitefi; cut open, mitefa; cutting open continually, mitchafa; one who cuts na bushli; to cut off the legs, nipalichi nipahli; to cut off at the shoulders, nipufli; to cut from the body, niplih; hair cut short, okkuhlonli; to cut the belly open, patufli, ph, petehlichi; to cut by scratching, shullifte; cutting a piece out, shulofah, to cut fine tihli; to cut a piece, tushuffi, tushli; to cut many pieces, tustuli, tushalichi; to cut to a point. telhhli; cut to a point, telha; to cut many off, teptuli; many cut off, tuptua.

Cutworm, n. Haigwenk.

Cypress, n. Shakola.

D

Daily, ad. Nitak moma, nitak atukma, nituk aiyuka.

Dale, n. Okfa, okuttuhaka; dell, okfa iskitini.

Dam, n. Oktepli; dammed, oktepa.

Damage. v. Okpeni. damaged. okpullo,

Damnation. n. Apelemi; damned, ai okpoloka.

Damp. n. Hotokbi; dampened. hotokbi.

Dance. v. Hihlah; a place to dance at. abibla; to dance for or to. ahihlechi; to make dance hihluchi; dancing hihlah; to dance with. ibahibla; a woman that sings a dance song. ihilhi; to dance with each other. ittihihla.

Dandruff. n. Nushkobo fochonli.

Dare. v. Pafi; I dare you, hump-hi;

Dark. a. Lusbi (color). okhilli: very dark,

tampki; darkness. ai okblilika, ai akhlika; to color dark. lusakbichi.

Darn, v. Akolli; darned. ulhkota.

Dart, v. Tibulli.

Daub, n. Apelusli; daubed. ulhpolusa.

Daughter. n. Ushi tek; grand daughter, ipoktek. daughter-in-law. ipok; my daughter-in-law. sapok.

Dawn. n. Onot okhllljchi.

Day. n. Nitak; daylight. onah; becoming daylight. onnot tcha: almost day. onnaghosi; all day long. shohbichi.

Deacon. n. Chuch nan isht im utta.

Dead. a. Illi. fiopa tepa; you are not dead; ikchilio; we are dead, pilli; I am about dead, si ai illi mak oke, sulli mak oke; I am dead, sulli.

Deaf. a Haksobish, haksi. ikhaklo; deaf-

ness, haksi, ikhaponaklo; deafen, haksu-
la, baksubachi.

Deal, *v.* Itatoba, kanchi; dealt. it ulhtoba;
good deal, fichna; to have mutual deal-
ing, ittimakaniohmi.

Dear, *a.* Holitopa; very dear. hilotompa;
it is dear to me; ghollo. to be dear to,
jholitopa; very dear to. jholitopa fehna;
a very dear friend, ittikana fehna; O dear!
okokko!

Death, *n.* Illi; to cause death, illichi; an occasion that caused death, ai isht illi;
a death bed, ai illi.

Debase, *v.* Kalaksichi; debased, kalakshi.

Debate, *v.* Itachowa.

Debt, *n.* Aheka; debtor, aheka im asba;
balance of debt not paid, aheka, takali.

Decay, *v.* Toshbi; to cause decay, tosbbichi,
shakbouvchi; decayed toshbi, shakbona.

Deceitful, *a.* Haksi.

Deceive, *v.* Haksichi; yimmichi, a deceiver;
haksichi, continually deceiving;haksihiu-
chi, hatak haksichi, deceived; haksichi,
jhaksichi, one who is deceive to or by
jhaksi; to deceive self, ilehaksichi; to
deceive with, isht haksichi.

Deck, *v.* Shemuchi; decked, shema.

Declare, *v.* Otuninchi. anoli; declared,
ouni; annowah, I declare! okokko! decla-
ra :on, aintokowa.

Decree, *n.* Anumpaulhpesa; nan ulhpisa.

Deed, *n.* Akaniohmi; deeds, nana akaniohmi puta.

Deep, *a.* Hofobi; somewhat deep. hofombi;
to deepen, hofobichi; to set deep, hofo
bichit hilechi; to plant deep, hofo bichit
hokchi, a deep place, hofobika; hofom-
bika. deep there. ahofombeka; not deep,
ikhofobo; hofobi keyu.

Deer, *n.* Issi; doe, issi iek; buck, issi nakni-
lapitta; fawn, issushi.

Defame, *v.* Achukushpeli; aholubi, Chakapa, a defamer, hatak naumcchi.

Defeat, *v.* Im aiycchi, i shahlechi; to cause
defeat, jhlakofichi

Defend, *v.* Apela, apipoa.

Defraud, *v.* Haksichit im ai ishi, defraud.
haksichi.

Defy, *v.* I sanali, pafi.

Degrade, *v.* Chakapa, hofahyalichi.

Degree, *n.* Ahika.

Deject, *v.* Hlipushichi; dejected, Hlipushi.
isht awiha.

Delay, *v.* Sulaha, hopakichi. to cause delay,
hopakeehcihi.

Delight, *v.* Yukpali.

Deliver, *v.* Ima, hlakofiebih, a deliverer,
hlakofichi.

Delude, *v.* Haksichih, yimmichih.

Deluge, *n.* Oka falama.

Demand, *v.* Asilhah, hoyoh.

Demolish, *v.* Akkuchchih.

Demon. *n.* Nanisht ahullo okpullo, setau.

Den, *n.* Chuka, hichukbi. bichukbi.

Denominate, *v.* Hochifo. *n.* Icnomination.
hochefo.

Dense, *a.* Sukko, tampki.

Dent, *n.* Habefa, hafakbi, hufikbi. dented,
habefoa, to make a dent, hofikbichi, ko-
fokbichi yafi, dented yafa.

Deny, *v.* Aha achih.

Depart, *v.* Kuniah iah, illi, illit. kunia, departed, chofah, departing. chuhafa, to

cause fo depart, cheflichi.

Depend. *v.* Anukchetoh, to depend on, ai
anukchito, dependent. anukchito, may
depend upon, anukchita hinla.

Deposit, *v.* Bohlih. continually depositing.
bohohlih one that deposits. bohli.

Depravity, *n.* Chukush im anukfila okpulo
ai imonua, okpullo.

Depress, *v.* Chukush akanlusih, depressed
chykush, akkglosi. isht awiha, depres-
sion, chukuvsh iknakno.

Decide, *v.* Isht, yopalah.

Descend, *v.* Aka iah, ak owah. ak kiah, a
descendeht. ai isht atiaka, chukachvfa.
isht atia, a descendant of the Choctaws,
chahta isht atia, a descendant, isht ai
onchuloli, isht atiaka.

Desert, *v.* Kuniah, issut iah, a deserter, ai
itupeha i falummi.

Desert, *n.* Chokushmi foka, yakni hayaka.
shinuk foka.

Desire, *v.* Ahnih bennah, polumunih, to
earnestly desire, ahni ghli, not to desire.
ikahnincho, desiring pollumma

Desk, *n.* Aholissochi, aianumpuli, ai o holissochi.

Despair, *v.* Yohma he ahni ik im ikshe,
yohma he ahni ik ai ithano.

Desperado, *v.* Hatak haksi atupa. nan
okponi.

Despise, *v.* shitilemah. isht ik i ahno. ika-
hoboloh, kunimmcchih.

Despoil, *v.* Okpenlh, wehpolih, despoiled.
okpulo, wehpoah.

Destroy, *v.* Okponih, destroyed, okpulo,
bakustoh, to destroy all, bakustolih, a de-
stroyer, nan okpeni.

Destruction, *n.* Ai okpuloka, isht ai okpulo mapalummi.

Desuetude, *n.* Aksho.

Determination, *n.* Achilita chilita to cause
determination, achilitcchi chititcchi, to
be determined, ai yimitah, moshollikah,
not determined, ikayiminto.

Detonate, *v.* Hilohah.

Develop, *v.* Hayakcchi.

Deviate, *v.* Folotah, to cause to deviate,
folotolih folotolichih folotowuchih, de-
viation, fitummi.

Devious, *a.* Fulumoa, folotah.

Devour, *v.* Upot tabli, isht upa, housa.
hopasa.

Dew, *n.* Fichak, Honey dew, fichak champuli, fichak kushgha. to fall as dew,fichak
lewili chohmi, dewberry, bissa untaluli.
haiuntaluli, sheu lap, wolaha, i welaha,
imbichyukohakshup.

Diagonal, *a.* Hanaiyah.

Disk, *n.* Heshi kanulli isht ulhpisa:.

Dialogue, *n.* Ittimanumpuli.

Diarrhoea, *n.* Ikfuh, issish hlopulli to
have diarrhoea isht ahlopulli to cause
diarrhoea, ikfiechi.

Dictate, *v.* Anumpa apesah.

Die, *v.* Illi, flopissah nusi, to die ut, ai illi.
may die, illa hinla, dead, illi, illitkunia
to cause to die, illichi. death, illi, to die
for another who was killed, itticili. I am
about to die, siaililih nuak oke. suli mak
oke. I came near dying, sullinghah. I am
dead sullih.

Differ, *v.* Itim lnla, ittachowa. ittimnukowa
to cause to differ, ittachowuchih, differ-

cut Ikliltillollo.

Difficult, *a.* Ahchiba kello, palemmi.

Diffident, *c.* Nukwiya.

Dig, *v.* Kulli, dug, Kula; digger, na kulli, to root or dig the ground with the nose, wosholichi.

Dike, *n.* Oka isht oktopa, yakni a kula, oaute, *v.* Chitolih.

Diligent, *a.* Ai ahli aiokpanchi, achunanchi; diligently, achukmalit.

Dilute, *v.* Ikhomecho, diluted, ikhomo.

Dim, *a.* Tohbi, kashofa, okhlilechi, tuhfokoli, to cause dimness, tuhfokolichi.

Dime, *v.* Iskeli, taia, time nehcfa ket sint pokoli.

Diminish, *v.* Koyu'flih, habofah, to cause to diminish habofcchi, habofichi habohlichi diminished, habohlih.

Dimple, *n.* Yikqwa.

Dine, *v.* Tahokoli impa upa.

Dint, *n.* Habefa, habiflichi, habifli, dented or indinted, habefah pl. habefoh, habifkvchi.

Dip, *v.* Chcbbili, to dip up, takefli, dipped up, taksfah, dipper, Ishtkcfa.

Direction, *v.* Pimma (yet when said the finger is always pointed) another direction, okhowaia, okhowatali.

Direful, *a.* okpullo,

Dirk, *n.* Bushpo isht ittibi.

Dirty, *v.* Litiha, to make dirty, litchli, itiihli, a dirty fellow, hnttak litcha, dirty face okhlitouli. I am dirty, salitlhah.

Disappear, *v.* Koniah, disappeared, akonia, halatah.

Disappoint, *v.* Yimmichih.

Discard, *v.* Kanchih, kanchichih, discarded kucha, kunia.

Discern, *v.* Akostininchih, undiscernable, nkostinincha hekeyu; discernable, akostinincha hinla.

Discharge, *v.* Hyssah, (i. e. a gun) issechi.

Disciple, *n.* Aiithana, ithona, nan ithona, uba anumpa ithona, discipline ai im abcchi, ai akostininchi.

Discourage, *v.* Chykcsh illichi, discouraged chykcsh illi.

Discourse, *v.* Anumpulih, the head of a discourse, anompa nushkoba.

Discover, *v.* Ahanchih, ahaynchi atonninchih, akostiniuchih. [haiyakcchih, okiahlih, discovered okfahah,

Discretion, *n.* Hopoyuksa.

Disdaln, *n.* Shittilemah, disdainful, shittilemu.

Disease, *n.* Abeka, llilli, contegeous disease, halcli, I have caught the contageous disease; sahalelih, to take or catch disease, elmollih, to give another disease, ulmollichih.

Disgrace, *v.* Hofahyalih, hofahycchih, disgraced, hofahyah, to disgrace self, llchofahyali disgraceful, hofahya, disgraced hofahya.

Dish, *n.* Ampo, amphcta, bread dish, puskaaicihto, a shallow dish, amp mahaia, amp malussa, a deep dish, ampo kolukbi, dishes, aiapushi, a flat dish, ampo patossa, a wash dish, ampo ai uchefa.

Dishearten, *v.* Chykcsh illichih, disheartened, chunkcsh illi.

Dishonest, *a.* Ikahlo, chykcsh ik ahlo, to be dishonest, ikaiahlo, to act dishonestly

isht akauomih, to act dishonestly with self; isht ilakanomichi, dishonor hofahya dishonorably, hofahyalit, a dishonorable man, hatak hofahya.

Dislike, *v.* Ikai okpachoh, ikahninchoh isht ikihono istikihahno, kaninmcchi.

Dislocate, *v.* Tahlollih, dislocated, tahlola, to cause dislocation, tahlofichi, dislocation, tahlofa.

Dismiss, *v.* Kuchchih, kanchih, dismissed, kuchah, kuniah, tiapah.

Dismount, *v.* Akkowah; dismounted, akkowah.

Disperse, *v.* Fimmih, fimiplih, dispersed, fimah, fimimpah.

Dispose, *v.* kanchih, disposed of, kuniah.

Disposition, *n.* Ai im ulhpiesa, a gentle disposition, bashka.

Dispute, *v.* Kulot itim anumpulih, it achowah, to cause a dispute, itachowcchi.

Dissertation, *n.* Holisso, annmpuli.

Dissoluble, *a.* Bilu binlu, indissoluble bilahe keyu.

Dissolve, *a.* Belochi, dissolvcable, bila hinla indissolvable, bila he keyu.

Distaff, *n.* Ponola kullo atakali.

Distance, *n.* Hopaki, a short distance, ikhopako, distant, hopaki.

Distemper, *n.* llilli, hlitika.

Distil, *v.* Holluyah, hoyah, distilled, holuyah.

Distract, *v.* Itta kcshkolih, a distracter, hattak, itta kcshkoli.

Distress, *v.* llbushalih, distressed, illvshah, Nukhaklo, Nukhvmah, Nahuttupa extremely distressed, issikkopa, to cause extreme destress, issikkopalih, I am distressed, sysikkopa.

Distribute, *v.* Hopclah, kushkoli, kushcpli, to distribute to each other, ittihopela, distributed, holhpcla, distribution, holhpela.

District, *n.* Ulhti.

Disturb, *v.* Ataklommih, Nukhakloch', afullih, aiullichih, anumpullichih.

Disuse, *n.* Aksho.

Ditch, *n.* Yaknl Kula, aka a yanulli,

Divan, *n.* Ai o binili.

Dive, *v.* Oklobushlih, pi, aklubbih, diver oklubbi.

Divert, *v.* Shanilih.

Divide, *v.* Itapahlcllih, kasheplih, kushkolih, iti hopela, divided it apablatah, itj holhpclah, holhpelah, divided iuto, bakapah, divide in branches, talaktuchi, divided in branches, falakto, to divide with, ittckuohupa, ittckushupli, a divider, kashvpli hopela, division-filamoli, holhpela.

Divorce, *n.* Holisso koshofa, itj kunia holisso, tekchi j kunio holisso.

Dizziness, *a.* Chukfoloha, yushtimilih, dizzy, to be dizzy, or being dizzy, yusht mili, to cause to be dizzy, chukfoloh chuh. chukfolohlih, I am dizzy, satasinoh.

Do, *v.* Yemmichih yamichih kaniohmih akaniohmih kaui ohmichi yohmih, to do so, ai yakohmi, a yakohmi, to do something with, akanimichi, doing something with, akanimih tahli, to cause to be done, akaniohmichi, a manner of doing, akaniohmi, (a fashion) to over do, ataplih, to do it over, ulbitilih, the same done over rebitet, doing or do, yemunohmi, have, shall or what must do, katimichih, katmichih.

Dock. *v.* Weshko ikhish

Doctor. *n.* Alikchi, a quack doctor, alikchi ila hobbi, a good doctor, alikchi achukma, alikchi impuuna, to doctor, alikchih.

Doctrine. *n.* Nan isht abechi, anumpa, nan isht hananchi.

Doe. *n.* Issi tek.

Dog. *n.* Ofi, his dog, ipcf. puppy, ofosik. a bitch, ofi tek, the owner of a dog, pushnayo, my dog, sapcf, dogwood, hakebopiihkupi, hakchopiihko.

Doll, *n.* Hatak holba isht washoha.

Dollar. *n.* Tcli holisso achufa.

Domestic. *n.* (cloth) Nantenna, nantenna tohbi.

Dominion. *n.* Apelichika, pehlichika.

Donate. *v.* Imissa, ipetah, donation, helbina.

Donkey. *n.* Issuba haksobish falaia.

Donor. *n.* Nahabencchi.

Door. *n.* Okhissa, aiabiha, aichliha aboha okhissa, a door shutter, okhisa isht okshilliihta, okhisa isht clbkuma, aboha isht okshilliihta door keeper, okhissa, atonih.

Dormitory. *n.* Anusi, aboh anusi.

Double. *v.* Puhlih, itelbilli, to double up, bounih bonulli doubled up. bonah, bonutah, doubled puhlah, bunni, itulbita, puihkachi, pohlomah (as a pocket knife) to shut or double up, as a pocket knife, pohlommih, pohlomolichi, continually doubling. pohlobommih. I am doubling up, sabonah.

Doubt. *v.* Anuktukl>, ikyimmo, doubtful anukwiah, chishba to be doubtful chishba, doubtless, ghlipulla, pulla, undoubtedly, ikahlokawa ikyohmokabeto.

Dough *n.* Tanche pushi lecha, sour dough shatemmi.

Dove. *n.* Puchi yoshoba.

Down. *n.* Abokbo, downs. Ilpismo, lipinto, to be thrown down, akkapilah, to throw me down, akkasepilah to come or get down, akkowah, down stream sokbish. downward, akkapilah, akcma. akimma, to go down, akkalah, akkaiah, to go down ward and hunt, akkahoyoh, to lie down, akkaittoloh, to fall down, akkaittulah fohopa akkckaha. fallen down, akkitulah, akkakahah, akkakohah, lying down, akkaittuyulah, laid down, akkakahut aisha, akkaksh tmgyah, botfalaid down, akkakaiyaha, I fall down. akkasutulah, you fall down, akkachittulah.

Drab, *n.* Lusbi.

Drag, *v.* Shallellichih halellih, akka shalellichih. dragging akka shalellichit halu-ili.

Drain, *n.* Holluya; holluyechi drained, holoya, yanolli.

Drake, *n.* Okfochush naknl.

Draw. *v.* Shalih, halcllih; to draw up through a loop, ahliffih ahliffichi: drown up, ahlifah; to draw out by hammering, bot shcplih; drawn out, bot shepah; to draw out,with a stick or finger, follih; to draw a liquid, bichilih: drawn, bicha; to finish drawing, bichet tahli; drawn

(from spasms,) halahlih; to cause to draw, halcllichih; to unravel or draw out. hiifa; to draw a chance or lot, mshuelih to draw water ochih; continually drawing water, olhchih; to draw down the ear, when made, as a horse, okmohlonlih; to draw out strands, shihlih; drawn out, shihab; to cause to draw out shihlichih; to draw up the hind part of the body suddenly. yefomokabehi; to draw up with heat, yekullih; drawnup, yikotah; drawing knife, isht shafa.

Dread. *v.* Komunta ikomuntah nukshopa, nukwio; to dread each other, ittikomuntah.

Dream, *v.* Holhpokunah; to cause to dream, holhpokunnuchih; to dream about, aholhpokunnechi; dreamed about, aholhpokunna; to dream,nusiku; I dream, sanusika.

Drench, *v.* Ishkochechi.

Dress, *v.* Fokkichit shema hlgfi; dressed fohka, hlgfa; to clothe or dress, fohkcehlchih; to dress for the grave, hattak illi isht afohllih; dressy, shemah; to dress in mourning, tabashih a dress, chikuma, cskuffa.

Drift, *v.* Hakchihpo, akehihpo.

Drill, *v.* Fatohlih: drilled, fotohah; a drill. teli isht fotohli.

Drink, *v.* Ishkoh; a place at which to drink, ai ishko; to drink with, ibai ishko; a drink, nan ishko.

Drip, *v.* Hoyah: dripped, hoiyah to cause to drip, hoiycehih, hallyuycehih; a dripping, hoiya.

Drive, *v.* Tihleiih pilhlihchih, ayah chufichih, clanwelih; driving in or to drive in, shenincllichil; to drive them. tihlilih; to drive them in, cbihlih; driven in, clbihkehi clbitkcehih: driven back, katapa, katapoa; to be driven in (as spokes) achushkcehi: driven, isht gya pehlichi; drover, nan olhpoa isht ayit.

Drone, *n.* Foi bila ishki hochito, hattak intakobi.

Drop. *v.* Hoyuchi, hoya, chilofah: dropped, holuya, kinahll, lewilih; to cause to drop, luoilichi; a drop, hoya; dropsy. oka atoba ililli, oka toba, oka [toba.

Dross, *n.* Hakhlopish.

Drouth, *v.* Chahto; to cause a drought, chahtochi; not drouthy, ikehahto.

Drown, *v.* Oka ai illi

Drum, *v.* Ahlipa chito olachi; a drum. ahlipa chito, ahlipa: drummer ahlepaboli; to beat a drum, ahlepa chitob lih; a drum stick ahlipa chito isht boti, ahlip isht boa, to sound the drum, ahlipa olah.

Drunk, *a.* Haksih; to be drunk haksi; oka haksih; drunkenness, haksih okishko haksih; somewhat drunk, haksi chohmi. shimmohah; not drunk, haksi keyu; to make drunk, haksichih; dead drunk, haksit illi: a drunkard, hattak okah ishko, okishko shahli; a great drunkard, hattak oka ishko shahli.

Dry, *a.* Shila beshshi, shelah; to be or being dry, shilah, chilakbi, chalakbi; to dry, shililih; dryness, shila; a place for drying, ahaka; to dry at, ashifilih; dried to or in, nshila; to cause to be dry, chahtochih, bushshichih; dried, chalokbih;

becoming dry, yauvllih; to make dry, yanuliehih, yuwvllichih.
Duck. *v* Oklobushlichih; ducked, oklobushlih; a duck. okfochush; drake, okfokchush nakni; a green head duck, bihlahchi, hakhoba; wood duck, hinluk; a diver, oklubbi kabaka; muscovy duck, muskoki okfochush; duck legged, akkutulla.
*Due. *a.* Aheka takali, ai ulhtoba ona; not due; at ulhtoba ik ono kisha.
Dull. *a* Ikhaluppe, tukbi; to dull, tukbichih; dullness, tuhfokoli, weki.
Dumb, *a.* Ikanumpolo, ikanumpulo.
Dumpling. *n.* Walakshi.
Dun, *n.* Bokboki.

Dung. *n.* Yelhki; dunghill, yelhki niashu; dung fork, yvlhki isht piha chufak.
Dusk. *a.* Okhlilahpi, okpolusbi, akshocho, bichi; shochobbi.
Dust. *n.* Botulli. hitok tohbi, hittukchubi, pushi; to dust, tetuhli.
Duty. *n.* Ai vihplesa, nana akaniomiha ulhpisa.
Dwarf. *n.* Hattak kawasha, hattak imoma; hattak ikchaho.
Dwell. *v.* Achykka; to dwell together. ittuchukuchi.
Dysentary *n.* Issish ikfia; to have dysentery; ikfihlichi; to cause dysentry, lkfiachi.

E

Each. *a.* Bika; each: aiyuka; each after his kind, ai immi aiyukali.
Eager. *a.* Achilita; to cause eagerness, achilituchih; to be eager. akomuntah, ayimintih; not eager, ikayiminto.
Eagle. *n.* Osi, Ossi.
Ear. *n.* Haksobish; ear lork, haksobish tapaiyi hishi,ampi, (corn); ear ache, haksobish hotupa roasting ears, nipushu; ear ring. haksobish: takahli; ear mark, haksobishbusha, marked ear. haksobish bushu; to mark the ear, hakso bish bushli; shrill sound in the ear, haksobish chasa; slit or split ear. haksobish chuhla; an ear slit, hakso bish chulafa; slit ears, haksobish chu hlahli; ear wax: haksobish hlitilli; a cropt ear, hakso bish hokofa;cropt ears, haksobish hokohli, hoksobish tupa, haksobish ulmo, haksobish tuptua; fox ear, haksobish ibakchufali; forked ear. haksobish chulakto; ear rings, haksobish takghli; the lobe of the ear, haksobish walohbi.
Early. *a.* Chike.
Earn. *v.* Asitubih.
Earth. *n.* Yakni lukfi, yakni; to be numbered with the earth, yakni uhulhtinu.
Ease. *v.* Nuktalali; eased nuktula; to take ease, fobah; easiness, nuktula; easy, nuktula: annktupah, nukehlto: quite easy, nuktaiyula, to make easy, nuktuali, nuktulalichi; to nuk all easy, nuktuluhlih; being easy, nuktula.
Eat. *v.* Impa, upa; to eat at or upon, ai impa; we eat, cpah; to eat with; ibai impu
East, *n.* Hushi akuchaka; eastern hushi akuchaka; casterly, hushi akuchaka.
Eaves, *n.* Ahoiya, ahoiya, chukka isht holmo uhli, aboha holmo uhili, oku ahoya.
Echo, *n.* Hobachi.
Eclipse, *n.* Heshi kunia.
Economical. *a.* Hatobah; economy, nan ila toba.
Eddy, *n.* Okfoyulli.
Edge, *n.* Alaka takcha, takchaka hallupa, uhli; two edged, hallupa tuklo, tahlahlaka hallupa.
Ediet, *n.* Nan ulhpisa, aunmpa ulhpisa.
Editor. *n* Holisso ikbi.
Educate, *v.* Holisso ithananchi; uneducated, holisso ikithano; educated holisso

ithana, holisso impuna
Efferversce. Honi
Effigy, *n.* Hatak hobuchih.
Egg. *n.* Akak ushi, akak ushi hlobon, akak ushi lobunchi: lobunchi; rotten egg. akak ushi shua; the yellow or yolk of an egg, akak ushi i lakna; the white of an egg, akak ushi i tohbi akak ushi i weluhu, akak ushi i wolakochi.
Eight, *a.* Untuchina; eight, auohuntuchna. eighty, pokoli untuchina; eight hundred, tahlepa untuchina; eighth, isht untuchina.
Either, *a.* Kanimampo; not either achuffahpi kia keyu.
Elate, *v.* Hawatah.
Elbow, *n.* Ibbak i shunkuni; elbow joint. ibbak i skukuni, itachukeli.
Elder, *a.* Buti, bashukchi, iksa akni, iksa pehlichi, iksa apesuchi; elderly, hatak assunochi,hatak tikba hatak,assunochikn the eldest or oldest brother or sister, akni.
Elect, *v.* Atokolih; elected, atokah, ulhtoka; election, vlhtoka; the place to hold an election, ui vlhtoka; an election by or with, nan isht vlhtoka; elector, atokoli, fotbohli.
Elegant. *a.* Isht imaka.
Elephant, *n.* Yulhkun chito; elifant.
Elevate, *v.* Chahachih; elevation, chaha; elevated, chahah; elevator, nan isht chahah.
Elm. *n.* Tohto;slipperyelm, balup.
Elope, *v.* Mullit kuniah.
Eloquent, *v.* Anumpuli impunna.
Elsewhere, *ad.* Kanimakinli.
Emaciate, *v.* Chunnachi hlepushich'n, hlipushih; emaciated, chunna, hlipush'.
Emasculate, *v.* Hobuk ikbi; emasculated, hobuk.
Embarrass, *v.* Anuktuklochih; embarrassed, anuktukloh unembarrassed, ikanuktukloh.
Embellish, *v.* Aiuklichi, akohlih; to embel, lish with, isht akohlih, isht ulhkohah, isht aiyklichih; embellished, ulhkohah.
Embers. *n.* Hitck yunha.
Embower, *v.* Hashontika ashuchi.
Embrace, *v.* Isht anukfokah shuolih; to embrace me affectionately, saprsholih.
Emetic, *a.* Hoetuchi, emetic wood, hiloka ikhish.

Emigrant, n. Wihut aya.

Eminence, n. Chaba | shahli, holitompa.

Emperor, n. Ulhti itibolhkaha | iniko.

Employ, v. Tohno; to employ me, satohno; employing, tohno, tohnoh.

Empty, a. Iksho, ikshot taha, staha, ikahobo, shahbi; to empty into, asitilib; to make empty, shabichih; (as a clean place).

Enamor, v. I hullochi, aiasitiah; enamored at or with, aiasitiah.

Encampment, n. Binah, binat asha, binot atasha; to encamp, binachih; encamping continually, binaltanchih.

Enchant, v. Afitiplih, afitiplichih, feppulih. afeppulih; enchanted, afitipah, feppulih an enchanter, hatak hulloka, isht ahullo; enchantress, ohoyo holloka.

Encircle, v. Apokfohlichih, apakfohlih, afolupli, afolnplichih; encircled, apakfohpah, afolupah afolotah.

Enclose, v. Fohklih; enclose fohkah.

Encourage, v. Atohnochih, atohnoh, naknichih, yimintochih; encouraging, nakni chih, yimintahanchih; encouraged, yimintah.

Ead, n. Ahokofa, ai uhli, hokofa, hokofifih, uhli; the extreme end, ai isht aiyop; to make an end, ai uhlichi ai yobbichih: endless, ai uhli iksho; to end something already commenced, ai yalbichih; ended, hokofa; the but end, sokbish.

Endure, v. Achunnachih, hlopullih.

Enemy, n. Tanampi, tunup.

Engage, v. Tohnoh itim apesah; engaged, itim ulhpisa

English, n. I klish, mhullo, englishman, iklish hutak; english language, nahullo im anumpa nahullo anumpa.

Engrave, v. Beshlit holissochih; an engraver boshlit holissochi; engraving, boshut holisso; engraved, bushut holisso.

Engross, v. Hochetolit holissochi; engrossed hochetolit holisso.

Enhance, v. Chitolichih.

Enigma, n. Nan ittim ikhum.

Enjoy, v. Yukpah; enjoyed one's self with, ai isht il ayukpah; enjoyment, ai isht il ayukpah.

Enlarge, v. Chitolih, chitolichih; enlarged. chito; to cause to be enlarged, chitoh lichih; an enlarger, hochetochi.

Enlighten, v. Ithananchih. | towikelichih. anukfohkih, enlightened, anuk fohkah, one that enlightenes, anuk fohkichi.

Enlist, v. Hohchifo ishih.

Enable, v. Chahachih.

Enormous, a. Chitoh.

Enough, a. Ulhpesa, lauu ulhpesa, yumma, not enough, ikono.

Enrage, v. Nokoachih, nukhobelochih, enraged, hukoah, anukshomuntah, to be enraged, anukshomuntah chukosh luah.

Enroll, v. Holisso takohlichih; enrolled, hohchifo holissot takohlih.

Enslave, v. Yukachi, a slave, yukab.

Entangle, v. Yushwichalih, to be entangled yushwichalih, ittufenah.

Enter, v. Chukowah, entered, chukowah, cannot enter; chukowa ho keyu.

Enthrone, v. Ai asha holitopa om binilichih, a throne, alasha kolitopa; seated on a throne ai asha holitopa ombinill.

Entice, v. Atonochih, anukpullichih.

Entirely, ad. Kemohmi, Kemmohmi.

Entomb, v. Aholluppi bohlih; entombed, holluppih.

Entrails, n. Iskuna; my entrails, suskona.

Entrance; n. Ai alota uchukkowa.

Entrap, v. Hoklichih; entrapped hoklih.

Entry, n. Achukkowa.

Enumerate, v. Holhtenah; enumerator, holhpenah, enumeration; holhtena, holhpina, hopenah.

Envious, a. Potonnoh, to cause enviousness, potonnohchi, envy, i nukkilli.

Epicure, n. Hattak impa shahli, issikopa.

Epilepsy; n. Halochi, holochichi.

Epistle, n. Anumpa holisso nowotaya.

Equal, a. Ittilani, lawi, lawichi; to be equal alawih,alawichi; lawih not equal ikalano; to equal, iti lauichi; to be equal to me; salawih; equal to aittilanih; equality, ai ittilauih.

Equip, v. Im atalhi; equipped, im ulhtaha.

Equality, n. Ahli.

Equ viente, v. Anumpa, apakfohlichih, anumpa folotowochih, anumpa ihiyuknchih; equivocation anumpa folotoah.

Eradicate, v. Ai isklachi.

Erase, v. Akcsha lih, akcshalichih; erasure akashafa

Erect, v. Hilechih; ikbi hiohlichi; erected, hikia, toba hiohlih, to erect at, ahilechi.

Err, v. Ashuchi; yoshoba; tp err at aiashuchi; error; aiashochika.

Erudition, n. Hattak nan impunna; hattak impunna, holisso impunia, nan impunna.

Eruption, n. Bokafa; foi ilweli.

Escape, v. Hlakoli; escaped ahlakolli.

Especially, ad. Ana, ak he, akheno, ak het, akheto.

Expound, v. Ittebohlih, itti halelih.

Essay, n. Holisso.

Establish, v. Hilichih, ghlichi; established; hikia.

Esteem, v. Ahninchi, holitobli, hih ahni-highly esteemed; holitompa, inestimable holitopa atepa.

Eternal, a. Bilia, bilivt bilia, bilia cha bilia, to cause to be eternak biliachichi.

Eucharist, n. Chitokaka im opiaka impa, opiaka impa holitopa, (Lord's supper.)

Eulogize, a. Holitopa isht anunpa; eulo, gized, holitopot isht anunpa; eulogy; holitoblit isht anumpull.

Eunuch, n. Hobak, hatak hobak.

Evacuate, v. Kuchut wiha, isset tamoa, holofah.

Evade v. Apakfopa, hlakofi.

Evangelist, n. Ubanumpa ithananchi; ubanumpa isht otta, ubanumpa tosholi, ubanumpa isht aya, holisso holitopa holissochi.

Evasion, n. Anumpa apakfopa.

Even, ad. Akkia ittilawi, hokakkia, makkia, yakkia; even as, akkia; it is even, ak makoka, akmokoke; akmakona; even this or that; ak oh kia to come even with; ittakshoh, lauechi ittakonia, to be even ittilauih; to make even, ittilauichi

Evening, n. Opia, opia ka shohbi, okyah, early in the evening, okhlilahpi shohbi kauli, till evening, okyachi, shohbi.

Ever, a. Bilia, aiimoma, chattuk, ever and ever, bilut bilia, billlucha bilia, forever, ont ahokofa wa bilia chabilia.

Ever-green, n. Okchamali bilia.
Ever-lasting, n. Bilia, bilia cha bilia, ai ulhliksho.
Every, a. moma, every one, moyuma.
Evident, n. Otuni.
Evil, n. Haksi, ai okpulo.
Ewe, n. Chukfi tek.
Exalt, v. Chuhachih, holitoblichih; oxalted, halitopa chaha, exaltation, isht aholitopa. •
Examination, n. Holisso apissa kucha, to examine pisa, pisa akostiniuchi. atanalichi, anukfillit pisa, bushlit pisa, to examine one's self ilanukfillet pisa, anukfillit ile pisa; examined, anukfillit.
Exasperation, a. Chukush lua.
Exceed, v. Ontiah. atupah, i shahlib exceeding, fichna,
Excellency, n. Chitokaka; excellent achukma hochukma, aiyoba, most excellent. achuyukma,hochukma,hochuyukma, excellencies, hochukma,
Exchange, v. It atobuchi, itatobah; exchanged, it ulhtobah.
Excite, v Afullichih to suddenly excite with anger, nukhlibishshikachi.
Exclude, v. Ikholhtino.
Excommunication, n. Akucha ulhpisa, eating with, ibai impa, we all eat, iloh impa; to eat together, ittibai impa; to make eat, upachih; still eating: ampah; to keep eating, ahampa, eatible or edible, apa.
Excrement, n. Yulhki.
Excuse, v. Imahaksichih, kashofi, hlakofichih: to excuse one's self, nan isht il i mihuchih.
Execute, v. Isht antah, attali; execute, isht utta ai ghlichi: executed, ulhtaha: exccutioner, hatak nuksitili; executive, miko
Exemplify, v. Haiyakuchih.
Exercise, n. Abuchi.
Exhaust, v. Tikambichih;exhausted,akuniah, kota, tikambi, taha.
Exhibit, v. Otuninchih, haiyakuchih, pisachih.
Exhortation, v. I mihiba. anumpa, nan

atohnohonchi. isht atonohchi.
Exile, n. Hatak kunia.
Exorbitant, a. Fiehna.
Expect, v; Ahnih; expectorate, hotilhko tofah kihhlafah.
Expedient, a. Ai ulhpesa.
Expel, v. Kuchichih, chuffichih; expelled, kucha.
Expensive a Iulli chito.
Expire, v. Fiopissah, illih, nusih.
Explain v. Otuninchih, anump tusholih; explained anumpa tushoah, otoni; explanation, anumpa tushowah.
Experience, n. Alimomaka.
Explode, v. Bokutlih, exploded, bokuffah, aksho.
Expose, v. Hohfahyuchih, walih; expositor, anumpa, tusholi; exposure, haiyakah
Expressman, n. Hatak anumpa isht aya.
Extend, v. Chitolih, chitolichih falafachih; extended, chitolih; extension falaia.
Extinct, a Iksho. mosholi, ai issa, akshoh.
Extinguish, v. Mosholichi, okpuni.
Extol, v. Holitoblichih, ai okpuchih.
Extract, v. Akuchichih, bushlih; extracted, akucha bushah.
Extravagant, a; Atupa. flehna.
Extreme, a. Fichna, ai i shali; ai i shahli.
Extricate, v. Hlakoffih; extricable, hlakofa hinla.
Eye. n. Nishkin; sore eyes, niskin hotupa. hulbubi; sunken eyes, ibakshohinli; watery eye, okhaiyanli; eye lashes, shillikchi niskin; near sighted or dull eye. nishkin tclhha, to have swolen eyes, eyes full of matter, okhlachonlih, okbosonlih okmosonli; eye ball, nishkin nihi; eye brow imosana; eye lid. nishkin itiulbi, sleepy eyes. okhlapunli; v. to eye peschi.o hopokoyu, atokot pisa;a squint eye, one out or cock eye, okshakinli; an eyesight holhponayoh, hoponaya; to wink the eyes, akmoshlih; to wink one eye. mochuukli; to cause eyesight, holhponaybhi. hopunnayuchi; nearly closed eyes okfakolih; blue eyed, oktalonli; hazel eye,okwalonli, okwelonli .

F

Face, n. Nashuka, nashshuka; a bald face, ibakhatanli; red face, ibak homali, itak homali; a dirty face or unwashed face, okhlichanli, okhlitonli; to make face at, okmislih; my face sunashuka; to face, ulutulih asahali it asanli; facing ulutah.
Fact, n. Ahli.
Fail, v. Shippa, akunia; to make a failure: ikahlicho.
Faint, a. Tikambi kotu; fainting, shimoha, illi; fainted, shimoha: 1 am fainting, sashimmohah.
Fair, a. Achukma, ai ghli, masheli.
Fairy, n. Kahikanchak: chukkishikanchiks
Faith, n. Na Yimmika, ai yimmika, ayimmi, yimmi; to be faithful, ai ahli; faithfully ai ahlika; very faithful, aiahli achukama. ai ghli fehna; faithful, nan ghli.

Fall, v. Akkittula, kinafa, pl kinahli, iklawot ia chilafah; to fall down. akka ittu laha, ittula pl. akka, kaha; fallen down. akkaittulah akka kohah; I fall down. akka suttulah; you fall down. akka chiitulah; to fall down from disease, akkummah, to cause to fall. chitohi chilofuchi; falling chilohgfa; to fall down. fihopa, hlitahah (as water); to fall down on the face, hliput ittulah; to fall with ibai ittulah: not fallen. as leaves. ikchilofo; the fall of the year. hushtulahpi onafahpi; fo fall into. ittuttulah; to fall (as fruit). lewilli; to make fall. lewilichi; to fall on. onotolah: fall of man. hatak ummona tobu yoshoba, hattak ummona ashuchi ummona.
Fallible, a. Haksa hinla, asucha hinla.

False, *a.* Ik ahlo! to be false, holubih; falsely, holubit, often used as an adverbial phrase, as, holubit ish nohowa nah, do not go about telling lies; falschood, holubi, anumpa holabi.

Falter, *v.* Anukchinto.

Fame, *n.* Aiannohqwa, annon; famous isht anoa, annoa achukma.

Family, *n.* Chukkachuffa; pertaining to a family, chukkachuffa ai ahaiaya, ai okla; the head of a family, hattak chukka chufa pehlichi; his family, į chukka achuffa.

Famine, *n.* Hopoba hohchufo.

Famish, *v.* Hohchufo, hohchufot illih.

Fan, *v.* Amahlichih; to fan at, amushlichih, ahmahlih, mushlichih; fanned, mushachih; fanning mushlihinchi; fanner, ufkoh; a fan isht amahlichi.

Fancy, *v.* Anush kunnah; a fancy, aunushkunna.

Far, *a.* Hapaki; farther, hopaki, į shahli; very far, hopaki fehna; to cause to go far, hopakichi, hopakichichih; not far, ikhopako, bilika; not gone far, ikhopakicho not very far, olanlih; close by, olalosi, olasi; long way off, olanlichi keyu; very near there, onghosi.

Farmer, *n.* Osapa tuksuli, hatak ossupa atok suli.

Fascinate, *v.* Chukush yukachi; fascination, isht ahullo.

Fashion, *n.* Ayohmi

Fasten, *v.* Akamussulih akullochi afachalih, takali, afachah; fastened, akamussa; fastened together, ittu fehnah; to fasten strong or tight, akullochi; tight or strong, akulloh akamussah; to fasten a latch, afachalih; fastened, afacha, to cause to fasten, afachalichih; not fastened or stopped, ikakamusso; fastened together, ittakamussah, to fasten together, ittaka mussulih.

Fast, *a.* Tushpa, pulhki. chahlih shinimpah, (used for walking,) walk fast, chahlih; to make walk fast, chahlichih; fast and fasting, ik impoasha, nuhullochi,; to fast, okissah; to make go fast, pulhkichich.

Fat, *n.* Nia, bila; somewhat fat, nia chohmi to fatt n, niachi, ipetot niachi; fattening, hlampko, niachi; fattened, niachi, ilhpitut nia; I am fat, saniah.

Father, *n.* Iki; my father, aki; your father, chiki; his, her their father, iki; our father, piki father or mother-in-law, ipolichih; grand-father. imafo.

Fathom, *v.* akka boyoh; fathomless, akkaiksho.

Fatigue, *v.* Hoyapli; to fatigue, hoyaplichi tikabichi; fatigued, kota, tikahbi.

Faucet, *n.* Oka abicha, oka abichili.

Faulty, *a.* Asuchi.

Favor, *v.* Iti holba, to go in quest of or one who receives a favor, habenut aya; a favorite, ainsitia,

Fawn, *n.* Isushi.

Fear, *v.* I nukshopa į komunta; to cause fear, komallichi, nukshoil; fearfulness, nukshopa; fearful, anukwiah; fearful, sakomotah, sanukwiah.

Feast, *n.* Chepuli, impa chito, impa ulhpissa, impa chinto; a great feast, chepuli; to make a feast, chepulichi.

Feather, *n.* Hushi hishi, hishi; a chicken feather, akak hishi; to grow f athers, hishi, tobah: soft feathers, apukbo, apukbo lipismo, lipinto; a feather bed, hushi hishi patulhpo; a quilt made of feathers, kasmo.

February, *n.* Febuoli.

Feebleness, *n.* Haknip kota.

Feed, *v.* Impuchi, upachi; fed ilhpita, feeder, nan epeta.

Fee, *v* Potoli, pl, pasholi.

Feign, *v.* Ilahobbi.

Fell, *v.* Kinulfi, pl, kinabli; fell down akka kohah; to fall, chant kinulfi.

Felon, *n.* Hukopa, felonious, hukopa.

Feminine, *a.* Tek imina.

Fence, *n.* Holihta; the side of a fence, holihtah apotaka; fenced up, holihta fohka; picket fence, holihta halupa; fenceless, hohlita iksho; one string of fence, hohlita okhowataka, holihta okfoataka; to fence, hahtuchi; fenced, holihta, aholihta; a staked fence, holihta itta fenah; to stake a fence, holihta itta fenilih.

Ferment, *v.* Chobokuchi.

Ferry, *v.* Peni kuchichi, peni hlopullichi, ahlaopulli; I ferried, ahlopulli li tuk; ferryman, peni in talaia.

Fester, *v.* Aninchi, aninchichi; to cause to fester, aninchichichi.

Fever, *n* Yunha; to have fever and ague, hochukwut yunha; fever cake (spleen) luksi, fever bush, iti kosoma; bilious fever, vunha chito, lakua chita isht abeka.

Few, *a.* Kanomosi, kanomosi iklauo, achafon; to be few, chubihah, chubihusih.

Fiat, *n.* Ai Yummohma.

Fib, *v.* Holabi.

Fiddle, *n.* Ahlipushi; fiddle bow, ahlepa isht olachi ahlop isht olachi; a fiddle string, ahlipah ushi ishtallakchi; a fiddler; ahlepa olochi, a base fiddle; ahlipushi chito.

Fie, *inj.* chwa! chwak.

Field, *n.* Ossapa; a hay field, hashuk abusha.

Fiend, *n.* Hatak haksi atupa.

Fierce, *a.* Yiminta, achilita; to cause fierceness, achlituchi; fierceness, homi.

Fig, *n.* Fik, a fig tree, fik upi.

Fight, *v.* Itibi; itibih, to cause a figh, ittibichi; fighter, nan itibi.

Figure, . Hobachi; to figure, hotihua.

File, *n.* Mihlolfi; filing mihlohofi; filed, mihlofa mohlohli, haluppa; filed at, amihlofah; a file or rasp. isht mihlofu; a flat file. isht mihlofa patussa; hand saw file. isht mihlofa iskitini; filing. botulli.

Fill, *v.* Alotuli; to fill up, alotolih, cause to fill alotulichi, full, alotoa, ulotowah, fullness, alota.

Film, *n.* Hakhlopish.

Filter, *n.* Aholya, aholuya, to filter, holuya holyuchi. hoyah; filtrated holuya, hoyah; not filtered, ik hoyo, ik busho.

Filthy, *a.* Litiha, chakapa; filthiness. litiha

Fin, *n.* Nuni sanahchi, nuni sanibehi.

Finally, *adv.* Ont isht aiopi, ont isht aiopiha, polaka.

Find, *v.* Ahauchi, pisa, ahayuchi; to find each other, ittahaynchi, to find me, siahayuchi.

Fine, *a.* Chipinta, lapushki, achukma haluppa; very fine or small, chipunta'

chipintasi; to be fine or soft, lipistoh; to cause to be fine or soft. lipistochi, pretty and fine, ainkli.

Finger, *n.* Ibbak ushi; forefinger, ibbak ushi tikba; middle finger, ibbak ushi ikluona, little finger, ibbak ushi ulhli; finger nail, ibbak chush; finger end, ibbak ushi wishakchi; thumb, ibbak ishki; finger ring. ibbak foka; finger rings, ibbak ushi ubiha; my finger. subbak ushi; my finger nail. subbuk-chush; my thumb. subbuk ishki.

Finish, *v.* Tahli, loshumi, ai ghli, aighli-chi, isht ahlophili; continually finishing, tahghlih; finished, ai ulhtahah, taha, loshoma; to finish off with alashummih.

Fire, *n.* Luak, hullushini; fired, bolukmi, hollushmi; to set on fire, hukmi, hushmi, luahanchi; make or kindle a fire. otih, tikbakahli; fire coal, tobaksi; fire wood, ulhti; fire place, ai ulhti, luak ai ulhti; fire dogs, luak in tikeli.

Firm, *a.* Kullo, ghli, kamussa.

Firmament, *n.* Shutika, uba shutik.

First, *a.* Tikba, ummona, ahpi, tikba, bilika; at first, ummona kuno, ummona hokuno.

Fish, *n.* Nuni; a black fish, nuni lusa; cat-fish nokishwana. nakishtali kushka; crawfish, shakchi; perch nuni patussa; gar fish, nuni kullo; sucker, nuni impu-sha homma;sun fish, nuni patussa; trout, sakli, shupik; buffalo fish; yanush, nuni kushina; whale, nuni chito okhuta asha, to fish, okwehlih, nuni ubi, nuni hokli.

Fist, *n.* Ibbak bonulli

Fit, *n.* Ahayah, halahli halochi; to have a fit, haiuchichi; to fit in together, ittahayah.

Five, *.* Tahlapi; five times, isht tahlapi, isht tahlapiha.

Fix. *v.* Aliskah, aliskiachi: to fix ones self. ilaiiskiachi; not to fix, ikaiisko.

Flag, *n.* Akshish balama, shupha.

Flail, *n.* Onush isht nihechi.

Flame, *n.* Libbika; to flame, libbi; to make a flame, libbichi.

Flank, *n.* Ikfichukbi, iffichukbi.

Flannel, *n.* Chukfi hishi tunna.

Flap, *v.* Hopobuchi.

Flash, *v.* Lipachi, malutha achi, bashuk mullih, shuhboklih.

Flat, *a.* Patussa latussa, takussa, (pl, patuspoa); to flatten, latustoli,patussuchi, takussachih; somewhat flat, matuhli; flattened, takussolih; flat lands, yakni matali, yakni patali; flatness, takussa; to flatter, anumpa ghli keyu kia isht aiok-puchi, holabit yupali.

Flatulence, *n.* Akeluachi, shutuplichi; flat-ulent, shutuplichi.

Flaw, *n.* Bitauli: to cause a flaw, betanlichi.

Flax, *n.* Ponola kullo; wild flax, nuchi.

Flay, *v.* Illufi, (pl hlohli); flayed, hlufa hlohla.

Flee, *v.* Chufah; fleeing, chuhafa; flight, chufa; fled, chufah.

Fleece *n* Chukfi hishi ulmo; fleeced, chukfi hishi ulmoh.

Fleet, *n.* Fahlkih, shinimpah, to cause fleetness, pulhkichih.

Flesh, *n.* Nipi, haknip; reduced ih flesh, chunnah.

Flexible, *a.* Walohbi, bikota hinla; inflex-ible, bikota he keyu.

Flimsy, *a.* Okshichanli.

Fling, *v.* Bohpuli.

Flint, *n.* Tussunuk.

Float, *v.* Okpulalih, takakant aya.

Elog, *v.* Fummi; flogged, fuma.

Flood, *n.* Okchito yakni tahli, oka chito.

Floor, *n.* Iti patulhpo, iti patupo; ground or lower floor, akka iti patulhpo.

Florid. *a.* Homma, hommuchi.

Flour, *n.* Bota, bota tohbi, onush bota pushi; corn flower, tanchit bota; cold flour, bota kapussa; parched corn flour, bota lushpa.

Flourish. *v.* Fahfolih.

Flow. *v.* Yanulli.

Flower, *n.* Pakanli; passion flower, hach-uktakaha.

Fluctuate, *v.* Bunukuchi.

Fluency, *n.* Anumpa i kucha achukma; to be fluent or fluent, anumpuli impunna.

Flush, *n.* Nashuka homma toba, homma.

Flute, *n.* Isht i pyfa, Uskolah; to play on the flute, Oskula alachi.

Flutter, *v.* Timiklih, timikmili; flytter-timikmikli.

Fly, *v.* Hika, (plural, heli); a house or blow chukani: a fly blow, chukanushi; to fly open, fachama, horse fly, ohlana, ohlana lakna, wublana; butterfly, hutapushik; large butterfly, opa shilup; a fly, shyshi; a gad fly, chunafilubi; large horse fly, ohlana chito; small horse flies, ohlana chipinta, spanish flies, shyshi wulh-korhi toba.

Foam, *n.* Pokpoki; to make foam. pok-pokichi.

Fodder, *n.* Tanchi hishi. tash hishi.

Foe, *v.* Tunup, tunampi, i sanali.

Fog, *n.* Oktohbi; to cause fog, oktobichi.

Fold, *v.* Puihhlih, pohlommichi; folded, puhlah, pulhkuchi, pohlomah; to fold up in, abonullih; to pen or fold, holiht uni, pened or folded, holihta ulhto; wrinkled or folded, yikifa; to wrinkle or fold, yikiffih; foliage, iti hishi.

Folk or **Folks,** *n.* Okla hattak.

Follow, *v.* Iakaiya; to follow up as a creek, afohkichi; followed, ahlioh; following after or next, achaka: future or following timehimmak, himmak pilla; following after (if one) iakaya, if two or more, iakaiyoha; to follow each other around, ittifollillichi; to follow uc, siakaiyah; to send to follow me, siakaiyuchi; fol-lower, im antia, iakaiya, im i thuna.

Fond, *a.* I hullo atupa; to be fond of, anushkunna; to fondle me, sapushohlih.

Food, *n.* Nan upa, ilhpak, illimpa. pinak.

Fool, *n.* Hatah lin anukfila iksho.

Foot,Iyi; foot of a tree, akishtula; hollow of the foot. iyi putta kalukbi; insteap, iyi putta pakna; heel, iyikotoba; sole, iyi putta; toe, iyushi; big toe, iyishki; little toe, iyush uhli; toe nail, iyakchush; a foot log or foot bridge, achup; my foot my feet, saiyi; my toe nail, saiyukchush; footman, akkayah, akka hekkit aya; footmen,akka hika; foot stool, aighikin; a foot path, hinushbi; a foot. print, ahabli.

Fop, *n.* Hatak ilak shema shahli.

For, *conj.* Abah! as for, in connection nominative, ak akuto.

Forbid, *v.* Im olubi, alumih, alumichi:

forbidden, alamah, alumah.

Force, *n.* Illamko; to force iu, shom-ollichi, kafollh.

Ford, *n.* Ahlopuili, akucha, hinakocha; to ford, okahika; I forded recently, ahlopulle li tuk; I forded there some time since, ablopullili tok; fordable, okahikah; not fordable, oka nowu he keyu.

Forefather, Iatak in tikba.

Forehead, *.n* lbi takla. immossona; prom-inent forehead, okussonli; high, broad forehead okkomuli.

Foreign, *n.* Yakni inla, oklush inla, ahalaya keyu; foreigner, okla inia, hatak iula.

Foreknowledge, *n,* Ai yummoma he im olhpesa.

Forelock, *n.* Ibisochi; a bang, okkochonli. okkahlonli.

Fornoon, *n.* Ik tabokoulo.

Foreordination, *n,* Ai yummoma he im olhpesa.

Forest, *n.* Haiyaka-yakulhaiyaka, itanuku.

Forever, *ad.* Bella, belia cha belia, ont ahokofa wa.

Forge, *n.* Aiulhti; to forge. bohli.

Forget. *v.* Imihaksi, ahaksi, ahaksichi, aiyukomah; forgotten, imihaksit kunia; forgetfulness, nan im ihaksi; to forgive, imihaksichi. kashofi; forgiveness. hashofa, kashofa, imihaksichi.

Fork, *n.* Falakto. iti falakto; at the fork, afu lakto; a fork, chulakto. chufak; to make a fork. chulatochih: a pitchfork, chufak hoshuk isht pchli; a table fork. chufak isht impa; a fork in a liub, falukto; to divide into forks or branches. falaktuchi; a fork in a stream or limb, i filommi; to fork, felommi felommin-chih; several forks. itakehulashli; a wide fork. itakehulali.

Former. *a.* Chashpo; formerly. chashpo.

Fort, *n.* Holihta kollo; to fortify, holihta kollo ikbi.

Forthwith, *ad.* Himmonali.

Fortnight. *n.* Nitak hullo tuklo.

Forwad. *n.* Pit, tikba pila,tikba pilla.

Foul. *a.* Litiha; foulness, litiha, kashofa keyu.

Foundation. *n.* Amiuti, intola, intolapi.

Foundery. *n.* Ai akmo; a founder, akmochi

Fountain, *n.* Aminti, koli; fountain head, wishakchi.

Four, *a.* Ushta, four times, ai ushta, ai ushtaba; fourthly, ont ai ushta, ont ai ushtaba.

Fowl, *n.* Iushi.

Fox, *n.* Chula; red fox, chula bomma.

Fracture, *n.* Koa, (of the skull); pokota, (of the limbs).

Fragments. *n.* Boshulli.

Fragrant, . Balama.

Frail, *a.* Hiipushi.

Frame, *v.* Foka itim olhpesochi.

Frank, *a.* Haigkah. frank-in-cense fila-kinsens; frakness. auumpa luma iksho.

Frantic. *a.* Holillobi, tasimbo.

Fraud. *n.* Haksichi; to defraud. haksichi.

Free. *a.* Yuka, keyu. i nahollo iksho; to give freely for nothing, pilla freely. fichna.

Freeman. *n.* Yuka keyu; freeman, toshka. ilap ahni-aya, hattak yuka keyu.

Freeze, *v.* Akglopechi. akalopi, kalampa, kalampi; frozen, akalopi; frozen akalopit taha: to cause to freeze. kalampichi; to freeze on me. siakoloplih; I am frozen. siakglopih.

French. *n.* Filanchi. tolanchi; frenchman, *•* filanchi hatak.

Frenzy, *n.* Holilobi.

Frequently. *adv.* Bekah.

Fresh. *n.* Okchaki, himona.

Fret. *v.* Nukocchi, misholichi; fretful, im anuk fila kollo. bushaya.

Friday. Flaite, falaite.

Friend, *n.* I kana itibapishi ittikana kana: very dear friends. Itti kanna fehna; pretended friends. itti kana ilahobbi; not friendly to each other. itti keyu; mutual friends. hattak ittikana; a friend of humanity, hatak i kana; friendly. bashka achukena, ikana; friendless, ikana ik im iksho.

Frighten, *v.* Nukhlakoshli, nukhlakanchali mahlali, nukshobli. anukhlakanchalih, nukhlakashli; frightened. nukshopa nukhlakancha mahlatah. frightened, anukhlakancha; to cause to frighten. mahlahlichi.

Frigid, Kapossa.

Frog, *n.* Kiba, shukottih; bull frog, halonlobi; young bull frog, shokotti, small frog, kaluska; toad frog, shilukwa, tree toad, chuk palantak, hachukpalantak; tad pole, yaloba.

Frost, *n.* Hotouti; frosty, hotonti; to cause frost, hotoutichi; white frost, okti hota; frosty color, shukshoki.

Froth, *n.* Pokpoki; frothy, pokpoki.

Frow, *n.* Iti isht shima.

Frown, Homechi.

Fruit, *n.* Uni nan uni: to bear fruit, anih; fruitless, uni iksho, ik ano, ik ahobo.

Fry, *v.* Auoshli. fried, olwosha, frying pan. aiolwosha ai ishi asha, ai asha, ai olwosha, apola.

Fuddle, *v.* Haksichi; fuddled, haksi.

Faltili, *v.* Aighlichi, aighle, imuighlichi; fulfilled, ai olhtaha, inaighblih.

Full, *a.* Alota, kaiya, alotowa; fullness, alota: brim full or bank full, alotowa: stomach full, kaiyah; I am full, safihopu; to be full, shatoplih.

Fundament, *n.* Hapullo nipi, isht biuli, nopullo.

Funeral, *n.* Ayokshochi, ayoya, hopi; funeral rites, hopit isht asha.

Funnel, *n.* Katoba ishtoni.

Fur, *n.* Na hishi lapushki-hish i lapushki.

Furlong, *n.* Falak, untuchina kot kowi achofa chatuk.

Furrow, *n.* Ilina; to furrow, boshli, buchali; buchaya, busha.

Further, *a.* Hopaki i shahli, mishihma, mishah, further time, himmak ma; furthest or farthest, hopaki i shaiyali.

Fusible, *n.* Bila binla.

Future, *a.* Himmak; a future time, himmak ma; future state, hatak illi shilom, bish ai asha.

G

Gag, r Itukhạ okshita.
Gain, c. Ahanchi, ishi, alapanlih; a gainer, ahanchi; to make additional gain, alapauliuchih.
Gall, n. Basunlush; to gall or inflame, ushunuchih, piko:fi; galled, pikofa.
Gallery, n. Iloshontika, ọhoshoutika, apushohla.
Gallop, r. Tabakli, abatullih, habataklih; to cause to gallop, abatullichi, habatullichi:
Gallows n. Anuksitili, anuksita, hatak unuksita.
Gamble, v. Kahli, iti kahli, buskah, bustoh; gambling, buskah; a gambler, hatak buska.
Gander, n. Shilaklak nukni.
Gang, ʼ. Hatak katonomouah, hatak kanohmi ona; a gang or herd, ittapeha.
Gangrene, n. Nipi toshbi.
Gap, n. Ahaluppa anukpilifa, pililil; a gap in a mountain; nuni ai ittu kolofa; to make a gap in tools, pillifichih.
Gape, r. Hawah, itakhabali; gaping frequently, hahạwah.
Gar r. Itukwahlichi, itukwuhlichi.
Garment, n. Nạfohka, ilefohka.
Garnish, v. Aiuklichih, akohlih, isht akohli, isht ulhkohah: garnished, akohah.
Garrison, n. Holịhta kullo:
Garter, a. Iyulhfou, iyafou.
Gas, c. Ilofullih.
Gash, n. Bushạ; gashed. chạyah, pilifah; to gash, pillifih.
Gate, a. Alabiha, aiulbiha, ai okshillihta, holihta isht ulhkuma, holihta okhissa.
Gather, r. Ittunahlih, itahobi, ulmo, gathered, itahobu, ulmo itunnaha; to gather at, ai ittuhobblih; to gather at, ai ittuhobah; to glue together, ai ulbochih; glued together ai ulboh; gathered in a heap, fohompạh; to live together, ittahayuchi.
Gaunt, a. Yahunnah; being gaunt, yohunnoah; to make gaunt, yohunnachi.
Gay, a Yukpa.
Gazette, n. Hollisso.
Gear, n. Isuba isht halulli.
Geese, n. Shilaklak; gander, shilaklak nukni; wild goose, hạkha; goose, shilaklak tek; gosling, shilaklak ushi.
Gelding, n. Hobuk, issuba hobak.
General, n. Hopali.
Generation, n. Ai ittishali, ittishali, ai unchululi isht ai uuchululi, hattak isht atla unchulolih; the present generation, himona hofanti.
Gentile, ʼ. Chintail okla, chintail, okla nan ik ithano, okla uba anumpa, ik im iksho-bulbuha.
Gentle, a. Honayo iksho, kostiui; to gentle, hopoyak salih, hopoyuksachi, kostininchi; to be gentle, kostinih; gentleman, hattak hollitopa, hattak ulhpesa, hattak hopoyuksa: gentleness, hongyo iksho; not gentle; ik honayo, ikkostiuo.
Germ, n. Aminti; to germinate, abusallih, busali, germinated, abusah.

Get, v. Ishi, ahanchi; to get down, akkowa; got down, akkowa; got in, or penued up, ulbihah, got or gotten; ạsha.
Ghost, n. Shilup, shilombish.
Gibbet, n. Anuksita, anuksitili.
Gift, n. Na hulbina, nạ holhpilla, holhpila, ima; received as a gift, habenah; to make a preset or gift, habenuchi; one who goes to receive a gift, habenut ạya: given, hulbina; a giver, nan ima.
Giggle, r. Yukpa, olulli.
Gill, n. Chil, ushta kut isht ishko achufụchatuk, chil achufa.
Gill, n. Impakti akạk impusha, (of a fowl); kaksun wakla, (of a fish).
Gimlet, n. Isht fotohushi; spike gimlet, isht fotobushi chito.
Gin, n Aulhi, anihilichi; cotton gin, punola anihechi
Ginger, n. Aksish homi; ground ginger, akshish homi botah.
Gird, v. Takchi, ashelichi, ashehuchi.
Girdle, v. Uskufuchi. yikuhli; girdled, yikuhla.
Girl, n. Ulla tek.
Girth, n. Ikfoka isht sita, ikfoka isht tullakehi.
Give, r. Ipeta, ima, habenuchi; to give recently, or quickly, ihima given, ilhpita, hulbiua; give here, auechih; give it to me, et uma, to give back, falummiut ibbak fohki falumiut ima; a giver, habenuchi, nan ima, nạ habenuchi; to give caution, haba; given, hulbiua; to give one's self up. as a criminal, ileyukuchi, to donate or promise to give, imissah; to give advice, nou i miah; lending or giving something,nan i potah,to give mụ, sapetah, to give boot, alapalinchi uluplichi; boot given alapanh, ulupuli.
Gizzard, n. Chakiffa.
Glad, ʼ. Yukpah; to gladden, yukpalih; to be glad, imachukma, yukpah, nạ yukpah: gladness, nạ yukpa, nan isht il ayukp; I am glad, sayukpah; gladsome, yukpah.
Glance, r. Anaktibuffih, anaktibulli, anaktibullichi; glanced, anaktibafah, anaktibuboa, anaktibatoa; to glance off, chassulih; to cause to glance off, chassullichi; not glanced, ikchassulloh; to glance and go obliquely off, tibullih, tibullichih.
Glaring, a. Tohchalalih, tohpokali.
Glass, n. Apisa; glassware, upisa toba; a a window glass, upisa kosshofu; a glass window, apisa kashofa okhisushi; sash for a glass window, upisa kashofa ai ulbiha; mirror, apisa.
Glean, v. Ulbulli; gleaned, ulbulah.
Glib, a. Ilalushki, haluski bụlushih.
Glimmer, ʼ. Malottakachi, tohkasakli, to glimmer this way, et tofohkoli.
Glisten, v. Tohpakali, chulhchulhchuki, malanchah to make glisten, chulhchulhchukichih; glistening, mạ ạtah, shohpakalih.
Glorify, v. Holitoblichit ai okpachih; holitobli, holitoblichi; glorified, holitopa

umpa; holituhompa; to cause to be glorified, holitopuchi.

Glory, *n.* Holitopa, aholitopaka, isht aholitopaka, shohpakali, holitoput annongglorious, aholitopaka; a place for honor or glory, aholitopa.

Glossy, *a.* Malantah.

Glove, *n.* Ibbak foka.

Glue, *n.* Kaueto; glue pot, kaueto ahonni; to glue together, ai ulbochih, ittulbochi; glued together, ittulboh; glutinous, shinushbi.

Gleet, *n.* Huta; to have gleets or whites, hutah antia.

Glutton, *n.* Hatak impa shabli.

Gnash, *v.* Noti it ai issochi.

Guat, *n.* Yikofa, shushe; buffalo gnats, hachulopushki; dog gnats, yikuffa.

Gnaw, *v.* Kilihih; gnawing, kilhih.

Go, *v.* Ia; if two, iti achi; if more than two, ilhkoli;go and stay, out anta out ai yashah; go by, ont ia; to go on farther, achakalichi; to go to, ai onah akkanulli; to go near, bilinkut ona, akkanallih; to go on foot, akkayah, akka noah; to go down, ak'ta ia; to go over or across' atanuplichi, ananapol'h;where to go over, atanapa; to go backward, falamoah; to go aside, fichupli, fichupah, fichupolih; to go slowly down, (as water) halata kullo; to go in, chukkowa; go on, (if one) mia; if more than one, hotepah; to go continually, ihiyah; to go back to, i falamao; about to go, iahosi,ia chintuk; to go in or unto, iba chukkowa; to go with, ibai ia, awant ia; we all go, iloh ia, iloh ilhkoli; to go by, im ia imaiya; to go over or above, abanuplih, tanublih, tanuplih, abauuplichi; go and bring, isht achi; both going or gone, itti achi; going side by side, ittaputah; several going about, ittanowah; to go back to each other, itti falamah; to go in or going in, maiah ubihah; to go out, as fire, mosholih; to cause fire to go out, moshbolich; to go in a wrong direction, naksika ia; to go down h ll, akuttchat; to cause to go fast, pulhkichih; to go under as water, yullullih; to go through, hlipulli, hlopulli; to go and return, falamut ula chi; to go back, falamut; going back, falamut ayat; I go, ia li; I can go, ia la hin ia; you go, isht ia; you can go, ish ia hinia; let us go, kil ia, let us all go, kil ilhkoli kilohia; to go off forever, biliachih; to cause to go off forever, biliachichi.

Goat. *n.* Isi kosoma; male goat, issi kosoma nakni; female goat, issi kosoma tek; kid, isi kosomushi, issi kosoma ushi.

Gobble. *v.* Temah, olah; gobbling, tohimah, olahanchih; gobbler, fakit nakni, fakit homutti.

God. *n.* Chitokaka, chihowa; godliness, chitokaka holitobli, chihowa holitobli; godly, chihowa nan ai ahni, holitopa; inspiration of God, chihowabut nakfokichi; kingdom of God, Chitokaka apelichika, chihowa aphlichika; love of God, Chitokaka isht i hullo, chihowa i hullo mercy of God, Chitokaka hokut i nukhaklo, chihowa nan isht i nukhaklo, ai i nukhaklo; omnipotence of God, Chitokaka nana okloha im aiya, Chitokaka nana moma im aya; omniscience of God,

Chitokaka nan oklyhaka ithana; omnipresence of God, Chitokaka himmona achufanli kantma moma anta; praise of God, Chitokaka ai im aholitopa, chihowa abnichi; son of God, Chitokaka ushi chihowa ushi; the throne of God, chihowa aiasha, chihowa abinili; to worship God chihowa aiokpuchih; a worship r of God, Chihowa aiokpuchi; God's laws, or the ten commandments, Chihowa im anumpa uihpisa pokoli; the lamp of God, Chihowa i chukfi ulhpo ush : an o pellence to God, Chihowa im atia; a disbeliever in God, (an athiest) Chihowa i yimmi keyu; an unknown God, Chihowa kuna ik itheno; the almighty God, Chihowa Chitokaka, Chihowa moma i shabli; rev lation of God, Ch howa isht otuni; gods, naholhut toba putta.

Gold. *n.* Tuli lakna, tuli holisso lakna; gold mine, tuli lakna akula, tuli holisso lakna akula.

Good, *a.* Achukma, aiyoha, hopoyuksa, hochukma, seemingly; good, achukma ahoha; good in the hightest degree, achuyukma, achukma; very good, achukma fehna, achukma aighli; better, achukma i shahli; best, achukma moma i shahli, achukma; st ll good, achukma moma; not good, achukma keyu, makali, ikackukino to improve or make good, achukmal'chih achukmali, aiyooali; to look good, achuk malit pisa; a good place, ai achukm i, a, yomba; a very good place, ai achukma, ai yo gka; a better place, ai achukmajka; to take good care, ai yooali; to be good, ai yoha, hocukma; good talk, anumpali achukma, anumpuli impunna; good nature, ogshka; goodness, hochukma, nana achukma, nana aighli; to make them good, hochukmalichih, hochukmalih; I am good, siachukma; b th good achuma bika, ittatyklot achukma; all good, achukma hieka, achukma moma, moma achukma; in good health, ayumogkah.

Goods, *n.* Ulhpoyak; groceries, ilimpa ulhpoyak; drygoods, nan toshbi, ulhpoyak.

Goose. *v.* Shilaklak tek; a wild goose, hakha; a tailor's goose, nafoka ishthumi chito; gooseberry, yuhlo ulhpoa.

Gore. *v.* Bahlih; to cause to be gored, bahlichih.

Gospel, *n.* Uanumpa, uba isht anumpa.

Gossip, *v.* Anumpa chukushpa shahlih; a gossiper, anumpa chukushp.ishali, anumpa chukushpa shali.

Gouge. *v.* Follih, fullih; gonged, fulah.

Gourd, *n.* Lokush, shukshohak; a water gourd or dipper, ishtkufa.

Govern. *v.* Pehlichi; governed, miko, ulthi i miko kufma; to make a governor at, amikochi.

Grab. *v.* Tihlifih, pl, tihlolih; grabbed, tihlifah, tihloah.

Grace, *n.* Chihowa holitobli, ayupa isht i kana; graceful (in manners), aiukli, isht imaka.

Grain, *n.* Uni, anih, tauchi, issubupa, onish lakchi.

Grand, *a.* Chito; to cause to be grand, chitolichi; grandeur, chaha, holitopa; grand-mother, ippokni; a grand daughter, ipokt·k; a grand son, ipoknankni; grand father, imafo.

Grant, *v.* Ima, aiokpachi.

Grape. *n* Paki; a grape vine, pakapi; grape juice, paki okchi, pakokchi; to pull down a grape vine, pakapi hliffih.

Grapple. *v.* Hokli, itti hokli, halulli; to grapple togethor, kiselih.

Grasp. *v.* Yichiffih, hokli, ishi.

Grass, *n.* Hashuk; crab grass, hashukputa, water grasses, hashuk ulhpoa; sedge grass, hashuk bassi; mowed or grass cut, hashuk busha; to cut grass, hashnk bushli; dry grass, hashuk busha shila; large grass, hashuk chito; grassy, hashukfoka to feed with with grass, hushuk isht ipetah; to cause to cat grass, bushuk ai impuchi; a grass blade, hushuk isht bushli; a grass roof, hushuk isht holmo; to rake hay or dry grass, hushuk shila ittanahlih; a grass or straw bed, hushuk patulhpo; to dry grass, hushuk shililiah; a grass cater, hashuk upa; a place from which grass has been cut, hushuk abusha; bear grass, pissah, pissah chula; grass hopper, hatafo, hatuffo, shakili.

Grate. *v.* Mihloffih; grated, mihlofah, mihlohah; continually grating, mihlohofflih; a grater, tanchi isht mihloffih, amihlofah.

Grateful, *a.* Alokpanchi.

Gratify, *v.* Fihoplih; gratified, fihopa.

Grave, *n.* Holluppi; to lay in a grave, ahulluppi bohli; to dig agrave, aholluppi kullih; a grave stone, aholluppi tuli hikia; a grave yard, aholluppi, hattak aholluppi aholluppi holihta; monument, isht ikhanahe; service at the grave, ahopi ka isht ai utta he ulhpesa; mourners, tabashi ulbleha; prayer, anumpa ilbusha.

Gravel, *n.* Tuli taloshik, tuli foka.

Gravy, *n.* Bila.

Gray, *a.* Tohbi, huta.

Graze, *v.* Hopohka; to cause to graze, hopoh kuchi.

Grease, *n.* Bila; to grease, fokkichi, litikfochih, bila, ahamnichi; greasy, bila bichah; melted grease, bila; unmelted grease, bila akmi; greased, litikfo, bila ahamah, to pour grease on, bila ohlalih; grease poured on, bila ohlayah; grease for a lamp, bila pula toba, to continue to grease, fokkihinchi; to grease at last, fokkicchi; greasy, litikfo; to make grease, litikfochih; I am greasy, salitikfoh.

Great, *a.* Hocheto, chito; greatness, chinto, hocheto; to be great, chitoh; to make great, chitolih; great ones, hocheto.

Greedy, *a.* Anuktupah iksho; to be or being greedy, anuktupah, issikopa. bunna atupa.

Green, *a.* Okchamali; pale green, okchakko, bright green, kilikoba; green, (not ripe) okchaki, okchukkochi walohah wulwuki.

Greet, *v.* Ai okpanchi; greeting, ai okpanchi; not greeting, ai okpanchi keyu.

Greyhound, *n.* Ofi puihki.

Griddle, *n.* Puska tuspuska anuna.

Gridiron, *n.* Tuli nip aiulhpusha.

Grief, *n.* Nanukhaklo, to grieve, nukhaklochi; grievous, okpulo. nukhaklochi.

Grind *v.* Fotohli, botohli, shohlichi; groud, fotoha, bota, shuachi; a place for grinding, afotoha; a back tooth or grinder, isht hopasa; a grind stone, tul ashuachi, tasheka, chashumpik, iskiffa ashuachi.

Grip, *v.* Yichili, kiseli.

Grist, *n.* Fotoha.

Grit, *n.* Lakchi; coarse grit, as sandstone, shikkulah.

Groan, *v.* Iliha, kiffaha; frequent groaning, hibiha, kiftahabah; to cause to groan kiffahoch.

Groom, *n.* Hatak himona ohoyo ittawaya.

Groove. *v.* Patahlichih; grooves, patahli.

Ground, *n.* Yakni; to ground, akkatulah; ground nut, waya, yaknukwaya, yakni i bula.

Group. *v.* Lokohli.

Grow, *v.* Hofantli, offo, aliktih, okpichililih; growing or grown, aliktih; to cause to grow, aliktichih; grown to manhood, hofantli; I am grown, sahofontih; just grown, himona hofantih.

Growl. *v.* Kilihah, tiklihah.

Grub. *v.* Itakshish kuchi; a grub worm yalah.

Grudge. *v.* I nukkilli.

Grunt. *v.* Illukah; grunting, hluka, hlukhluah.

Guard, *v.* Atoni; unguarded, ahaik ahno.

Guess. *v.* Im ahoba, himak fokalechit miha.

Guide. *v.* Apesanchi, ufonulih; a guide, apesuchi, tikba heka; guided, ufonah.

Guilt. *n.* Ai ashuchika; guiltless, haksi keyu; to flud guilty, onochih.

Guill. *v.* Haksichi; gullet, isht nauubli.

Gulp. *v.* Bulakachih.

Gum. *n.* Nuta balakchi, nuta hika; sweat gum, hika; wax or gum, hlittilli; black gum, hushupa, itunlh.

Gun *n.* Tanampa, tanapoh; gunsmith, tanamp ikbi, tanamp aiska.

Gurgle. *v.* Wuulohuchih; gurgliug, chubohuchi. chobohhauchi.

Gut. *n.* Iskuna; my entrails, suskuna.

H

Habit. *n.* Ai momuchi, ai yommohmi, ayommohmi, akaniohui, ayohmi; habitual, ai momuchi; habitation, aisha; habitually, chatuk, chokumo.

Hack, *v.* Chanuli; a hack, iti chanmli, iti chunaha.

Hail, *n.* Hatafo, hatuffo; hailstorm, hatuffo; to cause hail, hatafochih; to hail, hatafo.

Hair. *n.* Hishi; having hair, ishi asha; to be hairy, bishashah; long hair, hishi falaia; having much hair, hishi chito having no hair, hishi iksho; having hair grown, hishi toba; to grow hair, hishi tobah; lock of hair, haksun hishi; front or bang lock, ibishshuchi; hair of the head, pashi; hair of the hand or body, hishi; gray hair, pashi tohbi, yushbokoli; my hair, supashi; curly hair, yusbonoli wonoksho.

Hall. *n.* Aboha itti takla.

Halloo, *v.* Apahlichih, ali; to hollow, holitoblichi holitobli.

Hale, *a.* Achukmaka, nipi achukma.

Halt *a.* Kinafa, (lame) to halt or walk lamely, tabiklih; a place where to halt, ahilechi; halter, ibihcholo, foka.

Halve, *v.* Ita pahlulli; halved, ita pahlata.

Ham, *n.* Ohi.

Hames, *n.* Iti ikonla; hame string; iti ikonla foka isht talakchi

Hammer, *n.* Isht boa, nau ishtboa chufok isht boa; to hammer, bohli; hammered, boah; shoe hammer, isht boa iskitini; sledge hammer, tuli isht boa chito.

Hammock, *n.* Bokkoh, (ie hammock lan i).

Hamper, *v.* Anuktuklochih; hampered, anuktukloh.

Hand, *n.* Ibbak; to hand, ima, echi; to shake hands, ai okpechi; hand it here, auechi, echi; the right hand, isht imma: left, afabi; my hand, sebbak; handkerchiet, nan tapuski.

Handle, *n.* Ahalulli, ahakli, aieshi, ai ulphi, to handle in conversation, isht anumpuli; touched or handled pashohah to touch or handle, pashohlih, potoli, isht antua.

Handsome, *a.* Aiukli, pisa achukma, pl. hochukma, ayumba; not handsome, akaioklo, makali.

Hang, *v.* Takalichi, takali; if more than one, takohlichi taholi, takomaya, to hang by the neck, nuksitelih; hung by the neck, nuksitah; hang over, afabatah; a place for hanging by the neck, anuksita, anuksitili, hattak anuktilih; to hang on to, halanli; to hang many, nuksitohlih; to hana up, takalichi takolichi; hung up, takohli; hanging the head to one side, chiksanali; a hangman, hattak nuksitili.

Hank, *n.* Ponola shuna talakchi, ponola shuna, ponoshcna.

Happen, *v.* Akaniohmih; to have something happen, isht akaniohmih.

Happiness, *n.* Ayukpa, isht ilaiyukpa, nan, yukka, nan isht ilayukpa: the place of happiness, nan ayukpa: to be happy, imachukma.

Harbor, *v.* Fohah: a harbor for vessels, peni aiatuya, pen ataya.

Hard, *a.* Kullo, hakmo, kamossah, chalakbi chilakbih: hard as flint corn himimpa: to become hard, as a roasted potato, kachumbi: difficult or hard, palummih: to harden, as grease or water, akinichih: hardened, akmih, akmoh; to **Harden,** kullochi kamosuli; bardened, kelo kumossa; hardihood, chukush nakni; hardy, hattak nipi achukma; hardware, nan aholhponih.

Hark, *v.* Haklo, haponaklo; hark, (to call quick attention), nah.

Harlot, *n.* Ohoyo i lumaka; to play a harlot [haksia ihakloh.

Harm, Okpenih; harmed, okpulloh.

Harness, *n.* Issuba isht halulli; harness for a loom, pono shochoha.

Harrow, Onush isht ompoholmo, yakni isht lapuskichih.

Harsh, *a.* Kullo, homih, homichi haksuba.

Harvest, *v.* Hoyoh.

Hasp, *n.* Isht afacha.

Hasten, *v.* Tushpechi, tushpeli, tushpali-

chi, to be in haste, annukwaya; hastily annukwayot; to make haste, annukwayucb tushpalichih; hastiness, annukwaya; to haste, tushpa; hasty tushpa, abah ik ahno.

Hat, *n.* Shupo, shapo, to wear or wearing a hat, shapolih; put a hat an, shupolichit, his hat, i shapo; hatter, shappo ikbi.

Hatch, *v.* Hofellichi, fachanlichih: hatched, hofelli; hatching, hofelli a place for hatching, ahofellichih.

Hatchet, *n.* Iskif ushi.

Hate, *v.* Nukilli, isht ik i ahno, i hichchg- lih, ihichchulih, isht ikibahnoh, istiki- hahnoh, i nukkillih; hateful, okpulo, ikachukmo; hatred, iti nukkillih ai i nukkillih.

Haul, . Shalih; a hauler, halulli.

Have, *v.* Ishi, ishi, in asha, im alasba, in tonla; having ieshi: to have none or not to have, ik im iksho.

Haw, *n.* Chingfila.

Hawk, *n.* Hattak hlipush, akak ubi; fish hawk, chukcho; squirrel hawk, hasim- bish hommah, hasimbish hommak, hasimbichummak; large hen hawk, blakak; prairie hawk, iba fakchi, hutaba fakchi, heta pofukchi; pigeon hawk, hanon hunot; forked tail hawk, pasa falokto; a blue Pigeon hawl, tusobi, a small hen hawk, aiyichifichi; sparrow hawk, shikiliklik; night hawk, oksup afohli, oksup iba fohli; musquito hawk, haksobish nuli.

Hawthorn, *n.* Keti, (red); black hawthorn, chongafila.

Hay, *n.* Heshuk busha sbila, hushak sbila; to rake hay, heshuk ittenahlih; a hay cock, hushuk ittenahahchi; raked hay, heshuk ittenaha; to make hay, heshuk shililih; to mow hay, heshuk boshli; mowed hay, hushuk busha; a hay meadow, hashuk ai umo; to stow hay under shelter, hushuk ashadhi

Head, *n.* Nushkobo, noshkobo nishkobo; to lift the head up, akahchakalih; to bow the head, chunullih, yushchonoli; the back of the head, chushak, ia chushak; to raise the head high, shikklah; directly over head, tebokaka; to cause to hold the head down, yushchonolichi; my head sanushkoboh; head of a stream, ibitup, wishakchi; heads of a stream, bok atulohlih; head ache, nush kobo hotupah head land, yakni shokulbi, head long, himak fokkalechi; headless, nushkobo iksho; head stall, nushkobo foka; head strong chukcush kullo

Heal, *v.* Hlakofichi hlakofih, uttuchi, uttah masalichi, masalih; to heal at or from, ahlakoflih, to cause to heal at or from, ahlakoffichih; a healer, masalichi, na hla- koffichi; repeatedly healing, hlakofhin- chih; many are healed, hlakofoah, hla- kofot tchah; not healed, ikhlokofoh: to heal with, isht hlakoffichih; healed, uttah, hlakoffih.

Health, *n.* Nipi achukma, ikabeko; to be in health, nan i kanihmih keyu; to be in very bad health, nan i kanihmih chito; healthy, nipi a chukma, haknip achuk- ma, ikajabeko; good health, ayumbakah; healthful, ikalabeko; healthiness, hak- nip achukma.

Heap, *v.* Ittvnnahlichih; heaped, ittunnahah.

Hear, *v.* Haklon; hearing, haklo; a hearer hapouaklo, na haklo; repeatedly hearing, hahaklo; to cause to hear haklochih, haponaklochih; to make continually hear haklohonchih, a good hearer, haponaklo achukma; to hear from or at, ahakloh not hearing, ikahaklo; beyond hearing, ikahakloka, ikahaklokika; not heard, ikhakloh; cannot hear, hakla he keyu: deaf ikhaklo; to hear of self, ilehakloh.

Hearse, *n.* Hattak illi asbahli, illi a shahli.

Heart, *n.* Chukush; a good heart, chukush achukma; a true heart, chukush ahli; a depraved heart, chukush akkanlusih, an humble heart, chukush akkanlusi; a new heart, chukush himona; to renew the heart, chukush himoncchih: a wounded heart, chukush hotopa, chukush nahla; to disheartcn.chukush, illichih; disheartened, chukush illi; thoughts or affections of the heart. chukush im anukfilah; to captivate the heart, chukush eshih; a cold heart, chukvsh kapussa; hard hearted, chukush kullo; hardness of heart, chukush kullo; burning heart, chukush lua; burned heart, chukush luah; a bold heart, chukush nakni; a heart of flesh, chukush nipi: a fat heart, chukush nia; a sorrowrul heart, chukush nukhaklo; a timid heart, chukush nukshopa; a dispirited heart, chukush nusi; a bad or wicked heart. chukush okpulo; bad or wicked hearted, chukush okpuloh; to injure the heart, chukush okpcnih; a double heart, chukush tuklo; a grave or heavy heart, chukush weki; tender hearted, chukush wulwaki; hearty or zealous, chukush yiminta; a serious heart, chukush yubi; a joyful heart, chukush yukpa, to rejoice or console the heart, chukush yukpalih; the heart of a tree, chukush. ishkuna, heart burn, chukush lua heartily, fiehna.

Heat, *v.* Lushpuchih, lahbuchih, luspullih, libishlih; heated lesbpah, lahbah; to warm or get hot innih; a moderate degree of heat, libisha; prickley heat; tomushi, itombushi.

Heave, *v.* Wakelih, chitolit flohpah, chitot flohpah, hoetut pisah, honi; to heave up, vbapilah.

Heaven, *n.* Uba yakni, uba shutik; befeu, uba nlasha.

Heavy, *a.* Wekih; heaviness, weki; I am not heavy, sashuh hulah.

Heed, *v.* Akostninchih, ithanah; not heeding, ikyimmoh, aha ik ahno; to take heed, aha ahnih; caution or heed, aha ahni; to mistrust or take heed of him, aha im ahnih; heedlessness, aha ahni iksho, aha ahni keyu.

Heel, *n.* Iyikutoba.

Heir, *v.* Ishi, ai immih.

Hell, *n.* Ai ilbusha, ai ilbusha, ai ilbushaka, alok puloka; hel; hell fire, ai okpuloka luuk.

Helm, *n.* Isht afana, isht afina, a helmsman, afinili, peni afana; to turn a helm, afinilih, afinnih.

Help, *v.* Apeluchih, apelah, ibauechih; a help, apela ibauechi: frequently helping, apelohanchih; helper, apela ibauechi; helpless, apela ik im iksho.

Hem, *v.* Afohommih, apohlummichih; a hem, ufohuma; hemmed, afohomah, opohloma.

Hemp, *n.* Nuchi chito.

Hen, *n.* Akak ishki, akaka tek; hen roost, akaka anusi; guinea hen, akak kotlih; a setting hen, akak olata.

Hence, *ad.* Iluppa, henceforth, himmak a pilla, himmakpilla; henceforward, himmak pilla.

Hers, His, or It, *pro.* Ilup; herself, himself or itself, ilupinli ilup akiuli.

Herb, *n.* Haiyukpulo olba, the seeds of herbs, haiyukpulo nihi, olba nihi, herbage hushuk.

Herd, *n.* Ittapeha; to berd, pehlichih; a herder, peblichi, nan apistikeli. ulhpoba hoyoh.

Here, *ad.* Iluppa, yak; right here; iluppak inli; this here, yak; look here, yakch! hereafter, himmak, himmakpilla ka himmak pilla, ashba; to be hereafter, himmak a he, himmak ma, herein, iluppako hereafter tikba, tikbakash; heretofore, tikba ma.

Heresay, *n.* Iksa inla vbanumpuli iksa itti filnmohlih.

Hermaphrodite, *n.* Nakni ohoyo iklunna.

Hermit, *n.* Hattak haiyaka keyn,

Heron, *n.* Iti kushayaiya.

Hesitate, *v.* Anukchintoh, anuktukloh, aankwiah, nukwiah; hesitating, anukchintoh; without hesitation or unhesitatingly, anukchintoh iksho; hesitation anuktuklo, nukwia; to cause to hesitate, nukwinchih.

Hew, *v.* Tibilichih, tiblih; hewed, tihla; hewer, iti tibli.

Hic-cough, *v.* Nukfikonh, chukfikoah, chukfikolih; to cause to have hic-coughs. chukfikolichih; hic-cough, itukfikowa.

Hide, *v.* Luhmih, luhmicluh, aluhmichi; a hiding place. aiatuko; to hide one another, ittiluhmih; to hide from each other. ittilumah; hid or hiddeu, luhmah; the hide or skin, hakshup; having hides, hakshup asha; a raw hide with hair on, hakshup hishi asha; with hair off, hakshup hishi iksho.

High, *a.* Chahah; to heighten, chahachih, higher, chaha i shahli; highest, chaha moma i shall, chaha i shaliht tuhli, chaha i shalehchet tuli; high above, vba chaha; way up high, vba pillah; high minded, chukush chaha; height, chaha; high tempered, chukush haluppah.

Highway, *n.* Ai ittonowah, hinu chito, hina putha; highwayman, hina takla kahut hukopa.

Hill, *n.* Nenih; a mountain or high hill, nunih chaha; hillock, bokkochi, bokkoh; hillside, chakpatalika, akuttahaka: many small hills, boboki, bomboki; a range of hills, buehchali; a corn or potato hill, ibish; down hill, okuttahaka; to go down hill, okuttuhat la; to make potato hills, buntochih; a potato hill, bunte: made into hills, buntoh; hilly bombokih.

Hinder, *v.* Anukluklochih, ataklommi; hindered, atak lommah; to hinder self

with, isht Ilataklommih; to hinder each
other, ittatoklommih, ittatoklommichih;
a hinderer, nan ataklommi, nan otaklom-
michi; to stop or hinder, yokoplih; to
to cause to hinder, yokoplichih.
Hinge, *n.* Atakali; hinges, atakohli, okhissa atakohli.
Hip, *n.* Iyubi achosholi.
Hire, *r.* Tohnoh; hiring tohnoh; continually hiring, tohohnoh; a hireling ilhtohno;
to hire me, satohnoh.
Hit, *v.* Issoh, nchhih, to fail to hit, ihlakoffih; to cause to fail to hit, ihlakofflichih
Hitch, *r.* Takahlichih; plural, takohlichih.
Hither, *ad.* Iloppa; hitherto, tikba moma.
Hive, *n.* Foi ichukka; hives and croup,
fiopa tahli.
Ho, *intj.* Ale.
Hoarse, *a.* Nukshila; to be hoarse, nukshi-
lah; hoarseness, nukshila; to choke with
hoarseness, nukshiniffih, nukshikiffih; I
am hoarse, sanukshilah.
Hopple, *n.* Isuba iyi isht in talakchi, hob-
ble tabiklih, chahiklih.
Hobgoblin, *n.* Chukkishikauchik, kahshu-
kanchak, koshikanchank.
Hoe, *n.* Chahe. a hoe handle, chahopi,
chahe ai ulhpi; to hoe, alelih; hoed, liah:
a hoer, aleli; to hoe corn, tauchi lelih,
lelichih.
Hog, *n.* Shukha; a young hog. shukha himitta, young hogs, shukha himit hoa, pig,
shukhushi; sow, shukha tek; boar.
shukha hobuk.
Hoist, *r.* Wakeli; hoisted, wakaya.
Hold, *v.* Hoklih, ishih, halanlih, eshih halelih; holding halanli, halulli, noklih; to
hold still, hikia; to hold out to, iwelih; to
hold me in arms. sasholih; to hold out or
up, welih.
Hole, *n.* Choluk; a hole in the ground,
fichukbi, hichukbi; an auger hole, fatoha,
a touch hole haksun chuluk; to pierce
through and make a hole, hiyah, hlukaffih; a hole thus made, hlya, hlukafa;
holes, hlykachi; several small holes.
bored or punched, hlukaoli; to make
small holes, hlukanlichih hlunli, hlunli-
chih; to open a hole, hlumplih; a cave or
hole, hochukbi, hichukbi.
Holiness, *n.* Ai asuchi iksho achukma,
holitopa.
Hollow, *n.* Choluk, okfa, kalokbi; to make
a dent or hollow. kalokbichih bochaplih:
a hollow or ravine. kolukbi, warped or
hollowed, bochokuchih, bochopah; to
hollow with the mouth, tahpulah.
Holly, *n.* Hahlih, iti hishi haluppa.
Holy, *a.* Holitopa, chukush yubbih.
Homage, *n.* Holitoblih; to render homage,
holitoblichit ai okpachih.
Home, *n.* ¡chukka; homeless, ¡chukkaik-
sho; his new home, ¡ chukka himona;
former home, ¡ chukka tikba: to be like
his home,¡ chukka ohmi, ¡ chukka choy-
uhmi; homely, ikaiuklo, okpuloh; I am
homely, siokpuloh; homesick, pulatah.
chukka ¡ pulatah; to cause to be homesick, palatuchih; homestead, chukka
ossupa atolaya; homeward, chukka
pilah. chukka imma.
Hominy, *n.* Holhponi, tafula.
Hone, *n.* Bushpo ashuachih.
Honest, *a.* Ahli, chukush¯uhli; to be hon-

est, ai ahlih.
Honey, *n.* Foi bila; honey bee, foi ishki,
fobilishki; queen bee, foi bilishki ipokni:
honey comb, foi hakshup, drone, foi
ipokni.
Honor; Holitopa; desire for honor. holitopa benna; honored, holitopuchih
holitompa, holitopah; a place for honor;
aholitopa; honorable, aholitopaka; to
honor. holitoblichih, aiokpuchih, holitoblih: unhonored. ikholitopoh; to honor
each other, ittiholitoplih.
Hoof, *n.* Iyakchush.
Hook *n.* Teli chanakbi; to hook with
horns, bahlih.
Hop, *n.* Hanuhchi.
Hope, *v.* Pisa he ahni, yakohma ahui,
yohma he ahni.
Horn, *n.* Lapish; a horn to blow, isht pufa:
a powder horn, lopish; hornet, tohkel
pohkel.
Horrid, *a.* Okpulo fehna.
Horse, *n.* Issuba; mare, issuba tek, stud,
issuba nakni; colt, issubushi; race horse,
issubapelhkih; a sea horse, oka issuba.
Hospitable, *a.* I kana achukma.
Hot, *a.* Leshpah, aiohbih; at a hot place,
aleshpaka; to make warm or hot at,
aleshpalih; scalding hot, hukma hinla,
Hotel, *n.* Aboha ai impa chukka afoha,
chukka anusi, hattak afoha, ai impa.
chukka.
Hound, *n.* Ofi haksobish falaia; greyhound ofi pulhki.
Hour, *n.* Heshi kanelli, heshi kanulli
isht olhpisa
House, *n.* Chukka; a room, aboha; sides or
outside of the house, chukka onaksika;
a household, chukkachuffa; an adjoining house, chukka et apatunlih, aboha
et achaka; a high house, chukka chalia,
aboha chaha: a house keeper, chukka
achuffanboha im apistikili; the ruler of
the house, chukka achuffa pehlichi;
housed or put in a house, chukka fohkah:
a white house, chukka tohbi, chukka
hunta, to house or put in a house,
chukka fohkit; roof of a house, chukka
isht holmo; the eaves, chukka isht
holmo uhli, a plastered or daubed
house, chukka ulhpolusa; mortar or
plaster for a house, chukka isht ulhpolusa; a two story house, chukka ittueh-
aka tuklo; chukka ittuntula; rib of of a
house, chukka naksi; a small house or
closet, chukkushi, abohushi; a house
carpenter, chuk ikbi, chuk kikbi; a
deserted or waste house, chukkilissa;
an empty, vacant or desolated house,
chukka shahbi; to vacate or desert a
house, chukkilissuchih, chukka shab-
bechih; a house for gaming, or gambling
a boha abuska, abuska chukka; a house
of entertainment, aboha auusechi; a
bake house,or bakery, aboha apul loska:
a bath house, aboha ayupi; a large
house or room, chukka chito, aboha
chito: a red house, chukka homma,
aboha homma; a temple or palace, aboha
holitopa; a single house, aboha ilop
achuffa: a medium sized house or room,
aboha iskatuni; a small house or room,
aboha iskatuni, aboha isktini, chukka
iskitini; a tool house, aboha isht pilesa

aiasha.; a door shutter for a room or house aboha isht okshillihta; a door, aboha okhisa; a double house, aboha ittachaka; the foundation of a house, aboha į tula; a padlock for a house, aboha į luksi; household furniture. inachukushpa; a bed room, aboha anusi; a log house, chukka ittobana, aboha ittobana; to build a log house, aboha ittobeunih; a floored house, aboha iti patelhpo; a fallen house, aboha kinafa; a jail, fortress, prison or strong house, aboha kello; a notched house, aboha lanlaki: a yellow house, aboha lekna; a smooth or glistening house, aboha malushko; a shingle roofed house, aboha mismiki; House of Representatives, Aboha Nakfish; a wash-house or room, aboha nan ai achefa, under the house, aboha nuta, aboha nutaka; a cellar under the house, aboha nuta yakni kula; an indifferent or waste house, aboha okpullo; an old house, chukka sipokni. aboha sipkni; a wing of the house, chukka sanihchi; an ornamented house, chukka shema, aboha shema; a rotten house, aboha tushbi, chukka tushbi; a cottage, aboha shikkia; a gin house. chukka ponola anihchi; a store house, ai ittatoba; my house, a chukka; your house, chi chukka; his or her house, į chukka.

Hover, v. Illopohuchih.

How, ad. Katiohmi, katioht, kitimichit; how much or how great, katiohmi. kaniohmi; how? or what? hacha? cho? akcho?; how is it? hokako; however, umba.

Howl, v. Woha.

Huddle, v. Lokolih.

Hug, v. Sholih; to be hugged, ilolhputah; to hug each other, ittisholih.

Huge. a. Hocheto, chitoh.

Hull, n. Hakshup, hakhlopish; having a hull, hakshup asha; to hull nuts, hanlichih; hulling or stripping off the hull of nuts. hayah; to hull, pishaffih; hulled, pishaffah.

Hum, v. Shinihuchih, shimihuchih.

Human, n. Hattak isht a halaia; human race, hatak isht atia; human species, hattak isht atia; descended from the human race, hattak isht atiah.

Humane, a. į kana; a humane person, hatak į kana.

Humble, a. Chukush akanlosi, ilbusha; to be humble, akkalusih; to humble, chukush akkanlusih.

Humility, n. Imanukfila akkanlusih, ile akkanlusechih; humiliation,ai akkuhlusi, ilbusha ai ilbosha.

Hummingbird, n. Hlikuklo.

Hump-back, n. Kobokshi, kitikshi.

Hunger, v. Hohchuioh, impa bennah; hungry, hohchuio: very hungry, hohchofo fehna; while in hunger, hohchaioh; to be hungry, at last, hohchaiyafoh; to make him hungry, hohchufohih; to starve to death or kill with hunger, hohchufochit oblih; to die with hunger, hohchufot illib; to cause them all to starve to death from hunger, hohchufochih obit tahli.

Hundred, a. Tahlepah.

Hunt, v. Hoyoh, awottah; to hunt at or with, ai owottah, ai owottcenih; a hunting ground, ai owetta; to cause to hunt, hoyochih, hoyohouchih; go and hunt. hot ia; to hunt with, ibahoyoh; hunted with, ibahoyoh; one who hunts with, ibahoyo; to hunt each other, itti hoyoh; a hunter or huntsman, hattak owetta.

Hurricane, n. Apeli.

Hurry, v. Tushpuchih, anukwayochih, tushpa, tushpali; to be in a hurry, anukwayah; hurridly, anukwayat; to cause to be in a hurry, auukwiachih.

Hurt, v. Hottupah; a hurt, hottupa, bihlah, hurtful, botuppa, bihli; to cause to' hurt, hottupechi, hottupalih; one who hurts or gives pain. hottupeli; to feel hurt or to be hurt, imahlekah; nuhurt, ikhotopo; to hurt me, suttupah, sohottopelih; I am hurt, siaiokpulloh.

Husband, n. I hattak.

Husk, n. Hakshup, hakhlopish; to husk, luffih; husked, lufah; having husk, hakshupasha.

Hidrophobia, n. Holillubi.

Hymn, n. Ataloa; hymn book, holisso ataloa.

Hypochondriac, v. Chukush ik nakuo.

Hypocrisy, n. Nan flahobbi; hypocrite, nan ilahobbi.

Hysterics, n. Haiochi.

I

I, pro. sin. Li.—I pro. sin. la,— "li" is changed to la when connected with a verb in the future tense, i, sa, so, si, ono.

Ice, n. Okti, ákalapi; icicles, akalupi takohli.

Idiot, n. Itukholaya.

Idle, a. Intakobi. peh anta.

Idol, n. Nahuobattoba, chihowa hulbachi; idolator, na hulbut tuba aiokpochih; idolator, na hulbut tuba ai okpochi.

If, con. Akma, hatok meno, mot, hokmot; even if, hatok mako; if not, hatok mot; if it be, hokono.

Ignorant, a. Ikithunoh.

Ill, n. Abeka, okpullo, nan ikanihmi; ill will or ill nature, bolhpasha, ikso; ill natured, heshka iksho, hulpashi iksho, bashka keyu.

Illustration, n. Ishtapesa, ishtulhpesa.

Illustrious, a. Holitopa.

Image, n. Holba, chihowa hulbachi, na hulbohtoba.

Imagine, v. Anukfillih, ahnih, im ahobah.

Imbecile, n. Hlipushi; imbecility, hlipushi.

Imbibe, v. Ishkoh.

Imbitter, a. Homechih.

Imitate, v. Holbachih ahobachi. holba-

chih, inkaiyachit mihah; an imitation or
imitator; hobachi, hobachit ikbi holba;
to imitate in talking, hobachit anumpuli, hobachit miha; to imitate in writing, hobochit holssochi hlafit hobuchih,
to imitate the likeness of another, hobachit ikbi; to imitate the walk, hobachit
nowa, imitated, holba holbut toba, iakaiyachit mihah; to slightly imitate aho-
banlih; ilimitable, hobacha hekeyu.
Immediately, *ad.* Chekosi, ashalika, mih
mak inli ho.
Immemorial, *a.* Ai ithonaka misha,
Immense, *a.* Chitoh, hocheto.
Immodest, *a.* Hofahya iksho, ik hofahyo.
Immoral, *a.* Haksi; immortality, okchgya
bilia.
Impatient, *a.* Nukchinto keyu.
Impeach, *v.* Anumpa onochih; impeached,
anumpa onotulah; unimpeached, anum-
pa ik onotuloh.
Impediment, *n.* anuktulo.
Impenetrable, *a.* Chukkowa he keyu.
Impervious, *a.* Obukkowa he keyu.
Impiety, *n.* Chihowa ik im atio.
Implacable, *a.* Ifalama he keyu.
Important, *a.* Na fehna.
Impostor, *n.* Hattak haksichi.
Imprison, *v.* Aboha kullo fohkih; imprison-
ed, aboha kullo fohkah; imprisonment,
aboha kullo fohka; things captured or
imprisoned, nayuka,
Improper. *a.* Makali, ik ullhposo, ik i
mako.
Improve, *v.* Achukmalichih, achukmalih,
hochukmalichih, ho chukmalih; improv-
ed, achukmah, ho chukmah; improve-
ment, ai ulhtaha.
Imprudent, *a.* Hofahya iksho, ikhofahyo,
ahah ahni ik ithano.
Impudent, *a.* Hofahya ikso.
In, *prep.* His or their, i or in, are per. pro.,
3rd per., sing., "In," becomes nasal by
dropping n, thus, i for in; i chukka or in
chukka; his or their house; in the, keno,
hokuno, yokuno.
Inactive, *a.* Isht awiha; to be inactive, ile-
hobuk tobochih, hlepushih.
Inadequate, *a.* Nanihma he keyu; to adequate, alauwih, alauichih.
Incarnate, *a.* Haknip ant tobah; incarna-
tion haknip ant toba, haknip ant atoba.
Incendiary, *n.* Hushmi, hokmi.
Incense, *n.* Na balama lya, na balama
holukmi.
Inch, *n.* Inch, one inch, inch achuffa; one
foot, inch auatukloh, iyi achuffa.
Inclosure, *n.* Ilabefa.
Incite, *v.* Nan utohnochih.
Iclosure, *n.* Holjhta, aboljhta; to enclose,
holihtuchih.
Increase, *v.* Laua isht ia; to increase from,
isht achakah; to increase in stature,
hofantih.
Incubate, *v.* Alatah; incubation, alata.
Indecent, *v.* Chakapa.
Indeed, *ad.* Ukgh, muhli, ghli hoka; in-
indeed, wonderful, aumi.
Indent, *v.* Habifih, habifichih, yaffih; in-
dented, habifah, habefoah, habifkuchi
yafah.
Independent, *a.* Inla, ai anukchito iksho.
, Hattak upi homma; Indian
cheif, hattak upi homma miko,

Indigestion. *n.* Impa im okpullo.
Indizo, *n.* Nan isht okchakkochi, nan isht
okchamali; wild indigo, pakauli ok-
chamali.
Indiscernable, *a.* Akostinincha he keyu;
to discern, akostianichih.
Indiscreet, *a.* Ikhopoyukso.
Indispose, *v.* Ikahnoh.
Indissoluble, *a.* Bila he keyu.
Indissolvable, *a.* Bila he keyu.
Individually, *ad.* Achuffalit.
Indolent, *a.* Iutakobi; nan intukobi.
Inextinable, *a.* Holitopa, ghli, halitopa
atupa.
Infamous, *a.* Halakshi, makali.
Infant, *n.* Puskush, ullosi; infants, ullosi
puta.
Inferior, *a.* Amakalih, chukushpa.
Infinite, *a.* Ai uhli iksho.
Inflame, *v.* Chiletulih, pihloffih, piko'lih;
inflamed, chilitah, homma, pihlofah,
pikoffah; to cause to inflame, chiletuchih;
to inflame by friction, ashunachih; inflammation, na hotupa, nipi lua; inflammation of the breast, ik kishi hotupa;
inflammation of the bowels, ikfoka hotupa; inflammation of the liver, salakha
okpullo; inflammation of the lungs,
shilukpa okpullo; inflamation of the
spleen, takshi hotupa.
Inflict, *v.* Chussulohah.
Influenza, *n.* Ibi sheno,
Inform, *v.* Akostininchih, ottunichi; haklochih okfahlih; uninformed, ikakostinincho, ikhakloh, informant, haklochi;
continually, informing haklohonchih; an
former, hatak nan anoli'
Inhabit, *v.* Ai uttah; inhabitant, yakni ai
utta; inhabitants, yakni ai okla.
Inhale, *v.* Ila fiopa.
Iniquity, *n.* Ik ai ulhpisso,, vba nan ulhp-
isa kobuffih.
Inject, *v.* Fohkih.
Injudicious, *a.* Ikhopoyukso.
Injunction, *n.* Anumpa, ulhpisa, nan
ulhpisa.
Injure, *v.* hottupachih, bilhhlih, okpunih;
injured, notupah okpullo; to wound or
injure the feelings, bihliplih, bilhhlih;
to inflict an injury, hottupalih.
Ink, *n.* Isht holissochi okchi; ink, ik; ink
stand, isht holissochi okchi ai ulhto.
Inlet, *n.* Ai itabani.
Inmost, *a.* Anukaka fehna.
Inn, *n.* Aboha afoha, chukka anusi ai
imp, chukka.
Innumerable, *a.* Hohtenah atupa, aholhti-
nah iksho.
Inquire, *v.* Ponakloh; inquiring, ponaha-
kloh.
Insane, *n.* Tasimbo, holillubi; to cause in-
sanity, tasimbochih; I am insane, satas-
imboh.
Inscribe, *v.* Halissochi; inscribed, holisso;
an inscription, oholisso,
Inscrutable, *a.* Akostinincha hekeyu.
Insect, *n.* Shushi, kitak; a poisonous in-
sect, hattak halhpa; a hairy insect that
devours hides, in summer, shukuttih.
Insecure, *a.* Ahlakoffa he keyu.
Insensible, *a.* Chukush kapussa.
Insert, *v.* Achoshulih, achoshlih; to cause
them to be inserted, achoshlichih.
Inside, *n.* Anukaka; midway of the inside,

anukaka iklunna.
Insight, *n.* Haiąkah
Insnare, *v.* Hokli.
Inspiration, *n.* Mahli flopa; inspiration of God, chihowa hut nukfokichi; inspiration of the Holy Spirit. Shilombish Holitopa isht anukfokah; to inspire, ila flopah.
Instant *n.* Himak; instantly himonnali, yakosi, yakosi ittin tąkla, himonasi.
Instead, *ad.* Ulhtobah.
Instep, *n.* Iyi putta pakna.
Instigate, *v.* Teplih, nan utohnochih; instigating, nan utohnochih; instigator, nan utohnochi.
Instill, *v.* Anukfohkih, annkfokichih; instilling into the mind, anukfokihinchih.
Instruct, *v.* Im abuchih, ikhananchih, anukfokih; an instructor, anukfokichi, hattak imabuchi, hattak nan im abuchi; instructress; ohoyo nan im abuchi;
Instrument, *n.* Nan aiolachi, (i. e. a violin, etc.,) an instrument to weave or knit with, nan isht tunna; to play on an instrument, olachi.
Insult, *n.* Chukush hotupali; insulted, chukush hotapalih.
Integrity, *n.* Ahli.
Intemperate, *a.* Hattak oka ishko atupa, okishko shahli; temperate, okikishko, temperance, okikishko.
Intense, *a.* Fichna.
Inter *v.* Hoppih; interred holuppih.
Intercede, *v.* Isht anumpuli.
Interest, *v.* Haliayah; to be interested in, ahalayah; to draw interest, chelih; to be interested, ahalaiyah; concerned or interested, ahalayah; interested with, to, in, or on, ai isht ahalaiyah.
Interfere, *v.* Ittatuklummih, ittatuklummichih, to interfere with, olabichih.
Interior, *a.* Anukaka.
Internal, *a.* Anukaka.

Interpret, *v.* Anumpa tusholih; an interpretor, anumpa tusholi; interpretation, anumpa tushowa.
Intoxicate, *v.* Haksichib; intoxicated, haksih.
Intrude, *v.* Ataklummih, ataklummichib; an intruder, alaklummichi, ataklummi.
Intuition. *n.* Imilbik.
Inundation, *n.* Oka mitafa.
Invalid, *n.* Hatuk iksitopo.
Invaluable, *a.* Halitopa atupa; valuable, halitopa; very valuable, halitopa, febna.
Invective, *n.* Anumpa okpullo.
Investigate, *v.* Anukfillit pisah, aftnalichih.
Invite, *v.* Atonochih, imanolih; invited, im ahnoa, ilhtohnoh.
Irksome, *a.* Ahchiba.
Iron, *n.* Tuli; iron mine, tuli akula; iron bars, tuli fabussa bofoloha; iron rods, tuli fabussa chipunta.
Irreconcilable, *a.* Ifalama he keyu, huphla he keyu.
Irredeemable, *a.* Illakuffa he keyu, chumpa he keyu.
Irreparable, *a.* Ai iskia hekeyu.
Irretrievable, *a.* Ai iskia he keyu.
Irritable, *a.* Bąshka iksho, bąshka keyu; to irritate, chiletulih, nukoachi, hushayuchi: irritated, nukoah, hushayah.
Is, *v.* Ak osh. akot; strictly speaking the choctaw language, has no neuter verb, but in ak osh and ak ot, the verb is, understood, as wak osh; the cow is, because it is, ak okut; is it, fokka huto.
Island, *n.* Yakni tashaiya; island, yakni tulhkuchi.
Isthmus, *n.* Yakni oka itj takla.
Itch, *n.* Woshko, yaualichi; to cause to take or have the itch, wuskolih wuskochich; itching, yawolichi.
Ivory, *n.* Elephant noti,

J

Jacket, *n.* Ilefoka yuskuloli.
Jade. *v.* Tikambichih, hoyublichih, hlipushih;jaded, tckambih, hlipushi.
Jail, *n.* Aboha kullo; jailor aboha kullo apesuchi, aboha kullo apistekili. a prisoner in jail, aboha kullo fohka; to put a prisoner in jail, aboha kullo fohkih.
January, *n.* Chenuali.
Jaw, *n.* Nutakfa; jaw bone, Nutakfa foni.
Jealous, *a.* Nnktuhlab, potunnoh; jealousy, nutuhla, potunno; to cause jealousy potunnochih.
Jean, *n.* Chukfi hishi italata tunna.
Jeer, *v.* Hobachi.
Jehova, *n.* Chihowa.
Jerk, *v.* Halaklih, halahlichih; jerking. halahli; to twitch or jerk suddenly, yenullu, kuchih; continually twitching or jerking, yikuttokahanchih.
est, *v.* Yohpulah, lushkah, yopulachih; jesting, isht yopulla, lushkah; a jester, hattak yov ula; to joke or jest with each

other, ittiļhushkah, ittiyupulah.
Jesus, *n.* Chisus; the apostle of Jesus, chisus im uba numpeshi.
Jew, *n.* Chu; jewish, chu imma; jews, chu okla,
Jewel, *n.* Tuli holitompa isht shema.
Jews-harp, *n.* Tuli uskula.
Jingle, *v.* Olachih, ola, chusobuchih, chamak; jinggling, chamakahanchih; to make jingle, chamalichih; to jingle with a clear sound, solohuchih.
Job, *n.* Baha; jobbing, chikkihļha, baha; to job, fullih. chikkiļhah, bahlih, bahullih; jobbed, bahafah; to job with the point of a sharp instrument, teplih.
Jocular, *a.* Isht yopula, yukpa.
Jocund, *a.* Isht yopula, yukpa.
Join, *v.* Ibofohkah; to join to, ibulhtoh; joined to, ibulhtoh; to join together, ittihalulhih; joined together in marriage ittihalullih; to splice or join together, iituchukullih; to cause to join, ittuchuku-

lichit: a joiner, iti shafi; a joint, ai itta-
chakah, ittachakuli; joints, ittachakli; a
joint of a limb or tree, naksish; bone
joints, foni ittuchakuli, foni; a sholder
joint. iskistup: a high hip joint, kofulla:
to put out of joint, tahlofiih; put out of
joint, tahlofah; to cause to dislocate or
put out of joint. tahlofflchib.
Joke, *v.* Yopula, lushkah, yopulachih;
joking, isht yopula, lushkah; a joker.
hattak yopula; to joke each other, itti
lushkah, ittiyopulah.
Jole, *n.* Nutakfa.
Journey, *v.* Nowut ayah; when more than
one, itta nowut ayah.
Jovial, *a.* Yukpa.
Joy, *n.* Nan yukpa, nan isht ila yukpa;
joy bless you, yakoke, yoyful, yukpa;
joyous, yukpa; joyless, ikyukpo.
Judge, *n.* Hattak nan apesa, chuch, nan
apesa; to judge. anukfillih; judgment,
nan ulhpisa, nan ai ulhpiesa; judgment-

day, nau ulhpiso chnto nitak; final judgment, nan ai ulhpisa isht aiopi, nan
ulhpisa isht aiopi.
Jug, *n.* Lukfi kotoba, lukfi akotoba.
July, *n.* Chulai.
Jump, *v.* Hatonchih, hatulli, toluplih,
mulih; a jumper, hatonli; to cauc to,
jump. hatulichih; to jump up and down,
motuklih.
Junction, *n.* Ai ittibafoka, ai ittufama ai
ittusitcih.
June, *n.* Chun.
Junior, *a.* Nakfish, i himmak.
Jury, *n.* Chuli.
Just, *a.* Ahli, achukma, aiahli peh; justice
ai ulhpiosa, nan ulhpisa, nana ai ahli,
nana ulhpisa ai ahli, ai ulhpisa; the place
where justice is administered, ai apisa;
an office of the justice of the peace, ai
apoksia; justification, ai ulhpiesa; to
justify, ai ulhpiesuchi.
Juvenile, *a.* Ulla imma.

K

Kale, *n.* Tuhi.
Keen, *a.* Haluppa, chilitah, homi; to make
keen, haluppuchih chilituchih; keenness
halumppa, chilita.
Keep, *v.* Halullih, ilauwelih; to care for or
keep us, pieshih; caring for or keeping
us, pieshih; to keep me, sahulullih; a
keeper. apesuchi.
Keg *n.* Itafoushi.
Kernel, *n.* Foni, nihi, nipi.
Kettle, *n.* Asonak iyi; brass kettle, usonak,
asonak lakna.
Key, *w.* Isht tiwa,
Kick, *u,* Hablih, huhlih; to kick up; washs-
hanah: kicked. huhlah; to cause to kick,
huhlichih; to kick each other, ittibalhlih
to kick a horse wtih your heels, winni-
hah:
Kid, *n.* Issikosomushi.
Kidnap, *v* Hattak hukopoh.
Kidney, *n.* Hai ihchi, haiyihchi.
Kill, *v.* Ubih, abih, fiopa tuplih; we kill,
ebih; to assassinate, haksint ubih, hak-
sinchit ubih; not killing or not having
killed, ikboh; to try or want to kill, ubih
bunnah; to kill a man, hattak ubih.
Kind, *a.* I Kana, hulhpashi; kindness,
bashka, hulhpashi; unkind, hulhpashi
iksho, halhpashi keyu, hushka, bashka
keyu.
Kindred, *n.* Hattak i kanomih, i kanomih,
ittikanomi.
King, *n.* Miko; to reign or rule as a king,
amikoh; to make a king at, amikochih;
kingdom, pehlichika, apehlichika; kingdom of God, chitokaka apehlichika.
Kingfisher, *n.* Tushalali.
Kingsevil, *n.* Chiblanli.
Kinsfolk, *n.* Hattak i kanomih, ittikanomih.
Kinsman, *n.* Hattak i kanomih.
Kipskin, *n.* Wak ushi hapshup.
Kiss, *v.* Tukowah; to kiss caoh other. itta
tukowah.
Kitchen, *n.* Ahoponi.

Kitten, *n.* Kuttusi.
Knapsack, *n.* Bahta.
Knave, *n.* Hattak okpullo, hattak haksichi;
knavery, haksichi; knavish, haksichih
shahli, ikhaklo, haksi.
Knead, *v.* Yumuslichih, yumuslib; knead-
ed, yumuskah: knead tray, ayumuska.
Knee, *n.* Iyikulaha: knee joint, iyikulaha
ittachakuli; knee pan, iyin tulwashakchi
to kneel; hachukbihlipab; hachukbilh-
kah.
Knife, *n.* Bushpo; knives and forks,
bushpo chufak isht impa; butcher knife,
bushpo falaia, bushpo chitoh; drawing
knife, isht shata; pocket knives, bushpo
pohloma, bushpushi; a dirk, bushpo isht
ittibi; a knife handle, bushpo ai ulhpi.
Knit, *v.* Tuna; knitting needle, iyabi huski
isht tunna.
Knob, *n.* Pokshi.
Knock, *v.* Sokkohah; to knock once, sokoli-
chih: knocking, sokkohah; to knock
against. pokullib; knocking against,
pokuhafab; knocked against. pokufah; to
strike or knock me with the fist, sasa-
kulichih; striking or knocking me, sasa-
kahoh; to knock the breath out, nukbi-
pah; plural, nukbipoa; I am knocked out
of breath, sanukbipah.
Knoll, *n.* Bokkoh.
Knot, *n.* Pokshi, naksish. talakchi achuffa,
ulhpisa achuffa.
Know. *v.* Akostininchih. ithanah; unknown or not knowing, ikakostiniuchoh;
to know about, ai akostininchih; to make
known, ihaiakuchih; known. anukfohkah; knowledge, ai ithana, nan ithana;
the extent of knowledge. ai ithana ulhli:
retaining knowledge, anukfohkah; to
impart knowledge, anukfohkih, anukfo-
hkichih; continually imparting knowledge, anukfohkibinchih.
Knuckle, *n.* Ibbakushi abonuli.

La! *int.* Hush, hush ha! la me! alena! hushba!

Label, *n.* Hohchifo takalichih; labelled, hohchifo takali.

Labor, *r.* Toksulli, pilesah; gratuitious labor, yikowa; laborer, hattak na pilesa hattak toksoli; laborious, abchiba.

Lace, *n.* Sita shochoha.

Lack, *v.* Ikonoh, iksho, iklano.

Lacoule, *a.* Yushkololib.

Lad, *n.* Hattak himitta. ulla nakni.

Ladder, *n.* Atuya.

Ladle, *n.* Nakabila. isht kufa.

Lady, *n.* Ohoyo; ladylike, ohoyo imma, ohoyo holba.

Lae, *r.* Ulbul aya.

Lagoon, *n.* Hayip, haiyip okhutta i filumma,

Lake, *n.* Okhutta, haiyip; a lake caused by a beaver dam, hohtak; a small pond or lake, hohtak ushi; okhutushi.

Lamb, *n.* Chukfi, ulhpo ushi, chukfi ushi.

Lame, *n.* Tabikli, chabikli, hanahchi, shaloksholi, kingfa.

Lament, *v.* Yayah, tabashih;

Lamp, *n.* Bila pula,

Lampass, *n.* Nutakbachi.

Land, *n.* Yakni; land above,uba yakni.

Landing, *n.* Peni ataya akucha.

Lancet, *n.* Issish isht kuchih;

Lane, *n.* Holihta ittintakla.

Language, *n.* Anumpa; bad language, anumpa okpullo; good language, anum apa achukma; obscene languagk, chaka pa; to speak a foreign language, bulbahah.

Languid, *a.* Hlipushi, kotah, tikambih; to languish, hlipushichih; languor, hlipushi.

Lank, *a.* Yuhapa.

Lantern, *n.* Pula afoka.

Lap, *v.* Holukshih, ishkoh; the lap. iyobi pakna; lapstone, alullchi; lap board, abushli.

Larceny, *n.* Hukopa.

Lard, *n.* Shukha bila, bila; leaf lard, ihlapa.

Large, *a.* Chitoh hochcto; to make large, chitolih, chitolichih, hochetochbih hochctoli; to be very large or long, alakah, ayakah; to cause to be very large or long, ayakachih; not large, ikchito.

Lark, *n.* Shonolo, shonlolo.

Larynx, *n.* Ikolupi, kolumbish.

Lascivous, *n.* Ilaksi.

Lash. *v.* Fumini, hlukkahab; lashed, fumma; to give one lash, hlukalichih; to continue, hlukalihinchi.

Last, *a.* Ishtaiopi; at last himmakka, polaka; a shoe last, shulush atobah.

Latch, *v.* Afachalih; to cause to latch, afachalichi; latched, afachah.

Late, *a.* Ahchiba, cheki, himona; lately, cheki. cheki kash. chekosi kash.

Latent, *a.* Luma, ikhaiako.

Lath, *n.* Ulbuska, chukka ulbuska.

Lather, *n.* Pokpoki.

Laud, *v.* Hummohlib; laudable, ai okpancha hinla, abninchi ulhpesa.

Laudanum, *n.* Ishkot nusi, lotnum.

Laugh, *n.* Yukpah olulli; laughable, isht i yukpa ulhpesa; to cause laughter, yukpali.

Laundry, *n.* Nan ai achifa; a launderer, hattak nan uchefa; laundress, ohoyo nan achefa.

Laurel, *n.* Tushhlukna, kalmia.

Law, *n* Nan·ulhpisa, anumpa ulhpisa; a law book, nan ulhpisa holisso; a written law, anumpa ulhpisa holisso; a law maker, anumpa ulhpisa ikbi; lawless, anumpa ulhpisa iksho; to nulify or repeal the law, anumpa ulhpisa akshochih; a lawyer, anumpa ulhpisa isht utta, nan ulhpisa isht utta; to become a law, anumpa ulhpisa ahlit tobah; to break or violate a law, anumpa kobullih; a repealed law, anumpa ulhpisa kobaffah.

Lay, *r.* Bohlih hokchih; to lay down, akkabohlih, buchalih; to lay them there, at or on, alashachih; to lay across. ai yukhunnah; ahasalih, abanulih; laid across, ai yukhanayah, bushkuchih, bachayah, abasah, to lay across, as coru rows, ai yukhanilih; to lay them across, ai yukhannih; to lay down lengthwise, buchali; laid lengthwise, buchah buchayah; to lay them down, bacholi; laid down in rows, bachohah; to lay up or lay down, bohlih; continually laying up bohohlih, boyuhlih; laid up in rows side by side, buchohah, bushkuchi; to lay aside, to or by self, ilabohlih; to lay it down, kahpulih; to lay it on, unochih anashochih, ouochih; laid on top of each other, ittalata; to lay on top of each other, ittalatulih; laid several thicknesses on each other, ittalutkuchi; to lay across the tree or log, iti abunah, iti apanalih; to lay it down to or at, abuchalih; laid down to or at, abachayah; to lay across, ai okhonnilih; laid across, ai okhannayah

Lazy, *a* Nan intukobi, intukobi; laziness, nan intukobi.

Leach, *n.* Ahoya, aholyah, aholuya; to leach or filter, holluyah; leached or filtrated, holuyah, hollyah, hoyah.

Lead, *n.* Naki; lead mine, naki akula; white leac nakhuta.

Lead, *v.* Halullih, lauelih, pl, pehlichih, tikba heka; to lead by, ahalullih ahalullichih; leading, hulullih; to load me, sahullih; a leader of men, hattak i miko hopii; a leader or pilot, tikba hika; to lead astray, yoshublih; lead astray, yoshubah.

Leaf, *n.* Hishi, (of a tree) leaf of a book, holisso putta; leafless, hishi iksho; having leaves, hishi asha; to put out leaves, hishi tobah; dry leaves, hushtup.

League, *n.* Kowi tuchina.

Leak, *v.* Hoiyah. hoyah, oka hlopullih, hoya; leaked, hollyah, holuya; leaking, holluya; to cause to leak, holluyuchi; to leak ont, bichillih; leaky, hoya, oka blopulli.

Lean, *a.* Chuna; leanness, chunnah; to produce leanness, chunnachih; I am lean, sachunnah; to lean over, waiyah; several leaning over, waiyohah, waiyokuchih.

Leap, *v.* Hatonchih, mullih, tullih, tuluplih; a leaper, hatonchi.

Learn, *v.* Ikhunnah, ikhunanchih, akostininchih; to learn at, ai ithana; a learner, ai ithana, nan ithana; a place of learning holisso ai ithana holisso ai ithananchi; learning, holisso impunna; to learn from or of, imalithanah; educated or learned, impunna, nan impunna.

Leave, *v.* Impota, pota.

Leather, *n.* Wak haksup homma, nahakshuk lapushkit ulhtaha; sole leather, wak hakshup homma sukko; upper leather, wak hakshup homma; calf skin leather, wak ushi hakshup lapushkit ulhtaha; dressed buckskin, talhko.

Leave, *v.* Issah, kanchih, bohlih, left, kunia, chufah; to make leave; chuffichih.

Leaven, *v.* Nashutummichih, shatummnih; a leaven, nashutummich, shatummni, to make leave, shatummichih; leavened shatummih.

Lecture, *v.* Anumpulih; a lecture, anumpa.

Ledge, *n* Tuli iton tulhkuchi.

Ledger, *n.* Holisso.

Leech, *n.* Hallus, yallus; horse leech, hallus chito.

Leek, *n.* Hatofalaha.

Leg, *n.* Iyuppi, hanuli, hulhki, iyulhki; fore leg, fulup; the leg bone, hind leg, obala, hulhki foni; thigh, obi iyubi; calf of the leg, iyi bulhki, iyi i shilukua iyubi achosholi; joint, itachakuli joints, itachakli; knee, iyi kulaha; muscle, akshish; pastern joint, iyakiska; shank, iyi; shin, iyinchibako, iyinchampko; shin bone, iyinchibako foni; sinew, akshish; veins, issish i hina; ankle iyi inoksak, iyinosak; ankle bone, iyi inoksak foni; ankle joint, iyi tilokuchi; artery, chukush issish i hina; cross legged, iyi itontullichi; foot, iyi, tae, iyushi; big toe, iyishke; little toe, iyush ushli; toe nail, iyakchush.

Legal, *a.* Anumpa ulhpisa ai ulhpisa.

Leggin, *n.* Iyubbiha:

Legible, *a.* Ai itim anumpula hinla, haiakah otunih.

Legion, *n.* Laca febna, talhlepwh sepokni tuchina foka, lechun.

Legislate, *v.* Anumpa ulhpisa ikbih; legislated, anumpa ulhpisa ikbi; legislature, nan ulhtokut nan ulhpisa ikbih, nan apesa.

Lend, *v.* Impotah, i potah; lending something, nun i potah; a lender, impota.

Length, *n.* Falaia, hopaki; to lengthen, falalachih; great length, hoffuloha; to make them of great leuth, hoffulohuchih; lengthy, falaiah; lengthened, falaiah; to lengthen by splicing, achakachih, achakalih; not lengthy, ikfalaio.

Leprosy, *n.* Ilili okpullo, liplosi.

Less, *a.* Iklauo.

Lest, *conj.* Na.

Letter, *n.* Holisso inchuwa, hollisso, letta, anumpa holisso nowutaya; to mail a letter, holisso bahta chito fohkih; a letter or mail bag, holisso ai ulhto; a post office, holisso akaha, holisso nowut aya atlwa.

Lettuce, *n.* Okchaki upa, letis.

Level, *v.* Anumpisochih, ittilaucchih; to be levil, ittilauih, to make levia, ittilanechih; level land, yakni mutalih; to flatten and level, takussalih; flattened and leveled, takussa.

Lever, *n.* Isht afana, isht afina.

Lewd, *n.* Hawi, haui, haksi; to cause lewdness, baucchih haksichih.

Liable, *a.* Ilinla.

Liar, *n.* Holabi

Libel, *n.* Anumpa chukushpa; to libel, anumpa chukushpa ikbih, anumpa chukushpulih; libelant, anumpa chukushpa shahli.

Liberal, *a.* Ima im achukma.

Librarian, *n.* Holisso aiasha apesuchih, library, boliaso ai asha.

Licentious, *a.* Ilaksi; to cause licentiousnesa, haksichih.

Lick, *v.* Holukshih, shukah; to lick repeatedly, holuhakshih; a lick lukfupa.

Licorice, *n.* Ilotilhko kuchi.

Lid, *n.* Anpoholmo, isht ompohomo.

Lie, *n.* Holubi, anumpa holabi; to lie upon or over, ahlipa; to tell a lie on, ahalabih, to lie hard in the stomach, anukbikelih; to lic low or on the face, bihlepah blepah, hlipkuchih, lying on the ground with the face downward, bihlinpah, hlipiut, hlipit, bleplah; to lie down, akka ittolah, ittolah, tushkih; lying down, akka ittuyulah, kahah, ittolah; both laid down, akkakaiyaba; all laid down, akka kahut aiashah, akka kahut mayah; to lie with the back to the fire, alahkih; to make lie with the back to the fire, aiahkichih; lying lengthwise, bushkuchih, buchohah; to sit or lie, chiyah; a worshiper, that lies on his face, hli piut ittuluh; to lie (i. e. to tell) holubih; do not go about telling lies, as holubit ish nohgwa nah; to belie, holu bichi; to lie about each other ittaholuchih; to lie on back, tulluyah; to lie on the back with the face up watulhpit; to lie on, onatulah.

Lieutenant, *n.* Kapitunni iakaiya.

Life, *n.* Nan okchaya, okchaya, ilhfuopak, aiokchaya; to destroy life, fiopa tuplih; lifeless, illih, nusihha.

Lift, *v.* Wakclih; to be able to lift, lauih; to lift up, wakelih; to lift me, saluwih, sawaklilh, sawakelchit: to lift up the head, ubahchakalih; to cause the head to be lifted up, ubachakaluchih.

Light, *n.* Tohwikeli; to make a light, tohwikelichih; dim light, tohfokolih; sudden lights, (as those from a lightning bug), tohkuslih tokassalih, tohmaolih, tohkallih; to lighten tohmallih, tohmallichih hushuk mullih; lightning, tokmaslih, hushuk mulli, mulutha, tohkallih. continualIy lightning, malutmaya, to make light, by decreasing the weight, shohalalih, light (not heavy) shohhulah; brightning or getting light, shohmalalih; clearing up or getting light, shohmalalih; to cause to clear or get light, shohmalalichih; I am light, (not heavy) sashuhhulah; a light color, hutuchi huta; to light up this way, et tohwikclih; a lamp lit, bila tohwikcli, bila pula; light horsemen, issuba ǫ binili; about day light, onnut taha: light fingered, hukumpa: light headed, tasimbo, chukfoloha: to make light, (as lighting a lamp) palalih; a tree killed by lightning, hilohubi.

Lights, n. Shulukpa

Like, a. Holba, hobachit: to make like, hol buchih; made like, holbut toba, to be like achoyuhmih, bikah, chohmi, chomi; to love or to like, anushkunnah; to make exactly like, choyumichih; to mimic or talk light,hobachit anumpuli, to write like another, hobachit holissochih; to make like another, hobachit ikbih: alike, ittiholba, ittiobah; in appearance, like this, obmih; to liken, ohmihchih; te be like, ohmih: being like ohmih; unlike or not like, ikchohmo; likelv, hinla; perhaps or likely, hah, chohmi, chechuk, chechike. to speak like another, hobachit miha: tō walk like another, hobachit nowa; likeness, holba; to make a likeness, hobachit ikbih: to make somewhat like, ahobanli; to cause to appear like, ahobalih; likewise, akinli, mut; liking ahninchi; intensely liking, ahnicchi.

Lily, n. Napakanli, lilli.

Limb, n. Hanali (of an animal) limb of a tree, naksish; my limbs, sahanalih.

Limber, a. Wuhlohbi, pulokuchi: to make limber, walohbichih; to be limber, palolohhah, to make limber, palolohuchih i wulbhbichih.

Limestone, n. Tuli tohbi.

Limit, n. Ai uhli; limitless, ai ulhli iksho.

Limp, v. Kinngklih, tabiklih, chabcklib.

Line, n. Alatali, lapalichih, hlglih; a line or row, bachaya, hlgfa, isht folullichih, blackiug, to make a line with, nan isht lusachi: to face or line, ulutalih; facing or linig, ulutah.

Lineage, n. Chukka achuffa isht atia.

Linen, n. Ponola, kullo nantunna; linen thread, ponola kullo nan isht ahchywa; linen handkerchief, pono kullo nan tapuski.

Linguist, n. Anumpa tusholi.

Liniment, n· Nipi hotupa ikhisb, liniment.

Lion, n. n. Koi chito; lioness, koi chito tek.

Lip, n. Ittiulbi; thick projected lips, itakboshuli; upper lib turned np, ibakpishili, ibakpishasbli; my lips, satiulbi.

Liquor, n. Nan ishko, oka homi; a seller of liquors, ako homi kunchi.

Listen, v. Hoponakloh, hakloh; a listener, hoponaklo, hoponaklo nahaklo; a good listener, hoponaklo achukma; to cause to listeh, hoponakluchih; look out! listen! ma!

Little, a. Iskitini, kunomosi, (i. e. few) iklauo, chubchasi.

Live, v. Okchayah, anta, ahanta; to live by, ai okchayah; to live with iba chukkah: to live together in one house, itta chukkah; to live together, ittahayuchih; living, nan okchaya.

Liver, n. Salakha; my liver, sussulakha.

Lizard, n. Halgchalgwa, chalgwa; chame-

leon or green lizard; funi imalukusl; a small lizard that runs under leaves, bushtup yululli.

Lo! intj. Eheha! yakih! yaki.

Load, v. Alotolih; loaded, alotah, ulhpittah.

Loam, n. yakni paknali.

Loan, v. I'ota.

Loathsome, a. Okpullo.

Lobster, n. Shakchi chito.

Locate, v. Binilichih.

Lock, n. Ishtashana; to lock, ashunnichih; locked, ashana; a padlock, luksi; stock lock, aboha isht ashana; lock jaw nutakfakullo.

Locust, n. Hawa, hawa washa; black locust tree, kuti holba, kutbi lusa; honey locust tree, kuti; katydid; (a species of locust,) chashaiyi.

Lodge, v. Takglih, itonlah, antah; to lodge in a fork, kafulih; a lodge or camp, binah; lodging, anusi.

Lofty, a. Chaha.

Log, n. Iti; to lay across a log, itiabunah, iti abanalih: the upper side of a log, iti apakna, iti apaknaka; the under side of a log, iti nuta, iti nutaka; a hewed log, itipatussa; a rotten log, iti tushbi; a foot log, uhchup; house logs, chukka ittubuna; a log house raising, chukka ittabunni; a notched log house, aboha lanlaki; a rib pole for a log house, abo ha naksi.

Loin, Chushwa nipi.

Loiter, v. Chukka apullit aya.

Loll, v. Hahkah; to cause to loll, buhkuchih,

Lonely, ad. I chukkilissah.

Long, a. Falaia, hoffulloha; long and slender, fabussa; to make long and slender, fabussuchih; all long and slender, fabuskuchih; oblang, falaia kut awata ka i shahli, long winded, flopa i falaia; to make them long, hoffulohuchih; a long distance, hopa ki; a long time, hopaki; longer as to time or distance, hopaki i shakli; longest, hopaki, i shaiyahli. it will last a long time, hapaki hǫ tuha chi; to go a long distance, hopakichi; to take long steps, hopakichit haplih; to take very long, hopahkinchih; to increase distance, hopakichichih; by and by, if long, hopakikma; when it shall be long or far, hopakikmako, hopaki-.oh-mako; not long, ikfalaio, falaia keyu, yuskololi, yustololi, yushkololi; not a long distance, ikhopako, hopaki keyu; so long as, na; gone long distance, olanlichih keyu, olulichih keyu; long range, as a gun, pullikichih; I am long, safahlayah; long way off, pillah; long since or long ago, hopaki kash, hopaki pilla kash.

Look, v. Hopokoyoh, hopopoyo, hikiah, hoyoh; a look out, hopokoyo: to look about, ho pumpoyoh; to take one look, hopunngwoh; to look for, hoyoh; go and look for it, hotia; to cause to look after, hoyochih; to look repeatedly, hoyohonchih; to look for each other, ittihoyoh; look! a word of warning, ma, to look at me, sapisah; looking glass, apisa.

Loom, n. Nan atunna.

Loop, n. Ahlifuchi.

Loose, v. Yuhuplih, shohchupli, hlitofih,

hotofih,; to unhitch or get loose, mokof-
fih; unhitched or got loose. mokofah; to
be untied or get loos·, makohlih, hlitoa;
loose, mokohah; to loosen, fatokuchih,
yohaplih, yuhapolih; to become loose,
fatolichih, yuhapa; loose or loosely,
yohapa hoyopa; to untie or to loosen,
hlitolih; untied or loosened, hliton; to
loosen tilolichih shochohah; loose or
shaking, tilokuchi; to have loose bowels,
iktiah, okfiah; loosened, shochopah,
yuhapoh, hlitofah, holhtohfah.
Loquacious, a. anumpuli shrhli, itakhu-
poli.
Lord, n. Chitokaka; lordship, holitopa;
Lord's supp:r, chitok:ka im opyaka
impa; Lord God, chitokaka chihowa;
Lord's day, chihowa i nitak; Lord's
prayer, chihowa im anumpa ilbusha·
Lord's people, chihowa im okla; Lord of
hosts; ∪ba nan okluba flaieshi chihowa.
Lose, v. i kunia, yushublih; lost, kunia,
yoshoba; if more than one, i tamoah,
tanioa; a place for losing, akonia; to lose
sight of akeniah.
Lot, n. Ai olhtoka; to draw lot or chance.
na shuelih; a lot or chance. na shuela,
an inclosure or lot holihta; inclosed in
a lot, holihta ulbehah; to be inclosed in a
lot holihta ulbehah; to inclose in a lot,
holihta fohkih.
Loud, a. Chitolih; loudly, chitot chitoli
hosh; to speak loud, chitot anumpulih;
to ring or sound loudly, chitot olah; loud
sounding or loud ringing, chitot olah.
Louse, n. Issop; nit, issop nihi; lice, issop
laua.
Love, v. Anuksitah, anushkunna. i hullo
ahnichi; a lover, anushkunna, i hullo;

to love a man, hattak anuksitah; to love a
woman, ohoyo. anuksitah; not to love,
ikaninchoh; to love each other, ittachuk-
oibih; love. nan i hullo, peh ahnih; love
of God, chitokaka isht i hullo. chehowa
i hullo; love to God, chitokaka holitobli,
chihowa ya i hullo; loving, ahninchi
ahniechi,
Low, a. Akkutula; to be low in stature.
akkutulah; to be humble or low, akkalusih; vulgar or low, chakapa; a low
price, iulli ikchitoloh, iulli iklawo; to
low as a cow, mehah, wohah; down below, akka; the lower end, akkaishtula;
lowermost, akkafehna; to lower, akkiah.
akkaiah, akanlichi, akanlosichih; humble or lowly, chukush akkanlusi; low
spirit, chukush iknakno.
Loyal, a. Imantia, i shahli imantia.
Lucid, a. Kostini, malanta, tohwekelih.
Lucky, a. Im ohlah
Ludicrous, a. Isht yopulah.
Lukewarm, a. Lahba, libisha ummona.
Lumber, n. Iti busha, iti tihla; to saw lumber, iti bushli; to plane lumber, iti busha
halushkichih; dressed lumper, iti busha
haluski.
Luminous, a. Tombi. tommi.
Lunatic, a. Tasimbo, hattak tasimbo; a
lunatic asylum, hattak tasimbo aiasha,
hattak tasimbo aiasha chukka.
Lung, n. Shulukpa, shilukpa; my lungs,
sashilukpa.
Lust, v. Yushkummih; to lust after, ai
yushkummih; lustful, ai yushkummi:
lusted, ai yushkumah; to lust after each
other, ittayushkummih.
Lyceum, n. Holisso ai akhanna.

M

Mad, a. Nukoa, bashkiksho: crazy or mad,
holilubi; to get mad, to pout, hush ayab;
to cause madness, hushayuchih; madness or mad, chukcchi; I am mad, sanuk-
oah; to make me mad, sanukowuchih;
to madden, nukouchih. nukhobeluchih.
Madder, n. Nan isht hommuchih.
Maggot, n. Chukaoushi.
Magic, n. Fahpo, fappo; magician, fappoli,
hattak fappo.
Magnanimous, a. Imauukfila chito, holitopa.
Magnificent, d. Holitopa.
Magnify, v. Chitolichih.
Magnitude, n. Chito, chinto.
Mail, n. Holisso; to mail a letter, etc.,
holisso buhta chito fohkih; mail rider,
holisso shahli.
Majesty, n. Chitokaka.
Mayor, a. i shahli.
Make, v. Ikbih, tobachih; to make continually, ibikbih; maker, ikbi, isht utta,
nan isht uita; to make a mistake at,
aishuebt; to make or fix at, ai atahli; to
make a hole, hiyah; a hole made, hiya;
to make self known, ilehaiyakuchih; to
make self sullen, ilehasbayuchih; to

make self well, ilehinkoffichih; to make
self worthless, ilekalukshichih; to make
music, olachi; to make limber, palolobu-
chih; to make a pallet or bed, patalih;
to make speckle, tiktikichih; made, toba,
ikbi; not made. ikbo.
Mule, n. Hattak nakni, nakni.
Malignant, a. Homi fehna.
Mallet, n. nan isht boa, iti isht boa.
Man, n. Hattak; a grown man, hattak asunochi; an expressman, hattak anumpa,
isht aya; a talking man, hatak anumpuli;
a married man, hattak awaya; a profane
man, hattak chakapa; an old man, hattak sipokni; a young man, hattak himitta;
a strong man. hattak blampko; a large
man, hattak chito; a small man. hattak
iskitini; a bold man, hattak chileta; a
hard hearted man, hattak chukushkullo;
a lean man, hattak chuna; a bad man,
hattak okpullo. hattak haksi; a good
man, hattak achukma; a sick man, hattak abeku; a well man, hattak ikabeko;,
a dead man, hattak illi; ca
hattak im anukfila apessanli acbukina:
a talented man, hattak im anukfila
achukma; a feeble minded man, hattak

im anukfila ikkullo; a capricious man, hattak, im anukfila shanaia; quick witted man, hattak, imanukfila tushpa; a high man, hattak chaha; a low man, hattak ikchaho, hattak kawashu, hattak imonna; a lame man, hattak imomokpulo, a lazy man, hattak intakobi; a mean man, hattak kalukshi; a firm man, hattak kamassa: a worthless man, hattak ohchikimba; a wise man, hattak kostini; a black man, hattak lusa; a yellow man, hattak lokna; a white man, nahullo, hattak nipi tohbi; a dirty man, hattak litcha; a penurious or stingy man, hattak nan i holitopa; a learned man, hattak nan ithena; a rich man, hattak, nan i lawa; a poor man, hattak ilbusha; an ignorant man, hattak nan ik ithono: a poor sinful man, hattak nan ashuchi ilbusha; a healthy man, hattaknipi achukma; a sleepy man, hattak nusilhha shahli; a hangman, hattak nuksitili; a huntsman, hattak owetta; a severe man, hattak palummi; headman, hattak pehlichi hattak pehlichika; a boatman, hattak peni fohkot aya; an insane man, hattak tasimbo; a working man, hattak toksuli; a workman, hattak nan isht utta; a murdered man, hattak ubih; an imprudent man, hattak ufekommi; manhood. hattak oua,hattak toba; a gentleman, aattak holitopa, hattak ulhpesa: a red man, hattak upi homma, a ireeman, hattak yuka keyu; a bewitched man, hattak yushpakcma; a true man, hattak ahli, nakni ahli; I am a man, uakni sia hoke.

Manager, n. Hattak i miko; to manage, apesechi, isht utta.
Mane, n. Chushak hishi.
Mange, n. Washko.
Manger, n. Ai ilhpeta, ailmpa.
Mangle, v. Hliluffih; mangled, hlilafah.
Manifest, v. Haiakah; manifested, haiakah.
Manner, n. Ai yummohmi.
Mansion, n. Ai asha, chukka chito.
Manslaughter, n. Hattak uoi.
Mantel, n. Abatola, ubatola.
Mantle. n. Anchi.
Many, a. Laua, lawa; to make many; lawachih, a great many, apaknuchih; as many as, kaniohmi; I am many, salawah.
Map. n. Holisso yakni isht ulhpisa; map.
Maple, n. Chukcho; sugar maple, chukcho kollo, chukcho imoshi; soft or white maple, chukcho.
Maraud, v, Hukopa ittanowa.
Marble, n. Toli halushki; marble quary, toli halushki akula; a marble, toli lombo.
March, v. Ia, baiullit itanowa; to cause to march, baiollichih; marching, baiullit aya baiullit maya; march, (a month) mach.
Mare, n. Isuba tek.
Margin, n. Alaka,
Mark. n. Hlafa, ahlafa; to mark, blafih, hlalih, bushli; a marker, na hlafi bushli; to cause to be marked, hlalichih; to make streaks or marks, hasolih, nasolichih, busowachih; long marks, basosukuchih; a mark or gash from a cut, busha, marked, hlafah bushah; to mark a hollow mark, habillih, habiffichih; not marked, ikhlafoh; to mark a line with,

isht hlafi.
Marksman, n. Hassa impunna.
Marriage, n. Ittihalulli.
Marrow. n. Lupi, foni lupi.
Marry, v, Ittihalullih; ittauwaya, itauwayuchi, awaya.
Marsh, n. Okhlachako, hlabetah, hlafehah okhlachakoh.
Martin, n. Chuki: bee martin, hush puttak.
Martaingal, n. Yushchonolichi, issuba isht tibinachi.
Martyr, v. Atokowa kako isht illi. utakowa anoli.
Marvelous, a. Aunkblakencha.
Masculine, a. Nakni imna.
Mash, v. Litolih; mashed, litowah; I am mashed, salitowah.
Mason, n. Lukfi nuna isht utta.
Mast, n. Uni, nusi haiaka asha.
Master, n. Pehlchi, i nahullo; to master i shahlichih, lm aiyechch, pehlichih,
Masticate, v. Hapasa, hogsa, hopasu,
Match, v. Luak isht ikoi; to match, holba, itti laui; to make them match, holbuchih to be made to match, holbutoba.
Mate, v. Itti lau-chih, itti hoyochih.
Matter, n. Aninchichi; to matter aninchichih; to cause to matt u, aninchichichih, chah; to cause to matter, aninchichih. to cause to matter, aninchichih, Mattok, n. Chahe iskiffa, itakhish isht ulmo;
Mattress, n. Topa.
Maudline, a. Haksi, oka isht haksi.
Maul, n. Ishtbon, man ishtboa; to maul, bohiih; mauled boah.
Maxim, . Amiha.
May. n. Mc, ahinlah, chike hinla; maybe, chike.
Mayor, n. Hatak temaha pehlichi.
Me, pro. Sa, su, si.
Meadow, n. Hoshuk ai umo, hashuk abusha.
Meal, n. Tanch pushi, tanch bota; mealtime, ai impa ona.
Mean, a. Makali, kalakshi.
Means, n. Iskulli.
Meander, v. Pohlohommih; meandering. pohlomoah.
Measles, n. Chiliswa; to have measles or measly, chiliswa ubih.
Measure. n. Ishtapesa, isht ulhpesa; to measure, apesah; to measure with, isht apesah; measured, ulhpisah; measurably chuyohmi, chohmi chiyohmi
Meat, v. Nipi, ilimpa. ilhpak; hog meat, shukha nipi; beef meat, wak nipi; venson or deer meat, issi nipi; fresh meat, nipi okchaki; dried m at or bacon shukha nipi shila; meat house, nipi i chukka; meat market, nipi akuchii, nipi achumpa; roast meat, nipi ulhpusha, nipi ulbunih; baked m-at, nipi ulhpushu; barbecued meat, nipi ulbunii; boiled meat, nipi honnih, cooked meat, nipi blabochah; fri d meat; nipi ulwosh; stewed meat, nipi hounih; meat; nan ilhpak: good meat, nipi achuknm; sweet meat, nipi chumpuli.
Mechanic, n. Nan isht utta, isht utta chukikbi.
Meddle, v. Ataklemmih.
Mediator, n. Hattak nan olubichih, itti takla bikiut tosholih,
Medicine. n. Ikhish, okbish, ishhish.
Meditation, n. Anukfilli; to meditate,

anukfillih.

Meek, *a*. Chykosh yuhbih; meekness, chykosh yuhbi; to be meek, chykosh yuhbih; to cause meekness, chykosh yubbichih.

Meet, *v*. Ittofamah, afamah; met, ittofamah, ai itohobah, a meeting, ittahoba ittofama; to meet at, ai ittofamah ai itohobih; a place of meeting, ai itohoba, ai ittonaha, a church or meeting house, ai ittonaha chukka, oba isht anumpa chukka.

Melancholy, *a*. Chykosh iknakno.

Meliorate, *v*. Ai iskiah.

Melon, *n*. Okchgk; water melon, shuksbi.

Melt, *v*. Bilelih; melted, bilah: unmelted, bila akmi, ikbiloh, to couse to melt, bilelichih; the melt or spleen, tokoshshi, takushi.

Memory, *n*. Ai ithana, ai ithana olbli.

Mend, *v*. Akollih, aiskah, aiskiachih; a mender, nan apuskiachi.

Menses, *n*. Hullo; menstruation, hullo.

Merchant, *n*. Ittotoba nan chumpa.

Mercury, *n*. Ikhish kollo.

Mercy, *n*. Nan i nukhaklo. isht i nukhaklo mercy of God, chitokaka hokot i nukhaklo, chihowa nan isht i nukhaklo, ai i nukhaklo.

Mere, *a*. Banoh, beka, bieka; merly or to give for nothing, pilla; merely, pe.

Merit, *v*. Asitobih, imolhpesah; merit of Christ, klaist i nan isht aholitopa'

Message, *n*. Anumpa; to carry a message; anumpa isht gya, anumpa shabli; a messenger, anumpa shabli anumpa isht gya hattak anumpa isht gya.

Messiah, *n*. Messias; Klaist.

Metal, *n*. Toli.

Meteor, *n*. Palampa. palampa chito, pulgkpa.

Mew, *v*. Ygwah.

Mid, } Iklonna; the middle, ai
Middle, } iklonna, ai iklonnaka; midday tabokoli, nitak iklonna; midnight, ninok iklonna; toward the middle, ai iklonna imma; midway, iklonna, chakpa.

Mightly, *ad*. Fiehna; might have been, chin tuk chin tok: might be very, fehna hinla; mighty, kollo chinto.

Mild, *a*. Nuktanla, yohbi.

Mile, *n*. Kowi; a mile, kowi achofla·

Military, *a*. Tushka chipota, imma.

Milk, *n*. Pishukchi; to milk, beshlichih, ibishlichih, i wishlichih; milked, bishahchih; a milker, bishlichi; milk pan, pishukchi ai olhto, milk strainer, pishnkchi isht hoya; cream, pishukchi pakna nia; cream pitcher, pishukchi pakna ai olhto: butter, pishukchi nia butter milk, pishichi nia okchi; milky, pishukchi ohmih; milkyway, ofi hota kolofa i hina.

Mill, *n*. Afotoha; a saw mill, iti absoha; coffee mill, kafi afotoha; a mill (a coin) mill, pokoli kot sint achofla; miller, fotohli, fotoli.

Millenium, *n*. Afommi tahlepa sipokni achofla itti takla ka yakni momakot chisus klaist a im antia he bano. micha setan iksho ka he hoke.

Mimic, *v*. Hobachih; to mimic by talking, hobachit anumpuli; to mimic in walking

hobachit nowa; to mimic in writing hobachit holissochi.

Mind, *n*. Im anukfila; to mind, hakloh, ithanah, pisah, imantiah; mindful, hakloh; the mind of man, hattak im anukfila; a good mind, im anukfila achukma; a man of mind, hattak imanukfila gsha, a feebled minded man, hattak im anukfila ik kollo; being of one mind, ittachofla. ittaiachofla; to herd or to mind, pehlichih; a herder or minder, pehlichi.

Mine, *n*. Akula, toli akula; it is mine, ono yokah; mine, su, ommi.

Mingle, *v*. Ittaiyummih, ai yummi, ai yummichih: mingled, ittaiyummah; to mingle with, ai ittoyokommih; mingled with, ai ittoyohoma.

Minister, *n*. Obanumpeshi, obanumpa isht otta.

Mink, *n*. Oshon holba, shakihba.

Minor, *a*. Iskitini, ik lauo.

Mint, *n*. Shinuktibleli; mint.

Minute, *n*. Hopaki achofla; minit, minit achofla.

Minute, *a*. Iskitini, atokon: minutia, chukushpa.

Miracle, *n*. Nafchna, isht ahiulo; to work myricals, naiehucchih.

Mire, *n*. Haiyiko, hlabeta; miry, haismo, blabinta; to make miry, haismochih. hlabbetochi hlafehochih.

Miror, *n*. Apisa.

Mirth, *a*. Yukpa; mirthful, yukpa.

Mischievous, *a*. Acheba, isht achiba; to make mischievous, afikommichih; to be mischievous, afehkommih; too mischievous, isht achibochih.

Miser, *n*. Hattak nan i hullo, hattak nan i holitopa.

Misery, *n*. Apalommi.

Misfortune, *n*. Ishkonnapa; to cause to meet with misfortune ishkonnapachih.

Mislead, *v*. Yoshublih; mislead, yoshubah.

Misrepresent, *v*. Holubit anolih.

Miss, *v*. Anaktibollih, auaktibollichih ihlakoffih ashochi; missfinding game poaflih to cause to miss i hlakoffichih; to mis frequently, ittibatalih, ittibatulichih; to fail to meet or miss each other, itti hlakolfih; made unlucky or missed, poafah; missed or failed to hit, ihlakoifih.

Missionary, *n*. Oklushi obanumpa im abochih.

Mist, *n*. Okshimmichi; to mist, okshimmichih. oktobollih; misty. okshimmichi, ik baiako; to mist on, onoktobollih·

Mistake, *v*. Ashochih.

Mistletoe, *n*. Foni i shupha.

Mistrust, *v*. Aba im ahuih.

Mitigate, *v*. Yohaplih; mitigated, yohapah.

Mitten, *n*. Ibbak foka.

Mix, *v*. Ai yummih, ai yunmichih; a mixture with liquid, ahlata; mixed together ahlatah; to mix a liquid with something else, ahlatahih; mix̯d, ai yunmah; mixed with water, olhkommoh; to cause to be mixed, olhkomochih; a mixture, olhkomo; to mix together, ittaiyummih; mixed together, ittaiyumah; not mixed together, ikittaiyummoh.

Moccasin, *n*. Chunawha, (i e a snake), moccasin, (a shoe), taihko shulush.

Mock, *v*. Hobachih; to mock each other

ittihobachih; mocking bird, hushbulbahu.

Moderate, *v.* Chulosah, peh loma, nukt-anla: moderation. chulosa; moderately, chiyuhmi, chohmi, choyohmi; moderator hattak ittonahu peblichi, hattak ittonn-aha pehlicheka.

Modern, *a.* Himak, himona:modernize, himonuchih.

Modest, *a* Ahah ahni.

Moist, *a.* Anukyohbih, anukyohbichih, hokolbi hotokbi; to moisten, shummi-chih, holkulbichih hotokbichih; to be moistened with dew, okshachakmoh, oshachakmoh, shachokmoh; to moisten with dew, shachakmochih; moisture, shummi.

Molasses, *n.* Hupi champuli okchi, balasis.

Mole, *n.* Yuihkun.

Molest, *v.* Anumpulichih, ataklommichih.

Moment *n.* Yakosi, during the moment, yakosi ittin tgkla; this moment, himonasi.

Monarch, *n.* Miko.

Monday, *n.* Monti, manti.

Money, *n.* Tuti holisso; small money or change iskuli; moneyed iskuli in lawa, iskuli imma.

Monster, *n.* Nan okpullo, nan isht ahullo okpulo; monstrous, okpullo.

Month, *n.* Hushi; this month, himak hushi; one month, hushi achuffa; month-ly achuffakma, hushi aiyuka; by the month, hushi ulhpisa.

Monument, *n.* Isht ikhana he.

Moon, *n.* Hushi ninak gya; moonlight, hushi ninak-gya tohwikeli, nittuk omih, to eclipse or hide the moon, hushi lumih the moon eclipsed or hidden, hushi luma an eclipse of the moon, hushi kunia; full moon, hushi bolukta; to become full moon, hushi boluktuchih; the new moon hush, himona; like the moon, hushi holba; a circle round the moon, hush akohullih; the place where the moon shines, hushi ninak gya atomi, hushi atomi; the rising of the moon, hushi kuchah; disappearance of the moon, hushi loshumma; this moon, himak hushi.

Morality, *n.* Hopoyuksa, ahopoyuksaka, anuktanla; moral, hopoyuksa; moral law, isht ahopoyuksa he nan ulhpisa.

More, *a.* Laua i shahli, himak ma; more than common, afehna; to praise more than is due, afehnuchih; more added to, ibalhkahah.

Morning, *n.* Onnahinli; in the morning, onnahinlikma.

Morose, *a.* Bashka iksho, yukka iksho, bashkiksho, hashka keyu; moroseness, hulhpasha iksho.

Mortal, *a.* Illa hinla; illi im ulhtayak.

Mortar, *n.* Chukka isht ulhpolusa, i c mortar to plaster a house, a mortar for pounding corn, kitti, ahusi; pestle to to pound with, kittush.

Mortification, *n.* Hofahya, toshbi, nipi toshbi; to mortify, hofahyechih, nipi toshbichih; mortified, hofahya, nipi toshbi.

Moss, *n.* Shumo, iti sumo; moss in water, oktushi; mossy, shumo bano, shumo gsha.

Most, *a.* Laua moina i shahli. fiehna.

Moth, *n.* Nan ilayak shushi.

Mother, *n.* Ishki; my mother, hushki your mother, chishki; his her or their mother, ishki.

Mould, | *v.* Akmichih, akmochih; mold-
Mold, | ed, akmih, akmoh; a foundry or mould, aiakmo; mouldy, shukbuna, bokboki.

Mound, *n.* Yakui chishinto, bokkoh.

Mount, *n.* See mound.

Mountain, *a.* Nunih chaha, nunih, onch-uba chaha.

Mourn, *v.* Nuhakloh, isht nukhakloh, isht yaiyah, tabashih; to mourn for, tabashih, mourning; tabashih; mourner, tabashi; mourners, tabashi ulhleha; mournful, nukhaklo, ilbusha; days of mourning, tabashi nitak ulhpisa.

Mouse, *n.* Pinti; a brown mouse, pintukfi; a grass mouse, pintuksgla; mouse color-ed, toshbokoli hishi toshbi; a short tail mouse usually found in grass, yumbak.

Mouth, *n.* Itakha, itih; inside of the mouth, itakha anukaka.opening the mouth wide, itakhabali; open mouth, itakyabali; to make the mouth water, itukchubah. spittle sticking to the mouth, ituklapowa a yellowish collor about the mouth, ituklukna; to put in the mouth, ittih fohkih; to put it in the mouth, kupulih, black about the mouth, ibakinsonli my mouth, satih; sore mouth, itukha hutupa; the mouth of a stream, bok asetili.

Moveable, *a.* Kanuli.

Move, *v.* Kanullih kanullichih; to move to, kanullichih, akanullih; to cause to move to, akanullichih; to move away from, iwchah; moved or stirred as water, piakuchih poalichih; to move or stir, pialichih poalichih, poakuchih; moving rapidly, palhkih; to make haste or move fast, tyspalichih; moved, kunia ulhto-showah; removed, kanullih, akanullih, ulhtoshowah; to move away, wihah wibut kunia; moved away, wihah, to move slowly, yalullih; a mover, wibut gya; moving in ranks as soldiers, baiut bayah; moving in rank, baiullit gya, baiullit mgya; moving about, fulokahan-chih.

Mow, *v.* Bushlih, umoh; mowed, busha, ulmoh; a place mowed, hushuk abusha; to mow grass, hushuk bushli; mowed grass, hushuk busha; a mower, hushuk bushli, hushuk isht bushli; mown, ulmoh.

Much, *a.* Fehna, laua, apakna; very much, ai oklyha; to make much of, feuuchih; as much as, kaniohmi; I am much, sufehna; I am too much, sashahlih.

Mud, *n.* Lukchuk, hlatiko, hlatimo; mud-dy, hlatiko, hlafehah; to make muddy hlatikochi, hlatimochih hlafehuchih, hlabetuchih; mire or soft mud, hlabetah, haiyiko; a muddy or wet place, hlachiko, oklahsko; to make a muddy or wet place, hlachikchih, okhlachakochih, hlatiko-chih.

Mug, *n.* Ishtishko ampo, isht ishko, lukfi ampo chipunta.

Muggy, *a.* Hokulbi.

Mulatto; *n.* Nipi lakna, hattak lakna, hat-tak lusa nipi homma.

Mulberry, *n.* Bihi; mulberry-tree, bihi upi, bihupi.

Mule *n.* Issuba haksobish falaia.

Mullen, *n.* Hakchuma holba.

Multiply, *n.* Ittih akahlichih, lauuchi, lauat ia, lauat toba, isht itti bakahlih; multiplied, ittilb ulhkahah.

Mumps, *n.* Ikonla shatahli.

Murder, *v.* Hattak illichih, hattak ubih; a murderer, hattak ubi, hattak bika ubi; murderous, hattak ubi, hatjak bik ubi shahli.

Muscle, *n.* Akshish, shaha, okafolush; muscle shell, okafolush hakshup.

Muscadine, *n.* Sukko

Muse, *v.* Isht anukfillih.

Mush, *n.* Ashila.

Music, *n.* Taloa, ola; musical, taloa imma, nana olachi imma; musician, nan oluchi.

Muskmelon, *n.* Ochak; musk rat, kinta holba.

Muslin, *n.* Na tapushki.

Musquito, *n.* Sapontak; musquito bar, isht ahlipo.

Must. *v.* Chike: must have been, akutoh; must be, fotoh; must not, hatuk ohmi; it must be, omihah, pulla.

Musty, *a.* Toshbi, shakbona.

Mustard, *n.* Mustut.

Mute, *a.* Ik anumpolo, hattak ik anumpolo.

Matter, *v.* Anumpont ashah, anumpont iah.

Mutton, *n.* Chukfi nipi.

My, *pro.* A, um, su, minc, ummi.

Myrrh, *n.* Muh.

Mysterious, *a.* Inla, ik otano: mystery, nan ik otano, nana aluhma, na fehna chinto.

N

Nag, *n.* Issuba iskitini.

Nail, *n.* Tuli chufak, chufak; wrought nails, chufak boa; four-penny nais, holhtina ushta; eight-penny, holhtina untuchina; large nails, tuli chufak hochito; small nails, tuli chufak chipunta; to nail, anuhlichi; nailed, anahla, abonahla; nailed at, aishonohla; nailed to, anahla; to nail on, anulhhlichih; to cause them to be nailed on, abonulhhlichih; spike nails, chufak hochito; finger nail ibbakchush.

Naked, *a.* Banoh, fahko, nipi banoh, mih banob, nan iksbo.

Name, *n.* Hohchifo; name only, hohchifo bano, hohchifo bieka; nameless hohchifo iksho; to take a name, hohchifo ishi; a nickname, hohchifo okpulo; named, hohchefo takali, hohchifo, to name, hohchifochih; while naming or calling, hochifo; continually naming, hochihifo; to name each other, ittihochefoh.

Nap. *v.* Nusi, napkin, nantapuski.

Narrate, *v.* Anolih; narrated, annowah; narration, annoa; continually narrating, annohowah; to narrate a story, fappulih.

Narrow, *a.* Ik putho, atohlifa.

Nasty, *a.* Litiha; I am nasty, salitlhah.

National, *a.* Okla imina, ai okla.

Native, *a.* Ahofanti yakni yummakinli atoba, i yakni ahofanti; nativity ai utta.

Nature, *n.* Ai im ulhpesa; naturally so, ai ommo mali.

Naughty, *a.* Haksi, ik kost no, okpulo.

Nausea, *n.* Yuwala; to nauseate, yuwalachih; nauseating, yuwalah; I am nauseated, siyuwalah; to nauseate me, siyuwulichih; nauseous, ynwalah, okpulo.

Naval, *a.* Peni chito imma.

Navel, *n.* Hatambish, haiombish.

Navigable, *a.* Peni aya hinla, peni aya he ulhpesa; to navigate, peni isht aya, peni fokot aya.

Nay, *aa.* Keyu, ahah, ha, aheto.

Near, *da.* Bilika, ittuma; nearly, ahai, ngha, bilinchi; nearness, bilika; very near, bilikasi, olanlosi, olasi; places near to each other, ai ittibilika; near by, olan-

li, ittumasi, ibilika; near to each other, ittibilika; very near to each other, ittibelikasih; to come near, olanlichih; nearer, olalichih; nearest, bilikasi; to draw near, bilikuchih, bilinchih; to live near, bilika utta; near sighted nishkin tulhha.

Necessary, *a.* Yohma hopulla; necessitous, ilbusha, abunna.

Neck, *n.* Ikonla; short neck, okwiohillh; bow neck, tibbina; necklace innonchi.

Necromancy, *n.* Illi isht anumpuli, illi nan isht anoli ilahobbi.

Need, *v.* Bunnah; to be in need, ilbusha; needful, abunna needless, a yohma ulhpesa keyu; needy, abunna, ilbusha.

Needle, *n.* Chufak ushi, chufak ushi nan isht achunli; needle case, ai cibiha; knitting needles, iyubi huski isht tunna.

Neglect, *v.* Imihaksi, ahaksichih ik anukfillo, issah; neglected, aksho, ahaksi; neglectful, immihaksi, nan isht ik ahno; negligent, abah ik ahno.

Negotiate, *v.* Chumpah.

Negro, *n.* Hattak lusa; negress, hattay lusa ohoyo; a negro wench, hattak lusa ohoyo haui; a mulatto or half negro, hattak lusa iklunna; Africa, or the negro country hattak lusa i yakni; a negro boy, hattak lusa usbi; negro wool, hattak lusa pashi; a negro slave, hattak lusa yuka.

Neigh, *v.* Sihika, shuka, kileha; neighing, sibihikah, sohohoka.

Neighbor, *n.* Chukka apunta, b'lika utta; next neighbor, chukka et apatenlih; neigkbors, at ittibilika; his neighbor, i chukka apanta, i chukka alokuit; neighborly, chukka apanta ayohma he ulhpesa.

Nephew, *n.* Ibaiyi

Nerve, *n.* Illampko, kollx, au affection of the nerves, halohli; nerveless, ikhlampko; nervous, kullo, hlampko.

Nest, *n.* Ulhpichik.

Nestle, *v.* Binilih, alatah.

Nethermost, *a.* Akka fehna.

Nettle, *n.* Hattak bulhpa; to nettle, holhpuelih; bull nettle, hattak holupa chito.

Neuter. *a.* Aha'aia iksho, pe aya.

Neutral, *a.* Pe aya, ahalaia iksho.

Never, *ad.* Nitak nana wa. nitak nanakeyu; never will or never can. himma keyu; never before, chatoshba; never was or never has been. chatuk keyu, chatuk atushba, chatushba; nevertheless, amba, never to be, himma keyu.

New, *a.* Himona; to make new. himonuchih; somewhat new, himona chohmi; renewed himonah; renewable, himonucha hinla; newly, news, anumpa, annowa, anumpa kaniohmi; the place where news is told, nan aiannoa; news carrier, anumpa shahli.

Next, *a.* Himmak ma atukla; and next, cha.

Nibble, *v.* Kachelih. nip, kachelih.

Nice, *a.* Achukma, hochukma, koshofa.

Nickname, *v.* Himak fokalichit hochifo; a nickname, isht yopula hohchifo.

Nicotine, *n.* Hakchuma hliitilli.

Niggard, *a.* Hattak nan i hullo, nan i hullo.

Nigh, *a.* Bilika; well nigh, naha, ahosi.

Night, *n.* Ninak; dark night, ninak, okhlili; moonlight night, ninak nittukohmi; to night, himak ninak; midnight, ninak iklunna; fortnight, nitak hullo tuklo; last night. ninak asha; night before last ninak misha kash, nightly, ninak moma, ninak atukma, ninak aiyuka; I pass the night siononnah; night-cap, aihlipa; night clothes, nafoka fokut nusi; night mare, holhpokonna okpullo; night watch; ninak atoni.

Nimble, *a.* Tushpa.

Nine, *a.* Chakkalih; nineteen, abih chakkali; ninth, isht chakkali; nineteenth, isht abih chakkali.

Nippers, *n.* Isht kiseli.

Nipple, *n.* Ipishik; my nipple, sapishik.

Nit, *n.* Issep nihi.

Nitre, *n.* Hcpi kapussa.

No, *ad.* Keyu, aheto, ha ahah, chikimba; na! by no means, kaniohmi kia yohma, he keyu; in no wise, kaniohma be keyu.

Noble, *a.* Holitumpa; nobleman, hattak holitompa; nobly, chitolihosh, chitot.

Nod, *v.* Okfakolih, akkachimolih, akkachunni.

Noise, *n.* Yahapah. shakapah, tapulah, chobok, haksuba, hlachuk kabak; to make a noise from any object falling into water, chobokachih, hlobukachih; to make a gurgling noise, chobohuchih; to churn and make a noise, chobolichih; to make a noise by scratching the bark of a tree, fachohuchih; to confuse with noise, huksubachih; to make a noise like that of a knife or ax when it cuts anything, hlachak achih; to make noise by concussion, kabak; to make a noise with feet, as tramping of a horse, kitilichih kittikuchih; making a noise by pressure on the nose, okehoshonlih; making a noise by whooping, yahapah shakapah; to make a noise by hollowing, tapulah; to make a rumbling noise, wenihuchih, komohuchih; noisiness, yabapa.

Nominal, *a.* Hohchifo imma, peh hohchifo, hohchifo bieka, hohchifo buno.

Nominate, *v.* Wakelih, wakelichih; to nominate me, sawakelih.

None, *a.* Iksho; you have none, ikchim iksho.

Nonsense, *n.* Anumpa keyu; anumpah

makalih, anumpa kaniohmi keyu; non sensical, isht yopula, ik ahobalo.

Noon, *n.* Tabokkoah; tabakkoah. midday, tobokkolih.

Noose, *r* Anukhlifih; noosed anukhlifah.

North, *n.* Falummi; northerly, falummih imma, falummi chohmi; the north star, falummi fichik; northward or at the north, falummi pilah; way off north falummi pillah; northwest, falummi heshi aiokotula ittintokla; north-cast, chukfi ikpilo.

Nose, *n.* Ibishakini, ibiheholo; nostril, ibiheholo; mucus from the nose, ibilhkon; to bleed the nose, ibekolih; bleeds, ibikoah, my nose bleeds, sabikoah.

Not, *d.* Keyu, ha, ik, ahah, awa aheto; will not or cannot be so, chihchint; not so, chikimba, cannot be so, not possible, or probably not so, chiut: not often or not very, fehua keyu; would not or cannot, hokakant; it ought not, hotuk; does not, may can or must not, hotuk ohmi; do not, na! I am not, sia keyu; not at all, keyu kunmohmi; ought not or should not, yobat, cannot or will not, awa; not yet, keyu kisha.

Notable, *n.* Annoa achukma, isht annoa, it hannah hinla.

Notch, *r.* Chabt lamplih, lakofilh, lublih; to cut notches, chakoli; uotched, chakoah, lakowah, falukto, lakofah; notches, chakokokuchi, lukohil; to cause to cut notches; chakolichih, lublichih: a notch in a mountain, nenih itta hokofa.

Note, *n.* Holisso iskitini; noted, annoa achukma, holisso; to note, ikhana, holissochih.

Notice, *v.* Ai okpanchih, hakhlo; not to not to notice, ikaiokpacho.

Notify, *v.* Haklochih, imannolih; not notified, ik im cnnowoh; to be notified. imannowah; a notification. imannowa; notified imunnoah: to notify each other, ittihaklochih.

Notional, *a.* Imanukfila laua.

Notorious, *a.* annohowa, isht otoni.

Notwithstanding, *prcp.* Hobkia. atuk kia hokak, i. e. when followed by o, as umba hokako il iachi, which in English is, notwithstanding it is raining we are going.

Novel, *a.* Himona, a novel holisso; novelist, holisso ikbih; novelty, nana himona, a novice, himona isht utta.

Now, *ad.* Hinak, himo, himonasi, haha, himona, intah, tah; now-a-days, nitak himak a fohkali; now at this time, himakano; just now, himonasi hokak heno, hakak heto.

Nowhere, *ad.* Kanima keyu; not any where, kanima hoh keyu.

Noxious, *a.* Ai okpula, himla.

Nullification, *n.* Akshochi; to nullify, anumpa uihpisa akshochih.

Numb, *a.* Shimmoha chilhhlinah illi; to cause numbness, chilah hlinuchih; a great numbness, chilhhlinoha.

Number, *n.* Holhtena hopena hotinah; numbered. holhtenah; numberless, holhtena atupa; can or must be numbered, holhtena hinla; innumerable, holhtena he keyu, aholhtinah iksho; to be numbered with others, aholhtinah; numerable, holhtinah atupa; not numbered, ikholhtiuoh; to numbot each other, ittihotehnah, a numerator. hopena; numerous, laua.

Nurse, . Olla iskitini apesuchi, abeka apesuchi; to nurse, ilaueli, apesuchih, pishechih, hofantichih.

Nut, n. Dui; shaggy bark hickory nut, kapon; striped hickory nut, oksak shawiya; white hickory nut, oksak hutta; hard hickory nut. oksak kullo, aksak tuli; walnut, oksak hahe; pecan. aksak fulah, hickory nuts generally, oksak.

O

O, interj. Aichng! o ng! ahah! oh dear! aienahi; oh! on account of pain from water, aksnuki; oh! on accont of pain from fire. nkshupi; oh! indeed! aume; oh! painful, eha; oh! haha! oh. what! hau, hai, heigh ho, hauk; oh! from a sense of acute pain, humphe; oh! in time of danger, kaiho! oh! listen, look out, ma! oh! feeling contempt, makhaloka; oh! in defiance, ok; oh! when daring, okinta; oh dear, okokko! oh! it may be so, omiha! oh! well! when beginning to speak, omishke; oh! when suprised, owe! owi! oh! when a mistake is discovered, owih! oh dear! from pain, olle! oh don't! wehka! oh thanks! yakoke! oh alas! yakoke! aichng! O, that it might be, okbuno, hokbuno, yokbuno; o me, hok.

Oak, n. Nosoni; strictly speaking a red oak, black oak. nolokna upi noslaknupi; white oak, baiyi; spanish oak, chilbputha. yukhe; post oak, chisha; black jack, chiskelik, chokushmi; red oak, chishikta; chestnut oak, baiyi holba; over cup oak, bushto; water oak, chilbputha; jerusalem oak, lupchubi, haiyukpulo kosoma; oakon, nosupi osh toba.

Oat, n. Issuba upa, onush issuba upa.

Oath, n. Anumpa kullo; to testify on oath, anumpa kullo onotulut nan anolih, to take an oath, anump kullo, onochih, oath taken, anumpa kullo onotulah: to bind one's self under oath, anumpa kullo il onochih.

Obdurate, a. Chykush kullo, kullo.

Obedient, a. Iyinmi, imantia; obedience, im antia; to obey, imantia, iyimmi, imatia; not obeying, ikyimmoh, imatia keyu.

Oblidge, v. Yukpalih; obliging, i kana, yukpali.

Obliquity, n. Filommi.

Oblong, a. Falaia kut awata ka i shahli, shabbahki.

Obscure, a. Tuhfokolih. ik otano, hima; to cause obcurity. tuhfokolichih.

Observe, v Anumpulih holitoblih.

Obsolete, a. Kunia, aksho, ai issu, akshot taha.

Obstinate, a. Chykush kullo, ikyimmo, ikkosteno; obstinacy. chykush kullo.

Obstruct, v. Ikumglih, yokoplih; to cause obstruction, yokoplichih; obstruction, yokoplih, katapa; obstructed, katapah, katapoah.

Obtain, v. Ishih, ahanchih.

Obtuse, a. Ikbaluppo

Occasionally, ad. Bakah.

Occult, a. Ik otano, luma, ikhaiako.

Occupy, v. Aiashah, ainthwa, halullih;

not occupying, ikaiashoh, ikaiantoh.

Ocean, n. Okhutta chito.

October, n. Aktoba.

Odious, a. Okpulo.

Odor, n. Nabalama; a peculiar odor as the smell of fish, nakshobih. as of urine, kahlama; odoriferous, balama; odorous, balama; to cause odor, balamuchih.

Off, ad. Et, pit; off there or long way off. pillah; offspring, cheluppi; send this way or off this way, et pilih; send off that way. pit pillah.

Offend, v. Chykush hotopalih, nukhaklochih, nokoachih; offended, chykush hotopalih, chykush hotopah; offense, hottupa to give offense, hottupachih; offensive, okpulo. ai okpuninchi.

Offer, v. Bohlih, wehlih; offering, pit wehlih non ai ashuchi isht ulhtoba, uba pit isht ai okpuchi.

Office, n. Ai ulhtoka. nan isht utta, nan isht ai utta; officer, ulhtoka, isht utta, nan ulhtoka, tisha.

Officious, a. I kana, ataklummichih.

Often, ad. Chekohosi. chehiki; oft times or often times, himmong.

Oil, n. Bila, ngbilla; oiled. bila ahamah, ahamah; oily. bila bieka, litikfo, bila bano; to oil, bila ahammih. bila ahammichih; moistened with oil. bila ghlaya; to pour oil on, bila ghlalih; lamp oil, bila pulatoba; to melt oil, bilelichih: to anoint with oil, fokkichih; to oil frequenntly, fokkihinchih: to oil at last, fokkicchih; coal oil, tobaksi bila; coal oil can, tobaksi bila ai ulhto: an ointment or hair oil, ahama: to rub oil on, ahammih.

Old, a. Sipokni; chashpo, hopaki, kamussuli; older, sipokni i shahli; oldest, sipokui moma i shahli; the oldest brother or sister, akni; the olden times, chashpo; to wear out and make old, as a garment, hliplih; to be old. hliput, hliput taha. to make old, hlipuchih; to be aged or old, kamussulih, kaunshuchih; old or getting old, kaunsha; I am getting old. sakamussulih; I am old. sasipoknih; to be a year old, afommi.

Omen, n. Isht ulhpisa, isht ikhuna.

Omit, v. Ahaksih, ahaksichih.

Omnipresence, n. Himona achuffanlit kunima anta.

On, pr. Pit; onward, pit.

One, a. Achuffa; one at a time, achuffalit; not even one, achuffghpi kia keyu; not even one is, achuffghpi kia iksho; perhaps one, achuffona; to take here and there one, achafohlih, achafolih; just one with another, achanah; to become one with, ibachuffa, ibalachuffah; to make one as one of them, ibachuffalih; to add one to or, sent one more in. ibafohkih: once, himonna; just one, himonna; at once, himonna achuffanli, himonali; all at once, himoua achuffanlit himonali; to to be at once, himonali; once or one time. himona ha; let all talk or speak at once, himona achuffa momut ikanumpuli.

Onion. *n.* Hatofalaha, hatofalaha chito; ouion seed, hatofalaha nihi.

Only *ad.* Banoh, akbanoh, hakbano. akbano, yakbano, akbat, bat, beka pulla bieka, illa; only lately, biekah,

Ooze, *v.* Bichilih; to cause to ooze out, bichilichih; cannot ooze out, bichilla he keyu; to ooze out; hlitillih.

Open, *v.* Tiwih, fatummih, wakummih: opened, tiwah, fatomah, wakama, otuninichih; to cause to open, fatummichih; to crack open, fuchanli; cracked open, fuchanlih, bokanlih; to cause to crack open, fuchanlichih; not opened, as a knife, ikfatomoh; to reveal or open to him, imottunih ihaiyakah; an open place shuhbi, shahbi: empty or open, shahbih; open woods, tohwali; to open them, wakamolih: opened, wakamoah; opening as cotton, bokanli; to burst open, bokahlichih.

Opium, *n.* Nusechi kullo; opiate, nusechi, ishkot nusi.

Opportunity, *n.* Ai ulhpiesa.

Oppose, *v.* Ichapah, ichapoah i sanalih katuplih; to oppose each other as candidates. ittichapah; opposite, ichapa in tunnup.

Opossum, *n.* Shukhuta, possum; fat opossum, shukhuta nia.

Oppress, *v.* Ilbushalih; oppressed, ilbushah; oppressive, isht ilbushah, kullo.

Opulent, *a.* Nan in laua, holitompah.

Oral, *a.* Itukha ai anumps, anumpah; orally, anumpah bano.

Orator, *n.* Hattak anumpuli impunna, anumpa isht hika.

Orderly. *ad.* Achukmalit.

Ordinance, *n.* Anumpa ashuchit tusholih.

Ordination, .. Isht ai ulhtoka, isht ulhtokoa.

Origin, *n.* Ai isht ia ummona, aminti; an orgin of, ai isht auechi; original, ummona, himonna, ai isht ia ummona.

Oriental, *a.* Hushi akuchaka.

Orifice, *n.* Choluk.

Ornament, *n.* Isht shema; to ornament with, isht aiuklichih; ornamental. isht aiuklichi.

Orphan, *n.* Ulktaklah.

Orthodax, *a.* Ai ahli, yimmi ahli; orthodoxy, anumpa ai ahli ayimmi.

Ostensible, *a.* Haiaka hinla; ostensibly, haiaka hinla pulla; ostentation, haiyakah.

Other, *a,* Inla; and others, achomih; some other, inla.

Otter, *n.* Oshun; otter skin, oshun hukshup.

Ought, *v.* Yohma he pulla; it ought not, hotuk, hiobat, yobat.

Ounce, *n.* Ous; an ounce, ous achuffa.

Ours, *pro* Pimmi, pishuo; our, pi, pin, pimmi, hup, hupi, hupim, hupimmi, hupin; to be ours, hupimmit ours or ourselves, hupishno.

Out, *ad.* Haiakah. taha, iksho, out doors, kucha; to turn out, kohchih; to take out, kullih; taken out, kufah; to come out, haiakah; out let, asitili; to outrage, hottupachih, hottupalih; outrageous, okpulo, atupa, outset, himona isht ia; at the outset. mihmak inli ho, mashko; out skirt, ai ulhli,

Oval, *a.* Shabahki.

Oven, *n.* Apaluska, ai ulhpusha; oven lid; apaluska o hlipa.

Over, *pr.* Akuchchah, akuchah uba; to go over, ubanaplih; went over, ubanupolih; ulanupoah, annupolih; passing over, ai opitamah; ouercharge, iclli atuplih; overcharged, iulli atupah; over coat, nafoka chito; overcome, imaiyuchih, i shalichih; to overcome at, immaiyachih; overcup, bushto: overestimated, nafehnuchih; ovor flow, oka mitafa; overgo, i shalih, atupah, ontiah; overlay, lapalichih; overjoy. chukush yukpa atupah; to overlook, ahaksih, ahaksichih over seer, apesuchi; to overshadow, hoshontikachih; overtake, sakkih.

Owing, *a.* Ahika im usha; owing to, hona hocha.

Owl, *n.* Opa; horn owl, iskitini; prairie owl, opa shilup; screech owl, ofonlo; owlish, opah imma.

Own, *v.* Halullih; ishih immih; his own, ai immi ilapo; what is his own, ai immi ha; to or at his own or its own, aki akinli; every one owning, ai immi aiyukah; to own to, il anoli; owning or ownership, nan inmi; both owning; ai immibikah.

Ox, *n.* Wak toksuli; ox bow. waktoksuli ikoula ofohoma, wak toksuli ikonla afoka; ox yoke, yok, ikonla abana,

Oyster, *n.* Okafolush, chakla, opa haksun; oyster shell, akafolush hakshup.

P

Pace, *v.* Kiulih, kaiullih; a step or a pace, ahabli, uhali.

Pacific, *a.* Yohbi, nuktula, i kana, hopohla to pacify, hopuhluchih, chulosalih.

Pack, *v.* Shalih; packed shayah,

Paddle, *n.* Isht moffih; to paddle, moffih, moffih,

Padlock, *n.* Luksi, aboha i luksi.

Page, *n.* Holisso i tunnup achuffa, holliso putta in tunnup.

Pail, *n.* Ishtochi, ishtohchi.

Pain, *n.* Kommichi, hottupa, hihah; to be in pain, hottupah; painful, hottupa; nukhalochi; to cause pain, hottupuchih, hottupalib; afflicted with pains, nahuttupah; to pain me, sahottupah, suttopah. sahottupolih, suttupulih; severe pain, simiklih; painless, hottupa iksho, ikhottupoh.

Paint, *n.* Isht inchunli,anchaha; red paint, tishibomma, anchaha; to paint the face, anchahlih;to paint another, anchahlichih; a painter, anchahlichi, i chyli, in chyli.

Pair, *n.* Iloloh,

Palace, *n.* Aboha holitopa, chukka holitopa.

Pale,*a.* Huta, kashofa; iti shima holihta, holihta haluppa; a paled yard or lot, holihta haluppa; to make pales, holihta haluppa ikbi; to be pale white, hantah, paleness. huta, hauta.

Palid, *a,* Iluta, kashofa.

Palm, *a.* Ibbak putta.

Palmetto, *n.* Tala.

Palpable, *a.* Otuni.

Palpitate, *v.* Nuktimikuchih, michilhhah, nukwinakuchih; palpitation, nuktimikuchi; michilhha; palpitation of the heart ikfoka maleli, ikfoka baleli, chukush nukbimimkuchi.

Palsey, *n.* Haknip illi, nipi illi isht abeka, palsi; palsied. haknip illi.

Pamphlet, *n.* Holisso hakshup iksho.

Pan, *n.* Amp mahaia mulhha; frying pan, aiolwusha ai ishi asha; bake pan, apaluska; fire pan apula; tin pan, mulhha.

Pancer, *n.* Anumpa akpullo onochi.

anegyric, *n.* Holitoblit isht anumpuli.

Pang, *n.* Hottupa.

Pant, *v.* Fohuklih, fiopa tuha, bunnah; pants, breeches or pantaloons; obalafoka.

Panther, *n.* Koi.

Papaw, *n.* Umbi.

Paper, *n.* Holisso, aholisso; white paper, holisso tohbi; a slip of paper, holisso hilafa; blank paper, holisso ik a holisso; paper maker, holisso ikbi; paper cutter, holisso isht busha; to paper a room, holisso lupelichih; news papers, holisso chito nan annoa.

Parable, *n.* Anumpa nan isht ulhpisa, nan isht ulhpisa anumpa.

Parasol, *n.* Isht il o hhshontikachi iskitini

Pardon, *v.* Imihaksichih, i kashoflchih. i kashofih.

Pare, *v.* Luffih; parred, lufah.

Paregoric, *n.* Ikfoka hottupa ikhish; aparing. hakshup lufa.

Parley, *n.* Ittimanumpuli; parlor, pe aiasha aboha.

Paroquet, *n.* Kilikki; parrot, kilikki chito, kilikki ulhpoa.

Parsimonious, *a.* i hullo, nau i hullo.

Part, *n.* Kashapa; to be apart of, kashapah; to part from each other, ittifalommih; to part from, felommih; to cause to part from, filamolichih; partner, ai ittapela. **Partial,** *a.* Kanimanchi, i hullo, anuksita; to be partial to a man, hattak anuksitah.

Partridge, *n.* Kofih; parturition, eshi.

Pass, *v.* Ai opitummih; passed or passing over, ai opitumah; a ford or a pass, akuchcha; passed by, antiah,a highway or passway, hina; to pass through to, hlukaffih; bored through or passed, hlukafah; to pass through, hlopullit ona; to cause to pass through, hlopullechih; to come through or pass through, hlopullih; ratified or passed,hlopullih;passable, hlopul-

la hinla, ataya hinla; impassable, hlopulla he keyu; to pass quickly through, hlopohlih; to cause to pass quickly through, hlopohlichih; just passed through, hloponlih; to go by or to pass ahead, imalah, imayah; to pass each other, ittiopitummih; to pass with, ahlopullih; to pass the night, ononnah; passing by without calling, okhowatant aya; passion, anushkunna; passionate, im anukfila tushpa; the passover. ubanoblit ont ai impah; in the past, chikkih; pastor apesuchi, pehlichi,iksa inp hlichi.

Pasteboard, *n.* Holisso sukko.

Pasture, *n.* Hashuk ai impa; to pasture. hashuk ai impuchih; a pasture, holihta ulhpon aiasha.

Patch, *v.* Akullih; a thing with which to patch, isht ulhkata; patched, ulhkutah.

Pate, *n.* Nashuka, ibitakla.

Path, *n.* Hina ashi, hinushi. hina; pathless, hina iksho.

Patient, *a,* Nukchinto, nuktanla; a patient hattak abeka; patience, nuktanla; achunanchi.

Patriarch, *n.* Hattak iki chito, iki chito.

Pattern, *v.* Hobachih.

Paucity, *n.* Chubiha.

Pauper, *n.* Hattak ilbusha inla anukchito.

Paw, *n.* Iyi putta; to paw, shuilih, akohlahlih. •

Pay, *v.* Atobbih; to make him pay, atobbichih; to pay the debt, ebiloffih; paid the debt, chilofah, ulhtobah; the debt not paid, ikatobbah, ikchilofoh.

Payment, *n.* Nan ulhtoba; a time or place of payment, ai ulhtoba; not time for payment, ai ulhtoba ikono kisha; repayment falumut ulhtoba.

Pea, *n.* Tobihullo; garden pea. tobi hullo hikint uni; bush pea, tobi hullo abchla. peanut, waya; peacock, okchgwe la, chito

Peace. *n.* Chulosu, hulhpashi, hulhpasi na naiya; peaceable, hulhpashi, nuktanla, yukpa; peaceably, hulhpashit; to make or making peace, nguaiyachih; peaceful, nuktanla, hopohla, yukpa; a peace maker. hattak itta kushkoli.

Peach, *n.* Takon; peach tree, takonupi.

Peal, *n.* Binihuchi; pealing, binihuchi.

Pear, *n.* Takonchito holba; pear tree, takon chito holba upi; prickly pear, tulhpakha.

Pearl, *n.* Shyha, okafolush hakshup; pearl ash, hittuk.

Pebble, *n.* Taloshik.

Pecan, *n.* Oksak fula, pecan tree, oksak fula upi; pecan trees, oksak hofaloha upi.

Peck, *n.* Bushli ikluuma ya iklenna; pek, to peck, chanlih; to cause to peck, chanlichih; pecked, chayah; to peck each other, ittichanlih.

Peculiar, *n.* Chukush ilopissah.

Pedant, *n.* Hattak nan ithgna iluhobbi.

Peddler, *n.* Ulhpoyak shut aya.

Pedestrian, *n.* Akkaya, akka hikkit aya; pedestrians, akka hika.

Peel, *n.* Hoflih, hlohlih, fokoplih, lulih; peeled or to be peeled, hlofah; peeled off, hlohah lufah tinlah; fakohah, fakopah foenonlih; a peeling, hakshup lufa; unpeeled, hakshup asha.

Peep, *v.* Afanalichih· huiakah; peep at, afanatah.

Peevish, *v.* Namak keyu, nukoa; peevishness anuk' shomunta.

Peg, *n.* Isht anahla.

Pelican, *n.* Chalantak ahoba.

Pen, *n.* Ai cui, holihta, holiht unih; writing pen, isht hollisosochi; steel pens, tuli kullo isht holissosochi: gold pens, tuli holisso lakna isht holissochi; pent up, holihta ulbehah; penned, holihta ulhto, ulbihah, lead pencil, isht holissochi naki; penman, holissochi.

Penitent, *n.* Hattak yoshoba il o nukhaklochi, nukhaklo; penitence, ai isht nukhaklo.

Peniless, *a.* Ishkuli ik im iksho, ilbusha; penny, iskuli.

Pension, *n.* Afunmik ma ilhpeta; pensive, nukhaklo, asha.

Pentecost, *n.* Ubanublit ont ai impa asha nitak tuklo; pentikost.

Penurious, *a.* Ihullo, iskuli i hullo.

People, *n.* Ukla, oklushi.

Pepper, *n.* Tishi homi; red pepper, tishi homi homina; black pepper, tishi homi lusa; pepper box, tishi homi aiulhto.

Peradventure, *ad.* Yohba na, chishke.

Perceptible, *a.* Akostinincha hinla.

Perch, *n.* Nuni patussa; to perch, binilih.

Perchance, *d.* Yoba, yoba ka.

Percolate, *v.* Holluyah.

Perdition, *n.* Ai okpulloka.

Perfect, *a.* Ai ghlih, achukma ai oklgha; to perfect, tahlih; perfected, tahah ai ulhtah; perfection, ai ulhtaha.

Perforate, *v.* Hlopullih, hlgah, hlukuffih hlukanlichih; perforated, hlopullih, hlukanli; to perforate at, ahlukuliih; a perforation, ahlukasa; perforations, ahlukahli.

Perform, *v.* Yummohmih, tahlih; performing, yummohmih; performed, taha.

Perfume, *v.* Na balana; 'o perfume, balamuchih; perfumed, balamah.

Perhaps, *ad.* Chechik, chechukhah, ka; perhaps so, perhaps not so, chishba perhaps, as to time, place or degree, iokka.

Perish, *v.* Bushshih, illi, ilbushat illi; to cause to perish, bushichih; perished, bushih; perishable, okpula he ai imma, illa hinla, okpula hinla.

Perjure, *v.* Holubit anumpa kullo onochih.

Permanent, *a.* Ilikia billia he, amiha genuffa billia.

Pernicious, *a.* Okpulo, haksi.

Perpendicular, *a.* Uba apissant hikia.

Perpetual, *a.* Biliah; perpetually, billiah;

Persecute, *v.* Ilbushalih, ilbushachih; ilbushulih; a persecutor, ilbushali, hottupuli,

Persevere, *v.* Achebachih mahgyah, achunnachih, amosholih amosholichih, preserving, achunnachi, amoshohonli, perseverance achunnanchi; not perseving ikehilito.

Persimmon, *n.* Ukof,

Persist, *v.* Achunnachih, persisting, achunachi; persistence, achunnachi, amoshohonli.

Person, *n.* Hattak: persons, okla, hattak laua; personal, hattak ahalayah; a lean person, hattak chunna; a fat person, hattak nia; a sick person, hattak abeka; a good person, hattak achukma; a bad person, hattak okpulo; a pert person, hattak isht afekommi.

Perspicuous, *a.* Haiakah.

Perspiration, *n.* Laksha: to perspire, lakshuchih; to cause perspiration, lakshuchih; perspiring, lakshah; not perspiring, iklukshoh.

Persuade, *v.* Anumpulit nukfohkichih.

Pert, *a.* Tushpa, okcha.

Pestle, *n.* Kittush.

Pet, *n.* Ainsitia.

Petition, *n.* Holisso nan asilhha, anumpa asilhha.

Petrify, *v.* Tuli toba, kullo.

Petticoat, *n.* Uskuffa yoskololi.

Pettish, *a.* Namak keyu, nukoa, hushayah.

Petulant, *a.* Hushayah, namak keyu.

Pewter, *n.* Naki kullo.

Pharisee, *v.* Falisi.

Phlegm, *n.* Kahlafa ibilhkun, to raise phlegm, kahlafah.

Physician, *n.* Alikchi

Peazza, *n.* Hoshontika, jhoshontika, ohoshontika opeshchia.

Pick, *v.* Umoh; to pick out, fullih; picked out, fullah; picked, ulmoh, to open and pick out, fullih, lepimoh lepimochih; we pick, emoh; to pick them up, aiyoah, aioah, aiowah, a picket, holihta halappa, pickle, okulhchi; to pickle, okuchih, ukuchih; pickled, ulh kuchih.

Picture, *n.* Hattak holba (is, when a picture of a person); a picture of anything, holisso na holbut toba; to make a picture of anything, hobachit ikbi; a picture taken, hobachit ikbi.

Piece, *n.* Tushafuh, tushu; broken piece, tushahli; to cut a piece, tushuffih, tushlih; to cut many pieces, tustulih, tushalichih; a small piece, chinifa.

Pied, *a.* Bakoa; piebald bakou;

Pierce, *v.* Bahullih, hlumplih, hlifelichih houchlih, ahlumplih, hlukanlichih; pierced at, anchlah, ahlukuffih; a piercing sound, chasha; a place pierced, ahlumpa hlukufah; pierced through, hlukafah, hlumpah.

Pig, *n.* Shukhushi; shote, shukha himmitta; sow and pigs, shukha ilanclih.

Pigeon, *n.* Puchi; tame pigeon, puchi ulhpoba; squab, puchi ushi, puchi himohofulli.

Pigmy, *n.* Hattak, kawasha, hattak imoma, hattak ik chaho.

Pike, *n.* Bushah, i. e. a fish.

Pile, *v.* Pullih ittunnalichih; piled, ittunnabah; piled up, fohompah.

Pilfer, *v.* Hokupah.

Pilgrim, *n.* Pe nowut gya hattak.

Pill, *n.* Ikhish lumbo.

Pillow, *v.* Ulhpishshi; pillow case, ulhpishshi in shukcha.

Pilot, *n.* Hattak peni isht gya peni afana; pilot on land, tjkba heka;

Pin, *n.* Chufak ushi nushkobo asha, chufak ushi yushkoboli; wooden pin, iti isht anahla; pin cushion, chufak ushi ashamohli.

Pinch, *v.* Chiniffih; pinched, chinjfah, chinoah; a pinch, chinifa; to pinch them, chinolih.

Pine, *n.* Tiak; young pine, tiak himitta;

pine knot, tiak pishi; pine bark, tiak hakshup; dead pine, tiak illi; pine leaves, tiak hishi; pine pitch, tiak nia hlitilli; pine rosin, tiak nia; pine turturpentinr, tiak shua; to pine away, hlipushih; pined away, hlipushi, to cause to pine away, hlipushichih; pine lumber, tiak busha; to saw pine, tiak bushlih-

Pink, *n.* Tishepa; pink root, pakanlihomma, lupchubi.

Pint, *n.* Isht ishko achuffa.

Pious, *a.* Uba yimmi nuktanlut ayu.

Pipe, *n.* Hakchuma ashuka; an earthen tobacco pipe, hakchuma shuti; pipe an instrument to blow, isht i pufa.

Pique, *v.* Chukush bihlih; piqued, chukush. bihlah, chukush nuhla.

Pistol, *n.* Tanamp ushi, tanamp puskush.

Pit, *n.* Choluk, yakni; kernel or pit, foni; a cave or pit, hochukbi, hichukbi; to dent or to pit, hufikbih; to make a pit, hufikbichih,

Pitch, *n.* Tiak nia hlitilli; to pitch, hlilichih pit pilla; pitched, hikah; pitcher, picha, isht ishko chaha: pitchfork, chufak hushuk isht pehli hushuk isht piha.

Piteous, *a.* Nukhaklo. nukhaklochi; piti. ful, nukhaklo, nukhaklochi; pity, isht i nukhaklo.

Pithy, *a.* Ahli, shatummi.

Pi ot, *n.* Ai ontalut folohkuchi.

Place, *v.* Helichih; placed or set up, hikiah; to place at. ahelichih; an abandoned aiissah; another place. a iaksika; the place of departed spirits. hattak illi shilombish aiashah; to place side by side, ittichaplih; placed on or upon, ontulah.

Placid, *a.* Yohbi, yukpa.

Plague, *v.* Anumpulichih; plaguy. isht ahchiba, atuklommi, okpulo.

Plain, *a.* Haiakah; to make plain, haiyakuchih; a flat, level ground or plain. yakni matuli, yakni patuli; evident or plain, apissanli, otuni.

Plait, *v.* Atunuffoh, tunuffoh, pannih; to plait in, atunuffochih; plaited, punnah.

Plane, *i.* Isht halnshkichi, shafih; to plane, halushkichih; planed smooth, halushkih, shafah; to plane a plank. iti busha halushkichih; plank planed, iti busha halushki.

Planet *n.* Fichik, fichik chito; the orbit of a planet, fichik ataya.

Plank, Iti busha; dressed plank, iti busha halushki; to dress a plank, iti busha halushkichih.

Plant, *n.* Hokchih; a planter, na hokchi, nokchi; planted, holokchih; a weed or plant, haiyukpulo holokchi; seeds of plants, haiyukpulo nihi; to plant seed out of the same year's growth, afelimmin; a place for planting, aholokchi; planted with or to, aholokchih.

Plaster, *v.* Apaluslih; plastered. ulhpolusah; mortar or plaster, isht ulhpolusa.

Plat, *v.* Pannih, tunuffoh.

Plate, *n.* Ai inpa, amp huta; pewter plate, naki kullo am o; platter, amp huta chito; to plate, akolih; plated, akohah, ulhkohah.

Platform, *n.* Aianumpuli.

Play, *v.* Ilbhlauullih, wushobah, olachih,

to cause to play, ilhhlauuelichih, wushohuchih; to play at a game, achuhpih; to play on an instrument, olachih; continually playing, olahanchih. played. olah; a play ground, ai ihlawulli, to play to or for, iwushobah; playful, isht achiba.

Plead, *v.* Isht anumpulih, isht im uttah, asilhah; a pleader, hattak auumpull.

Pleasant, *a.* Yukpa, achukma, hochukma: to please, yukpuchih; to be pleas d with, imalachukma,

Plentiful, *a.* Laua, chitoli, apakna; plenty, chubiba keyu.

Pleurisy, *n.* Chunukko ubi, chunukkubi; to have pneumonia or pleurisy, chunukkubih; the chest or pleura chunukkko; pleurisy root, chunukko ubi ikhish.

Pliable, *a.* Anukyohbi, anukyohbichih; to render pliable, hokulbichi: made pliable by wetting, walashah; pliant, walohbi, nuktula.

Plow, *n.* Yakni isht putafa, issubi i chahe, plow beam, yakni isht, putafa; plow stock, yakni isht putafa aiulhpi; plow share; yakni isht patafa; plow handle, yakni isht putafa, ai ishi; to plow corn while very young, alelih; plowed while young ullah; to plow, yakni bushli, bushli patudih; to plow corn, lelichih, to plow among corn, lihah, patafah.

Pluck, *v.* Fullih, plucked, fulah, to pluck up by the roots, chukuffih; plucked up, chukafah.

Plug, *v.* Kamalih; plugged, ulhkumah.

Plum, *n.* Takon ushi; wild plum, isi in takon ushi; tame plum tree. takonlush upi: wild plum tree, isi in takonlush upi.

Plume, *n.* Shikopah: a red plume, shikopa homma: black plume, shikopa lusa: white plume, shikopa tohbi; blue plume shikopa akchukko: to wear a plume, shikoplih.

Plummet, *n.* Naki isht hlafa.

Plump, *a.* Hlampko, hloboah, hlobukta.

Plunder, *v.* Hokupah.

Plunge, *v.* Oklobushlih: plunged, oklubbih.

Ply, *v.* Isht ahantah.

Pneumonia, *n.* Chunukko ubi, chunukkubi.

Pocket, *n.* Shukcha: poket book, holisso i shukcha, holisso nan aholisso.

Pod, *n* Hakshup.

Poignant, *a.* Haluppa.

Point, *v.* Bilhhlih, bilhliplih, haluppuchih: a pointer, bihli, bilhhliplih: drawn to a sharp point, ibakchufauli, ibakchufashli: to point one's self, ilebihliplih: to point at or out, nabilhhlih: to point at me, sabilbhlih: running to a point, tepah.

Poison, *n.* Isht illi.

Poke, *n.* Koshiba: poke root koshiba akshish: poke berry, koshiba ani: to poke the fire, chilhlichih: a poker, luak isht chilhhlichi.

Pole, *n.* Iti fabussa, fabussa: pole cut, konih,

Polite, *a.* Hopoyuksa, ai ulhpissa, ai okpuchi impunna.

Pollen, *n.* Pushi.

Polygamy, n. Ohoyo ¦ lawa, hattak ¦ lawa.
Pommel, n. Chanwona, ¦ chanwona.
Pompous, a. Ilauata, ile chahuchi.
Pond, n. Haiyip, hohtak: a small pond, hohtak ushi.
Ponderous, n. Weki.
Pool, n. Aiyupi.
Poor, a. Chunna; ilbicsha ik abobo: to cause to be poor in flesh, chunnachih: poor in purse, ilbushah: not poor in flesh, ikchunno: we are poor in purse, pil busha; 1 am poor in flesh, sachunnah.
Pop v. Basahuchih, basahlih, to cause to pop, basahlichih: popping, basa kuchih bashahahanchi basasahkahanchi; popopen, bokalih, hlukali; to make pop, hlukalichih; poplar, sipsi; poppy, haiyuk pulo nusechi; populace, okla moma.
Per n. Hoshontika ¦ hoshontika, o hoshontika, opushshia.
Pork, n. shukha nipi; fresh pork, shukha nipi okchaki.
Porringer, n. Isht ishko, ulla im isht ishko.
Positive, a. Abli, kullo, apissanli.
Positive, a. Hinla, hinla chechuk; to be possible, chishke; possibly- chishha, yoba; might possibly be, yobah ka; perchance or possibly, hinlakma, yobakma nana chishha.
Post, n. Tonnink, tonik, ahika; ball posts, ai ulbi; postman, holisso shali; postmaster, holisso atiwa apesuchil; post office, holisso atiwa, holisso nowut aya atiwa, bolisso akaha.
Pot, Iyasha, ampo; a pottery ampo ikbi, ampo tuna; a pottery, ampo, atoba: earthen pot, shuti; pot lid, ohlipa; pot hooks, iyusha isht talakchi; potash, hittuk; potsherd, ampo koa, shuti koa.
Potato. n. Ahe; potato patch, ahe aba aholokchi; a potato hill, ahe bunta, ahe ibish; to make a potato hill, ahe buntochih; to boil potatoes, ahe bobih; boiled potatoes, ahe bolbi; a potato house, ahe in chukka; wild potato, ahe nukshupa, lukchuk ahe; a yam, ahe kushaha, yem; Irish potato; ahelumbo, ahe hluboa; seed potatoes, ahe pehua; roasted potatoes, ahe ulhpusha; a potato vine ahe upi; fried potatoes, ahe ulwushah; potato peelings, ahe hakshuk.
Potent, a. Ai ahli; hlampko, kullo, potentate, hattak pullommi.
Poultry, n. Akaha
Pound, n. Weki achuffa; to beat or pound, hopysib, husih, bolih; pounded, hosh, botah, hollussih: to pound fine; botoli; to pound to powder, botullichih, to pound the husks off corn, chilhhlichih. pounded in a mortar, holbpnsi, hollunsi, pounder; isht oka boa.
Pour. c, Hlalih, fohoblih, hlatublih, bichelih, hlatuplih, fohopah, yanullih, hlatapa, umbah; to cause to pour, blalichi. to pour upon, hlablulih. o hlalih to pour them on the ground, akka hlalih, akka hlepolih; poured on the groud,akka hlayah, to pour out, fohoblih, to pour upon, ofoholichih, ohlatuplih; poured, fohopah, hlatapah,

Pout, r. Hush, ayah.
Poverty. n. Ai ilbusha, chuna.
Powder, n. Hittuk; powder flask, keg. canister or horn, hittuk ai ulhto, powder mill, hittuk atoba; scattered powder, hittuk hlaya, to scatter powder, hittuk hlali; a powder charger, hittuh isht ulhpisa; to powder fine, botolih; powdered fine, botah.
Power, n. Aiuhlika, ibbak foka, nan isht im ai ahli, nan isht ai ahli; the power. isht imaiahlika; powerful, ai ahli, kullo hiampko; powerless, ikkullo, hlampko iksho.
Practice, r. Isht uttah abuchih, ulbuchih; an excercise or practice, abuchi; to cause to practice, abuchichih; to teach by practice, abuchichih.
Prairie, n. Oktak; a small prairie, otak ushi.
Praise, r. Afehnachih, ahnichih, habliitoblit isht annmpulih, hummahlih; to prise self, ilahnichih, ilanatah.
Prance, r. Hatulli, hatonli; to make prance hatullichichuh; prancing, mullih.
Prate, r. Anukchiblafah, anumpuli shahlih, himak fokalechit anumpuli; prattle, anukchihlafa.
Pray, r. Anumpa ilbusha, anumpuli; a prayer, anumpa asilhha, anumpa ilbusha.
Preach, r. Anumpulih, ubanumpa isht anumpuli; preacher; uba anumpa isht anumpuli, obanumpa isht uttu, isht anumpohonli
Prerint. n. Nan alatokoli, clekshun isht aiasha.
Pecious, a. Holitopa, ai itti chito.
Precocious, r. Ik ai ono.
Prefer, r. Aiahnichin; preferable; achukma ¦ shahli.
Pregnant, a. Chakalih, ushi kaiyah; pregnancy, chakali; to cause pregnancy, chakalichih: not pregnant ikchakalo.
Premature, a. Ik ai ono.
Prenare, r. Atahlih, ulhtaba; prepared, ulhtaha.
Present, n. Hulbina; to receive a present. banenuh, to make a present, habenuchihi to go in quest of a favor, habenut ayah; to give me a present, sahabinchih: a present, nan hulbena; to present, welih, imah, habenuchih; presently, himonasi, chekikma, chekosikma; present time, himak.
Preserve, r. Halullih; preserved for future use, ulhpoah.
President, n. Ai ¦ pehlichi, nahullo ¦ miko.
Press, r. Akantalih, katussulih, intohno: pressed, akantah, to press together, akantalichih, akapulih, akapulichih: to press or lie hard upon the stomach. anukbikelih, to touch or press on object over head, bikclih. bikclichichih; to press ones self, ilaktanlichih: pressed together, ittakamussah: pressed hard with the hand,obitipah ombitipah, obitito press in, shumullih; pressed, shumullih: to cause to press in, shumullichih; urgent or pressing, acheba. akomuntah.
Presume, r. Abui: presumtuous, himak fokalechi, ili yimmi, ahah ik ahno.
Pretend, v. Ilahobbih, a pretender, hattak

nan ithanailohobbi.

Pretty, *a.* Pisa achukma, ai okli, achukma; not pretty, ikaioklo, pisa achukma keyu, ikachukmo. .

Prevaricate, *v.* Anumpa folotowuchih fulohkuchit anumpulih, anumpa apok fohlichih, anumpa shanaiolih, anumpa ilaiyukachih: prevaricated, anumpa shanaioah, fulokuchih; a prevaricator, anumpa shanaioli fulokuchi;a prevarccation, anumpa shanaioa, fulokuchi; prevaricating, fulokahanchih.

Prevent, *v.* Alumih, alumichih, prevented, alamah.

Previous, *n.* Tikba.

Price, *n.* Ai ulli, ullbi, iulli, nan ulhtoba; to price, ai ullih, iulli onochih; a high price, iulli chaha; to raise the price, iulli chabuchih; high priced, iulli chito, cheap or low price, irlli ikchitoloh, iulli iklawo; a small or insufficient price, iulli ikono: a price too high, or an overcharge, iulli atepah; to price too high or to overcharge, iulli atcplih.

Prick, *v.* Bilhhlih, bilhhliplih; pricked, bihlah; pricking, bihlah, bihli.

Pride, *a.* Ilefehnuchi; proud, ilefehnuchi; to be proud; ilefehuuchih

Priest, *n.* Hattak kullo, hattak na holitompa isht utta.

Prime, *v.* Haksunchilih haksun onchilih; priming, hittuk haksun ouchiya: prime, (first or good), achnkma, ommoma.

Prince, *n.* Chitokaku; principal, i shaht tahli, mona chohmi; principle, ai yummohmi, ayemmohmi.

Print, *v.* Holisso ikbi toli isht hollissochih: printed, holisso toli isht holisso; a printer, holisso ikbi, toli isu holissochi, a print, oholisso.

Prior, *a.* Tikba, tikba.

Prison, *n.* Aboha kullo; prisoner, aboha kullo fohka, hattak yuka, yuka; to imprison, aboha kullo fohki; imprisoned, aboha kullo fohkah; a prison keeper, aboha kullo apisuchi, aboha kullo apistekili; to arrest a prisoner, hattak yukachih.

Private, *a.* Luma; private parts of a female iyubchtakla; privately, ikahaklo.

Privilege, *n.* Nan isht il ai yukpa.

Prize, *n.* Isht ulhtoba.

Probable; *a.* Hinla chechik, chichik; hinla; probly, achili, chechuk, hatuk ok; probably so, chechike; probably, (may be hoped), chishke, chi chishke.

Probe, *n.* Bushlit pisa.

Proclaim, *v.* Anolih, continually proclaiming, annohowah, anohonlih; a proclaimer, annoachi, hattakpaya.

Prodigal, *a.* Isht yopoma.

Produce, *n.* Nuwayn; to produce, nawayuchih, a producer, nawayuchi, producing, na wayuchih.

Profane, *a.* Chakapa, okpulo; profanity, chakapa.

Profess, *v.* Miha kut il otuninchi, il ahobbi.

Proficient, *a.* Hattak impunna, nan impunna.

Profit, *n.* Ai isht il apisa; to profit one's self, ai isht il ahauchih, ai isht il ahayuchih, ai isht il ayukpa; unprofitable, ai isht il apisa keyu; gain, boot or profit, alapanli; profitable, nan isht ahaucha hinla, nan isht im ai achukma.

Profligate, *a.* Isht yopoma, okpulot kunia, hattak okpulo.

Pro'ound, *a.* Hofobi, impona.

Prognosticate, *v.* Anumpa tikbanli anoli.

Prohibit, Alumih; prohibited, alamah.

Prolific, Chcli impunna.

Prolix, *a.* Salaha; prolong. falaiah.

Prominence, *n.* Haiakah.

Promise, *a.* Immissa, nan im issa; to promise to give, imissah, anumpa im issah; a breech of promise; anumpa kobafa; prompt, tushpa.

Promulgate, *v.* Anolih; promulgated, annoachih.

Prone, *a.* Ai imoma.

Prop, *v.* Tikulih, tikohlih; propagate, chelih; propagator, anumpa fimmi; proper, aiolhpesa.

Prophet, *a.* Hopaii; prophecy, anumpa tikbanli anoli.

Propitiation, *n.* ulhtoba.

Prosecute, *v.* Anumpa onochih.

Proselyte, *n.* Nan im ithana. ebannumpa unkfoka.

Prosperous, *a.* Achukmrt mahaya.

Prostitute, *n.* Hawi, haui: to cause prostitution, hawichih.

Prostrate, *v.* Akkuchchih.

Protection, *n.* Aiatokko.

Provide, *v.* Im atahlih; provided, lui ulhtaha; providence, nana moma ka apihisa.

Protrude, *v.* Chauwonah; to cause to protrusion, chauwenuchih; protruded chauwonah.

Prove, *v.* Abuchit pisah, imahlihchih; to prove at, aiatokolih; proved, ai atokowah, aiulhtokowah, imaiahlih, ulhtokowah.

Provender, *n.* Nan upah; province, pehlichika, apehlichika.

Provision, *n.* Nan upah, pinnak, ilhpak, illimpa.

Provoke, *v.* Chiletulih nukouchih, chilillih, teplih; provoking, nan utohnochih; provocation, chukush lua.

Proximate, *n.* Bilika; proximity, bilika, ibilika.

Prudent, *a.* Ahah ahni, nuktanla, hopoyuksah hopokynksia.

Pry, *v.* Afinilih, afinnih, hoyoh; pried, afinah.

Psalm, *n.* Ataloa, uba isht taloa; psalmist, ataloa ikbi, uba isht taloa ikbi.

Pshaw, *intj.* Anontl! ehwa! ehwak!

Public, *a.* Otvul, okla imma; publish, anolih haiakuchih, hoilsso ikbi.

Pucker, *v.* Shikidih, shikolfih shiniffih; puckered, shikifah shekofah, shinofah, takba.

Pudding, *n.* Asheia, bahpo; to make a pudding, bahpulih, bahpochih.

Puff, *v.* Chitolit fiopah; chitot fiopah, shubboklih.

Puke, *v.* Hoctah, howitah; to make puke, hoctuchih; to try to puke, hoctut pisah.

Pull, *v.* Halullih; to pull up, lobafih hlilifih lobahlichih; pulled up, lobafah, lobahlib pilifah; to pull off the hair, boaflih: hair pulled off boafah; to pull the m up by the root. chukllh, tchlih; pulled up by the root. chukablih, tchah; just commencing to pull, himona halulli; to pull off by the hand, hlchli; unraveled or pulled out, hlifah; to pull out or pull down, hlifi:h; continually pulling out. hlihililh; to pull or drawout, hlifichih; pulled off, hlohah; to pull from the stalk, nalhlichih; continually pulling; nahlihinchih; to pull out straws, shehlih; to cause to pull out, shehlichih; pulled out, shehah;

Pullet, *n.* Akaka tek himitta.

Pu'pit, *n.* Ahikict anumpulih, ai anumpuli.

Pulsate, *v.* Mitikllh, michiklib.

Pulverize, *v.* Botolib, pushichih, pulverized botah.

Pumpkin, *n.* Issito.

Pun, *n.* Nan ittim ikhena.

Punch, *n.* Ish hlumpa; to punch, fullih; punches, isht hlunchi.

Punctual, *a.* Ai ahii; puncture, hlumplih

Pungent, *a.* Ilomi, kisli; pungency, homi.

Punish, *v.* Nan im apesah; femmi, nann i kanichi; punished; femu; punishment, ai issikkopa, nan isht ilbusha, nan ulhpisa onutula.

Punk, *n'* Tashukpa, teshshukpa.

Puny, *a,* Ikhlampko.

Pupill, *n.* Im ithaua.

Puppet, *n.* Hattak holba isht washoha.

Puppy, *n.* Ofusik, ofunsik.

Purchase, *v.* Chumpah; purchaser, nachunpa.

Pure, *a.* Ai ghli, kashofa.

Purgative, *a.* Ishkot hlopulli.

Purify, *v.* Keshoffichih; to purify on's self ilekeshoff'h.

Purple, *a,* Homayi.

Purse, *n.* Teli holisso i shukcha.

Pursue, *v.* Illiohlih; pursued, ahlioab, achunanchih.

Pus, *n.* Aniuchichi. unichichi,

Push, *v.* Toblih; to push cachother, ittituplih.

Put, *v.* Polih, kahpulih; to put on iablipelichih; n place for putting on, aleplelli; to put carefully away, achukmalit ashahchih, achuk malit bohlih; to put in, aiohki; to cause to put in, aiohkichih; a place to put things in, aiohka; to put, down, akkabohlih; to put a hand on.
'   '   ', on as a dress, fohkih fohkechi; to cause to put on, fohkvchichih; to put up hiohlichih, hilichih; to put on, as shoes, holuh, holuchih; to put across, abanulih, abenkachih; to put u p at, ahilechih; to put side by side, itta putali; to put together, itte bafohkib; to put in the mouth, itti fohkih; to put in, malachih; to put to stay, kahpolih; to put cover on, ompuhomoh; to put upon, onashachi, ontulalih, to put to one side, shanilh; to put out of joint, tahlufih, put out of joint. tahlofah, tablofichih; to put into water, akuchih; to put it on, onuchih; to put more on, ulbitilih; ulbitale; to put iu trough. ai impa fohkih; to put in a bad place, okpuloka fohkih; to put out as fire, mosholichih.

Putrid, *a.* Toshbi, shua; putty, apisa isht akmo.

Puzzle. *v.* Aiyukomah; puzzled with, ai ittuyokomah.

Q

Quaff, *v.* Chitot ishko, chitot nullin.

Quail, *n.* Kofi.

Quake, *v.* Wennichih, winakuchih, winnalichih, winnachih.

Quarrel, *v.* Ittachowah, itti nukkowah, to cause to quarrel, ittachowuchih; quarrelsome, nukkhuoshahli. ittachowa shahli; quarry, teli akula, querulous, nan miha shahli.

Quart, *v.* Kowat, isht ishko tuklo; quarter, hanali achufla; a quarter of a dollar. iskelli tuklo; a quarter eagle, teli holisso tuklo iklenna afena, teli holisso tuklo iklunna atuchina; quarterly, hishi tuchinakma.

Queen' *n.* Ohoyo miko, miko tekehi; queer, ehukushi ilupissah.

Question, *n.* Panakloh; questioning, panahakloh.

Quibble, *v.* Fulokechit anumpulih; a quib-

bler, fulohkechi.

Quick, *a.* Tushpa; to be quick, anukwayah, to cause to be quick, chekichih, anukwayuchih. anukwiachih; quick motion, palhkih; to cause a quick motion, palhkichih; quickly, chikke.

Quiet, *v.* Cholusah, chulhsah a hopohlechih; to make quiet, cholusachih; to become quiet, hopohlah, nuktolah; quieted. hopohlah; quiet, nukchito, nuktola; being quiet, nukchintoh; quietness, nuktola.

Quill, *n.* Hushishi.

Quilt, *n.* Neu itulhketta.

Quinine, *n.* Yunba kobufli.

Quinsy, *n.* Ikonla shatili; choking quinsy, nukshinila.

Quit, *v.* Issah, issachih, ai issuchih; we all quit. iloh issah; to quit repeatedly, ihissah; I quit, ai issechi lih.

R

Rabbit, *n.* Chukfilluma, chukfi, chukfi haiaka asha; swamp rabbit. chuk fi patakitta.

Rabble, *n.* Hattak yahapa laua.

Rabid, *a.* Holillubi; to be crazy or rabbid, hollille bih.

Raccoon, *n.* Shaui.

Race, *v.* Ittimaiyah; to cause to race, ittimaiyuchih; tribes or races, oklushi. a generation or race, ai unchululi.

Rack, *v.* Kaiulllh, kiullih.

Radient, a. Tommi, malutha.

Raft, n. Akchihpo, hakchihpo, pehta.

Rag, n. Hlilafa; rags, hlilalakuchi; I am ragged, salito tukcchih.

Rage, n. Auukshomunta; to rage, anukshomuntah, nukoah, nukoah, nukhobelah.

Rail, n. Holihta, puhla; rail road, toli hina.

Rain, n. n. Umba; to make rain, umbachih; a rainy place, aiumba, aiumbaka; rainbow, hinak bitepuli, nakatepuli; rainy, umba shahli.

Raise, v. Apowah, (such as cattle, etc.,) just grown or raised, himoua hafanti; to rear or to raise, hofontichih; reared or raised, hofanti; continually raising, hofantihinchih; to produce or raise a crop, nawaycchih; raisin, paki shila; to raise, wakelih, tanichih; raised, wakayah.

Rake, n. Hashuk isht ittunnali, hashuk isht pihli; to rake, ittunahlih.

Ram, Chukfi uakni: rampart, holihta kullo.

Ranch, n. Imaiasha imayasha.

Rancid, a. Kotomah, kalancha; to cause rancidity, kotomochih.

Random, n. Himak fokali; to act at random, himak fokalichih, to talk at random, himak fokalechit anumpuli.

Rank, a. Kosoma.

Rankle, v. Aninchih, aninchichih.

Ran som, r. Chumpah.

Rant, v. Chitot anumpuli.

Rape, v. Hoklit ai issah, ohoyo hokli.

Rapid, a. Pulhki, rapidly, fichna; rapids, fopah, yanr'lit kullo

Rapture, n. Chakusha eshi.

Rascal, n. Hau..k haksi; rascaily, haksih.

Rash, a. Tushpa, ahah ik ahano; to act rashly, himak fokalechih; rashness, ahaahni iksho.

Rasp, n. Isht mihlofa chito, isht mihlofa; rasped, mihlofa; to rap, mihloffih; continually rasping, mihloho uh.

Raspberry, n. Bissa upi tohbi; a raspberry bush, bissupi tohbi.

Rat, n. Pichahli; a large long tail rat, toshkaluhli; rattiy, hlopullih.

Rational, a. Hopoyuksa.

Rattle, n; Chasha, washalichih, washahochih: rattling, chashah; to rattle, chashah, chusokuchih; to cause to rattle, chashahachih, chusolichih; rattling as a chain, chusohqhah, chusohah, chusohuchih, not rattled, ikchashahuchoh: rattle snake, sintullo; ground rattle snake, chukfitih tolohli, chukfitoh tolohli.

Raven, n. Fula chito, felushto.

Ravenous, a. Anuktupah iksho.

Ravine, n. Kalakbi, kolukbi.

Ravish, v. Hoklit ai issah, ai issah: ravisher, hoklit ai issa, ravishment, ohoyo hokli,

Raw, a. Okchaki, pikofa.

Razor, n. Nutakhish isht shafa, razor strop, nutakish ist shafa a shuachi.

Reach, n. Ai onah, onah, onanchih, ulah: to arrive or reach with ibai onah: not reached, ikaionoh, ikonoh.

Read, v. Ittimanumpulih, holisso, ittimanumpuli: read or reading, ittimanumpah: a reader, holisso ittimanumpuli: readiness, ai okpanchi achukma.

Real, a. Ahli, mih fehna, really, ahli, fehna, ba.

Reap, v. Bushlih, umoh: reaped, bushah ulmoh: reaper, isht bushlih, bushli.

Rear, r. Hofantichih; to carefully rear, holi toblichit hofantichih.

Reasonable, a' Ulhpesa; to reason with, nan isht anukfillih.

Rebel, n. Anumpa kobolfi.

Rocede, v. Falamah.

Receive, v. Eshih: a receiver, aiashachi.

Recent, r. Himona, chiki: recently, chekosi, cheki, chekosi kash.

Recep'ucle, n. Afohka, aiashachi.

Reckloss, a. Himak fokalechi

Recon, '. Hotihnah, mahoba, amahoba. hopenah: reconed, holhtinah holhpenah, Reclaim, v. Falamint boyoh, falumuint i hoyoh.

Recluse, n· Hattak baiaka keyu, hatak luma.

Recoil, v. Falamah.

Recollect, v. It hanah, it haiyanah.

Reconcile, r. Hopohlcchih, aiiskah, aiiskiachih; reconciled, hopuhiah; unreconciliation, isht itti nan aiyuchi, iskt ulhtuhomba.

Record, n. Holisso atakali: to record, holisso atakalechi; recorded, holisso; a recorder holissochi.

Recover, v. Masalih, blakoffi; to cause to recover, masalichih, hlaxoffichih; commencing to recover, hlako lit isht ia recovered, hlakoffih, ahlakoflih, hlakofoah, hlakofot tuhah; I recovered, sahlakoffih; I am recovering, sahlakoffit tuhah.

Recruit, v. Fohah: recruited, fohah.

Rectify, v. Achukmalih, achukmalichih; rectified, achukmah.

Rectitude, n. Hopoyuksa.

Rectum, n. Kobish.

Red, a. Homma, homma; to be red hommah; somewhat red, homma chohmi, homakbi; reddish, homaiyi, homakbi: a red spot. homma talaiya; very red, homma fchna, homma tishepa; to color, tan, paint or blush red, hommachih; reddened, hommah; I am red, sahummah; red bird, bishkommak.

Redeem, r. Falcmmint chumpah; redeemer falcmmint chumpa, chumpa, to redeem self, ilechumpah; The Redeemer, Chumpot alakofichi, chumpot na hlakofichi; redemption falcmmint chumpa, nanulhtoba; redemption for us, ai okchaiya pin chumpa he keyu.

Reduce, v. Haboffih, ikhomechoh, koyuffih, shiollih; to cause reduction, haboblih, habofcchih habofichih, shiollichih; reduced, habofah shiotah; to reduce in valua, kalakshichih; reduced in value, kalakshih.

Reed, n. Uski chuhla.

Reel, n. Aholhtota; to totter or reel, faiokuchih; to reel as thread, hotoffih.

Refer, v. Isht umihub.

Reform, r. Apoksiachih, hopoyuksalih ai iskiachi, hopoyuksachi, hopoyuksuli; reformation, ile kostinuchi.

Refuge, n. Ahlakolli.

Refund, v. Falamut attobbih, falcmmint attobih; refunded, falamot ulhtobah.

Refuse, n. Ashittilema; to refuse, ikaiokpachoh, ikhakloh, kanimmuchih.

Regard, v. Ai okpanchih ahninchih, ahnib, holitoblih, ithanah; regarding, ai okpahanchih.

Regenerate, v. Chukush himonuchih; regeneration, chukush himona, himona toba, atuklant utta.

Registry, n. Holisso anumpa atakali.

Regular, a. Biliah, regularly, biliah.

Regulate, v. Aiiskiachih, aiiskah; regulator, ai iskinchi.

Rehearse, v. Hobachit miha.

Reign, n. Amikoh, miko.

Reimburse, v. Falummint attobih.

Rein, n. Kapali isht talakchi, to rein, halullih; reins, haiihchi, haiyihchi.

Reinstate, v. Falummint fohki, falummint hilcchih.

Reiterate, v. Auohou111h; reiteration, anohou111h.

Reject, v. Ikaiokpauchoh, ikhakloh, shittilemah; to reject me, sushittilemah.

Rejoice, v. Yukpah, yukpali, ngyukpah; rejoicing, ngyukpah.

Rejuvenate, v. Himonachih.

Relapse, v. Afelimah, falamah; relapsed, afelimah; a relapse, afelima, falamut abeka.

Relate, v Anolih; related, auoah, anowah; continually relating, annohowah; related too much, annoah atupah; to narrate a story, fappulih; relating news, fappulih; relation, ittikauomi, ikanomi, hattak i kanomih,; related to each other, ittikanomih; relative, ikanomi.

Relax, v. Shochoplih; relaxed. shochopah, shochohah.

Release, v. Illakofiih; released, hlakofiih

Relieve, v. Illokofiichi; relieved, hlakofiih. anuktopah.

Religion, n. Ubnumpa anukfoyuka, ubanumpa yimmi, ubanumpa.

Reluctant, a. Anukwiah, ikbunnoh, nukwiah.

Rely, v. Anukchitoh, ai auukchitoh.

Remain, v. Autah, abantah; remaining. takkalih; remains, uipi illi itola.

Remedy, Ai iskiachih; remedied, ai iskiah.

Remember, v. Ithanah, ithaiyanah, ikhanah; remembered, anukfohkah,; still remembering, anuk fohkah.

Remind, v. nukfohkih; reminded, nukfohkah.

Remnants, n. nan utaha.

Remote, a. Hopaki; remotely, hopaki; remoteness hopaki.

Remove, v. Kanullih, wihah, wihachih, kanullichih; to remove to, kanullichih, akanullih, akanullichfh; removed, kanullih ulhtoshowah.

Rend, v. Hlilcchih, hlilichih, hlilufiih, hlilahlichih: rent, hlilofah, hlilahlih; a rent, hlilafa; to rent land, yakni impotah.

Rendezvous, n. Ai ittufama; to rendezvous, ai ittufamah.

Renegade, a. Hattak baksi okpulo.

Renew, v. Himonachih; renewed, himonah, himonah toba; renewable, himonacha hinla.

Renovate, v. Himonachi; renovated, himonah.

Repair, v. Ai iskiachih, ai iskiachih; repaired, ai iskiah: a repairer, ai iskiachi, achukmali, nan apuskiachi; not to repair or not repaired, ikaiiskoh; reparable, ai iskin hinla; irreparable, ai iskiah he keyu.

Repay, v. Falummichi, falumolichih, falummin' attobih; repaid, falamut ulhtobah; repayment, falamut ulhtoba.

Repeal, v. Akshochih; repealed akshoh, akshottaha.

Repeat, v. Ulbitclih, atuklanchih; repeated, ulbitah, atuklah.

Repel, v. Falummichih, falumolichih.

Repent, v. Ile kostininchih; the place of repentance, ai ile kostiniuchi.

Replenish, v. Alotulih; replenishep, alotah.

Reply, v. Afulummichih, falumminchih mihah, anumpa falummichih; replied, afulumah, anumpa falamah; a reply, afuluma, anumpa falama, replying, anumpa falummihinchih.

Report, v. Anolih; reported, annoah, annowah; a report, annoa, annowa; a good report, annoah achukma; a bad report, annoah achukma keyu; reported continually, annohowah, annoah atupah; to be reported at, ai anowah; the report, ai annohowa; a reporter, anoli.

Represent, v. Ahobachih, aboballih; representative. aboha nakfish utta ulhtoka.

Repremand, v. Isht i fappulih.

Reproach, v. Posilhhah, posilhhuchih; reproachful, hattak hofahyah: reproached with,, ahohfahyah.

Reprove, v. Isht i fappulih.

Reptile, n. Na balali, shushi balali.

Request, n. Nan asilhha; a written request, holisso nan asilhha.

Rescue, v. Hlakofiichih; rescued, hlakofii.

Research v. Hoyo fehua.

Resemble, v. Aholbrehih; made to resemble, holba; resembling, holba; resembling to,ahoyulba; resemblance to, aholba

Resentment, Iali okha.

Reserve, v. Ulhpoah.

Reside, v. Biuilih, utta, while residing, binilih takla; not residiu, biuilih keyu; residence, ai ahauta, ai utta: resident, ai utta, anta; residiug, uttah.

Resignation, n. Uba Piki i nutaka lummot asha.

Resin, n. Tiak nia.

Resist, v. Ichapah, cchapoah; resisted, ichapah.

Resolute, a. Achilltuchih, aloshumah; to be resolute, amosholih, amosholichih, chilitab, yiminta, nukwia iksho, hoyopa; resolution, achuunachi,

Respect, v. Ahninchih, ahuih, holitoblih, ithanah;to have self respect, ileholitoblih; to be respected together, ittiba holitopah: to mutually respect each other, ittiholituplih; I am respected, saholitopah; respectful, ai okpauchi, ikana.

Respire, v. Fiopah; respiration, fiopa.

Respond, v. Falumminchit mihah, falummint mihah.

Rest, v. Fohah itunlah. a place of rest, afoha; restless, afoha iksho. komunta, peh anta, himma keyu; resting at or on, afoha: to cause to rest, afohochih; rested, fohah; a rest, foha; to give rest, fohuchih, **Restitution**, n. Falummichih, falumolichih.

Restore, v. Hlakofiichi, falummichih, falumolichih: restoration, hlakofii.

Restrain, v. Halanlih, halullih; to cause restraint, halullichih.

Resurrect, v. Falamut okchayah; resurrection.

tion, falamut okchaya, illi falamut tani, illi a falaminchit tanichi.

Retaliate, *v.* Atobbichih, okbah; retaliation ilai okba.

Retort, *n.* Anumpa chunkush nolbhli; to retort falumminchit mihah, falummint mihah.

Return, *v*; Falamut iah, falamoah, falamah falamut ulah: to return to, falamut onah; a returner, falamolichi; returned, falamah; falamoah; to go and return, falamut ulachih; to restore or return back, falummichih, to return from afalamah; to to return to, ¡ falamah: not returned, ikfalamoh; will not return, falama he keyu.

Reveal, *v.* Imottunih, ihaiyakah, okfahlih, ottonichich; revealed, oktahah; not revealed, ikim ottunoh; revelation, nan otuni, uba anumpa otuni, nan isht otuninchi; book of revelation, nan otuni holisso.

Revengeful, *a.* Ilap ma attobi bunna, okha bonna, nukkilli.

Revere, *v.* Ai akpanchih; to reverance, holitobih; revered, holitopah; reverend, holitopa; reverential, nuktaula.

Revert, *v.* Falamah; reverted, falamah.

Revile, *n.* Chakapah; reviling, chakahapu; a reviler, chakapa.

Revive, *v.* Falummint okchulih, falamut okchah, falamut ochayah; revivalist, falummint ubanumpa isht okchull; revived, falamut okchayah; a revival, falamut okcha.

Revolt, *v.* Anumpa kobuflih: revolted, anumpa kobafah.

Reward, *a,* Isht ulhtoʼba. nan ulhtoba; to reward, attobih; reward, ulhtoba.

Rheumatism, *n.* Foni hotopa, iti chakli hotopa, na hishi ubi.

Rib, *n.* Naksi; a rib pole. aboha naksi: rib bone, naksi foni; my rib, sanuksi; ribbon, sita lapushki, sita futtaha, sita putha.

Rice, *n.* Onush ashila toba, onush lakchi: rice bird, konabinuli.

Rich, *a.* Holitopah, nan ¡ lawa; richly, fichna.

Rickets, *n.* Noli kobafa.

Riddle, *n.* Isht yuha tash puhla isht yuha; a pun or riddle, nan ittim ikhuna.

Ride, *a.* Ombinilit ayah, o ashut ayah; ridden or rode, ontulah; to ride or riding with, ibai ombinilih, ibai ontulayah; to ride double, ai ittisbolih; rider, on talaia o binile.

Ridge, *n.* Buchchah, onchuba; to ridge. bunaiyuchih; to make a ridge, buchchah ikbi; ridged, bunaiya; the top of a ridge buchchah puknaka; a straight ridge, buchchah apissah.

Ridicule, *v.* Namihuchih; ridiculing. namihuhachih.

Rifle. *v'* Patahlichih; rifled, patahlih; a rifle gun, tanamp patahli.

Right, *n.* Ahli, ai ulhpiesa ulhpesa ai ulhpesa: right time, ai Ulhpesa: righteous, hopoyuksia, hopoyuksa; the righteous, hopoyuksa; righteousness, nan ulhpesa, nana ai ulhpiesa, ahopoyuksaka.

Rigid, *a.* Kullo, palummi.

Rill, *n.* Bok ushi.

Rind, *n.* Hakshup.

Ring, *n.* Tuli chanaha; finger ring, ibbak uhsi foka; finger rings, ibbak ushi ubiha; to ring, chamak, olnchih; continually ringing, olahanchih, chamakahauchih; rang, olah; ringing loud, chitot olah; ringworm. hullampa; to have ringworm, hullampubih.

Riotous, *a.* Yahapa.

Rip, *v.* Illiluflih, hillichih; ripped, hlilafa, hillahlih; to ripple, bunukuchih; to cause to ripple, bunutkuchichih; a ripple, banutha.

Ripe, *a.* Hanta (as grain) hatuchih, nuna, tubachi; ripeness, hatuchi: to ripen; hatuchih. wayah, alaknah. alaknuchih; to begin to ripen, alaknut ia, alaknut isht ia; ripened, alaknah; being ripe, nunah: green or not ripe, okchukkochi, waloha, wulwukl.

Rise, *v.* Wakayab. tanih, uba iah. shatummih; to rise again. falamut tunlh; to leaven and cause to rise, shatuminichih; to rise up, bokonolih; raised up, bakkonnoah; risen, tahanih;to cause to rtse, as a blister, wokkolachih; raised up as a blister. wokkolah; rose or risen, wakayah.

Rive, *v.* Shimmib; riven, shinah; one who rives, shimmi.

River, *n.* Bok, huchcha, okhina; channel of a river, bok ayanulli; the source bok wishakchi: the mouth, bok asetlli: junction of rivers, bok ai ittusetlh: tributary. bok chuhlufli; tributaries, bok chuhlahli, bok chuhhli: river bottom, bok anyka, lussa; a long, river. bok falaia; the fork, bok falakto; one side, bok ¡ tunuup; the other side, bok mishtunnup; this side, bok ola tunuup; rivers heading together, bok ittitikohll; the main river. bok upinli; a deep river, bok hofobi; a shallow river, bok ikhofobo

Rivet, *v.* bot apiliflih, bot apiliffichih; riveted. boat apelifah.

Rivulet, *n.* Bok ushi.

Roach, *n.* Nuni patussa, (a fish) cock roach, nia chupka; bila chupka nuni chupka.

Road, *n.* Hina, ai ittunowah; a large or wagon road, hina chito, hina putha: the fork, hina falukto; to make a road, hina ikbi, a cross road. hiha akfoata, hina ubanubli, hina okhowata hina o hanubli; to cross another road, hina o hanublih, hina ittaiokhuhah hina ubanublih: an old deserted road, hinaksho; to measure or lay off o road, hina apesa: along the road, hinabaiyah, binali, hina takla; a narrow road, hina ikputho; a path hiuushi.

Roan, *a.* Bukboki.

Roar, *v.* Bimikuchih, bimihuchih, fopah, chopah, fopah, winnehuchih, kilehah; to make roar. bimihuchichih; roaring. bimihuchi, chopa; to roar, as wtnd fopah, fapah, fokah, komohuchih: to roar as water, chopah; to cause a roar, a a storm, fupuchih.

Roast, *v.* Apushlih: to roast at, aiapushlih; roasted over a fire, ulbunih,; roasted, ulbpushah.

Rob, *v.* Wehpullih, hukopah, nawehpulih; to rob him of, ¡ wehpulih; a robber, nawehpuli, hattak hokupa, hattak wehpoli: robbed, nawehpoa, wehpuah; caused to be robbed, nawehpuachih, wehpulichih.

hokupah; robbing, nqwehpulih.

Robe, *n.* Anchi.

Robin, *n.* Bishkohkok, bishkonluk; wake robin, hichi.

Robust, *v.* Hlampko, kullo; to cause robustness, hlampkochih.

Rock, *n.* Tuli: a large rock, tuli chito: large rocks, tuli hochito; whet rock, tuli isht shuahchi, tul ashuahchi; a rocker or rocking chair, ai obinile faiokuchi; to rock, faiokuchih faiolichih; rock salt, hapi kullo; rocky, tuli ai asha.

Rod, *n.* Fuli, ahapli tahlapi.

Rogue, *n.* Hattak haksi, issikopa, hokopa; roguish, haksi, isht akanomi, okpulo yopula.

Roll, *v.* Faiokuchih, banuthuchih, bunukuchih. chanullih, tonullih, tonullicbih; waving or rolling, poakcnhanchi, banuthah; to roll up, bonnih, bonullih; not rolled up, ikbonutoh; rolled up, bonah bonuntah, bonutah; a bundle or roll, bona bonuta, ugbunota; bundles or rolls, ugbunkuchi; to make a rall, bonullichih; to roll a wheel, chaunichih; not rolled, ikchanulloh; to roll up in, ubonullih; to cause to be rolled up together in, abonullichih; rolled up in, abonutah, abonkuchih; to roll them up in, abunnih; rolling, tonolih; continually rolling, tononolih. tonullichih; rolls, ponola shiahchi.

Roof, *n.* Aboha isht holmo, isht holmo chukka isht holmo, holmo; the eves of a roof, chukka isht holmo uhli, aboha isht holmo uhli; a shingle roof, mismiki; to roof, oholmochih.

Room, *n.* Aboha, chukka; one room, aboha achuffa, aboha ilup ochuffu; dining room, aboha ai impa; bed room. aboha anusi: bath room, aboha ayupi: a large room, aboha chito: high room, aboha chaha: an adjoining room, aboha et achaka: a small room, abcha iskitini. abohushi: a medium sized room, aboha iskatcni: a wash room, abohauah ai achifa: an old room, aboha sipokni: roomy, putha, chito.

Roost, *n.* Auusi: a hen roost, ukaka anusi: rooster, akak nakni.

Root, *n.* Akshish, haksish, akkishtula: to take root, akshish tobah.

Rope, Aseta tanuffo, ponola hcnula chito, pono kullo honula, ponolah kullo, pono kamussa, ishtullakchi: ropiness, hlikaha: ropy, chincshbi, hlikaha.

Rose, *n.* Napakanli ulhpoa: rosy, homma.

Rosin, *n.* Tiak nia, tiak nia paluska, hlitilli.

Rostrum, *n.* Ahikiut anumpuli, hattak ai anumpuli.

Rot, *v.* Toshbichih shakbonuchih; rotten or rottenness, toshbi, shua, litowa; shakbona shumba.

Rotund, *a.* Lumbo, bolukta.

Rouge, *n.* Anchaha, tishi homma; to color the face with rouge, anchabiih, tishi homma achahlih; to color anothers face, anchahlichih.

Rough, *a.* Babukih, haluppa; bambokih sbikkulah, bambakih, bunutkuchih; to produce roughness, babukichih.

Round, *a.* Bolukta; lumbo, hlaboa, halaba loboah; to make round. hlohoachih, lombochih; short and round, hlobukta: to make short and round. hlobuktuchih;

roundish, lobuhko; roundness, kulaha, hloboa.

Route, *n.* Aiaya, auowa.

Row, *n.* Atia, bachaya, hina; to make a row foJ planting, hina ikbi, hina apesa; to row or paddle, moflih.

Royal, *a.* Miko imma.

Rub, *v.* Amishuflih, pushohlih, kosholichih mishoflih, pibloflih; to rub on, akasholichih; akashoflih amishoflih; to rub out or against. akushuflih, akoshullichih, amishohlichih, amishokuchih; rubbed on, amishofah; rubbed, amishoub; a place to rub at, amisholichi; to rub on, as salt, yummichih, fohkichih; to brighten or rub smooth, halulukuchih; to rub gently with hand, hummih; rubbed, humah; to rub with, isht ukohlih, isht ulbkoah; to rub off, mishoflih; rubbed off mishofah; continually rubbing, mishoboflih; to rub off the skin, pikoflih, moflh, pishufflih, pikohlih; rubbing off the skin, mulah, pishuhkuchih; rubbed the skin off, pishuffah; my skin is rubbed off, sapishofah; to rub over me, sopushohlih; rubber holisso isht kashuffl.

Ruddy, *a.* Homma.

Rude, *a.* Haluppa, okpulo.

Rue, *v.* Ittifalcinmichih.

Ruffian, *n.* Hattak haksi atupa.

Ruin, *v.* Okpcninchih, okpcnih; ruincd, okpulo; ruinous, ai okpcui, isht okpulo; I am ruined, siaiokpulob, siaiokpulokah.

Rule, *v.* Amikoh. hlaflh; a rule, auumpa ulhpisa, nan ulhpisa; ruled, hlafah; a ruler, atoni, na pehlichi, pehlichi. isht hlafa, hattak i miko, holisso isht bluffl.

Rumble, *v.* Komohuchih, fomohab, fomohuchih: to rumble in the stomach, nukchawah, rumbling, fomohah.

Ruminate, *v.* Ilopasa, hoasa.

Rumor, *n.* Anumput aya.

Rump, *n.* Hapullo, bopullo, hutip, ishkish; a high rump, chishina.

Run, *v.* Balelih, tihlih matelih. bulullih, yihlepah, yanulli chufah, tihlaiah, a runner, baleli. maleli, chufa, auumpa isht aya, auumpa shali; to ruu as a vine, bulullih; to run away, chufah; running chuhafa; to cause to run, chuflichih malelichih; to run about, fidhkuchih; a place for running, achafa ayanulli; to ooze or run out, bletillih. running together, ittapeha: to cause to run continually, malelihinchih; to run out in a small stream, bichillih. pechillih; running down, shippuh; to cause to run down, sheppulichih; to run one down, amihochih; to run off, lihlih; to run as water, yanullih; all run, yihlipah; to run them, yihliplih; to make them run, yihliplichih; continually running them, yihlihimplih; to run under, as water, yululih; running under, lululi; a runagate hattak haksi okpulo: a runner, hattak chufa.

Rural, *a.* Haiaka imma.

Rush, *v.* Amosholichih, amosholih; rushing, amoshohoulih; a rush or bul rushes, kushahuchih.

Russet, *a.* Lakna, homma.

Rust, *v.* Alakna, alaknachi.

Rustle, *v.* Fomohab, fomohuchih, kushahuchih.

Ruth, a. Nukhąklo; ruthless, nukhąklo iksho.

Rye, n. Onush lusa; rye flour, onush lusa bota; rye bread, onush lusa paloska.

S

Sabbath, n. Nittak hullo, foha nittak.
Sable, a. Lusa,
Sack, n. Bahta, shukcha;a corse sack, buncha; "grip" or traveling sack, nafoka ashali.
Sacrament, n. Nan isht ulhpisa holitopa, okyaka impa.
Sacred, a. Holitopah; holitopa, ai ąhli: sacredly, holitoput; sacrifice, uba isht ai okpuchi.
Sad, a. Nukhąklo, im anukfela.
Saddle, n. Issuba ompatulhpo; saddle skirt, haksobish; horn or pommel of a saddle, chauwuna, i chauwuna, stirrup, tuli ahupli, tuli hupli; stirrup leather or strap, tuli hupli isht tullakchi; girth, ikfoka isht sita; saddle bags, wak hakshup shukcha; to saddle umpatulih; saddled, umputah, umputulhpoh; saddler, issuba umpatulhpo ikbi.
Sad iron, n. Nakfoka isht huma tuli patussa.
Safe, a. Ilakofh, achukma ąsha.
Sagacious, a. Kostini,
Sage, a; Hopoyuksa.
Sail, n. Kohta, sails, nąhutah.
Saint, n. Ubanumpuli, ubanuunpą yimmi, ubankmpa isht holitopa; sainted holitopah, ubanumpah isht holitopah.
Salad, n. Okchąki nan upa.
Sale, n. Achumpa,akanchi, kanchi, akunia saleable, kaucha hinla.
Saline, n. Hupi atoba, hupi ai ikbi.
Sallow, a. Lakna.
Salt, n. Hupi; salty, hupi homechi; salt works, hupi atoba, hupi ai ikbi; salt celler, hupi ai ulhto; like salt, hupi holba; salts, hupi holba; salt petre, hupi kapussa; salt spring, hupi kulih; coarse salt, hupi lakchi; salt water, hupi oka; fine salt, hupi pushi; salted, hupi yumini to salt, hupi yummichih; to make strong by salting, homechih; somewhat salty, hominchih; to salt at, ai yaminichih, fohkichih; to salt with, ai yummih, ai yummichih; saltish, takba.
Salubrious, a. Ikaiaboko.
Salute, v. Ai okpuchih; saluting, ai okpahauchih; a saluter, ai okpanchi; not saluting, ai okpauchi keyu; a salutation hau.
Salvation, n. Ai okchąya, isht ai okchlinchi nan aiokchąyah; sufficient for salvation, ai okchąya he ulhpesa.
Salve, n. Ilachowa abama.
Same, n. Amiha chuffa, hasi, hash inli, inli; of the same kind, bika; same as, ohmih.
Sanctify, v. Hullochih, hotoblih, kasbofih, yohbichih, holitoblichih; sanctity, holitopa; sanctification, isht akashofa, nan ashuchi ik im iksho, shilombish holitopa isht yohbi, sąktifikeshun; not sanctifying, fkholitoploh; santuary, chukka holitopa, ai ittunaha chukka;

Sand, n. Shinuk; quick sand, shinuk haismo, sand stone, tuna shukwa; sandy, shinuk fokah.
Sane, a. Kostinih; I am sane, sakostinih.
Sap, n. Okchi; sapience, hopoyuksa; sapsucker, biskinik, oktik, chukchuk, biskinik chito, biskinik iskitini.
Sarcasm, n. Anumpa chukush nuhhli.
Sarsaparilla, n. Akshish lakna
Sash, n. Apisa kashofa ai ulbiha, ishtuskofuchi.
Sassafras, n. Iti kufi, kufi iti.
Satan, n. Nan isht ahullo okpulo; Satan.
Satchel. n. Huchik, bahta, shukcha.
Sate, v. Yummih, yummichih; to satiate me. siyommichih.
Satisfy, v. Fihoplih: satisfied, fihopah, shatuplih: satisfactory, fihopah; to cause satisfaction. fihoplichih, shatuplichih; I am satisfied, safihopoh.
Saturday, n. Nittak hullo nakfish, satuti.
Saucer, a. Tasimbo, haksi, isht akanumi.
Saunter, v Chukka apellit ąya.
Saurian, v. Kitiulbi.
Savage, n. Nukhąklo iksho, kullo.
Savana, n. Oktak.
Save, v. Okchalinchih, ilatombah. hlakofichih; saved, ahlakofih, hlakofh, apouchih, okchąyah; a place of safety, ahlokofh; to cause to be saved at. ahlokofichih; saved with, ai isht okchąyah; salvation, ai okchąyah; hlakofh; saved by, ai okchąyah; The Savior, Hlako'lichi, Okchalinchi; saving, ilatobah, ilatobah impuuna, okchalinchi; savory, champuli kushaha.
Saw, n. Itti isht busha; cross cut saw, isht busha chito; a circlar saw, ishtbusha chunaha; hand saw, isht busha iskitini; whip saw, uba itula isht busha; to saw, bushlih; sawed, busha; sawyer, bushli, iti bushli; saw mill, abusha, itti abusha; sawed lumber, iti busha.
Say, v. Achih, mihah, ah, anumpulih; say no, ahą achih; not to say, ikachoh; not saying, ikachoh; to say after, iakaiyachit mihah; it is said, miah, mihah; achih; saying, nąmibah, amibah; to say something toward this way, nun et achih; said, iakaiyachit mihah.
Scab. n. Liahpo; scabby, kochonlih; scabbard, i shukcha; the scab of a sore, hlachowa hokshup.
Scald, n. Holhpa; scalded, holukmi; to scald, oka lushpa isht hokmi; scalded, oka lushpa isht hokmi; scalds, oka lushpa holhpa.
Scale. v. Fachanlih, isht weki, isht wekichi; to scale or peel off, fochonlih; scaled 'off, fulah; scales, hakhlopish.
Scalp, n. Hattak pashi.
Scan, v. Hoyoh; scandal, anumpa okpulo; scandalous, hofabyah.
Scars, n. Basosukuchih, misa, lasa, misofa.

Scarce, *a.* Iksho. chubihasih, chubihah; scarcity, chubihah.

Scare, *v.* Mahlulih, nuksboblih nukblokushlih, mahlalichih, yihlik achih; scared, nukshopah, nukblakanchah, mahliah.

Scarify, *v.* Illafih, hlalichih; scarified, hlafa; to scarify one's self, hlalih.

Scarlet, *n.* Homma.

Scatter, *v.* Fimmih, fimimplih hlelih fimkuchih, hlalih, hlatuplih; to scatter them, hlablulih, o hlalih; scattered, hlaya: a scatterer, hlali, hlcli, na fimmi.

Scent, *v.* Ahchishih, huwah, ai ishuah; to scent after me, siahchishih.

Schism, *n.* Itta kushkowa, ubanumpa isht itta kushkown.

Scholar, *n.* Holisso ithana, holisso ikhana: scholarship, holisso ithana.

School, *n.* Holisso ai ithana, holisso ai ikhana holisso apisa; large school, holisso apisa chito, aolisso ai ithana chito; school house, holisso ai ikhana chukka, hilisso apisa chukka; school mate, holisso ittiba pisu; school teacher, holisso pisuchi, holisso ikhunanchi, holisso imabuchi.

Scissors, *n.* Ishkalashna, ishkachaya; shears, ishtkalasha chito; to cut with scissors, kachelih, kalasha.

Scold, *v.* I nukoachi; to be scolded at, i hiyyah.

Scollop, *v.* Kachunlih, lanlakichih; scolloped, kachunlih, lakowah, lanlakih.

Scorch, *v.* Anaksholih, anakshuflih; scorched,anakshofah,anakshohah; unscorched, ikanakshofoh, ikanakshowoh.

Score, *v.* Baklih, baklichih; to chop and score, chant buklih.

Scorn, *v.* Shitilemah, nukkillih, isht ik i ahnoh; scornful, shitilema.

Scorpion, *n.* Halambia,; a stinging scorpion, halambia hasimbish isht nulbhli.

Scoundrel, *n.* Hattak haksi.

Scourge, *n.* Hlukata; to scourge, hlukahah, hlukalichih; a scourger, hinkaha: continually scorging, hlukalihinchih.

Scout, *n.* Napisa; to go on a scout, napisut ayah; going on a scout, napisut aya.

Scrape, *v.* Shaffih, pchlih, shuffih blahhih; scraped, shafah, boaiah, pihah, shuffah, hlahah; to scrape off the hair, boaffih; a scraper, akushulichih.

Scratch, *v.* Hlafih, kullih, kululih, shuffih, yicholih; scratched, hlakuchih, kulafah, ullufih; scratches, hlakuchi: to cause to be scratched, hlolichih; a place for scratching, akulli; not scratched, ikhlafoh; scratching or to scratch me, sakulih, sakullichih; to scratch up, shuffih; scratched up, shufah; continually scratching up, shuhaflih; to scratch with claws, yicholih.

Scrawl *v.* Himak fokalechit holissochih.

Screan, *v.* Chalakah: screamnd, chalakah; screaming, chalahakah: a scream chalak chilak, chalaka; a screamer, chalakuchi.

Screen, *n.* Hoshohtika; to screen, hoshontikachih.

Screw, *n.* Tuli isht shuna; scr w plate tull isht shuna ai ikbi; screw driver, isht ashunichih; screw threads, yikoha: to cut

screw threads, yikohuchih; to cause to cut, yikolichih.

Scribe, *n.* Holissochi, hattak holissochi, anunpa ulhpisa isht utta, na holissochi.

Scripture, *n.* Holisso holitopa: scriptural. holliso holitopa takali.

Scrofula,*n.* Chihlanli, shatohpa; to be scrofulous, shatohpuh, chihlailih: to produce scrofula, shatohpuchih, s atohpulih, shatohpullichih, chihlanlichih,

Scrutinize, *v.* Achukmalit pisah.

Scuffle, *v.* Ittimmufoah, haiclih, afoah; a scufflcr, haicli.

Scurrile, *a.* Chakapa, okpulo; scurrility, anumpa makali.

Scurvy, *n.* Noti ahika litowa.

Scythe, *n,* Hashnk isht busha hashuk isht bushli hashuk isht umo: scythe blade, bushpo hashuk isht umo.

Sea, *n.* Okhuta chito: sea board, oka ai ulhli: arm of the sea. okhuta i filummi.

Seal, *n.* Nan isht ulhtokowa; sealing wax holisso isht ai akmo kullo.

Seam, *n.* Ai ahchuwa, ai ulhchuwa: scamless, ai ahchuwa iksho; seamstress, ohoyo nan achunli.

Search, *v.* Hoyoh; to search closely, achukmalit pisah; to research, hoyo fehna.

Season, *v.* Fohkichih, yummichih; to season at, ai yummichih; weather or season, kucha: time or season, ai ona.

Seat, *n.* Aiasha, ai qbinili, ai ombinili, ai qnasha abinili: a long seat. ai qbinili falaia ai ongsha: a sacred seat ai qbinili hanta: a mercy seat, ai qbinili holitopa; an arm seat, ai qnasha shukba. ai asha: seated, binilih; not seated, binilih keyu; to sea°, binilichih; to cause them to take a seat binohlichih; to cause him or her to take a seat. binilichih, to be seated, chiyah; his seat, imaiasha.

Second, *a.* Ilitukla atukla; second ttme, atuklahma atuklant, atuklachih: to do it the second time, hitukluchit: secondly, ont atukla, ont atuklaha; a second (time), yakosi itti takla. sikan.

Secret, *n.* Aluma; alumaka, luma; secretly, ikkahaklo; to secrete, alaluhnih aluhmichih.

Secretary, *n.* Holissachi: aholissochi; his secretary, i holissochi.

Secular, *a.* Yakni isht ai utta imma.

Secure, *a.* Isht ai okpuloka hinla iksho: security, ihikiah.

Sedate, *a.* Nuktanlah.

Sedentary, *a.* Binili bilia.

Sedge, *n.* Hushuk bassi.

Seduce, *v.* Haksichih; seduced. haksichih.

Seduloux, *a.* Achunnanchi.

See, *v.* Pisah, holhponayoh, noponayoh, hopumpoyoh, hopokoyoh. hopopoyo; to see visions, holhpokunna; to cause to see, holhponnayuchih. hoponnayuchih; to see together, ittibapisah: to see me, sapisah; to suffer me to see, sapisuchih.

Seed, *n.* Nihi. nakhuta; seeds, nanihi; to save seed, pehnuchih; seed for planting, pehna, nihi pehna.

Seek, *v.* Hoyoh, bunnah; unsought, ikhoyo seeker, na hoyo.

Seem, *v.* Ahobachih, ahobalih, chinih; seemingly, chinih. achini.

Seer, *n.* Hopali.

Seesaw, *n.* Ittintakanha.

Seethe, *v.* Honih; seethed, honnih, nusecthed, ikhonnoh.

Seldom, *ad.* Fehna keyu, kanimikma.

Select, *a.* Ulhtoka; to select, atokoli; selected, atokoa, ulhtoka.

Self, *pro.* Akiuli, akint; self to, ile ak osh; that is self, (is understood) as, uno ak osh pisa li; I see myself, self examination, anukfillet ile pisa; self denial, ile kanchi, ile kaiyanchi; self esteem, ilefehnochih, to show self, ilchaiyauchih; to hear of self, ilchakloh; to deceive self, ilehaksichih; to cure self, ilchlakoflichih; to renew self, ilchimonuchih; to make self young, ilchimettuchih; to break one's self, ilekobuffih; to purify one's self, ilekushoffih; to wipe ones self, ilekusholichih; to tie ones self iletakchih; to give one's self up, ileyukuchih; by itself, ila; made by its lf. ila atobah; to make one's self sick, ilabekuchih; to wash self, ilachifah; to have self esteem ilanichih; boiled by itself, ilahonnih; to fix one's self, ilaiiskinchih; to tell on one's self, ilai anolih; to squeeze one's self, ila katanlichih; to think of self, ilanukfillih; to examine self, ilanukfillit pisah; to talk to one's self, ilanumpalih, selfish, ilapokpulu, ilapunla; to praise self, ilawata; to cut one's self, ilebushli, ilechanlih; to redeem self, ilecumpah; selfishness, ikhaponaklo.

Sell, *v,* Kanchih, kampilah; sold, kunia; a seller, kunchi; to sell on credit, ahokachih; to sell back, falommint i kanchih.

Senate, *n.* Aboha akni; senator, aboha akni utta ulhtoka.

Send, *v.* Pilah; sending, pilah; to cause to send, pilachih; to send after, ikai yachit pilah, ikaiyachit chu.lichi; to send back, falominchit pilah, falommint pilah.

Senna, . Id hishi holba.

Sensible, *a.* Kostini, imponna; senseliss, ikkosteno, im anukfila iksho, I am senseless, satasimoh.

Sentence, *v.* Anumpah onochih; to pass sentence, anumpa ulhpisa onochih, nan im apesah; continually passing, nan im apihisah.

Sentiment, *n.* Ai abni.

Seperate, *v.* Ittifilommih kashuplih; seperated, kashuplih, a seperator, kashupli; a separation, filamoli; to cause a separation, filamolichih; a place of separation, ai i filommi.

September, *n.* Siptimba.

Sepulcher, *n.* Aholuppi, hattak ahollupi.

Sccene, *a.* Yohbi, nuktanla.

Serious, *a.* Ahli, ubanumpa yimmi, abanumpa anukfilli, abanumpa ahni.

Sermon, *n.* Ubanumpa isht anumpa.

Serve, *v.* Isht uttah, toksulih, holitoblichih to serve faithfully, holitoblichi aighli; servant, tishu.

Set, *v.* Alatah akatulah, talalih, talahli, hilechih, ashachih, lapalichih; setting, alata; to set out, apowah; to set at or on, abinilih; to set up; hilchih hiohlichih, er.cted or set up, hiohlih; to set down. takkalichih; to cause to set (as a hen), alotalih; set; tallah, talohah, talomayah, hiklah, ashah, lapalih.

Settle, *v.* Ilinilih, binohlih; settlers, binohli; settlement, ai oklah, abinili; settled, binohlih, binilih, okla ai ashu; to settle at, ai oklochih, abinilih, abinohlih, achukkah, ai oklochih; to settle on, abinilih; to cause them to settle at, abinohlichih, ai oklochichih: a colonizer, binohlichi; unsettled, abinili keyu ikabiniloh; to settle lately, himona ai aklachih; to settle to one's self, ilabinilih; settled (as sediment), oka tulah.

Seven, *a.* Untuklo; seventh, isht untuklo, seventeenth, isht nuahuutuklo.

Sever, *v.* Ililuffi hokohlichih; severed, hokohlih; several, kanohmi.

Severe, *a.* Kullo, palommih; to be severe, pollommih.

Sew, *v.* Achunlih, non achonlih; to sew together, ittachuulih; sewed ulhchowah; sewing machine, isht achunlih, nan isht achunlih.

Sex, *n.* Male, nakni; female, tek; sexton, hattak itti hopi, nan hopi.

Shade, *n.* Hoshontika, ohoshontika, opushshia; to make a shade, hoshon tikachih hoshontichih ohoshontikuchih: to place under a shade, hoshontika ashachih shady, hoshontika, very shady; hoshon; tika iawa, shaded, ohoshontikah.

Shadow, *n.* Hoshonti, ahoba, ugholba; to make a ahadow, hoshontichih; to overshadow, hoshontikachih.

Shaggy, *a.* Fachanlih; shaggy hair, bishi chito.

Shake, *v.* Fahalichih, faiokuchih, faiolih, faiolichih, tahtulih, tahtulichih, wunnichih winnachih, winakuchih, wonnichih, shaking, faiokahanchi, winnakuchih; shaken, faiokuchih, tahtuah; to shake by the root, fotoklih; to shake self, as a dog, ilewilohlih; shook or shaken, tahtuah.

Shall, *v.* Hinlah, ahinlah, chike, himma, (as hlakofa himma keyu; he shall never recover.)

Shallot, *n.* Hatofulaha.

Shallow, *a.* Ikhofoboh, malossa, okchonak, paknali; to be shallow, malossah.

Shame, *v.* Hofahyuchih; to make one ashame, hofah yalichih; ashamed, hofahyah; shamefulness, hofahya; shameless, hofahya iksho, ik hofahyo; shamefully, hofahyalit; shemeful, hofahya, hattak hofahya.

Shank, *n.* Hanali foni, iyi foni.

Sharp, *a.* Haluppa, homi; to be sharp, haluppah, sharpened; haluppah, shuahchih; sharpness, haluppa homi; sharply, haluppa; to sharpen, haluppuchih, shohlichih,, haluppulih: the sharp edge. ahaluppa; sharp edge turned up, ahalupa anukpilifa; to utter sbrill or sharp, sounds, chasah; not sharp haluppa keyuo ikhaluppo; not sharp yet, haluppa keyu kisha; to cut to a point or sharpen, tulhlih; a sharper, hattak kasichi.

Shave *n.* Isht shafa, iti isht shafa; to shave, shafih; shaved, shafah.

Shawl, *n.* Anchi, innochi, nantapuski chito; to put a shawl on, auchih; black shawl, auchi lusa; cotton shawl, anchi ponola; light colored shawl, anchi huta; purple shawl, anchi homakbi; red sbawi, anchi homma, homma; silk shawl, silk anchi; white shawl, anchi tohbi; woolen shawl, chukfi hishi anchi.

Shear, *v,* Cmoh; shorn, ulmoh; to shear sheep, chukfi hishi umo; a shearer, chukfi hishi umo; shears, isht kachaya, isht kalasha chito, chukfi hishi isht tulmo,

Shed, *n.* Ulhtipo, hushoutik, aboha uba takali; shed room uboha et achaku; to make a shed, hoshontikachih; to shed tears,hlatuplih; to shed the hair, buy-ufflh, buaflih; shed off, boyafah, buafah,

Sheen. *n.* Chukfi, chukfi ulhpoba, rain.

chkfi nakni; ewe, chukfi tek; wether, chuk bobuk; lamb, chukfi ushi, chukfu-shi; sheep wool, chukfi hishi; sheep shears, chukfi hishi isht ulmo; sheep skin, chukfi hakshup; shepherd, chukfi apiscchi; sheep fold, chukfi aiasha; mut-ton, chukfi nipi; fleece, chukfi hishi ulmo; fleeced, chukfe hishi ulmoh; to shear sheep chukfi hishi umoh; a sheep shear-er, chukfi hishi umo;

Shelf, *n.* Abatula, ubatula, ai onasha, ai ontalaia; a shelf for crockery, ampoatula, ampushi atuloha; a long shelf, uba tula falaia.

Shell. *n.* Hakshup; to shell, lufflh, huchih, uibechih, niheflchih, chiluhka; to shell, as corn, chiluhka; shelled, cheluhkah, nihit tuhi; corn sheller,. nan isht chilu-hka; a charm shell, fullush hakshup; to shell nuts, banchih, hanlichih.

Shelter, *n.* Ai atukko.

Sheriff, *n.* Hattak yukachi, hattak takchi, shulif.

Shield, *n.* Ai atokko.

Shin, *n.* Iyinchibako iyinchampko, iyi-chumko; shin bone, iyinchibako foni, iyichumko foni.

Shine, *v.* Chulhchulhchukichih. malan-chuh, tohchallih, tohchullalih, tommih; shining bright, malatah, tohchalalih, tohpokolih; snn shine, hushi tommni

Shingle *n.* Iti shima yushkololi, aboha isht holmo: shingla roof, mismiki.

Shin. *n.* Pchta, peni chito.

Shirt, *v.* Nafoka lumbo:hunting shirt, nafoka patafa.

Shiver. *v.* Chuhlih wunnichih, wunnihin-chih; shivered, chuhlah; to shiver with cold, wanannahuchih; shivering; wanan-nahhah; shivering, hochukwachi, wunni-hinchi.

Shoal, *n.* Okchuwuha.

Shoe. *n.* Shulush, shilush; shoe maker, shulushikbi; shoe brush, shulush isht kasholichi: shoe blacking, shulush isht lusachi; shoe string, shulush isht talak-chih; shoe maker's apron, tikba takali; shoe hammer,isht boa; shoe knife, bush-po:lup board. abushli; shoe last, shulush atoba; shoe punch ▸holush isht hlumpa; shoe tacks, tuli chufak chipunta; shoe thread, pono kullo isht ahchqwuh; shoe bench, shulush ai ikbi ai q asha; rubber shoes, shulush shepu; brogan shoes, shu-lush kullo; shoe cobbler, shulush, akulli; mended or repaired shoes, shulush ulh-kuta; slippers, shulush malossa; boots, shulush chaha; ladies shoes, ohoyo ishu-lush: Children's shoes, ulla i shulush; to shoe (as a horse,) shulush lapalib, lapoh-lichih: shod all round, shulush lapohlih.

Shoot, *v.* Hussah, tokufflh; shooting, toka-fah, hussa; shot, hussah, tokafah; shoot-ing off, tokahlih; to shoot off, tokahli-chih; a marksman, hussa imponna; to shoot at, anulhblih; where shot, anuhlah; a shooting place, anuhla; to shoot as a bud, bikoplih; to cause to shoot, bikupli-chih; anything te shoot with; isht hussa; to shoot with a blow gun, bahpulih, shot, bahpoah; to shoot off obliquely, tibulli-chih,

Shop, *n;* Atoksahlih, ai ittuloba.

Shore., *v.* Alaka, oka alaka, oka uhli on-tulaka.

Short, *a.* Yuskololi, yustololi, yushkololi, ikfalaio toluski, kolukshi, akkalih; to be short, yustololih; shortness, yustolollih; to shorten, yustololichih, toluskichih.

Shot, *n.* Nakushi, nakushi; buck or grape shot, nakpaki.

Should, *v.* Chin tuk chin tok; should not, yobat: should have been, achin tok; should have, ahetok.

Shoulder *n.* Tahchi, fulup; stoop shoulder sokkono, tokkono; shoulder blade, ok-putha; back of shoulder blade, shanakha; shoulder joint, tahchit avetili; shoulder of man, tahchi—of a beast, fulup; my shoulder, suttuhchi; my shoulder blade, sashannukha,

Shout, *v,* Yuhapa; to shout at, apahlichih.

Shove, *v.* To.lih; to shove each other, itti-tuplih.

Shovel, Ishtpcha; fire shovel luak isht piha, hittuk chubi isht piha; dirt shovel, lukfi isht piha: to shovel. pchlih; shovel-ed, pihah

Show, *v.* Haiakah, walih haiyakuchih, obuuinchih, pisachih, [haiyakuchih; shown, halakah, otunib. pisah; to show, self, ilchaiyakuchih; showing, walih; a show, ayopisuh.

Shrill, *a.* Haluppa chasah, samampa, kam-ampa.

Shrine, *n.* Itombushi holitopa.

Shroud, *n.* Hattak, illi ulb foa nantumua abonuuta, hattak illi isht afohlih. ill i nukioka; to shroud, hattak illi isht afoh-lih,

Shrub, *n.* Bushukchi; shrubby, itakshish laua.

Shuffle, *v.* Tulohkuchih, fulohkuchit anumpulih; shuffling, fulokahanchih; shuffled, fulohkuchih.

Shut. *v.* Akamulih, ukummih akummih, okshihtah, okshillihtah, okhishtah; shut, akamah, ulhkamah, akamah, okshilita; shut up or in, ai okshillihtah; ta fasten or shut as a bung, ikumalih; to shut as a pocket knife, pohlommih; shut, pohlom-mah; to cause to shut, pohlomolichi; shut-ting continually, pohlohommih; still shut, ulhkamah; shut in, ulhtoh; shut-tle. nan isht tunna i peni isnt piha.

Shy, *v.* Nukshopa; to shy off, puncllukah-chih.

Sick, *a.* Abeka, nan ikanihmi; to be sick, abekah: sickness, abeka; to cause sick-ness, abekuchib; to sicken one's self, ilabekuchih; I am sick, siabekah; a sick-ly place, aiabeka; not sick, ikabekoh, abeka keyu, nan i kanihmi keyu.

Sickle, *n.* Hashuk isht bushli, isht ulmo.

Side, *n.* Chunukko ikfeksa naksi: inside, anukaka: side of, alapalika, lapulika; to put side by side, ittaputalih; going side by side, ittaputah; to stick on the side, lapalih; each or both sides, tahlahlakka; on this side, takla, i tunup; this side, ola; on this side of ola in tunnup olehma.

Seive, *n.* Isht yuha; sifter, isht yuha.

Sift, *v.* Yohlih; sifted, yohah.

Sigh, *v.* Chitolit fiopah, chitot fiopah.

Sight, *n.* Aianompisa; to take aim or sight, anumpi sahchih; an eyesight, hofhponayo, hoponayo, hopokoyo.

Sign, *v.* Hohchifo takalichih, lupalichih signed, hohchifo takalih, lupalih; signal isht unnon, isht otuninchi.

Signature, *n.* Hohchifo takali; signer, hohchifo holissochit takalichih.

Silence, *n.* chulosa, nuktanla; to silence, chulosuchih, chulo salih; silent, anumpa ik i lauoh, anumpa, ik im iksho, chulosa, loma, nan ik acho, ikanumpuloh; I am silent, sasammatah, sammatulih.

Silk, *n.* Silik; sewing silk, silik isht abchunlih; silk handkerchief, innochi; to silk, as corn, okshunlih; silking, okshoulih; silk worn, silik shushi.

Sill, . Aboha i tula, silly, ik kosteno, haksulba.

Silver, *n.* Tuli huta; silver mine, tuli huta akula; silver ware, tuli huta.

Similar, *a.* Cholant, bolba, ittihobah,

Simmer, *v.* Shinillih, shinillichih, simmering, shinillih.

Simply, *ad.* Banoh, biekah, pe peh: to simplify, haiyakichih, halakuchih.

Sin, *n.* Ai ashuchika, nan ai ashucheka, nan ashuchi: to sin, ashuchih, yoshubah, to sin at, aiashuchih; a sinner, nan ashuchi, yoshuba, hattak nan ashuchi: to cause to sin, yoshublih: sinful, ashuchi, haksi.

Since, *prep.* Hoka, ka ba, kamba, kama.

Sincere, *a.* Chukush ghli.

Sinew, *n.* Akshish, hakshish: many sinews, akshish laua, chushwa: his sinew, i chushwa.

Sing, *v.* Taloah, olachih: a song book, holisso ataloa: to sing at a dance by a woman, hihih: singing at a dance, hihihih; to sing to, at a dance ihihih: to sing the death song, tulwuchih: singing or sung, taloah; continually singing, talahowah.

Singe, *v.* Anaksholih, abakshafih; singed, anak shuah, anakshohah, anakshofah; not singed, ikanakshofah, ikanak showah.

Single, *a.* Achuffa; singly, achuffalih, akba noh, akbat; singletree, iti okhowata.

Singular, *a.* Inla, achuffa.

Sinister, *a.* Ik achukmo okpulo.

Sink, *v.* Oka akuniah, akuniah; to sink down akka ia; a sink or dent, hufikbi: to dent or sink, hufikbih; to make a dent or sink, hufikbichih.

Sister, *n.* Ittibapishi: my sister, antek, your sister, chin tek; his sister, i tek.

Sit, *v.* Binilih, chiyah binohlih aiashah; to sit down, binilih; while sitting, binilih takla; not sitting down, binilih keyu; to make sit down, binilichin; to sit at or on, abinilih onashah, ai o binilih; continually sitting, chihiyah; to sit or sitting with, iba binilih, ibai ombinilih; not sitting at, ikaniashoh; to sit facing each other, itta-

chiyah, ittabinilih; to sit about, kananalih, abinohlih, sitting about, kananalih; to sit as a tailor, puchukkoh; to sit among or with, takla binilih, takla ibabinilih, sitting there, tullayah, tulohmayah.

Six, *a.* Hannulih, hunnah; to make six, hannulichih; let it be six, hannulih ho; sixth, isht hunnali; sixteen, auahunnali.

Skein, *n.* Falama achufa.

Skeleton, *n.* Haknip foni, nan illi foni; a mere skeleton, hattak chunna.

Skill, *n;* Imponna; skillful, imponna, hopo yuksa, hopoyuksia, ikhana.

Skillet, *n.* Oka awanlulli iskitini, apaluska.

Skim, *v.* Okpehlih; skimmed, okpihan; a skimmer, isht okpiha.

Skin, *n.* Hakshup; having skin, hakshup asha; a skin with hair on, hakshup hishi usha, to skin, hlulih, lullih; skinned, hlufah, lufah.

Skirt, *n.* Ulhkona akka takalichi, hasimbish.

Skittish, *a.* Nukblakancha, nukshopa.

Skunk, *n.* Konih, a small striped skunk, Konih chukcho, konih shupik.

Sky, *n.* Shutik.

Slack, . Yuhapa, sulaha, to slacken yuhaplih; slackened, yuhapah; slackuess, yuhapa.

Slander, *v.* Aholubih, aholubichih achokushyalih, namihuchih, anumpa, chokushpa ikbi; slandered, achokushpah, chukushpah; a slanderer, achokushpali, anumpa chokushpali; to cause slander, achokushpolichih; slandering, namihah, chukushpalih; slander continually, namihuchachih; slanderous, chukushpa imma.

Slate, *n.* Aholissochi, islet; slate pencil, is let isht o holissochih, islet pisil.

Slave, *n.* Hattak yukah, yukah; to enslave, yukachih.

Slaver, *v.* Itukholayah.

Sled, *n.* Iti shalulli; sledge, tuli isht boa chito.

Sleek, *a.* Halushki, haluski, to slicken, halushkichih.

Sleep, *v.* Nusih; sleepy, nusilha; to sleep in, at, or on, anusih; to sleep with, ibanusih; slept with, ibanusih; sleeping with, ibanusih; to sleep together, ittibanusi; I sleep, sanusih; to sleep on, ousih.

Sleet, *n.* Pucha lushshah, pucha lushah; to sleet, okpachalushah, pachalushah.

Sleeve, *n.* Ilefoka shakba.

Sleigh, *n.* Iti shalulli; to sleigh, shulullih.

Slender, *a.* Fabussa, fabasfoa, hlibatah.

Sley, *n.* Uski chuhla.

Slice, *v.* Bushlit tushuflih.

Slide, *v.* Shalallih shululih; to slide away, hanaklih; to slide down; tibuflih; slidden down, tibafah; sliding along, yullullih.

Slim, *a.* Hlibatah, fabussa, fabasfoa.

Slimy, *a.* Hlikanli, hlikaha, to be slimy, hlikahanchi, hlikanlih, to cause sliminess hlikahuchi, hlikanlichih; sliminess, hlikaha, hlikanli.

Sling, *n.* Hunaweli; to sling, bahpohlih; to sling at, bohlih; slung, bahpoah, fahummih.

Slink, *v.* Akahmohlolih.

Slip, *v.* Shalullih, shalakli, shakkulullih; I slip, sashakkulullih; slippery, halusfih; to slip off, as leaves, hlehlih.

Slit, *v.* Chuhlih; slit, chuhla; to make a slit, chuhlichih.

Slobber, v. Itukholayah; 'slobbering, ituk-holaya.

Slothful, a. Intakobih; slothfulness, nan intakohi.

Sloven, v. Hattak liteha; extremely sloven, litaha o'kpulo; slovenly, liteha.

Sluggard, a. Hattak intakobi; sluggish, intakobi; sluggishness, nan intakobi.

Sly, a. Apahli, alahlichih.

Small, a. Isk'tini, chipinta, kitini; not very small, chipinta, chopunt; to be very small, chipintah, chopuntah, chi-p'utasih; small ones, chinta, chipintasi qu te small, ch'pintasi; to make them quite small chipintochih; small children, chipotah, chopotah; small things, chuk-ushpe; small but long, hibatah; a small t ing, nanes.; a small quantity, kenomosi; to make the waist small, ynnushkichih; small arms, tanampo, tanamp ushi, tanam-pa yushkololi; small pox, ebalakwa; to have the small pox, chalakwa.

Smart, a. Kostinih; to smart, shimolih nuksimilih, nuksimilichih, mohlih, muf-kachih; to cause to smart, mohlichih; smarting, mohlichih, mufkachih shimo-lih.

Smash, v. Wuhlih; smashed, wuhlah; be-ing continually smashed, wuhqhlah.

Smell, v. Ahehishih, hewah, huwah, bala-mah, kosomah, shuah, bomih; a fetid, disagreeable or old smell, bitemah; to smell bad, bitemah shuah; to cause a bad smell, bitemuchih, shouchih; a sour smell, as of urine, kahlqmu; smelling strong, as of musk, kosomah; to cause a musky smell, kosomachih; a rank smell, kotomah; to cause a rancid smell, kotomrchih; to stink or smell bad, shuah, shoah.

Smile, v. Yukpah.

Smite, v. Issoh, bolih, smite or smitten, boah.

Smoke, n. Shobohli; to smoke, shobohlih, shobohlichih; continually smoking, sho-bohohlih; to omit smoke, kofullih; smoking of fire, kofotah; a place for smoking, as curing of meat, aiqshoboh-lichi; to smoke tobacco, hakchuma shuk-ah; smoky, shubohli.

Smooth, a. Halushki, haluski, hlimimpa, hlimishka, lisemo; to be smooth and ly-ing flat, lisemoh; to make lie smooth, lisemochih; smoothness, hlimimpa, ha-lushki lisemoh; to make smooth, hlim, ishkuchlh, hlimimpuchih, halulqkuchih, halushkichih; to smooth over, a difficul-ty, hummohlih.

Snack, a. Pinak, nan ilhpak, nan upah.

Snail, n. Hatta yoshubli; snail shell, hatta yoshubli hakshup

Snake, n. Sinti; adder, hahtah; black snake, sinti lysah; chicken snake, ubak-shah; coach whip sinti koyufa tohbih; copper head, chahlakwah; garter snake, sinti basoah; green snake, pash falakto i sinti, king snake, sinti pohkni; joint snake, sinti kolokumfih; moccasin, chunnashah, shaui imanchahah; rattle snake sintullo; diamond rattle snake, tiak i sintih; ground rattle snake, chuk-fitohtololih; striped snake; sinti basoah; viper, sinti chilitah, sinti okpolob;

water snake, nan upah; snake root, tiak shuwa.

Snap, n. Chahlak, basahli; to snap, chah-lalichih, basohrchih; continually snap-ping, chahlakahanchih, basahahanchi, basasahkahanchih; snappish, bassah-vchih; a snappish noise, basak; to cause to snap, basalichih.

Snatch, v. Hhachuk et eshih.

Snath, n. Hashuk isht busha aiclhpi.

Sneeze, v. Habishkoh; to make sneeze, habishkuchih; sneezing, habihishko; a sneeze, habishko; I sneeze, sahabish-koh.

Snipe, n. Okchus, lopinah.

Snore, v. Hlabakah; snoring, hlabakah; a snore, hlabaka.

Snort, v. Hlotukah; snorting, hlotuka; a snorter, hlotuka.

Snow, n. Okti pushi; to snow, oktushah, a snow bird, Inksakina.

Snuff, n. Hakchuma bota; to scent or snuff, huwah; a snuff, hubishkochi; snuff color, lakna; snuff box, hakchuma bota aiolhto; snuffers, pula isht tubli.

Snug, a. Atakluin iksho, katuli.

So, ad. Hacha hoke; as, truly so, ahli hacha; usually so, ai imomali; to be so, or lik-so, ai ohmichih; is it so? ayomeh? ayoh; said so, achihhoke; so be it, or let it b; so, ikahli; let it be really so, ikah; fehna, not so, ikahlo; will surely do so, ikahlichoka he keyu; because it is not so, ikahlo kamba; it is so, or is so, mohlih, was so or did so, kashkint, kashkin, as, ali kashkin, I said so and you know it; so long as, na; surely it was so toshke.

Soap, n. Isht ahchifa, isht ulhchifa, soap box, isht ulhchifa aiolhto; bar soap, isht ahchifa kullo; shaving soap; isht ulhchifa bulamah; soap stone; talhpa.

Sober, a. Oka homi ik ishko, kostini; sobri-ety, kostini, nuktanla, ili oktampli.

Society. n. Iksa.

Sock, n lycobohoski, iyabihuski.

Soda, n. Paska shatommichih, sote.

Soft, a. Lapushki, yatushki, yabushki, haiemo;soft ground, hlatimo;to soften by moisture, hotokbichih; softened, hotok-bi; to soften, lapushkichih, yatushki-chih, yatushkichih, lopushkichih, yub-uskichih; softened, lapushkih lopush-kichih; softness, lapushki; to soften by wetting, walushcchih; softened, wal-ashah; all soft, yaboboah. yatotoah; soft feathers, hpismo, hpinto; to be soft, hpistoh; to cause softness, hpistochih.

Soil, n. Lukti; to soil, litchlih; soiled, liti-ha.

Solace, n, Hopohta; to solace, hopohlu-chih; solaced, hopohlah,

Solar, a. Hushi ahalaiya,

Sold, v, Kunla.

Solder, v. Aiakmochih, aiolbochih; to solder together. ittai akmochih, ittak-mochih, ittolbochih; soldered together, ittolbon, ittalakmoh.

Soldier, n. Tushka. tushka chipota.

Sole, n. Iyi petta, achufia, ilap bano, ilap achufia.

Solemn, a, Nuk tanla, chanumpa isht nuk tanla; to solemnize, holitoblichih; sol-emnly, holitoput.

Some, a. Chubbiha, kanimih; some of,

akanimi; somebody, kunah. kuna; I am somebody, safchnah; somewhere, kanimma; sometimes. kanimikma, kaniohmikma; somewhat, chohmi.

Son, Ushi, isoh; my son, sasohnakni; your son, chiso; grand son, ipoknakni; son-in-law, iyup; my son-in-law, saiyup; my grand son, sapoknakni.

Soon, *ad.* Chikosi, cheki, chekosikma, chekikma; to cause to be soon, chekichih, chikkichih; very soon, chekosi, chekosi fehna, chekosikma, chikke; as soon as, makinli.

Soothe, *v.* Hopohluchih; soothed, hopohlah.

Sorcerer, Hottak isht ahullo; nuseka, hattak, holhkunna; sorcery, holhkunna; to enchant by sorcery, hottosih, hottosichih.

Sore, *n.* Hlachowa, liahpo, hatluppa.

Sorrel, *n.* Pihchi, osonak ontulali.

Sorrow, *n.* Nanukhaklo, nukhaklo, sorrowful, nukhaklo; to be or being sorrowful, nukhakloh, libushah; to produce sorrow, nukhaklochih; I am sorry; sauukhahloh; a place of sorrow, anukhaklo; an occasion of sorrow, anukhaklo; to be sorry from, anukhakloh; to cause to be sorry from., anukhaklochih.

Sot, *n.* Hattak okah ishko, okishko peh atupa.

Soul, *n.* Shilombish; to have a soul, shilombish im ashah; my soul, sashilombish: soulless, shilombish iksho.

Sound, *v.* Olachih, olah, pofuchih-iktoshbo, achukma; continually sounding, olahanchih; to fathom or sound, akka hoyoh; to sound loud, chitot olah; sounding loud, chitot olah; shrill sound, chumakuchih.

Soup, *n.* Nahonni okchi.

Sour, *n.* Hauoshko, kushkaha, homi, homechi; to make sour, hawoshkochi, hominchih; sourness, hawoshko; not sour, ikhawoshko; sourness, nahomi.

Source, *n.* Ibetup, aminti.

South, *n.* Oka mahli; south wind, oka mahli; southerly, oka mahli imma, oka mahli chohmi; south west, oka mahli hoshi ai ok tula ittintakla; south east, oka mahli hoshi ai akuchaka ittintakla; southerner, okla mahli yakni ai otta.

Sow, *w.* Shukha tek; boar, shakha nakni; pig, shukhushi.

Sow, *v.* Fimmih, hlahlih, fimimplih, hokchih; sown, fimah fimimpah, hlayah; a sower; na hokchi, fimmi; to sow thinly, fimkuchih; thinly sown; fimimpa.

Spa, Oka alikchi.

Space, *n.* Hopaki; spacious, chito, achito.

Spade, *n.* Lukfi isht peha, isht peha.

Spanish, *a.* Ispani imma; Spaniard, ispani hattak; Spanish oak, chilhputha.

Spare, *a.* Chunna; to spare, apouchin.

Spark, *n.* Pohlota; to sparkle, shohpakalih, pohlohlih, chaulhchukih; sparkling, pohlohlih, chulhchulhchuki; to cause to sparkle pohlohlichih, chulhchulhchukichih; to shine or sparkle, tohchallih; sparkling, tohpokalih.

Sparrow, *n.* Hushi iskitini, chusa; sparrows, hushi chipunta; cock sparrow, hlufintini.

Sparse, *a.* Fimimpa; sparsely; finimpa.

Spasm, *n.* Haiochi, haiochichi, halahli; to have a spasm, haiochichih, holahlih. to cause to have spasms, haiochichichih, halahlichih; I have a spasm, sahalulih.

Speak, *v.* Anumpulih, achih, imhah; a speaker, hattak anumpuli; a fluent speaker, anumpa i kucha achukma; frequently speaking, anumpaholih, na mihah; evil speaking, anumpa chukushpa, a short speech, anumpa ikfalaio, anumpa kolofasih, anumpa kolofah, short speeches, anumpa kolohli; speechless, anumpa ik im ikso; to deliver a speech anumpa isht hikah; very brief speeches, anumpa tilohli; a very brief speech, anumpa tillofah; to speak in a foreign language, bulbahah; speaking in a foreign language, bulbahah; to speak loud, chitot anumpulih; to speak back to, falommichit anumpulih, falomminchit mihah; let all speak at once, himonna achuffa momut ik anumpuli; not speaking, ikanumpoloh; to speak in undertone, woluhuchih; speaking under tone, woluhah; to speak in a very low voice, woshohuchih; speaking in very low voice, woshohuhanchih; speaker, anumpeshi.

Special, *a* Atokoa, specially, hatak heno, hokak het.

Specify, *v.* Hochifoh.

Specious, *a.* Achukma ahoba.

Speckle, *n.* Blikoa; to speckle, hlikokolichih, hlekolih; to be speckled. hlikoah, chikchiki, tik tiki; to make speckle, chikchikichih, siksikichih; specks, chikchiki siksiki, a frosty speckle, shukshoki; spectacle, nishkin alata; spectacle case, nishkin, alata atoka.

Spectator, *n.* Hattak yopisa, yopisa.

Speech *n.* Anumpa isht hika; a long speech, anumpa falaia; a short speech, anumpa ikfalaio; short speeches, anumpa kolohli; speechless, anumpa ik im iksho; to deliver a speech, anumpa isht hikah.

Speed, *a.* Pulhkih, shinimpah; to cause speed, pulhkichih, chekichih; speedy, tushpa, ashalika chekosi, cnike; speedily; cheki, hokak heno, hokak het.

Spell, *v.* Holisso hochifot ittim anumpolih; spelling book, holisso ai ishtia ummona, ispilin buk.

Spend, *v.* Kanchih; spent, kuniah.

Spice, *n.* Na balama.

Spider, *n.* Chulhkun; a spider web, chulhkun i chukka.

Spike, *n.* Chufak; spike nails. chufak hochbito; hand spike, isht tonolichih; spikenard, spaiknut.

Spill, *v.* Akkafohoplih, hlatuplih, hlalih, hlatapah, hlayah; spilled, spilt, akkafohopah, hlatapah, hlayah; to spill them on the ground, akkahlatuplih, akka hlipelih, akka hlaiih; spilt them on the ground, akkahlatapah, akka hlayah; to cause to spill, hlalichih; to spill shot or beads, hlelih; not spilt, ikhlatupoh; to spill upon, ohlipiah, ofoholichih, ohlatuplih, ohlipilih; spilt upon, hlaya, ohlayah, ohlipiah.

Spin, *v.* Nashunnih, shunuih, honolah,

spuu, shonah, honnolah; spinning, sholiannih; a spinner, nashonni, honola; spinning wheel, ponola ashona, ahonola; chonaha; spindle, tuli fabossa.

Spirit, *n.* Shilombish, oka homi; my spirit, sashilombish; spirited, chilitah; spiritual, shilombish imma; spirit world, shilombish ai asha yakni; to be spiritless, ilehobok tobochih, hlepushlh.

Spit, *v.* Tofah, tufah; spitting, tuftuah; continually spitting, tuhofah, tuftuhoah; spitting blood, issish tufah; spittle, itukchi; spittoon, itukchi ai olhto.

Spleen, *n.* Takushi, tokoshchi, luksi; spleeny, namak keyu, nukoah.

Splice, *v.* Achakalih, achakalichih, ittochokka ili spliced, achakah, olhchakah; to caus to be spliced, achakachih, ittochahkachih, ittochokolichih; the place spliced at, ai ittachaka; to splice them together at, ai ittachakalih, ai ittachaklih; not spliced, ikittachukoh.

Splinter, *n.* Chuhlafa.

Split *v* Chublih, pahlallih, pablatochih. puhlih, shimolih; split, chuhlah, cholaktoh. pablatah, chuhlatah, shimafah, pchlah: to split off, chuhlulli, chuhlolilh. shukulilh shibahlib, shimahlih; split off, chublafah, shibofah, chuhlatah, bakapah, shukafah; a split, chuhlafa, bokafa, cholakto; one who splits, chuhli; one who splits into, chuhlolli; to split blocks, bakahllh, baklih; split into halves, bakapoa; split open, bokufah, patahlih; to split open, bokulilh. patahlichih: to split off, shibolilh, shimolilh, obakoplih.

Spoil, *v.* Okpunih; spoiled, okpulo, bakustoh.

Sponge, *n.* Islet isht kasholichi.

Spool, *n.* Pouala iti olhfou.

Spoon, *n,* Ishtimpa, tuli isht impa, fulush; teaspoon, isht impushi; horn spoon, lupish isht impa, fulush. big spoon, isht impa chito; ladle, isht kufa.

Sport, *n.* Yukpa; sportive, isht achiba.

Spot, *n.* Bakoa, hlikowa; spotted, bakowa; large spots, bakowa, bakokukochih; small spots, chikchiki, tiktikih siksiki; to make spots, bakolih, bakowochih; in bunches or spots. luklukih, luklukit; small spots or speckles, hollsso, chikchiki siksiki; to make small spots, siksikichih, chikchikichi; I am spotted, sabokoah; very spotted, hlikokoah; to make speckled or very spotted, hlikokolichih. hlikolih, tiktikichih.

Spout, *v.* Wishillih; to cause to spout, wishillichih.

Sprains, *n.* Tahlofa naha.

Spread, *v.* Fimmih, fimimplih, pollih; to spread out, potolichih; to spread as a flock of birds; hlapah; spread. hlapa; to spread a pallet or bed, patolih.

Sprig, *n.* Fuli, broken sprigs, fuli kaua.

Spring, *n.* Kolih, ai ochi; hot spring, oka wahlclll; medicinal, oil or sulphur spring, oka alikchi; to spring; bichullih; sprung, bichotah; spring of the year, toifuhpi; to spring open with a stick, fachammih; sprung open, fachamah.

Sprinkle, *v.* Fimmih, fimmimplih, pushkah, okshimmichih oflimini; sprinkled, fimah, fimimpah; to sprinkle with, isht

dashkah, isht pashkalih; to sprinkle on, oflmmih; sprinkling, as raiu, okshimmihichih.

Sprout, *v.* Abosalih, offoh; sprouted, abosah, bosah; to sprout from, ai unchululih, unchulolih; a sucker or sprout, apotut offi, unchulolih; sprouted from, unchuloah.

Spruce, *a.* Kashofa, ilapokslachi.

Spur, *n.* Chukfak iyafoa, chukfak iyolhfoa; spurstrap. chufak, iyafoa isht taklakchi; the spur of a chicken, in chahe, chahi; the spur of a mountain, nuni filommi; to spur, bahlih; spurred. bahafah.

Spy, *n.* Lumot akostininchi, lumot apesochi.

Squab, *n.* Puchi ushi, puchi himo.

Square, *a.* Bolukta chukbi ishta folota; a square, a carpenters instrument, isht olhpisa, isht apesah; squares, bolbokih, to make squares; bolbokichih, to square, boluktochih, to be square. boluktab.

Squash, *n.* Ussi, isito, isitushi.

Squat, *v.* Bikuttokohchih.

Squeal, *v.* Chikah. chilika; squealed, chikah; a squealer, chika;

Squeeze, *v.* Katossalih, tihlillih, tihlolih; squeezed, tehloah, tihlifah; to squeez out, bushlih; squeezed out, bushah; to squeeze the hand, bocholih; squeezed, buchopah.

Squirrel, *n.* Fuci; a gray squirrel, funi okchokko, funi toshsbo, funi toshshi; a fox squirrel, lakua, fanukla, falakua; a black squirrel, funi lusa; a stripped ground squirrel, chinisa; flying squirrel, puli; red squirrel, funi homma.

Stab, *v.* Bahlih, hlifelichih; stabbed, bahah; to stab several times, hlillijha: one that stabs. blillijha, hlilelichi.

Stable, *n.* Issuba i chukka, kollo, kamossa.

Staff, *n.* Tubi; walking with a staff, tubalih.

Stag, *n.* Lapitta: to stagger, faiakochih.

Stair, *n.* Atuya; stair case or stair way, oba chaha atoyya; up stairs, oba chaha.

Stake, *v.* Ittofinilih; staked, ittofenah; a stake for a fence, holihta haluppa; to stake a fence, holehta ittafenilih; a staked fence, holita ittafena.

Stale, *a.* Sipokni, stale as old bread, shilut kollottaha.

Stalk, *n.* Ubi.

Stall, *n.* Ai lhpeta. abikia.

Stammer, *v.* Anuktukloh, anumpah anuktukloh, stammered anumpa anuktukloh; a stammerer, anumpa anuktuklo,

Stamp, *n.* Habcfa; to stamp, habifflih, habiflichib, huhlih, buhlichih, hufikbih; stamped, habcfoah, huhlah.

Stanch, *v.* Kollo. yiminta, achillta.

Stand, *a.* Ahikia; a speakers stand, ahikiot anompuli; to stand in, achushkachih; that which stands in, as spokes, achushuwa; to stand on the ground, akkah. to stand erect, akochakalih; to stand facing, et hiklah; to stand, standing or to stand still, hiklah; to make stand, hilochi; to be standing, that is, any number over one, hinli, hinlli; they stand, hiohlih, hiyuhlih; standing, hiohlih; to stand up several, hiohlichih: to stand

about, hiohm iyu, hiohtmaya, hioht
hiohlit asha; to stand in place of, ihikiah; one who stands in place of. ihikia;
to stand upon, ohikiah; to stand erect
with the head high, shikkiah; to stand
at a place, ahclichih; a small table or
stand, ai impa iskitini; standing facing,
pithikiah.
'ale, a Ai afacha.
Star, n. Fichik, fochik; a large star, fichik
chito; shooting stars, fich.k heli; starry,
fichik asha. fichik haiyaka; the orbit of
a star, fichik atuya; a flying star, fichik
hika; the great bear or dipper. fichik
issuba; seven stars.fichik itolhpi; the
north star, fichikhomma: a fiery star,
fichik luak; a sparkling star, fichik poh-
lulli; a comet, fichik shobota, fichik sho-
bulli; a constellation. fichik lokoli; star
light, fichik tohwikeli,
Starch, n. Nafoka isht chalakbichi.
Starve, v- Hohchufoh; to cause starvation,
hohchufochih; starved, hohchufo; to
starve anything to death, hohchufochit
abih; starved to death. hobchufot illi; to
starve them all to death, hohchufochit
obit tabli; starvation, hopoba. hohchufo.
State, n. Uhtih.
Sta ute, n. Nau ulhpisa, anumpaulhpisa
Stay, v. Antau, ashau. ashwah, ahantah,
otta ; to be contented to stay, achayah;
to stay with, ahinma ; a place to stay at,
ai otta, aiahasawa, ai oshua, aianta; to
stay around, ai yahantan, ai yantah; to
to stay with, ibai antah; staying with,
ibai antah; not contented to stay, ika-
chayon: not staying at, ikaiashoh; staying, ottah; to stay with me for company,
siaidinuah; to steady or to stay, halanlih.
Steady, u. Nuktanla, kostini, apissoli; to
steady, halanli.
Steal, v, Hokopah, hukopah; stolen, hukopah; to steal the heart, chukosh eshi.
Steam, v Hobechih; steaming, hobechi; to
steam self, ilehobichih; to emit steam,
kofullih; steamboat, peni oka wahlullih;
steam engine, oka wahlullih, nan isht
bushlih, nan isht botolih.
Steel, n. Toli kullo; steelyard, nan isht
weki, isht weki. isht wekichi.
Steep, a. Chabah; to steepen, chabuchih;
very steep. chaha fena.
Steer, n. Wakhobak; a steersman, that is
of a boat, hattak peni isht aya.
Stem, n. Isht takali.
Stench, n. Shuah; to cause stench, shouchih.
Step, a. Ahabli, ahali; to step on, ahulhhli-
chih. ahalelichih, hablichih; to step,
hablih; stepped, hablih; to take long steps
hopakichit haplih; to step lightly, yupullih, yupullichih; stepping lightly, yupullih; to step boldly, yuwukuchih; stair
steps, attuya.
Stew, n. lioni; stewed, houuih; stewed
victuals, honnih; to cause to stew, honi-
chih; not stewed; ikhonnoh; a steward,
chukka achuffa pinak im ahauchi,
chukka achuffa nan upa im ahanchi.
Stick, n. Balih, ulboh, ai ulboh, ulbochih;
stuck, bahah, okfayah, ulboh, ittibalul-
lih; to stick it, achoshulih, shemulli-

chih: to stick them in, achoshlin ulbihlih;
to cause them to be stuck in: achoshlichih; to stick to, alapalih, alapalloh:h; a
place for sticking on, aluprli; to rub on
or stick on, alepulichih; to stick them on,
lapohlichih: stuck them on, lapohlih: a
walking stick, tobi; walking with a stick,
toblih; to stick poles, ubilbhli.h; stuck in,
uchushkuchih; to stick them for ther,
ittihalulih; to stick in cracks or crevices,
kofohlih; sticky, shinushbi, uiashmo; to
make sticky, shinushbichih.
Stiff, a. Kulloh, kamussah. chan'o lih,
chilokbih; to stiffen, chihhl'nah. chilluh-
linuchih; stiffened, chibhl nah, chala
kblih; a numbness or stiffness, chilhhlinoha.
Stigmatize, v. Hofabyalih; to stigmatize
with, isht hohfahyalih.
Still, a. Cholosah, chollusah; to still, cho-
lussuchih, chulosalih; yet or still, immo-
muh, moina; stillness; chulosa,
Sting, v. Nuhli; stung; nuhla; to cause to
sting, nublichih; stings of insects, shushi
nehli.
Stin y, a. Nau i bullo; to be stingy, i
hulloh.
Stink, v. Shuah; to cause to stink, shouchih.
Stir, v. Tiwalichih ilhkolechih; stirred,
ulhfulah, tiwalichih; stirring, tiwalihi-
chih; to stir water, poulichih, pialichih,
pokuchih; water stirred, poalic li, pioki-
chi; to cause to stir, pialichih, poalichih;
to stir a liquid while it is cooking, afullih, afullichih.
Stirrup, v. Ahubli, ahali; stirrup leather
or strap, ahupli isht tolakchi
Stich, v. Achunlih, nan achonlih; a seam
or stich, ai ulhebuwa; stiched, ulhchu-
wah.
Stock, n. Nan ulhpoa nampoa; to stock,
uppih; stocked, ulhpih, ulhpih; a stock-
ing, iyabi huski falala.
Stomach, n. Takobba, ikfoka, tukubbo; a
large stomach, bahauoh shittina, shutt-
una; a very large stomach, bihunnayah,
shittinjoah; to make a large stomach,
bohunnochih; full stomach, kaiyah; my
stomach, sukfoka; pit of the stomach,
wulwa, i wulwa; the crop or stomach of
rowls. impafukchi; stomach ache, ikfoka
hottuppa.
Stone, n. Toli; lap stone, wak hakshup
abuslih; ston brulse, chukfi nishkin;
stone cutter, toli bushli; stony, toli iana,
toli foka.
Stool, n. Abinili. ai obinili. obinili yushkololi.
Stop, v. Issab; a cessation, obstruction or
a stop. yokopa; to cause to stop, issachih
yokoplichih; to stop up. akamullh, ulhkamoah, akummih; to stop as a bughole,
ikomalih; a stopper, akumami i kemali,
yokoplichi; to stop and stand, hikiah
checked or stopped, hilichih, ikumalih;
to dam or stop water, okhataplih, oktu-
blih, oktuplih; dammed or stopped,
okhatapah, oktupah; to obstruct or stop,
yokoplih; obstructed or stopped, yokopah; stop! take care! ahah; a stoppage,
anukbikeli, bikoli, oka bikeli.
Store, n. Achumpa, aittutoba; a' store

house, ai ittctoba chukka; to lay up or store away, boblih; a store keeper, ai ittctoba apesvchi.

Storm. *n.* Umba okpulo; cold and stormy, hushtula chohmi, kucha okpulo.

Story, *n.* Anumpa nan amoli isht anumpa.

Stout. *a.* Illampko, kolloh, kilimpih; to make stout, blamkochih; I am stout, sakullo.

Stove, *n.* Toli ai ulhti: cook stove, toli ahoponi; stove pipe, toli ai ulhti a shoboblli.

Straggler, *n.* Hattak kenia.

Straight. *a.* Apissunli, cihpisa: to straighten, chisbichih straightened, chisbih: not straight; shanuyah; immediately or straightway cheke, chokosi, mih makinli ho ashalika.

Strain, *v.* Illi ih, holluyochih, hoiycchih, hoyah, boiyah strained, hlifah, hoiya. boluyah: to strain out. bichillih, pichillih; I am strained, sahlifah: a strainer, ahoiyyah, ahoyyu;notstrained, ikbus toh.

Strange, *a.* Ahalaya keyu, inlah, himounh a stranger, hattak inla, inla, hattak ik ithano.

Strangle. *v.* Anukhlamcllih, anukhlamcllichih nukhlamcllih; strangling, nukhlamcllih; to cause to strangle, nukhlamcllichih; strangulation, anukhlamcllih.

Strap *n.* Chulaia, isht talakehi.

Straw, *n.* Hashuk shila; straw bed, hashuk patclhpo; straw berry, blyko.

Stray, *v.* Folotah, tamon, kunia, yoshoba.

Streak, *n.* Bason; streaked. basowah; to make streass, basowahchih, basollchih, basolih; not streaked, isbasowoh; a striped or streaked face, okhlawinlih; long stripes or streaks basosykuchih.

Stream. *n.* Bok, bokushi, ayamclli, okhina, hvchcho; up stream, ibitop, wishakchi; streamlet bokushi.

Street, *n.* Hina: a narrow street, hina ikputho; wide stre t, hina putha.

Strengthen, *v.* Hlampko; to strengthen, hlampkochih; strengthened, hlampkoh; a str ugthener, isht hlampkochih.

Strenuous *a.* Chiletah.

Stretch, *v.* Hlapah, shepolih, sheplih, chisbichih chisemoh: stretched, hlapa, shepah chisehmoh; to stretch at, ashiplih, ashebbih; a place to stretch at, ashiplih; to stretch one's self, chisbih; to stretch the limbs, chisemoh, chisemolih; to cause to stretch the limbs, chisemochih, chisemolichih; stretched limbs, chisemoah; to stretch one's self, chisemoh hika; to stretch by the legs, mamplih; stretched by the legs, mampa; to stretch either body or legs, mampolih, stretching, shepoah

Strew, *v.* Fimmih, fimimplih; strewn, fimah, fimimpah.

Strike, *v.* Issoh, fahamah, bolih; struck, fahamah; to strike at or on, afahama; to strike with a stick bakalichih, fahamah, striking with a stick, bakkaha; to strike a blow, fahamah; struck a blow, fahamah, to strike continually, fa'foah; striking with force, fahfoah; to strike against each other, ittai issoh; to strike each other, itti bohlih itti fahamah; to strike against, komollchih, pokc'lih; striking repeatedly against, kommohah, pokcha-

fah; to strike once with, litclichih; to strike with the palm of the hand, pesalichih, lesallchih; striking, pussahah; struck against, pokofah; to strike w th or against, in order to sprinkle, pushkah, olimmi; to strike me, safa'iamah, sessoh, to strike on the nose, wokkohah, wohlo, hah.

String, *n.* Isht talakehi; a rawhide string, asita; a bucskin string, hlibata; a string on which anything is strung, aholhtcpi: string, holhtanpih, holhtcpih; to string on a string, hotampih; rooty or stringy, akshish laua, a string or ropy string, hlikaha.

Strip, *v.* Fakoplih, fellih hlilih; to strip off, blchlih; to cause to strip, hlilichih stripped off, hlihah; stripped or skinned, blyfah, blofah; to skin or strip, hly lih, hlolih; stripped off, as bark, hlohah; to strip off the bark, hlolih; to ca se to strip off, blollchih.

Striped, *a.* Besowa, basoah, basowah, chenisah; to make striped, besolih, basowachib, basollchih; long stripes, basosykuchih; to be striped, chinisah: striped face, akblawinlin.

Strive, *v.* Achhunnachih, yichiuah, ittachowah, ittafehnah.

Strong, *a.* Kello kamessa, hlampko, kalaucha, kil mpi; to be strong hlampkoh; to make strong, hlampkoshih; to make strong with salt, homechih, strong as spiritual liquors, homa; very strong, homi icnah; somewhat strong, homi chohmi; not strong or not woven strong, yohapa, hoyapa; raucid or strong, kalaucha; to be strong or stout, kamessah; I am strong, sakullo; stroug, as red pepper, shekanlin.

Struggle, *v.* Shiksulah; to struggle for, haichih; to struggle against; ainokuiah.

Strut. *v.* Wekkenah, yowckuchih, ihawatot nowah; to strut as a turkey, temah; strutting, tohiah.

Stubborn, *a.* Ikhapounaklo.

Studious, *a.* Holisso aiokpanchi, achnunachit pisa.

Stud, *v.* Pisah, anukhhinlih.

Stuff, *v.* Alotulih; to cause to stuff, alotulichih: stuffed full, aluttowah.

Stumble, *v.* Ibctoblih, ibctoplih.

Stump, *n.* Iti kolofa: stumpy, kanasha;

Stun, *v.* Haksubachih; stunned, haksubah; stunning, haksuba.

Stupid, *a.* Im anukfila weki.

Sty, *n.* Hushilcbi, kushilcbi; a pig sty, shukhushi i chukka.

Style, *n.* Akaniohmi; his style, ai im ulhpesa; to name, specify or style, hohchfoh.

Subdue, *v.* Kostinuchih, im aiyochih, atablih, i shahlichih

Sublime, *a.* Chaha, chaba i shahli, pisa achykuta.

Subordinate, *r.* Holubichih; subordination, holubichi.

Subscribe, *v.* Hohchifo takalichih; a subscriber, hohchifo takalichi.

Subsequent, *a.* Himmak.

Subside, *v.* Chulosah, shiollih habofah, hopohlah, haboflih; to cause to subside, habofcchih, shiollichih habollchih, habohlichihih, hopohlcchih; subsided.

habofah, habohlih, hopohlah; sniotah, Substitute, r. Ulhtobah, ulhtobah, ulhtoboah.
Sub'le, a. Haksi.
Sacculent, a. Hokolbi.
Such, a. Ayomi, chomi: such ·as, chomi kut, chomi kg, choyohmi kut: such as are, chomi kuto, chomi hokuto: such as the, chomi kakosh: such as whom, chomi kako.
Suck, r. Pishih; sucked out, hlahah; a sprout or sucker, aputut offi: sucker (a fish), neni impusha humma·
Sudden, a. Haksinche, yakosi takla; suddenly, haksiuchi; to surprise suddenly, haksint eshi.
Suffer, r. Nukhumnih, pullummih, suffering, nukhumah. hottupah: to cause to suffer, pullummnichih, hottupa.
Suffice, r, Fihoplih: suffieed, fihopa: to cause to suffice, fihoplichih: sufficient, ulhpesah: su Deiently, ulhpesa.
Sugar, n. Hupi champuli; white sugar, hupi champuli tohbi: sugar bowl, hupi champuli· aiulhto; sugar cane. hupi champuli upl: sugar mill: hupi champuli atoba, hupi champuli ai ikbi: to sweeten with sugar, hupi champli, yummichih; sweetened with sugar, hupi champuli yummi: molasses. hupi champuli okchi.
Suitable a. Ahayah, ai ulhpesa.
Sulky, a. Hushaya; to produce sulkiness, hushayuchih.
Sul!en, a. Bashka iksho, nukog, nukfoka; to be sullen, bashka ikshoh; sullenness, hatlak nukowa shahli; to get sullen. ilchashayuchih.
Sulphur, n. Hittuk lakna pushi, hittuk lekna.
Sultry, a. Loshpa fehna, alluhbih; sultriness, alahbi, to produce sultriness, alahbichih.
Sumach, n. Bashukcha, bushshukcha; a sumach bush, bashukcha upi; white sumach, buti, bashgkchi.
Summary, n. Anunpa nushkobo.
Summer, n. Toffa, yohbi; last summer, toffa yash; next summer, toffa atukla, toffa atuklakma; summer set, hachonushshi, hachowanushshih; to cause to turn a summer-set, bachowanushichih.
Summon, r. Hoyoh, im ulhpisa tuk o hoyoh.
Sun, n. Hushi; pertaning to the sun, hushi ahalaiya; a circle around the sun, hushi akonullih: a sunny place. hushi atomi; resembling the sun. hushi holba. to warm with the sun, hushi innih, tomimih, the moving of the sun. hushi kanulli: sun rise, hushi kucha: the rising of the sun. hushi kuchah; to obscure the sun, hushi kuaiah; an eclipse of the sun, hushi kunia: to get warm in the sun, hushi labisha: warmth of the sun: hushi libesha, sun burnt, hushi lua: to be sun burnt, hushi luah: sun eclipsed, hushi luma, hushi itti opitemmih: to eclipse the sun. hushi luhmih; sunset or sun down, hushi oktula, to sun, hushi ontombichih. hufkah; a sun beam, hushi tombi a sunflower, hushshi; dried by the sun, or sunned, holufkah: that which is sunned, holufka; not sunned, ikhofkoh: sunshine, tobih; sunday, nittak hullo nittak,

nittak hullo, nit'ak holitopa; a sun dial, hushi kanulli isht ulhpisa; sunless; hushi luma.
Supple, r. Walohbi, lapushki.
Support, r. Ai ataya, halullih. ai okchaya, halanlih; a support, bikeli, tikeli; to support with a prop, tikelih, tikohlichih; supporting, tikelih tokohlih.
Suppose, r. Imahobah, mahofah.
Suppurate, r. Aninchih, aninchichih; suppuration, aninchichi, unichichi.
Surcingle, n. Ikfoka isht tulakchi, c unukko isht tulakchi.
Sure, a. Ahli, ai ahli tokn,: surely, ahli, pulla; to make sure, ahlichih; he will surely not do so,ikahlichoka he keyu; assuredly, pulla: surely it was so, toshke; surety, atoni.
Surfeit, v. Anukbikelih. nukbikilih; yummih: surfeited, yummih; I am surfeited, siyummih; to surfeit or satiate me siyummichih.
Surly, a. Hushaya.
Surpass, r. Imaiyachih.
Surprise, r. Anukhlakanchalih; anukblakashlih; by surprise, haksinchi: surprised.anukblakanchah; to take by surprise, haksint eshi; a surprise or taken by surprise, haksint eshi.
Surround, v. Afoluplih, afoluplichih; surrounded, afolupah, aiolutah; entirley surrounded, afollotah.
Survey, r. Chuhlih; to survey land, yakni chuhlih; surveyor, yakni chuhli, nan apesuchi.
Sustain, r. Halullih; sustenance, ai ok-. chaya.
Swale, n. Okfa.
Swallow, r. Nallih, nanuplih, lup na nublih, bulak achih, nunuplih, nulih; swallowing, nallih; continually swallowing, naluhamplih; to swallow largely, chitot nullih; a caimncy swallow, chopihlak, chukoba; to cause to swallow, nunuplichih.
Swamp, n. Bok anuka, lussa, lussah anuka.
Swan, n. Okak.
Swap, a. Ittatobah; itta tobuchih; swapped; it ulhtobah; to swap back, ittifalummnichih.
Swarm, r. Wihah, lawah, swarmed, wihut kuniah.
Sway. v. Chassulah; swayed, chassulah.
Swear, r. Anumpa kullo onochih, (this means to swear as a witness); sworn, anumpa kullo onotulah: to curse or swear chakapah; swearing, chakabgpah; a profane swearer, hattak chakapa; not swearing, ikchakapo.
Sweat, n. Laksha; to sweat or make sweat, lakshechih; sweating. lakshah; a place for sweating. alaksha; sweated at, alakshah; a place to produce sweat. alukshuchih; to sweat to cure the sick. hobechih; not sweating, !klekshob.
Sweep, r. Bushpulih, pashpullh pushpolih; swept. bushpoah, pashpoah.
Sweeny, n. Shulla.
Sweet, a. Champulih, kushghah, sweetness, champuli kushaha; to sweeten, champulichih; sweetened, champulih; to be sweet, champulih; loves to eat sweet things, ichampolih· not sweet, ikcham-

pulo; to sweeten at, ai yammichih; sweetened at, ai yaminih; to sweeten with; ai
yommichih, ai vommih: sweet salt, (sugar) hopi champu i; to sweeten with sugar, hopi champuli yommichih, iohki-
chih: sweetened with sugar, hopi champuli yomni: sweetish, itukowisli, ituk-
wislichi.

Swell, *v.* Shatalih, shofohlih, oshonachih,
chitolih; a swelling, shatali; swelling or
swelled, shatasholih; to cause to swell,
shatalichih, shofohlichih, chitolichih;
to swell from a sprain, shofohlih: swolen,
shofohah; I am swelling or swolen, sash-
atolih; I am afflicted with swelling; sosh-
otolih; to swell in spots, polkochih;
swelled or swolen, mitibilchi; swelled up,
bokkonoah, to swell up, bokk-
onolih, bokkonolichih.

Swift, *a.* Chahlih, polbki, shinimpa; to
cause swiftness, chahlichih.

Swim, *v.* okshinillih, oka okpolalih, oka
okyuhlih, yuplih.

Swindle, *v.* Haksichih; swindled, hqksih;
a swindler. haksichi.

Swine, *n.* Shukha.

Swing, *n.* Afahata, ofohata; to swing at, in
or on, afahatah; to swing, fahatah, fahalichih, sahlih; to swing slowly, fahakochih;
swinging slowly, fahakohahchih; to
cause to swing slowly, fahakochichih; to
swing off. fahottokohcih.

Switch, *n.* Fuli; to whip with a switch,
fuli isht fommih; switched, fuli isht
fomah.

Sword, *n.* Boshpo falaia; sword scabbard,
boshpo ishukcha.

Sycamore, *n.* Sinih; sycamore bark, sinih
hakshup.

Syllable, *n.* Silebil.

Sympathize, *v.* Nukhqkloh; to sympathize
with, iba nukhqkloh.

Synagogue, *n.* Chu okla oba isht ai anumpa chukka, sinikak.

T

Tabernacle, *n.* Olhtipo, tabanekil, chu okla
olhtipo i holitopa.

Table, *n.* Alimpa; a writing table, ahollis-
sochi: a table leg, ai impa iyl; table cloth;
ai impa o hlipa; a table cover, ai impa o
patolhpo, ai impa o pohlomo: a work
table, atoksoli; table land, yaknl matali
chahah; a long table, ai impa falaia, a
small table. ai impa iskitini, ai impushi.

Tacks, *n.* Chufak chipinta; to tack togeter,
ittahonolhhlichih; to tack on, onolhhli-
chih: tacked on' ouolhah; a tack, chufak
ushi.

Tad pole, *v.* Yaloba.

Tail, *n.* Hasimbish; to whisk the tail,
hasimbish fahlih; wisped the tail, hasimbish falah a short tail, hasimbish topa,
to cut the tail hasimbish toplih; to shave
the tail, hasimbish amoh: busby tail, po-
hota; tailor, nafoka ikbi; tailoress, oboyo
nafoka ikbi.

Take, *v.* Ishih, yokachih, hoklih lishi; to
take from or out, ai isni; to take altogether, ai oklyhanchih;to take also, al
oklyhalih to cause all to be taken together, ai oklyhalinchih; to take root,
akshish tobah; taken from, akucha; to
take them out, akuchawehlih; to take out
from, akuchichih; to take the hair off,
booilih, boyoilih; to take all, bakostolih;
all taken, bakostoah; to take off, fakoplih
fakolichih; to take back, falommint isht
in: to take by surprise, haksint; to take
out, as honey, holhta. hota; to take the
bark or skin off, hohlih; takon, ieshi;
one who frequently takes, ihishi; to take
in with, isht chukowah; to take through
with, isht hlopuli h; to take away from
by force, olobih; to take up, pehlih; taken
up, pehah; to take down, takoffih, taken
down takufah, tiapah; to take out of me,
siakuchih.

Tale, *n.* Anumpa annowa, anumpa nan
anoli; a tale bearer, anumpa chukush pa,
ikbi, hattack nan anoli.

Talent, *n.* Toli holisso laua isht olhpisa,
weki non isht olhpisa chito, nan imponna.

Talk, *v.* Anumpulih; talked, anumpah;
to talk incessantly, anukchiblafah: a
anumpa; a round-about-talk, anumpa
folotoah, anumpah ilanjakah; talkative,
anumpa i laua, anumpah shohlih; not
talkative. anumpa ik i lanoh; a short
talk, anumpah kolofasih, anumpa kolofo;
vile talk, anumpa okpulo; a fluent talker,
anumpa i kucha achukma; to talk back,
folomminchit anumpulih; talking ire-
quently, anumpohollih; a great talker,
anumpa shabli; to sit and talk, auum
pulit ashah; to talk to one's self, ilanum-
pulih; to talk about self, isht ilanumpu-
lih: to talk together, ittibai anumpulih;
to talk about, isht anumpulih, isht ittim
auumpulih, posilhhah, talking about,
namihah.

Tall, *a.* Chahah; taller, chaha i shahli;
tallest, chaha moma i shahli, chaha i
shalichit tahli; to make tall, chahachih :
long or tall, falaiah ; to lengthen or make
taller, falaiachib ; not tall. ikchahoh.

Tallow, *n.* Wak nia.

Talon, *n.* Hushi iyakchusb.

Tame, *a.* Kostini ; to tame, kostiniuchih,
hopoyuksachih apoa; to be tame and
gentle, hanayoh iksho, hopoyuksa: untamable, hopoyuksa he kuyu; to civilize
or to tame, hopoyuksalib : tamed, hopoyuksa olhpos ; untamed. ikhopoyuso.

Tan, *v.* Hummachih ; tanned, hommah ; a
tanner, wak hakshup hommochih ; tan-
nery, hakshup homina atoba.

Tangle, *v.* Yushwichalichih ; tangled, yushwichalih.

Tansy, *n.* Tqsi.

Tap, *v.* Hlumplih ; tapped, hlumpah.

Tape, *n.* Situshi ; tapes, sita chipunta.

Taper, *a.* Chysah ; tapering, chysah.

Tapster, *n.* Bicheli.

Tar, *n.* Tiak nia ; tarantula, chulhkun khito.

Tardy, *a.* Sulaha; very tardy, sclaha fehna.
Tare, *n.* Haiyukpulo.
Target, *n.* Tehlipa iskitini.
Tar.y. *v.* Autah, abantah; to tarry there, ai a bantah.
Turt, *a.* Hawushko, haluppa.
Tartar emetic, *n.* Hoitochih tohbi.
Taste, ". Ishkot pisah, upet pisah; tasteless, ikhomokit tuba.
Tattle, *v.* Achokushpolih, chokushpolih, a tattler, anumpa chukushpa ikbi, aunmpa chukushpalih
Tavern. *.* Chukka afoha, chukka anusi. hattak afoha, ai inpa chukka.
Teach, *v.* thananchih, imabuchih, ulbuchih, hopoyukselih, nan ithunanchih; teaching, nan it hunanchih; a teach-r, nan ithananchi, hattak ikhunanchi, hattak nan ikhunanchi, hattak im abuchi, hattah nan im abuchi, ithunanchi.
Tea, *n.* Ti; b'ack tea, ti lusa; green tea, ti okchamali; hyson tea, haison ti; ten cup, kaf ai ishko; tea saucer, in talaia; tea pot, ti ahonni; tea table, ai inpa iskitini; tea spoon, teli isht impushi
Tear, *n.* Nishkin okchi; tearful, annkhgklo.
Tear, *v.* Hlilulih hlilichih; torn, hlilafah. hlilahlih; to tear a part, hlilafah; torn in small piec s. hlilali; to tear in small pieces, hlilahlichih; to tear apart or into, ittahlilafah, itta hliluilla; to tear down, ticbli, ticplih, yuhlih; torn down, tlapah, yuhlah; continually tearing down, yuhuhlih.
Tease, *v.* Im achibuchih, achunnachih im usilhha; teasing, isht ahchiba.
Teat, *n.* Ipishik; my teat, saplshik,
Tedious, *a.* Uhchiba uchchibah, ahcaiba; to be tedious, ahchibnchih, ahchihbalih.
Tell, *v.* Anolih, imunol h; befug told, imunnoah; told, annoah; to tell at, annolih; to be told at, aiannowah; continually told, annohowah; told too much, annoah atupah; to cause to be told, annoachih; continually telling, annolionlih; telling ft at last, anoyulih; cannot tell, anola he k yn; to tell on one's self, ilaf anolih; we all tell, iloh im anolih; to tell tales on, nan alanolih; the place for telling news, nan annoa; to tell a lie on me, siaholebih; to tell on me, sianolih; to tell a tale, fappulih: a teller, anoli.
Temnerate, *a.* Okikishko, nuktalanli, hopoyuksa; temperance, okikishko, ile okianepli, ile nuktalanli.
Temple, *n.* Chukka hunta, aboha holitopa; the temple, haksun tubaiyi, haksun tolulyi.
Tempt, *v.* Nukpullichih, anukpullichih, imomaka pisah; tempted, nukpellih; temptation, nukpelli, anukpullika, isht imomaka pisah, anukpulli; to be tempted at, ai anukpellih, ai annukpullika; the place of temptation, aiannukpelli; to tempt at, aiannukpullichih.
Tend, *v.* Apesuchih.
Tender, *a.* Lapushki, kanliksha; tender growth, walohah, wulwrki, walubbi. waloa; tender loin, anukbakchi, anukblakchi, anukbakchi.
Tent, *n.* ulhtipo; tenth, isht pokoll.
Tepid, *a.* Labisha ummona, lahba.
Term, *v.* Hochifoh; termed, hohchifo.
Terrapin, *n.* Luksi.

Terrible, *a.* Okpulo palummi.
Ter ify, *v.* Nukshoblih; terrified, nukshopah.
Territory, *n.* Tellitoli, ulhti.
Testament, *n.* Holisso holitopa; testament, nana ittin; ulhpisa, hattak im anumpa isht aiopi ilap elhpoyak imma, nan isht ulhpisa; New Testament, testament himoua.
Testator, *n.* Anumpa isht aiopi ikbi.
Testify, *v.* Atokot anolih; to testify at, aiatokolih; testified at, ai atokowah; testimony, ai atokowa, annowa; to testify on oath, anumpa kello anotolct nan anolih; insufficient testimony, annoah ikouo.
Tetter, *n.* Halampa, hellampa; to have tetter, hullampubih.
Text, *n.* Anumpa unshkoko, uba anumpa takali ai anumpet isht ia.
Thick, *a.* Sukko, sokkoh; thickness, sukko; to thicken, sukkochih, sukkoh.
Thicket, *n.* Bafelli, bafelli talaia, b'taha, abohli; to become a thicket, abohlichi.
Thie', *n.* Hattak wehpoli, hattuh hukopa. hokopa; thievish, hukopah, hykompa.
Thigh, *n.* Obi iyubbi; upper side of thigh, obi nihi; thigh bone, obi foni; socket of the thigh, eyubachushuli; my thigh, saiyobi.
Thimble, *n.* Ihbak ushi foka.
Thin, *a.* Chunna, fimimpa, tapuski, okchauwi, shachahah; to make poor or thin, chunnaohih, yohunnachih; to thin out, shachahchlih; sparsely or thinly, fimimpa; to make thin, tapuskichih; gaunt or thin, yohunnah.
Thine, *pro.* Chinimi, chin, chi; to be thine, chimmih; to become thine, chinmui tobah.
Thing, *n.* Nana, ng; anything, uana; small things, chukushpa.
Think, *v.* Ahnih, mahobah, annkfillih; to think about, isht annukfillih; to think deeply, ahni ghli, ahnit anukfillih; will or would not think, ahni he keyu; not thinking, ikahnoh; not thought of, ika-nukfilloh; to think much of self, ileichnuchih; to think much of each other, ittohnih; to think of him or herself, ilanukfillih; a thought, anukfilli; thoughtful, anukfilli, imanukfila.
Third, *a.* hituchina, hituchinaha, atuchina; thirdly, ont atuchina, ont atuchin-una.
Thirst, *n.* Ituklapowa; thirsty, itukshila, nukshila.
Thirteen, *a.* Auahtuchina; thirteenth, isht auatuchina.
Thirty, *a.* Pokoli tuchina; thirtieth, isht pokoli tuchina.
This, *pro.* Illeppa. yakohmih, yakomichih; this side of or this way, ola, olema; just on this side of, eletoma, oletomasi.
Thistle, *n.* Shomettih, shumo.
Thither, *ad.* Illeppa pilla, yumma, yummimma, illeppimma.
Thoug, *n.* Illibata.
Thorax, *n.* Haknip.
Thorn, *n.* Kotih; red hawthorn, knti; black hawthorn, rhcuailla.
Thou, *pro.* Chi, chia, chim, chisuo; thou art, chia hoke, chiushkc.
Though, *ad.* anu conj. Hatok okia, hohkia hok, hatok okeno, hokakosh, hokakot.

Th'ash, *v.* Bolih; a thrasher; auihi, auihi-chi, anihilichih.

Thread, *n.* Ponola nan isht ulhchuwa, po-nolah nan isht auchuwa; home spun thread, ponolah ilupint shunni; twisted thread, ponolah shuna, pono shuna; thread case, ponolah ai ulbiha; hank of thread, ponolah shuna talakchi; flax thread, pono kullo isht ahchuwa; skeins of thread, ponola pakassa; spools of thread, ponola iti ulhfoa; silk thread, silik isht achunlih; shoe thread, pono kullo nan isht ahchuwa.

Three, *a.* Tuchina; three times three, tuchina bat tuchina; three score, pokoli hau-nali; thrice, hituchina, hituchinaha; to do it three times, hituchinachi.

Throat, *n.* Nelup, i nuluppi ikonla; his throat, inaluppi; sore throat, ikonla hottu-pa.

Throb, *v.* Mitiklih, michiklih; throbbing, michilbhah.

Throne, *n.* Aiasha holitopa, ai obinili han-ta, miko im ai obinili; to enthrone, ai asha holitopa ombinilichih; enthroned, aiasha holitopa ombiuilih

Through, *prep.* Ai ittitakla; to go through, hlopulli, hlipulli; hluku lih; to go quickly through, hlopohlih; to cause to go quick-ly through, hlopohlichih; just through or those just through, hlopohlih; going through, hlopulli; to come through, hlo-pullih; to cause to go through, hlopulle-chih; to pass through, h'opullit oua; to pierce through, hljah, blumplih; pierced through, hlukafuh hlumpah; worn through, punched through, bored through or perforated through, hluka-fah; to bore or work throug, hlukanli-chih; to break through, hlukullih.

Throw, *v.* Pilah, pilachih, bohpulih; thrown kanchih; to cause to throw, pilachih; to throw down, akkabolih, akkapilah, akbu-chchih; to throw me down, akkasupilah; to throw back, ialummint pilah; to throw them down, foboblih; to throw·each other about, itti fabfulih; to throw away, kanchih; to sling or to throw, bohpolih; to throw at, bohlih; thrown, bohpoah; to throw up with a stick, fachammih, fach-ummih; thrown up with a stick, facham-ah; to continually throw up, fachihali-chih; to throw mud with a stick, fahkoh, fahkulih; to throw upward, uba pilah-

Thrush, *n.* Taluktak.

Thrust, *v.* Bahlih, chikkihah; to thrust foiward, chauwenah; thrusting, chuki-hah; to thrust out the tongue from heat, hahkah; to cause to thrust, hahkuchih; to thrust in, maiahchih.

Thumb, *n.* Ibbak ishki; my thumb, subbek ishki; thumb nail, ibbakchush; my thumb nail, subbuchush.

Thump, *v.* Timiklih; thumping, timikmilih, tiuikblih; to mak·thump, timiklichih.

Thunder, *n.* Hilohah, tasah; thundering, hilohah; a shasp peel of thunder, hilo-hah tusa; a thundercloud, hilohah hosh-onti; a thunder shower, hilohut umba; to cause thunder, belohuchih; a thunder-bolt, huchuk molli, molutha, tasah.

Thursday, *n.* Hlusti.

Thus, *a.* Yak, yakohmih, yakohmichih; to be thus, achoyuhmi.

Thy, *pro.* Chimmi chin; thine, chimm chin; thyself; chishno akinli.

Tic'k, *n.* Shutunuih; seed ticks, shutunuu-shi.

Ticket, *n.* Holisso blilafa.

Tickle, *v.* Chukchulih, chukchulichih; tick-led, chukchuah; a tickler, chukchuli.

Tidings, *n.* Anumpa annowa.

Tidy, *n.* Kashofa, litiha keyu.

Tie, *v.* Takchih, sitelih, sitohlih; tied, tuk-chih, sitohah; to tie a knot, ittashikonu-plih, ashikonoplih; tying a knot, ittashi-konupah, ashikonopah; to tie together, (as seed corn,) shikolih; tied together, shikowah; to tie one's self, iletakchih; to tie to, asitilih; tied to, asitiah; I tied him, her, it or them, takchili; I tied you, chi takchi li, (If "you," refers to more than one use, huchi takchi li,) you tie me, is sa takchi; you tie him, her or it, ish tak-chi; you tie us, ish pi takchi; you tie them, ish takchi or okla ish takchi; he or she ties me, sa takchi; he or she ties you, chitakchi; he or she ties him, her or it takchi; he or she ties us, pi takchi, (pi) he or she ties you, huchi takchi; he or sne ties them, takchi or okla takchi; they tie me, sa takchit okla; they tie you, chi takchit okla; they tie him, her or it, tach it okla; they tie us, pi takchii okla; they tie us all, hupi takchit okla! they tie you all, huchi takchit okla; they tie them, okla takchit okla; we tie you, e chi takchi; we tie him her or it; e takchi; we tie you (pi) e huchi takchi; we tie them, okla e tak-chi; we all tie him, her, it or them, eho takchi; ye or you tie me, hus sa takchi; ye or you tie him her or it, hush takchi; ye or you tie us, hush pi takchi; ye or you tie them, okla hush takchi; they tie me, sa takci, or oklat sa takchi; they tie you, chi takchi; they tie him, her or it, takchi: they tie us, pi takchi; they tie us all, hupi takchi; they tie you, huchi; they tie them, oklat takchi; or takchi; I tie him, her, or it for you, chin takchi li; I tie him, her or it for him or her, in takchi li; I tie him, her or it for us, pin takchi li; I tie him, her or it for us all, hupin takchi li; I tie him, her or it for you, huchin takchi li; I ti tie him, her or it for them, in takchili or okla iu takchili; you tie him, her or it for me, is san takchi; you tie him, her or it for him or her, ish in takchi; you tie him, her or it, for us, ish pin takchi; you tie him, her or it for us all, ish hupin takchi; you tie him, her or ir, for them, ish in takchi or okla ish in takchi; he or she ties him, her or it for me, au takchi; he or she ties him, her or it for you, chin takchi; he or she ties him, her or it, for him or her, in takchi; he or she ties him, her or it, for us, pin takchi; he or she ties him, her or it, for us all, hupin takchi; he or she ties him her or it for you, huchin takchi; he or she ties him, her or it, for them, in takchi, okla in takchi; we tie him, her or it, for you, e chin takchit: we tie him.'her or it, for him or her, il in ta kchi; we tie him, her or it, for you, e hu chin·takchi: we tie him, her or it, for the m, okla il iu takchi; we all tie him, her or it, for them,

floh in takchi; ye or you tie him, her or
it. for me, hussan takchi; ye or you tie
him, her or it, for me, hussan takchi; ye
or you tie him, her or it, for him or her,
hush in takchi; ye or you tie him her or
it. for us, hush pin takchi; ye or pou tie
him. her or it, for us all, hush hupin
takchi; ye or you tie him. her or it, for
them, okla hush in takchi; they tie him,
her or it, for me, oklat an takchi; they tie
him, her or it. for you, chin takchi; they
tie him, her or it, for him or her, in takchi; they tie him, her or it, for us, pin
takchi; they tie him. her or it, for us all,
hupin takchi; they tie him, her or it, for
you, huchin takchi; they tie him, her or
it, for them, in takchi or okla in takchi;
I am tying, takchi lishke; you are tying,
ish takchishffe; he or she is tying, takchishke; they are tying takchit okushke
we are tying, e takchiske; we all are tying, eho takchishke; you are tying, hush
takchiske; they are tying, takchishke, or
oklat takchishke, ("ishke" is simply a
definite and emphatic way of expressing
anything), I do tie, takchilihoke; you do
tie, ish takchi hoke; he or she does tie,
takchi hoke; they do tie, takchit okla
hoke; we de tie, e takchi hoke; we all do
tie, eho takchi hoke; ye or you do tie,
hush takchi hoke; they do tie, oklat takchi hoke or takchi hoke: I tied or have
tied, takchi li tuk: you tied or have tied,
ish takchi tuk: he or she tied or has tied,
takchi tuk; we tied or have tied, e takchi
tuk; we all tied or have tied, eho takchi
tuk; ye or you tied or have tied, hush
takchi tuk; they tied or have tied, oklat
takchi tuk; tak chit okla tuk, takchi tuk;
if the time is very remote, tok; is used
instead of tuk; I did tie, (it was so) takchili
tuk oke; if sp aking of a tying that occur-
ed long since, it would be thus, takchili
tok oke; as tok refers to time remote and
tuk to time recent, I shall or will tie, takchi la chi; her or she, shall or will tie, takcha chi; we shall or will tie, e takcha chi;
we all shall or will tie, eho takcha chi;
ye or you shall or will tie, hush takcha
chi they shall or will tie, oklat takcha chi
takchit okla chi, takcha chi; If the time
is remote and indefinite, it is thus, I
shall or will tie, takchi la he; you shall
or will tie, ish takcha he; her or she shall
tie, takcha he; we shall or will tie, e takcha he; we all shall or will tie; oklat takcha
he; ye or you shall or will tie, oklat takf
cha he, takchit okla he or tak cha he; i-
you wish to speak regarding the future
and strongly express purpose in an imperative sense, it goes thus, I shall or
will tie, takchi lashke: you shall or will
tie, ish takchaske; he or she shall or will
tie, takchashke; we shall or will tie, e
takchashke; we all shall or will tie, eho
takchashke; ye or you shall or will tie,
hush takchashke; they shall or will tie,
oklat takchashke, takchit oklashke, takchashke: I can or may tie takchi la
hinla, you can or may tie, ish takcha
hinla; he or she may or can tie, takcha
hinla; we may or can tie, e takcha hinla;
we all may or can tie, eho takcha hinla ye

or you can or may tie, hush takcha hinla,
they may or can tie, takchit okla might
oklat takcha hinla, takcha hinla: I might
or could have tied takchi la hinla tuk;
you might or could have tied, ish takcha hinla tuk; he or she might or could
have tied, tacha hinla tuk, we mig t
have tied, eho takcha hinla tuk; ye or
you might have tied, hush takcha hinla
tuk; they might have tied, oklat takcha
hinla tuk or takcha hinla tuk; I was
about to tie, takchi la chin tuk, you were
about to tie, ish takcha chin tuk: he or
she was about to tie takcha chin tuk; we
all were about to tie, eho takcha chi tuk:
ye or you were about to tie, hush takcha
chin tuk; they were about to tie, oklat
takcha chin tuk or takcha chin tuk; I
should or would have tied, takchi la he
tuk: you should or would have tied, ish
takcha he tuk; he or she should or would
have have tied, takcha he tuk, we should
have tied; e takcha h tuk: we all should
have tied. eho takcha he tuk: ye or you
should have tied, hush take a he tuk;
they should have tied, oklat takcha he
he tuk or takcha he tuk: (if you wish to
refere to a remote time, use hi tuk in
place of he tuk), when or as I t c, takchi
li mut; when you tie, ish takchi mut;
when he or she ties, takchi mut; when
we tie, e takchi mut; when we all tie, eho
takchi mut; when they tie, oklat takchi
fflut, or takchi mut; if you wish to imply
a future contingency, when I tie, (if I ti),
takchi likmut; when you t, if you tie),
ish tokchikmut; when he or she ties, takchikmut; when we tie c, etakchikmut;
whn w all tie, eho takchikmut: when
ye or you tie, hush takchikmut; when
they tie, oklat takchikmut, takchikmut;
if I had tied, takchi li tukmut; if you had
tied, ish takchi tukmut; if he or she had
tied, takchi tukmut; if we had tied,
etakchi tukmut; if we all had tied eho
takchi tukmut; if ye or you had tied,
hush takchi tukmut; if they had tied,
oklat takchi tukmut or takchi tukmut;
if you wish to refer to time far in the past
use tokmut instead of tukmut; if I shall
or will tie, takchi la chikmut; if you shall
or will tie, ish takcha chikmut; if he or
she will tie, takcha chikmut; if we shall
tie, e takcha chikmut: if we all shall tie,
eho takcha chikmut; if ye or you shall
tie, hush takcha chikmut; if they shall
tie, takcha chikmut; this refers to tying
that will occur in the immediate future,
if the time is more remote, it goes thus,
if I shall or will tie, takchilihokmut; if
you will tie, ish takchi hokmut; if he or
she will tie, takchi hokmut; if we shall
tie, e takchi hokmut: if we all shall tie,
eho takchi hokmut; if ye or you tie, hush
takchi hokmut: if they tie, takchi hokmut; if I shall have tied, takchi la hinla
tukmut; if you shall have tied, ish takcha hinla tukmut; if he or she shall have
tied, takcha hinla tukmut; if we shall
have tied, e takcha hinla tukmut; if we
all shall have tied, eho takcha hinla tukmut; if ye or you shall have tied, hush
takcha hinla tukmut; if they shall have

tied, takcha hinla tukmut; let me tie, ak takchi; let him or her tie, ik takchi; let them tie, takchit ik okla; let us tie, ke takchi; let us all tie, keho takchi; tie ye or you, ho takchi; let me tie, I will tie, takchi lashke; you shall tie, ish takchashki; let him or her tie, takchashki; to untie, hlitolih, hlitoflih, hotohlichih; united, hlitua, hlitofa, hlitofkuchih, hotohlih, hlitoha; to untie many, hlitohlih; to cause to be untied hlitohlichih, mokohlih.

Tiger, *n.* Koi basoa, koi; tigress koi tek.

Tight, *a.* Katanlih, yubapa keyu, kullo; okishkot haksi; to tighten, katanlichih, akullochih; to fasten tight, akullochih; to butten up or tighten, akamussalih; tightened, akamussah; to set or stick in tight, ahlachalih, alachalichih; to be fixed in tight, ahlachah, ahlachavah-

Till, *ad.* Na; a till, iskulli itombeshi; to till land, okchahli, okchuhlih; till this time, hinak ano.

Timber, *n.* Iti, iti chaya.

Time, *n.* Taim, nitak, ai ona; a proper time ai ulbpesa; a time or place of payment, ai ulotoba; not time for payment, ai ulhto'ba ikono kisha; time or place of appointment or election, ai ulhtoka; a short time, chekosikma, chekosi hokma; present time, himonasi himak, himona, inib mak inli bo, ashalika; oft or often times, himmong; some times, kanimikma, kaniohinikma; times, (used in repeating the multiplication table) bat, time or times, used after ordinals, ha; as atukla ha; second time, the third time, out atuchina ha; at this time, himak, himak ano; about this time, himak foka, himmak foka; at a future time, himmak ma; the comingtime, himmak pilla; one time, himonna ha; at the same time, himmonna achuffa; let all talk at one time, himmoua achuffa momut ik anumpuli; a long time, hopaki; a longer time, hopaki i shahli; it will last a long time, hopaki ho tuba chi; when a long time, hopakikmako, hopakihokmako; not time, ikaionoh; to bring forth before time, ikaiono ho chelih; a short time, ikbopako; to have time, shaklah, i haiyakah; time piece, hush kanulli isht ikhuna; meal time, ai impa onah.

Timid, *a.* Anukwiah; I am timid, sanukwiah, sakomotah; to be timid, komontah; timidity, komonta; to produce timidity, komollichih; timorous, hobak toba.

Tin. *n.* Asonak huta; tin ware, asonak huta; tin basin, mahaia iskitui; tin bucket, asonak tohbi isht ohchi; tin canister, asonak huta ai ulhto; tin cup, isht ishko; tin pan, asonak mahaia; tin plote, asonak amp huta; tin wash pan, ai okami; tinner asonak huta ikbi,

Tingle, *v.* Sumahuchih.

Tinkle, *v.* Sumampah.

Tip, *n.* Wishakchi; tipsy, okishkot haksi; tip toe, shikkiliklih. •

Tire, *v.* Tikambichih, hoyublichih, tikahbichih, kotah, hoyaplichih; tired, hoyaplih, tikahbih kotah; continually being tired tikohahbih; to tire out ai intakobih, ai intakobichih.

To, *pr.* Ak okuno; as to, ak okuno; to or

unto, ako, hak o to-pit, toward, pit to yoka; as, "come to Jesus." okchalinchi yoka oh im ulah.

Toad, *n-* Shilukwah; a tree toad, chukpalantak

Toast, *r.* Anaksholih, anakshuflih; toasted, anakshuah, anakshohah.

Tobacco, *n,* Hakchuma; chewing tobacco, hakchuma paluska; a pulg of tobacco, hakchuma paluska; smoking tobacco, hachuma bota; tobacco snuo, hakchuma bota; to smoke tobacco, hakchuma shukah; a tobacco pipe, hachum ashuka, au euithen tobacco pipe, hakchuma shciti; a cigar, hakchuma shuna; a roll of tobacco, hakchuma ulhfoa; nicotine of tobacco, hakchuma hlitilli; a tobacco worm, hachumpa upa, hakchuma shushi tobacco seed, hakcuma nihi, give me some tobacco, hakchuma sapetah; tobacconist, hakchuma kanchi.

Toe, *n.* Iyushi; big toe, iyishki, toe nail, iyukchush; my toe nail, sulyukchush; my big toe, sayisaki; my toes, sayushi; little toe, iyush uhli; my little toe, sayushi uhli; to tip toe, shikkiliklih.

Together, *ad.* Aieninchit, ittachaklih; to splice together at, ai iliachakalih; to come together at, ai ittufama.

Toll, *v.* Toksulih, pilesah.

Tomahawk, *n.* Iskiffushi

Tomb, *n.* Ahollopi aboha, aholuppi; tombstone, aholluppi tuli hikia.

Tomorrow, *ad.* Onna, onnaba, onnakma tomorrow, onnahinlikma.

Ton, *n.* Weki tahiepa sipokni tuklo.

Tongs, *n.* Luak isht kiseli, isht kiseli.

Tongue, *n.* Isunlush; to put out the tongue okchilabih; pulling out the tongue rapidly like a snake, okchillubi; my tongue, sasoulush;languages or tongues, anuinpa wagou tongue, iti chanulli tikba hikia; buil tongue, wak isuulush.

Tonic, *n.* Nipi isht hlampkochi ikhish.

Too, *ad.* Akiulih.

Tool, *n,* Isht toksuli, nan isht toksuli.

Tooth, *n.* Noti; foretooth, uoti tikba; eye tooth, noti isht itivi; corner tooth, noti chukbi; molar tooth, noti pokta; tooth brush, noti isht kasholichih noti isht achefa; tooth ache, noti hottuppa; toothless,noti iksho;tooth pick,noti isht shinli; my tooth, sanuti; my teeth, sanoti; toothsome, impa achukma.

Top, *n.* Wishakchi, paknaka; tophet, ai okpuloka.

Torment, *n.* Apullummi, ai okpuloka; to torment, apullummichih, pullummichih; the place of torment, aiissikopa.

Tortoise, *n,* Luksi hachotakni; tortoise shell, lukshakshup.

Torture, *v.* Hottupah, hottupuchih.

Toss. *v.* Pilah; tossing, fuhummih.

Total, *a.* Momah, banoh okluha; totality, moma, banoh; totally, banoh.

Totter, *v.* Faiokuchih;tottered, faiokuchih.

Touch, *v.* Pashohlih, potolih, hulilih; to touch me, sahalelih; touched. pashohah; to touch the bottom, akkahikah; touching continually, pashohghlih; not reached or touched, ikbikiloh ikhaleloh, to touch over head, bikelih, to cause to touch; bikelichih.

Tough, *a.* Kullo, I am tough, sakulloh.

Two, *v.* Halut isht ayah; towing. halut isht ayot.

Toward, *pr.* Et; auet, pit pilah; towards the speaker, auet: to light up toward this way, et towekelih; to whoop toward this way, et toshah; to call out this toward way, et tohpalah; to stand with face toward this way, et hikiah; towards, aheh, imma, pilah; standing with face toward, pit hikiah.

Towel, *n.* Nashuka isht kasholichi.

Tower, *n.* Chukka chaha; to tower, chahah.

Town, *n.* Tomaha, a small town, tomoha iskitini; a village, tomohushi; a city, tomoha chito.

Trace, *v.* Hinay, hinushi; to tract or trace, silhhih; to trace a line, hlafih; traced, hlafa; traces or trace chains, isht halulli.

Trachea, *n.* | Kolumbish, | kolupi.

Track, *n.* Hina, ahapli; to track, silhhih; a small book or tract, holisso hokshup iksho.

Trade, *v.* Ittatoba; trader, ittatoba shahli, na chumpa, ittotoba: tradesman, ittotoba.

Tradition, *n.* Anumpa isht auchinchi.

Traffic, *n.* Ittatoba; a trafficker, ittotoba.

Trail, *v.* Silhhi; a irail, hlohama.

Traitor, *n.* Na haksichi.

Trample, *v.* Ahahlichih, ahablichih, hablih, hablichih.

Tranquil, *a.* Hopohla; to tranquilize, hopohluchih, cholusuchih; tranquillity, cholusa.

Transgression, *n.* Asochi, anumpa olhpisa obaneblit kobodi: a transgressr, anumpa kobodi.

Transient, *a.* Ch·kosi ant iah: transitory chekosi koninihyuh, vakosi ittintakla.

Translate, *v.* Anumpa tusholih, tosholih: translation, anumpa tushowa atoshowa, holisso atoshowa: translat.d, anumpa tushoah; a translator, anumpa tusholi: to translate incorrectly, anumpa ashochit tusholih.

Transparent, *a.* Shohkullalih, shohkauwalih.

Transverse, *a.* Nan aiyukheng.

Trap, *n.* Hoklih; a trap, ishtolbi, nan isht hoklih.

Trash, *n.* Chopilbkush.

Travail, *v.* Nottupa.

Travel, *v.* Nowot ayah, nau obinit ayah; to travel on foot, akkayah, akkanoah; travelers on foot, akka hika; to cause to travel fast for me, auchablichih; travelling fast for me, auchablih; to travel through, anowot hlopullih; traveled on, anowah.

Transverse, *v.* Hlopullih; transversed, hlopullih.

Tray, *n.* Iti ampo, ai olhto ayammoska.

Treachery, *n.* Haksi, treacherous, haksichih.

Tread, *v.* Hablih, hohlih; tread on, hablih, ahakichih, aholhhlichih; to cause to tread, hablichih, hohlichih; a treadder, ahablichih, habli, hohli; to tread down, hlohommih; to cause to tread down, hlohommichih; trodden down, hlohamah: trodden, hohlah; to tread on each other, ittihalhhlih; a treaddle, ababli, ahali, ahohlit.

Treasurer, *n.* Iskoli | sholi, holisso sholi.

Treat, *v.* Halollih: to treat so, yakahmichih; to treat cruelly, issikkopat.n.

Treaty, *n.* Chulite.

Tree, *n.* Ipi, opi; to mark the tree, iti | chylih; a forked tree, iti falokto,; to lay across a tree, iti abonah, iti abanalih; a high tree, iti chaha; the bark or a tree, iti hakshup; a young tree, iti himitta; a s:ump of a tree, iti kalofa: a hard wood tree, iti kullo; an alder tre·; itukawaloha: an ash, shinop; white ash, sh.nop holba; prickly ash, iti kapossa, iklish potasopi; willow, tokojsha: weeping willow, itokowisha, tohominsan; whortleberry, shiopha; sheki fennehi; pine, tiak, long leaf pine, tiak faya; white pin tiak hota; young pine, tiak himitta, tiak ushi: yellow pine, tiak lakua: peach tree, takonopi; apple tree, takon chito opi; persimmon, ykof; pecan .ree, oksak fola opi; pecan trees, osak hofaloha opi: pear tree, lakon chito holba opi; plum tree, takonlush opi; wild plum, issi | takonlush opi; poplar, sipsi; sycamore, sinni, foni ik oyo: thorn, koti; walnut tree, hahe opi, hahe, papaw, ombi: red hawthorn, kot. black hawthorn, chunahila; white oak, baiyi; water oak; chiluputha, nusichipuntopi, red oak, nusopi; overcup, busnto: chestnut oak, baiyi holba: spanish oak, chishikta: post oak, chisha, black oak, nuhloknopi; black jack, chiskillik: dwarf black jack, chokushmi; mulberry tree, bihopi; soft maple, chukchu; supar maple chukchu kullo, chukchu imoshi; hon·y locust, koti; black locust, koti lusa; linn, pishshunnuk; hickory, oksak opi. oksak kapko, oksak takba opi, oksak toli: swamp hickory, hobilhkopi; iron wood; iyanobi, oka hiloha; holly, bishi halupa, hali; hackberry, kapko; sweet gum, hika: black gum, itoni hushupa: fig tree. fik opi; elm, tohto; slippery elm, balup: cotton wood, shombola: chiua tree, itolhpoa opi; chineapin hachulaktopi: dogwood, hakchopilhkopi: cypress, shakulo: cedar, chuahla: bois d· are, koti lakna: cherry, ittolikchi: tame cherry, ittollikehi ol hpoa: chestnut tree, atopi: beech, hatonbolaha.

Tremble, *v.* Wannichih, wauaoahuchih.

Trot, *v.* Yahyochih: trotting, yahyohanchih: a trotter, yahyochi.

Trouble, *v.* Ataklommih, anumpulichih, ilbushalih; troubled, ilbushah, ataklamah; to be troublesome, afekommih; to cause trouble, afekommichih; troublesome, ahehiba, ataklommi, nau isht atopa, olhchiba isht akanomi; troubling self, isht ilakanomichich; greatly troubled nan i kanihmi chito; to trouble water, pialichih; troubled water, piakochih.

Trough, *n.* Ai ilhpeta, alimpa penli; to put into a trough, ai impa folikih.

Trout, *n.* Saklih; a large trout, saklih chitoh.

Truck, *n.* Iti kolaha; truck wheels, iti kulaha.

True, *v.* Ahli· not true, ikahlo; to be true, ai ahli; truly, ai ahlit, ahli, akot, mohli. pulla, ta; it is true, ai ahlishke ahlishike: to make true, ahlichih; to fail to make true, ik hluchoh; because it is not true, ik ahloka; because it is not true, ik ahlo kamba; faithful or true, nan ahli, truly so, chahlok.

Trunk, *n*. Itombi; body or trunk, haknip.

Trust, *v*. Anukchitoh, abskuchih, į yimmih, nianukchitoh; trusty, anukchita hinla; confidence or trust, anukchito; not to trust, ikanukchetoh; trustee, nan apistikeli uihtoka.

Truth, *n*. Ahli; to establish the truth; ahlichih; the truth nan ai ahli, nan ai ahlika, truthful, ai ahli; a truthful man, hattak ai ahli.

Try, *v*. Ilahobbih, pisah.

Tub, *n*. Nan ai ache̊fa, iti kolofa, aiachefa.

Tuesday, *n*. Tusti.

Tug, *v*. Halut isht ayah.

Tumble, *v*. Tonollih, akkatulah, akumah, tohuollichih filummih; tumbler, ai ishko.

Tumor, *n*, Shatali; tumult. haksuba.

Tunnel, *v*. Kotoba isht oni.

Turban. *n*. Bitah, ishbitah; to wear a turban, ishbitilih bitilichih.

Turbid, *a*. Lukchuk asha litiha.

Turkey, *n*. Fokit; a gobler, fakit nakni, fokit homctti; a hen, faket tek; young turkeys fokit ushi; half grown, fokit himmit hou; a young gobler, fokit kuchukak, turkey buzzard sheki.

Turn, *v*. Filemah, filimmih, chunahah, chanahuchih, tonolih, halellih; turned, folatah; to turn at, afalamah; a turning row, afalama; to turn inside out, anukpilidih; turned inside out, anukpilifah; to turn them out from, aku chawehlih; to turn back or return, falamah, plural, falamoah; to cause to turn back, fola molichih; turning back, falamut aya; to return to, falamut onah; to turn aside, ilchapah; a turning, fichapa; to turn self about, fulokuchih; to turn another about fulolichih; turning about, fulokahanchih, fulumon: to turn quickly, fulottokuchih, to turn aside, folatah; to turn them off from, folotolih; turning off, folotoah; to turn over on the face, hlipelih; turned over on the face, hlipiah; to turn them over, hlipohlechih; turned over, hl'pohlih, (if only one,) hlipolih; to turn off to go aside, fichuplih, fichuplichih, fichuyah, fichupolih, fichupolichih; to cause to turn from, filamolichih; to wander or

turn about, filihkuchih; wandered off or turned away, filamah; turned round or over, filimah; plural, filemoah, to turn them over or around, filemolih; to cause to turn them over or around, filemolichih; to turn over, filimmih; to separate or turn away from, filummih; to cause to turn away from, filummichih, to twist or turn aside, shanaiyah;· turning aside, shanayah: to make turn aside, shaugyuchih: to turn the edge, pilihlib, turned, pilifah: to turn them out loose, tihllih: to turn over and over, tonullih, tonullichih: to continue turning over and over, tononolih.

Turnip, *n*. Tunip: wild turnip, woha.

Turpentine, *n*. Tiak shna, tiak bila, tiak uia.

Turtle. *n*. Hachotukni: a water turtle, abushka: a soft shell turtle, holwa; a striped head turle, luksabashka: loggerhead turtle, hachotukbi, terrapin, luksi; terrapin shell, luksi, hakshup.

Tusk, *n*. Noli isht, itibih.

Tutor, *n*. Hattak ithananchi, nan it hunnanchi.

Twire, *ad*. Hitukla, bituklaha.

Twig, *n*. Tnli; to whip with a twig, fuli isht fummih.

Twilight, *n*. Nittakih, okhillinchi okpulusbi.

Twin, *n*. Palokta, pokta, hainp, hayup.

Twine, *v*. Pono kollo honula.

Twist, *v*. Honolah shanaiyah, punnih, na shunnih, tuneffoh: to warp or to twist, bochussachih, bochits salih; warped or twisted, bochokuchih, bochussah, to twist cotton, na shunnih: twisted, punnulah, punnulohab, shanayah; to cause to twist, shaugyuchih; to twist from one side to the other, yikuttokuhchih; continually twitching or twisting, yikuttokahauchih.

Twitch, *n*. Halablih, yikuttokahchih; to cause to twitch, ha ahlichih; convulsive twitches, yalalaba, yallaloha, yalalahbuchi: continually twitching, yikuttokahanchih.

Two, *a*. Tuklo; the two, ittatuklo; to make two, tuklochih.

Type, *n*. Na holba, tell isht holissochih.

U

Ubiqaitp, *n*. Himmonna achuffanlit kunimma anto.

Ugly, *a*. Ikaioklo, okpulo, aiokli keyu, ik į mako, tasimbo; I am ugly, siokpuloh.

Ulcer. *n*. Hlachowa, liahpo.

Umbrage, *n*. Hoshontika.

Umbrella, *n*. Isht olohoshontikuchi.

Umpire, *n*, Hattak nan olubichi.

Unable, *a*. Na nihma he keyu.

Unadvisable, *a*. Achukma keyu.

Unaware, *a*. Haksinchi,; unawares, hakinchi.

Unbecoming, *a*. Eakali, ikaioklo.

Unbelief *a*. Ik į yimmo, nau ik į yimmo; an unbeliever. nan ik į yimmo.

Unbent, *v*. Ikbikolloh, bikotah keyu

Unbind, *v*. Kotoffih, hlitoffih; unbound, kotohlih, hlitofa; many are unbound. hlitobah; to unbind many, hlitohblih: too many to be unbound, hlitohlichih.

Unbuckle, *v*. Mokofih; unbuckled, mokofah. ·

Unceasing, *n*. Billia

Uncertain, *a*. Achukma ik aksotiuiucho, ai ahli ik ithano, chishba, ik ahlo, nana chishba.

Uncivil, *a*. Ik kosteno, ik hopoyukso; uncivilized hapoyuksa he keyu, ik kosteno, ikhopoyukso.

Uncle, *n*. Imoshi, imushi.

Uncontrollable, *a*. Ikachukmo.

Unction, *n*. Ai ahaina.

Under, *ps.* Nuta; to be under, ai inutah, undergo, hlopulli; to undermine, akkish tula kullit kinuffih; understand, akosti ninchih, ikhanah, inponnah; understood anukfohkah; understanding, im anukfila; an undertaker, hattak illi hoppi isht utta; unkervalue, chuknshpa: undervalued, chukushpah, holitoblih keyu.
Undone, *a.* Ik ulhtaho, ai okpulo.
Undoubted, *a.* Ai ghli, ik ghlo ka hetoh: undoubtedly, ik ghlo ka wa, ik yohmo ka hetoh; doubtless, ghli pulla, pulla.
Undue, *a.* Ik ulhpeso, atupa; undulate, bunukuchih.
Uneven, *a.* Ik iti lauo bombokih, bakukih; to make unevon, bubukichih.
Unexpected, . Haksinchi; unexpectedly, haksinchi; taken unexpectedly, haksinteshi; to arrive unexpectedls, bakstut ulah; unexpectedly (to the speaker) afo hofo.
Unfaithful, *a.* Ik ai ghlo.
Unfashionable, . Ai yummohmi keyu.
Unfit, *a.* Ik nihpeso, unfixed in habits, ai ullu ikitbano.
Unfortunate, *a.* Ik ahobo, ai i hlakofi. poyafo.
Unfriendly, *a-* Ik i kano, ik ni okpacho.
Ungrateful, *a.* Ikaiokpanchoh.
Unhappy, *n.* Ilbusha, nukbaklo, yukpa iksho.
Unhitch, *v.* Mokofih; unhitched, mokofah.
Unholy, *a.* Ikholitopoh.
Unity, *v.* Itiba fokih ittiba fokah; united, itiba foka, ittibai achukulbih ittibai achuffa; a unity, achuffa.
Unkind, *a.* Bashka keyu, hulhpashi iksho, hushka iksho.
Unknown, *a.* Ik ai ikhano, chishba, humah.
Unlawful *a.* Ai ulhpesa keyu, ik ai ulhpeso.
Unlearn, *v.* Im ahakstih; unlearned, ikimpunnoh.
Unlike, *a.* Ikahuboh, ikkittiholboh ikcho-

hmo; unlikely, tokomi.
Unload, *v.* Kuchih: unloaded, kuchah
Unlucky, *a,* Ikahoboh, ai i blako:fih; to make unlucky in hunting, poaffih; made unlucky, poafah.
Unman, *v.* Hobuk ikbi, hobuk; unmanly, hobuk toba.
Unmanerly, *a.* Hopoyuksa keyu.
Unprincipled, *a.* Haksi.
Unravel, *v.* lilifah, shelih: unraveled, hlifah, shelah-
Unripe, *a.* Okchekkochi.
Unruly, *a.* Haksi.
Unskillful, *a.* Ikimpunnoh.
Untamable, *a* Hopoyuksa he keyu.
Unto, Ako, hako, mako yako, ak ona, okokuno.
Untrue, *a.* Ik ai ghlo, ai ghli keyu; to be untrue, holubih; untruth, holubi; because it is untru, ikghlo kamba.
Unutterable, *a.* Anola he keyu.
Unwelcome, *a.* Ikaiokpanchoh.
Unwilling, *n.* Ikahnoh, ikbunnoh, ai okpanchi keyu.
Unwise, *a.* Ikhopoyukso.
Unworthy, *a,* Ikholitopoh.
Unwritten, *a.* Ikholissochoh;
Unyielding, *a.* Bikota hekeyu.
Unyoke, *v.* Yok i shofih; unyoked, yok i sbufah.
Up. *d.* Uba; upward, ubah.
Upbraid, *v.* Posilhhah, posilhhuchih.
Upholder, *n* Halulli.
Uppermost, *a.* Chaha i shallhehit tuhli, chaha i shulibt tuhli.
Urge, *v.* Atohnoh, atohnhchih, intohno yimitcchih; urgency, achiba.
Urine, *a.* Hoshuwah, to urinate hoshuwab
Us, *pro.* Hupi, ki, kil, pi.
Use, *v.* Isht antah, isht ayah; usually, chokusho, biekah, chatuk; usual, chokumo, hokomoh; hokumoh atak,
Utensil, *a.* Isht toksuli.
Utter, *v.* Anumpulih, achih anolih; utterly, banoh.

V

Vacation, *n,* Foha.
Vagabond, *n.* Ai uttpa iksho, chukka abaiya, hattak kalakshi kunia, hattak haksi akpulo.
Vagrant, *n.* Chukka abaiyah, chukka abaiyuchi.
Vain, *a.* Ilefehnuchi, ik ahofoh, intakobih; vanity, ilefehnuchi.
Vale, *n.* Okuttuhaka.
Valiant, *a.* Ahli, nukwia iksbo.
Valid, *a.* Kobafa he keyu, achukma, ai ghli.
Valise, *n.* Nafoka asbali.
Valley, *n.* Okfa.
Valuable, *a.* Holitopa; to value, ai ullih, iulli onochi, ai illichih, holitoblichih, i holloh; undervalued, holitoblih keyu; invaluable, holitopa atupa.
Vanish, *v.* Kuniah, kashofah, iksboh.
Vapid, *a.* Ikhomokit tuha.
Vapor, *n.* Kofota.
Various, *a.* Ilaiyuka; to vary, aiyukachih, aiyukalichih.

Varnish, *n.* Itombi isht malantuchi.
Vast, *a.* Chitoh, hocheto; vastness, chinto.
Vegetable, *n.* Haiyukpulo, ulba; vegetable, hofantih.
Velu, *n.* Akshish, hakshish, issish i hina.
Venerate, *v.* Holitoblih; venerated, hblitopah.
Venison, *n.* Issi nipi.
Venture, *v.* Amosholih, amosholichih; continually venturing, amoshohonlih.
Verbal, *a.* Anumpah; verbally, anumpah banoh.
Verbose, *a.* Anumpa laua.
Verdant, *a.* Okchamalih.
Verge, *v.* Bichotah, tobunah; the verge, ai ubli.
Verily, *ad.* Ahli, ghli, ho, ghli hosh.
Vemifuge, *n.* Hushwush ubi, hushshowush ubi, lupchubi; vermifuge weed, hushun.
Vermilion, *n.* Tishepa.
Verse, *n.* Anumpa ulhpisut holisso, holisso anumpa tupa; uerses, holisso anumpa tuptua.

Vertigo, n. Chukfokoha.
Very, a. Ai ahli. illuppak atuk, akluha, aiehuah, iehun, fehnah, kush, hacha, (as, achukma hacha; it is very good,) very much, fiehna. okluha, ai oklyhah; would be very, fehna, hinla; not very, fehna keyu.
Vessel, n. Ahlabocha, ahlabushli, nana ai ulhto; vessels, nana ai ulbiha nana ulhpitta; a vessel to pickle in, aiulhkachih; a milk vessel, abishlichi; a vessel to boil in, aholbi, pan abonui; a boat or vessel, pehta, peni.
Vest, n, Nafokushi nafoka shakba iksho.
Vibrate, v. Fahakuchih: vibrating, fahakhauchi.
Vicinage, n. Bilika: vicinity, bilika.
Victuals, n. Nan upa, illpak, ilimpa, holhponi; boiled victuals, honni.
View, v. Hopokoyoh, hopopoyo, pisah.
Vigilant, a. Okcha, il anuk tahla.
Vile, a. Chakapa. haksi: to act vilely, haksih; to vilify, chakapah.
Village, n. Tumuhushi.
Vine . Baluli: a grape vine, pakapi: muscadine vine, sukkoupi.
Vinegar, n. Oka hauashko.
Violin, n. Ahlipushi; bass violin, ahlepushi chito; a violin bow,, ahlepah isht olachi; violin strings, ahlipah ushi isht-talakchi; the sound of a violin, ahlepah olla; to play the violin, ahlepah olachih;

a violin player, ahlepah olachi.
Viper, n. Sinti okpulo, sinti chilita.
Virtue, n. Ahli, ai ulhpisuchi, nan ulhpisali, nana ai ulhpiesa; virtuous, holitopa, ai uhli, ai ulhpesa.
Virulent, n. Homi fehna.
Viseid, a. Hikaha.
Vise, n. Isht kiseli chito; thumb vise, isht kiselushi.
Visible, a. Haiakah.
Visit, v. Chukalahah, i nowut ayah; to make a visit, chukalahuchih; a visitor, chukalaha chukalahuchi, nowut aya.
Vital a. Ai okchaya.
Vitrial, n. Toli holuya okchamali.
Voice, n. Im anumpa ola, ola.
Volcano, n. Nuni lua.
Vomit, v. Howita, hoeta; to make vomit, hoetuchih; to try to vomit, hoetut pisah; you all vomiu, bohoetah; you all cause others to vomit, hohowituchih; vomiting, hoeta; vomiting blood, issish hoeta.
Voracious, a. Anuktupah iksho, issikopa, impa shahli.
Vote, v. Atokolih, lotimah voted. atokoah, ulhtokah: a voter, atokoli, fot bohli.
Vow, v. Anumpa kullochit mihah, anumpa holitopa il ouochih, anumpa, il onochih, im issa.
Vulgar, n. Chakapa, makali; not vulgar, ikchakapo, vulgarity, chakapa.

W

Wade, v. Oka nowah, oka hikah, anowah; to wade through, anowut hlopullih; waded through, anowah.
Wafer, n. Holisso isht akulo, holisso isht akamussa.
Wag, n. Hattak yopulla.
Wagon, n. Iti channoli, iti chunaha; wagon body, iti channoli o talala. wheel, chunaha; fore wheels, chunaha tikba hlli; hind wheels, chunaha ulbulaka huli; tongue, iti chauelli tikba hikia; wagoner, iti channel, isht aya; wagon whip, isht fuma chito.
Wall, v. Yaiya isht yaiya.
Waist, n. Ikfeksa; waist coat, nakfokushi.
Wait, v. Hoyoh; waiter tishu
Wake, v. Okcha, to waken, okchali.
Walk, v. Nowah, akkaya; walking nowah; a walker, nowa; a walk, anowa; to walkt on, anowah; to walk through, anowah hlopullih; to walk fast, chahlih; a a fast walker,chahli:to cause to walk fast, chahlichih; to walk with, ibanowah ittibanowah; walking together, ittibanowah; one who walks with another, ittapatuli; to walk with a cane, tabilih; to walk lamely, tabiklih; to walk lightly, yupullih, yupullichih; walking lightly yupullih; to walk grandly, yuttulah yowukcchih.
Wallet, n. Bahtushi, bahta, shukcha.
Walnut, n. Hahe, oksakhahe: walnut tree, hahe upi; oksakhahe upi
Wander, v. Folokahanchih, fulohkuchih, filihkuchih, hinak fokalechit aya, fitihkuchih; wandered off from, filamah, filom-

mih; to cause to wander off. filamolichih, filummichih: a wanderer, filihkuchi, titihkuchi: wandered off, filommih filomolih.
Want, v. Bunnah, ikonoh, polummih, ikshoh; wanting, bunnah. polumah; one who wants, bunna; to come to want, as food or water, baiyonnah: not wanted, ikbunnoh: to be in great want for meat, pushkunoh: I want, sabunnah: you want, chi bunnah; he or she wants, bunnah: we want, e bunnah; we all want, eho bunnah; I may want, bunna la hinla; you may want, chi bunna hinla; we may want, ebunna hinla: we all may want, eho bunna hinla.
Wanton, n. Haksi.
War, n. Itin tanampilh,itibi chitoh: to cause a war, tanampih: warrior, tushka: red warrior, tushka homma; a war song, hoyopa taloa: a war whoop, hoyopa tessaha.
Warily, d. Aha ahnit: wariness, aha ahni.
Warm, a. Likema, libisha, yohbih: to warm, libeshah, libisblih. innih; warming, libisbuh: warmth, libisha: to warm by the sun, likemah: to cause to warm, likemuchih: to warm at, ai innih: a place to warm at, ai iuni; moderately warm. lahba; to be warm, labbah, yohbih; warmed, lahbah; to make warm, lahbuchih, lubbuchih, yohbichih; to warm up from anger, muklibishlih; warmed up, nuklibishah; to cause to warm up, nuklibishshiakhchih; I am warm, salibeshah.
Warn, v. Imunolih, anolih; warned, imunnoah, annoah.

Warp, *v.* Bochussalih, bochussachih, chassulah, kofussah; warped, bochokuchih, bochussah, chassulah. kofussah; to cause to warp, chassaluchih, kofussachih; not warped, ikchassuloh; a weaver's warp, upi. ponola upi; warping bars, ponola aholptcchi, ponola ahotachi, woof ponolah isht tunna, isht tunnah.

Wart, *n.* Shalukwa.

Was, *v.* Tuk, tok; surely was. chahlih; was there, kamo, kumo.

Wash, *v.* Achefah; washed, achefah, ulhchifah; to wash the head, aiehlih; a washer woman, ohoyo nan achifa; to wash one's self, ilachifah; unwashed, ikachefoh; face not washed, ikokamoh; to wash the face, okamih; to wash the face at or in, ai okamih; a wash pan, ai okami a wash tub, ai achefa. itl kolofa, nan ai achefa; washed clothes, nun ulhchifa.

Wasp *n.* Chanushshik, chushshik; black wasp or dirt dauber. tekhanto; large red wasp, chanushshik homma; striped wasp, koalabi; yellow jacket, nakni foi.

Waste, *v.* Isht yopomoh, okponih; wasted, okpulo; wasteful. isht yopomo shohli.

Watch, *n.* Hushi kanulli isht ikhona, hushi isht ikhona; watch chain, hushi konulli isht ikhona ishtallakchi; watch key, hushi kanulli isht ikhona isht ashania a watch maker, hush isht ikhoun ikbi; to watch, atonih,apistikelih,aicechih,apesuchih; a watchman, atoni, nan apistikeli, ngpisa, hopokoyoh; watchful, hopokoyoh shahli.

Water, *n.* Oka;not water,oka keyu;no water, oka iksho; good water, okachukma, bad water, oka okpulo; sweet water, oka chumpuli; sour water, oka haushko; cold water, oka kapossa; warm water, oka libeaha; hot water, oka lushpa; red water, oka homma; yellow water, oka lakna; black water, oka lusa; clear water, okshawgli, oka tawgli, oka tawgli, oka shohkaugli; bad smelling water, oka shuwa;sweet smelling water. oka;balama, fresh water, oka hinona; hard or limestone water, oka takba; like water, oka ohmi; back water, oka bikeli, oka fulama; high water, okchito; deep water, oka hofobi; shallow water. oka ikhotobo, oka hofobi keyu, okchuwoha; rain water, oka umba; river water, bok oka; creek, brook or branch water, bok ushi oka; spring water, kuli oka, salt water, hupi oki; sea water, okhcba oka; slack water, oktimpi; boiling or hot spring water, oka wahiulli; sulphur, oil or medicinal waters, oka alikchi; well water. kuli hofobi oka; frozen water, oka kalampi; ice, okti; icicles. akalupi takohli; eddy water, okfoyulli; a pond of water, baiyip. okutuch; a pool of water, aiyupi; a lake of water, okhota; a sea or ocean of water, okhota chito; a gulf of water, okhota shokuibi; the fountain head of water. aminte, kuli, bok atiaohli ibetup, wishakchi; a stream of water, ayanulli, okhina. hucna. bok, bok ushi, okhinushi, oka abachaya; mouth of a stream of water, bok asetili asetili; overflow of water. oka mitafa; a whirl pool of water, oka fuyohu; a hole of water, oka chuluk; heavy water, oka weki; strong water, (whiskey)

oka homi; Tom Fuller (tifula) water, oka holoshka; water having a fishy smell, oka nuk shobi; water in a vessel, oka talaiya; a place for water. oka ai asha; a place to get water, oka ai ohchi. ai ochi; ripple of water, oka banotha. water rapids, yanelli kullo; a water fall, cascade or cataract, oka chopa; in or under water, okangkaka; a water spout, oka abicha, oka abnhili; on the other side of water, oka mishtunnup, oka misha, water that is fordible, okabinka; water not fordible, oka nowa hekeyu; lying in water, oka bachaya; water gruel, okchani, asholck chabahg; water proof oka ikhlopullo; to put into water, akuchi, oka akuchi; to mix with water, okomih; to fall into water, okettulah; to swim in water, oka. okpulalih, oka okshinilllih, oka okyullih. to drink water, oka ishkoh, oka nanapiih; to swallow water. oka nullih; swallowing water, oka ngbgllih; to draw water through a faucet, oka bichilih; drawn, oka bicha; to drive into water, oka kenchih; to hold over water, oka o wehlih; holding over water, oka wiebiih; to wet with water, oka isht luchulih;to make water,oka toba; top water, oka pakngli, oka pakna, oka pak naka; waterman, pini isht gya; watermelon, shukshi; watery, chubohbih, okchushbah; water tight, oka ikhlopulloh.

Wattle, *n.* Wulakuchi, ǀ wulakuchi, impaktl.

Wave, *v.* Bunukuchih, faholichih, banuthuchih fahlih; to cause to wave, bunutkuchichih, fahakuchichih; to wave in the air, fahlolih; a wave, bunuthah; waved, fahah; waving, fahakuchauchi, ponkahanchi: wavering, faioka hauchi, ai utta ik ithuno.

Wax, *n.* Ifititili; wax of the ear, haksobish hlitilili; bees wax. foi hakmo; shoe maker's wax, puno kullo isht ahama.

Way, *n.* Aigya, anowa; the way to go, ai in; mid-way, iklunna; the mid-way of the inside, anukka ikiunn: this way, et auet: to appear this way, et baiyakah; to call out this way, et luhpalah: to whoop toward this way, et tusahah; a narrow way, hina ik putho; by way, hina takla, takla: that way, pimma, (point direction when you say, pimma;) long way off, pillah: going every way, putulichih; between or on the way, takla: to way lay, aiichih, aiyichih.

We, *pro,* E as e takchi, we tie, hupi,as hupi nusih; we sleep, hupi talachih; we are tied, hupia, as, hattak upi homma hupia hoke; we are Indians, bupishno; that you and all of us, pi, piah, il, as, il iah, we go.

Weak, *a.* Ik hlampko, kullo keyu, tikambih, tikabbih, kanliksho, ikhomo; to weaken, ikhomechoh; to be weak, hotah; weakly, hlampko keyu.

Wealth, *n.* Nan ǀ lawa; wealthy, holitompa

Wean, *v.* Pishi issuchih; weaued pishi issah.

Weapon, *n.* Nghaluppa, nan isht itibih.

Wear, *v.* Folikah: a wearer. fohka; to wear out, hliplih; worn out, hlipa; to be worn out, hliput toha; to wear a strap or sash on sholder; hunawelik.

Weary, *a.* Hoyubli, tikahbi· to weary: hoy-ubiichih: wearied. hoyublih, kotah; to be weary, hoyaplih, tikahbih; wariness, hoyapli.

Weather, *n.* Kucha; good weather, kucha achukma; bad weather, kucha okpulo; cold weather, kucha kapussa; warm weather kucha libesha.

Weave, *v.* Natunah tunnih; weaving, natunah: a weaver, natuna' tuna; woven, tunnah.

Wedge, *n.* Tuli isht puhlah; to wedge, akullochih; to wedge in, shamullichih.

Wednesday, *n.* Witniste, winsti.

Weed, *n.* Haiyukpulo, uiba; to hoe or weed aislih; weed seed, haiyukpulo nihi.

Week, *n.* Nittak hul·o. wik; last week, nittak hullo ash: week before last, nittak hullo atuklakash; next week, nittak hullo atuklakma nittak hullo atukla; weekly, nittak hullo aiyuka.

Weep, *v.* Yayah, yaiyah; to cause to weep, yayuchih; weeping, nishkin okchi mihiti.

Weevil, *n.* Hapulak, tauchi shalunkuchi; weevil eatan, shuluka.

Weft, *n.* Isht tunna.

Weigh, *v.* Wekichih; continually weighing, wekihichih; weighty, weki; weighed, wekih; weights, weki isht uihpisa.

Welcome, *v.* Ai okpanchih; unwelcome, ikai okpancho; a welcomer, ai okpuchi; to cause to welcome, ai okpuchichih.

Weld, *v.* Ulbochih, ittalakmochih, ittakmochih; welded, ulboh; to weld together, ittulbochih, welded together, ittulboh.

Well, *n* Kuli hofobi; all well, achukma asha; still well, achukma moma, achukmaka; well known and definite, chokusho chokush osh, well? (this or that) hakcho, akcho; mighty well, fiehna; to make one well hlakoffichih, masalichih; to be weli, hochukma, imachukma; to get well, masalih, talakyffih; to be well nau i kanihmih keyu; very well, (when the same. as yes) ome! well! it may be (so, but it is new to me) omiha! well! I (calling attention) ome, omishke; very well, (when admitting it to be right) uihpesa.

Wen, *n.* Shatohpa.

Wench, *n.* Ohoyo haul; a negro weuch, battak lusa, ohoyo haul.

West, *v.* Hushi aiokatula: hushi ai okatulaka; western or westward, hushi ai okatulaka; westerly; hushi ai okatula imma; hushi ai okatula pilah; a long way west, hushi ai okatukla pillah; a west wind, hushi ai okatula imma et mahli; western folks, hushi ai okatula okla.

Wet, *n.* Lucha, lacha, hotobi: to wet, luchalih; to be wet, luchah; wet ground, hlatimo; I am wet, saluchah.

Whale, *n.* Nuni chito okhuta osha.

Wharf, *n,* Peni aiatuya.

What, *pro.* Akcho, cho, ha, ho, hah. kush; what is it, hah? hai? nanta ho? what or how?katiohmi, nautah, natah: what then, ak muno, ak muto; somewhat· chohmi.

Wheat, *n.* Onush, howit; wheat bread, onush palushka.

Wheel, *n.* Chunaha; to roll a wheel, channichih; iron wheel, tuli chunaha; spinning wheel, ponola ashunnah, ahonola; fore wheels, chunaha tikba heli; hind

wheels, chunaha ulbul aka heli.

When, *ad.* Ka, katiohmikma, kauiohmikmi kash, na, okma, yokma, hokma, achikeh. akma, ak mak o; when is it, ak mak ocha, ak mak ona; whence, katima kanima.

Where, *ad.* Katima, kanima, muto; anywhere, kanima kia; no where, kanima keyu: not anywher, kanima hoh kevu; elsewhere, kanimakinli; some where, kanima: wherein, yummako; whithersoever, kanima yoh kia; wherefore, katiohmi, katiohmi ho.

Whet, *v.* Shohlichih, shuahchih, shublichih; whetting, shuhlihinchih; whet stone, tuli isht ashuahchih.

Whether, *pr.* akcho, katimampo, katima ko.

Which, *pr.* Kuta; which one, katim ampo.

While, *ad.* Takla, na; a short while since, ash, yash, hash, kash; a good while ago, chamo.

Whine, *v.* Bikbiah; a whine, bikbia; a whiner, bikbia.

Whip, *n,* Hlokata, isht fuma hlukata; whip lash, isht fuma wishakchi takali, hlokatu wishokchi takali; an ox whip, isht fuma chito; to whip. hlukahah, fummih; whipped, fumah; a whipper, hlukaha, hlukalichih; whipping, hlukalihinchih; to pop a whip, hlukalichi, hlukata olachi; sound of a whip, hlukata ola; to whip with a switch, tuli isht fummih; whipped, fuli isht fumah; a place for whipping, afuma; to whip while running, mokulichih; to whip with one stroke, tiplich; whipping, tippihah; riding whip, issuba isht fuma; wagon whip, isht fuma chito, whipping with a rod, teppihah; whippletree, iti okhowata.

Whippoorwill, *n,* Wohwulih, chukkilakbila.

Whirl, *v.* Fatahuchih, to whirl around, hunnanokih, fitihuchih; to cause a thing to whirl round and round, hunnanokichih; whirling, futahuchih, fafohlih; to whirl about, fitihah fafohlih: to whirl rapidly, fitihlichih; to whil with a stick, fatahuchih; whirling, fatahah: whirl pool, okafoyuha; whil wind, kpanukfila; whirligig, nan isht washohah.

Whisker, *n.* Nutakhish.

Whiskey, *n.* Oka homi: to sell whiskey, oka homi kanchih: a whiskey seller, oka homi kunchi.

Whisper, *v.* Woshobuchih: whispering, woshohuhanchih.

Whistle, *v.* Kontah, kuntah; whistling, hohotah

White *n.* Tohbi; to whiten, tohbichih: a bluish white, tohbokolih; a greenish white, tohbokkoli; a pale white, hanta, huta; to make a pole white, hantuchih; whites, hutah ont iah: to turn white, hutachih: a yellow white, huta lakna; to color a yellow white. huta laknanchih; a white man, na hullo; a white woman, nahullo ohoyo; I am white, tatohbih; I am a white man, nahullo sia.

Who, *pro.* Kutah; whoever, kuna hohkia.

Whole, *a.* Bonoh, momah; wholly, bonoh, momah.

Whoop, *v.* Tasahlih, tussahah, whooping, tasahahlih, tasahah; whooped, tasahah;

to whoop at, apahlichih; to whoop toward this way, et tusahah; awar whoop, hoyopa tassuha; whooping cough, hotilhko fjka.

Whortleberry, *n.* Shiupha, yuhlo. a huckleberry bush, shiuphupi; a winter huckleberry, aksak ohchi.

Why, *ad.* Katihma, nantihmi, nakatimi, atukǫ.

Wicked, *a.* Haksi, tasimbo, okpulo; to act wickedly, isht akanomi; wickedness, ai ulhpesa keyu, ai okpulo.

Wide, *a.* Putha, auatah, hoputha, katupah; widley, hopakichit; to be broad or wide, hopulbkah; width, hopulhka; to widen, puthuchih, auatuchih; scattered wide apart, shachahah; to scatter wide apart, shachabulih; to spread the legs wide apart, wakchalulih; toowide, wakchah to widen out, yatuplih, yatupachih; widened, yatupah; to stand with the feet wide apart, yuttulah.

Widow, *n.* I hattak illi; widower, tekchi illi.

Wife, *n.* Tekchi; my wife, satekchi.

Wiggletail, *n.* Hattak chukush upa; wigwam, hattak upi homma in chukka.

Wild, *a.* Nukshopa; to be wild, honayoh; wildness, honayo; not wild, ikhonnayoh; wild cat, shakbutina; wilderness, baiaka, yakni hulaka kǫwi.

Will, *v.* Aiahni wil, shall or will, hinla, chike.

Willingness, *a.* Ai okpanchi achukma; unwilling, ai okpanchi keyu.

Willow, *n.* Tukǫbishshah, tukǫwishah.

Wilt, *v.* Bushih; to cause to wilt, bushichih; wilted, bushih; not wilted, ikbushoh.

Win, *v.* Im ubih; to win back, okbah.

Window, *n.* Okhisushi, okhisa ushi; window, blind. okhisushi isht okshillihta okhisushi aiakmo: window glass, apissah. apisa, kashofa; window curtain, okhisushi, i holmo: window sash, apisa kashofa ai ulbiha; a glass window, apisa kashofa okhisushi.

Windpipe, *n.* Ikolupi, kolumbish.

Wine, *n.* Oka pǫki; wine glass, oka pǫki ai ishko; wine bibber oka pǫkisnko.

Wing, *nr* Na sanihchi, sanihchi.

Wink, *v.* Mochuklih, okmoshlih, mushmolih; winking, mochuklih; continually winking, mochukmolih, mochuhǫklih.

Winnow, *v.* Amahlih. amahlichih; a place to winnow. amolichih.

Winter, *n.* Hushtula, onafa; wintery, hushtula chohmi; the first of winter, hushtula ummona. onafahpi; to winter, hushtula antoua hlopuljih.

Wipe, *v.* Kashofih; to wipe off, kasholichih, kihlih; to wipe on, akashotichih, akashoflih; to wipe self, ilekusholichih, wiped, kashofah; a wiper, nan isht kasholichih..

Wire, *n.* Tuli fabussa, wire fence, tuli fabussa hulihta.

Wisdom, *n.* Hopoyuksa; to cause wisdom, hopoyuksalichih; having wisdom, isht hopoyuksaka.

Wise, *a.* Hopoyuksa, kostini; to be wise, hopoyuksoh; not wise, ikhopoyuksoh, hopoyuksa keyu; to make wise, hopoyuk-

sachih, hopoyuksalichih; I am wise, sakostiuih.

Wish, *v.* Bunnah, polummih, ahnih; wishful, bunnah anakfilli; a wish, bunna, wishing, polumah.

Witch, *n.* Aholhkunno, ohoyo aholhkunno isht ahullo; a wizzard, hattak ahalhkunno, hattak holhkunna, hattak ahnlhkunna, hattak yushpokummi; a witch, ohoyo yushpakummi. to bewitch a man, hattak yushpakummih; a man bewitched, hattak yushpakuma; witchcraft, hulhkunna, ikhish isht yuhpakama; a hobgoblin or witch, kashikanchak, kashikanchak; a place at whitch to become a witch, ai isht ahullo; to place at which to make another a witch, ai isht ahollochih.

With, *pro.* Ishit, isht ibai tǫkla iba awaut, itta.

Wither, *v.* Bushshih bilakhlih; withered, bushshi, bilakhlih; not withered, ik bushshoh; withered, shullah; withers; ya wushka.

Witness, *n.* Aiatokowa, nan anoli; to witness together, ittibapisah.

Wolf, *n.* Nashoba, wolf county, Nashoba kaunti.

Woman, *n.* Ohoyo; a young woman, ohoyo himitta; young women, ohoyo himithoa; a pretty woman, ohoyo pisa achukma; a married woman, hattak awaya; a single woman, hattak ikawayoh; a good woman ohoyo achukmah: not a good woman, ohoyo achukma keyu; a white woman, nahullo ohoyo; a choctaw woman, chahta ohoyo; a negro woman, hattak lusa ohoyo; a worthless woman, ohoyo ikahobo; a poor woman, ohoyo ilbusha. an old woman, ohoyo sipokni, kasheho; my woman, umohoyo: his woman, im ohoyo: your woman, chim ohoyo.

Womb, *n.* Ushuto,

Wont, *a.* Chokumo.

Wood, *n.* Iti; fire wood. iti ulhti, iti olulhti; woods, kǫwi, iti anuka, yokni haiaka; wood chuck, shanoktukosh, shanishttukoshi; wood cock, issinia pichechi; wooe pecker. tikti, chakchuk; red head wood pecker, bakbak; smaller redhead wood pecker, chilantak; a small speckled wood pecker, biskihik; the common wood pecker, hushi iti chanli; rotten wood, iti toshbi; hard wood, iti kullo; to chop wood, iti chalih; iron wood, iyanubbi; dry wood. iti shila; honey comb wood, shal akpa.

Woof, *n.* Ishtunna, ponalash isht tunna.

Wool, *n.* Chukfi;hishi lambs wool, chukfushi hishi; woolen cloth, chukfi hishi nantunna, chnkfi hishi tuna; woolen goods, chukfi hishi nantunna toba; woolen yarns, chukfi hishi shunni; home spun woolen yarn, chukfi hishi ilapint shunna; home spun woolen goods, chukfi hishi ilapint tunni; a wool sack, hishi ai ulhto; "niggar" wool, hattak lusa pashi; wooly, wuksho; to make wooly, wukshuchih.

Word, *n.* Anumpa; one word, anumpa achuffa; a sound or good word, anumpa ai ulhpesa; only a word, anumpa banoh; a new word, anumpa himona; a word maker, anumpa ikbi; topass many words. anumpa itti lawachih; a word of some

sort, anumpa kaniohmi; a word of no
sort, anumpa kaniohmi keyu; short
words, anumpa kolohli; an oath or hard
word, anumpa kullo; wordy, anumpah
lawa; an old word, anumpa tikba; the
first word, anumpa tikba takanlih,
anumpa ummona; to make a word,
anumpa ikbih; God's word, Chitokaka
im anumpa.

Work, *v.* Toksulih, pilesah; to mak work.
toksalichih; to work or ferment, as liquid
chobokuchih; to work with, itabatok-
salih, isht toksulih; working with, iba-
toksalih; to make me work, satoksali-
chih; a work house, chukka atoksuli; a
workman, ai iskiachi, nan isht utta; a
worker, nan isht utta, hattak nạ pilesa.

World, *n.* Yakni, yakni chunaha folota
hattak moma, yakni moma; the world
above, uba yakni.

Worm, *n.* Shụshi; tape or grub worm,
lupchn; a hairy worm, (that destoys
hides) shokutti; glow worm, hulba, angle
worm or fish worm, lupchu; silk worm,
silik shụshi; tobacco worm, hakchuma
shụshi; small worms that affect children,
hushowush hushwush; worm wood,
hushun.

Worry, *v.* Anumpulechih, ataklununih.

Worse, *a.* Okpulo į shahli, okpulo fehna,
okpulo į shaht tahli, okpulot taha; to
make worse, aiyubichih, made worse, ai
yubbih.

Worship, *v.* Holitoblichit ai okpachih ai
okpuchih; a place at which to worship,
aholitoble; worshipping ai okpahanchih;
worshiper, ai okpuchi, hlipint ittula; to
cause to worship. aiokpuchichih; wor-
shipful, ai okpuchi ulhpesa.

Worthy, *a.* Holitopa, ulhpesa: worthily,
holitoput; worthless, ikahoboh.

Would, *pv.* Hetuk; would have, hinla tuk;
would be very, fehna hinla; would have
been, chin tok, chin tuk.

Wound, *v.* Nuhlih; to wound at, anulhhlih
wounded, nuhlah; wounding continually
nuhạhlah; the place where wounded.
anuhlah; feelings wounded, chụkush
hotopalih; to wound. honuhlih; wounds
of various kinds anuhla, alitowa, ai
okfạya, ahoa, achạya, abaha, abushau, to
wound in various ways, bushlih, chanlih
bolih, litolih; wounded, bushah, chạyah
nuhlah, boah. litowah.

Wrap, *v.* Bonullih; wrapped up, bonuntah;
to wrap up, ubonullih, ubonullichih.

Wrath, *n.* Isht į nukkilli, ai į nukilli;
wrathy, nukbobela, nukoa shạhli,

Wren, *n.* Okchiloha; small wren, chikchik.

Wrestle, *v.* Ittishih; to wrestle with me,
satishih.

Wretch, *n.* Hattak okpulo; wretched.
ilbusha, ikahobo.

Wriggle, *v.* Fatahuchih; wriggling, futahuchih.

Wirng, *v.* Bushlih; not wrung, ikbushloh.

Wrinkle, *v.* Shikoffih, shinifih yikifih;
wrinkled, shikifah shikofah, yikịfah, a
wrinkle, shikofa.

Wrist, *n.* Ibbak iska; wrist joint,
ibbakf tillokuchi ibbak ittachakuli;
wrist band, ibbak arohoma.

Write, *v.* Holisnochih; continually write-
ing, holissohouchih; a writer, holissochi;
to write upon, ọholissochih; wrote or
written, holisso.

Wrong, *a.* Yoshoba, ashuchi, okpulo.

Y

Yam, *n.* Yum, ahekushạha.

Yard, *n.* Holịhta, wanuta, kusbihiyi tuchina; to put in a yard, holihta fohki; a
yard stick, isht ulhpisa, nan isht ulhpisa.

Yarn, *n.* Chukfihishi honnola, chukfi hishi
puna nashuna, home; spun yarn, chukfi
hishi ilupint shunna; one hank of yarn
chukfi hishi ittupuna achuffa: to spin
yarn, chukfi hishi shunnih; spun yarn,
chukfi hishi shuna.

Yawn, *v.* Hawa.

Year, *n.* Afummih; yearly, afummi aiyu
kalih; a yearling, afummi: to go over one
year old, atunuplichih; over one year old
atunupa; this year, himak afummi; next
year, afummi atukla; afummi atuklakma
new year's day, afummi himona nittak;
last year, afumash.

Yell, *v.* Tahpulah; yellow jaoket, yakni į
fal,

Yellow, *n.* Lakna; to turn yellow, ataknah,
alaknochih; to make yellow, laknuchih;
made yellow, laknuttuha; yellow hammer. fitukhak.

Yelp, *v.* Wobwah, wohlichih.

Yes, *ad.* Ah, omi, yau, į įh, ukah; yes indeed, ụkah; yesterday, pilashash, pila-

sha kash.

Yet, *con.* Hokakạno, immomah, kịsha,
moma, kị; not yet, keyu kịsha: not there
yet, ikaiono kịsha; not come yet, iklo kị.

Yoke, *n.* Abunalih, abunkachih, yok fokih
yoked, yok fokah; an ox yoke, wak toksuli ikonla abana, yok.

Yonder, *a.* Yummah pillah.

You, *pro.* Chi, chia, chishno; to you chim,
chishno: you not, chik; yourself, chishno
akinli; because to vou, chishno yọka;
you are, chishno yokut; you (plural).
huchia, huchisno; not you, huchik.

Young, *a.* Himitta; to make self young,
ilehimittachih; I am young, sahimittah:
somewhat young, himittah chobmi: very
young, himittosi; to make young, himitt-
uchih; to be young, himittah.

Youth, *n.* Himmittah, youthful, himmittah.

Your, *pro.* Chin chị, chin huchị huchim,
huchim huchimmi, huchishno yoka;
yours, chimmi, chisno; yourself, chishno
akinli; to become yours, huchimmi toba;
yourselves, huchishno akinli, huchishno
akint, huchishno akinli hosh; because
it is yours, huchishno yokạ.

Z

Zeal, *n.* Aiyiminta, achilita, amoshuli; zealot, hattak ai yiminta; zealous, achilita, yiminta, chilita; to cause to be zealous, achilituchih, ai yimitachih; to be zealous, ai yimitah, determined or zealous, chukush yiminta; not zealous, ik-ayimintoh, ikchilitoh.

Zenith, *n.* Tubokaka.

Zephyr, *n.* Hushi aiokatula imma et mahli.

Zigzag, *a.* Yayakih; to cause a zigzig, yayakichih.

NUMERALS.

1. One, Achuffa.
2. Two, tuklo.
3. Three, tuchina.
4. Four, ushta.
5. Five, taihlapi.
6, Six, hannali.
6. Seven, untuklo.
8. Eight, untuchina.
9. Nine, chakkalih.
10. Ten, pokoli.
11. Eleven, auahchuffa.
12. Twelve, auahtuklo.
13. Thirteen, auahtuchina,
14. Fourteen, auahushta.
15, Fifteen, auahtahlapi.
16. Sixteen, auahhannali.
17. Seventeen, auahuntuklo.
18. Eighteen, auahuntuchinoh.
19. Nineteen, ahbichakkalih.
20. Twenty, pokoli tuklo.
21. Twenty one, pokoli tuklo akucha acuffa
22. Twenty two, pokoli tuklo akucha tuklo
23. Twenty three, pokoli tuklo akucha tuchina.
24. Twenty four, pokoli tuklo akucha ushsta.
25. Twenty five, pokoli tuklo akucha tahlapi.
26. Twenty six, pokoli tuklo akucha han-

nali.
37. Twenty seven, pokoli tuklo akucha untuklo.
28. Twenty eight, pokoli tuklo akucha untuchina.
29. Twenty nine, pokoli tuklo akusha chakkali.
30. Thirty, pokoli tuchina.
40. Forty, pokoli ushsta,
50. Fifty, pokoli tahlapi.
60. Sixty, pokoli hannali.
70. Seventy, pokoli untuklo.
80, Eighty, pokoli untuchina,
90. Ninety, pokoli chakkali.
100. One hundrek, tahlepa achuffa.
200. Two hundred, tahlepa tuklo.
300. Three hundred, tahlepa tuchina.
400. Four hundred, tahlepa ushta.
500. Five hundred, tahlepa tahlapi.
600. Six hunkred; tahlepa hanuali.
700. Seven hundred, tahlepa untuklo.
800. Eight hundred, tahlepa untuchina.
900. Nine hundred, tahlepa chakkali.
1000, One thousand, tahlepa sipokni achuffa.
2000. Two thousand, tahlepa sipokni tuklo.
1.000.000. One million, tahlepa sipokni bat tahlepa sipokni achufa.

Ordinal Numbers.

1st. First, tikba.
2nd. Secoud, atukla.
grd, Third, atuchina.
4th. Fourth, aiushta.
5th. Fifth, isht tahlapi.
6th Sixth, isht hannali.
7th. Seventh, isht untuklo.
8th. Eight, ish, untuchina.
9th. Ninth, isht chakkali.
10tb Tenth, isht pokoli.
11th Eleventh, isht anahchuffa.

12th. Twelfth, isht auahtuklo.
13th Thirteenth. isht auahtuchina.
14th. Fourteenth, isht auahushta.
15th. Fifteenth, isht auahtahlapi.
16th. Sixteenth, isht auahhannali,
17th. Seventeenth, isht auahuntuklo.
18th. Eighteenth, isht auahuntuchina.
19th. Nineteenth, isht ahbichakkali.
20th. Twentyteth, isht pokoli tuklo.
21st. Twentyfirst, pokoli tuklo isht akncha achuffa.

APPENDIX.

CONJUGATION

—OF—

TWO TRANSITIVE VERBS:

Buy,—Chumpah.   Sell,—Kanchih.

INDICATIVE MOOD, PRESENT TENSE—INDEF-
INITE

1st per. sing., I buy, Chumpa li.
"   "   I sell Kanchi li,
2d "   "   You buy, Ish chumpa.
"   "   You sell, Ish kanchi.
3d "   "   He or she buys, Chumpa.
"   "   He or she sells, kanchi.
"   dual They buy, i. e. two persons,
           chumput okla.
"   "   They sell   "   "
           kanchit okla.
1st per. plu, We buy, E chumpa.
"   "   We sell, E kanchi.
"   "   We all buy, Eho chumpa.
"   "   We all sell, Eho kanchi.
2d "   "   You buy, Hush chumpa.
"   "   You sell, Hush kanchi.
3d "   "   They buy, Oklat chumpa. or
               Chumpa.
"   "   They sell, Oklat kanchi, or
kanchi.

PRESENT TENSE, DEFINITE AND   C.

1st per. sing. I am buying, Chumpa lishke.
"   "   I am selling, Kanchi lishke.
2d "   "   You are buying, Ish chum-
               pashke.
"   "   You are selling, Ish kanch-
               ishke.
3d per. sing. He or she is buying, Chum-
              pashke.
"   "   He or she is selling, Kan-
              chishke.
"   dual They are buying, Chumput
           oklushke.
"   "   They are selling, Kanchit ok-
              lushke.

1st per. plu. We are buying, E chumpa-
               shke.
"   "   We are selling, E kanchi-
               shke.
"   "   We are buying, Eho chum-
               pashke.
"   "   We are selling, Eho Kanch-
               ishke.
2d "   "   You are buying, Hush chum-
               pashke.
"   "   You are selling, Hush kanchi-
               shke.
3d "   "   They are buying, Oklat
               chumpashke.
"   "   They are selling, Oklat kan-
               chishke.

PRESENT TENSE—EMPHATIC.

1st per. sing. I do buy, Chumpu li hoke.
"   "   I do sell, Kanchi li hoke.
2d "   "   You do buy, Isht chumpa
               hoke:
"   "   You do sell, Ish kanchi hoke.
3d "   "   He or she does buy, Chumpa
               hoke.
"   "   He or she does sell, Kanchi
               hoke.
"   dual They do buy, Chumput ok-
           la hoke.
"   "   They do sell, Kanchii okla
               hoke.
1st "   plu. We do buy, E chumpa hoke.
"   "   We do sell. E kanchi hoke.
"   "   We all do buy, Eho chumpa
               hoke.
"   "   We all do sell, Eho Kanchi
               hoke.
2d "   "   You do buy, Hush chumpa
               hoke.

" " You do sell, Hush kanchi hoke.

3d " " They do buy, Oklat chumpa hoke, chumpa hoke.

" " They do sell, Oklat kanchi hoke.

PAST TENSE—IMMEDIATE OR RECENT.

1st per. sing., I bought, I have bought, chumpulituk.

" " I sold, I have sold, Kanchi li tuk.

2d " " You bought or have bought, Ish chumpa tuk.

" " You sold or have sold, Ish kanchi tuk.

3d " " He or she bought or has bought, Chumpa tuk.

" " He or she sold or has sold, Kanchi tuk.

3d " dual They bought or have bought, Chumput okla tuk,

" " They sold or have sold, Kanchit okla tuk.

1st " plu. We bought or have bought, E chumpa tuk.

" " We sold or have sold, E kanchi tuk.

" " We all bought or have bought Eho chumpa tuk.

" " We all sold or have sold, Eho kanchi tuk.

2d " " You bought or have bought, Hush chumpa tuk.

" " You sold or have sold, Hush kanchi tuk.

3d " " They bought or have bought, Chumpa tuk, oklat chumpa tuk.

" " They sold or have sold, Kanchituk, oklat kanchi tuk.

PAST TENSE—REMOTE

1st per. sing. I bought or have bought. Chumpali tok.

" " I sold or have sold, Kanchili tok,

By changing tuk to tok all the numbers and persons can be conjugated.

PAST TENSE—EMPHATIC.

1st per. sing. I did buy (it was so), Chumpali tuk oke.

Add oke to the number and persons for the rest of these two forms of the past tense.

FUTURE TENSE—IMMEDIATE AND DEFINITE.

1st per. sing. I shall or will buy, Chumpa la chi.

" " I shall or will sell, Kanchi la chi,

2d " " You shall or will buy, Ish chumpa chi.

" " You shall or will sell, Ish kancha chi.

3d " " He or she shall or will buy, Chumpa chi.

" dual They shall or will buy, Chumput okla chi,

" " He or she shall or will sell, Kahcha chi.

" dual They shall or will sell, Kanchit okla chi.

1st " plu, We shall or will buy, E chumpa chi.

" " We all shall or will buy, Eho chumpa chi.

" " We shall or will sell, E kancha chi.

" " We all shall or will sell, Eho kancha chi.

2d " " You shall or will buy, Hush chumpa chi.

" " You shall or will sell, Hush Kancha chi.

3d " " They shall or will buy, Chumpa chi, oklat chumpa chi.

FUTURE TENSE—REMOTE AND INDEFINITE.

1st per. sing. I shall or will buy, Chumpa la he.

" " I shall or will sell, Kanchi la he.

By changing chi to he all the numbers and persons can be conjugated.

FUTURE TENSE—REMOTE,

Strongly expressing purpose, and used in an imperative sense.

1st per. sing. I will buy, Chumpa lashke.

" " I will sell, Kanchi lashke.

2d " " You will buy, Ish chumpashke.

" " You will sell, Ish kanchashke,

3d " " He or she will buy, Chumpashke.

" dual They will buy, Chumput Oklashke.

" " They will sell, Kanchit oklashke.

1st " plu We will buy, E chumpashke.

" " We will sell, E kanchashke.

" " We all will buy, Eho chumpashke.

" " We all will sell, Eho kanchashke.

2d " " You will buy, Hush chumpashke.

" " You will sell, Hush kanchaske.

3d " " They will buy, Chumpashke, oklat chumpashke.

FUTURE TENSE—EMPHATIC.

1st per. sing. I shall or will buy. Chumpa la chi hoke.

" " I shall or will sell, kanchi la chi hoke.

In the same way add hoke or oke to the other persons, in all the numbers—they are one and the same, and are simply changed to preserve the euphony.

POTENTIAL MOOD—PRESENT TENSE.

1st per. sing. I can or may buy, Chumpa la hinla.

" " I can or may sell, Kanchi la hinla.

2d " " You can or may buy, ish chumpa hinla.

" " You can or may sell, Ish Kancha hinla.

3d " " He or she can or may buy, Chumpa hinla.

" " He or she can or may sell, Kancha hinla.

" dual They can or may buy, Chumput okla hinla.

" " They can or may sell, Kanchit okla binla.

1st " plu We can or may buy, E chum-
    pa hinla.
" " We can or may sell, E Kan-
    cha hinla.
" " We all can or may buy, Eho
    chumpa hinla.
" ' We all can or may sell, Eho
    kancha hinla.
2d " plu You can or may buy, Hush
    chumpa hinla.
" " You can or may sell, Hush
    Kancha hinla.
3d " " They can or may buy, Oklat
    Kanchahinla, chumpa hinla.
" " They can or may sell, Oklat
    Kancha hinla.

PAST TENSE—IMMEDIATE OR RECENT.

1st per. sing. I might or could have
    bought, Chumpa la hinla
    tuk.
" " I might or could have sold,
    Kanchi la hinla tuk.
2d " " You might or could have
    bought, Ish Chumpa hinla
    tuk.
" " You might or could have sold,
    Ish kancha hinla tuk.
3d " " He or she might or could
    have bought, Chumpa hin-
    la tuk.
" dual They might have bought,
    Chumput okla hinla tuk.
1st " plu. We might have bought, E
    chumpa hinla tuk.
" " We might have sold, E Kan-
    cha hinla tuk.
" " We all might have bought;
    Eho chumpa hinla tuk.
" " We all might have sold, Eho
    kancha hinla tuk.
2d " " You might have bought,
    Hush chumpa hinla tuk.
" " ' You might have sold, Hush
    kancha hinla tuk.
2d " " They might have bought,
    Oklat chumpa hinla..
" " They migkt have sold, Oklat
    kancha hinla.

PAST TENSE—REMOTE.

1st per. sing. I might or could have bought,
    Chumpa la hinla tok.
" " I might or could have sold,
    Kancha la hinla tok.
By changing tuk or tok all the numbers
and persons can be conjugated and translated as above.

PAST TENSE SECOND FORM—IMMEDIATE.

1st per. sing. I was abought to buy, Chum-
    pa la chin tuk.
" " I was about to sell, Kanchi la
    chin tuk.
2d " " You were about to buy, Ish
    chumpa chin tuk.
" " You were about to sell, Ish
    kancha chin tuk.
3d " " He or she was about to buy,
    Chumpa chin tuk.
" " He or she was about to sell,
    Kancha chin tuk.
3d " dual They were about to buy,
    Chumput okla chin tuk,

" " They were about to sell.
    Kancha chin tuk.
1st " plu. We were about to buy, E
    chumpa chin tuk.
" " We were about to sell, E kan-
    cha chin tuk.
" " We all were about to buy,
    Eho chumpa chin tuk,
" " We all were about to sell, Eho
    kancha chin tuk.
2d " " You were about to buy, Hush
    chumpa chin tuk.
3d " " They were about to buy,
    Chumpa chin tuk.
" " They were about to sell, Kan-
    cha chin tub.

PAST TENSE. SECOND FORM—REMOTE.

1st per. sing. I was about to buy, Chumpa
    la chin tok, etc.
By changing tuk to tok, all the numbers and
persons can be conjugated and translated
as above.

PAST TENSE, THIRD FORM—IMMEDIATE.

1st per. sing. I should or would have
    bought, Champa la he tuk.
" " I should or would have sold.
    Kanchi la he tuk,
2d " " You should or would have
    bought, Ish chumpa he
    tuk.
" " You should or would have
    sold, Ish kancha he tuk.
3d " " He or she should have
    bought, Chumpa he tuk.
" " He or she should have sold,
    Kancha he tuk.
" dual They should have bought,
    Chumput okla he tuk.
1st " plu We should have bought, E
    chumpa he tuk.
" " We should have sold, E kan-
    cha he tuk.
" " We all should have bought,
    Eho chumpa he tuk.
" " We all should have sold, Eho
    kancha he tuk.
2d " " You should have bought,
    Hush chumpa he tuk.
": " You should have sold, Hush
    Kancha he tuk.
3d " " They should have bought,
    Chumpa he tuk.

PAST TENSE, THIRD FORM—REMOTE.

1st per, sing. I should or would have
    bought, Chumpa la hi
    tok.
By changing hetuk to hitok, all the numbers
and persons can be conjugated and translated as above.

FUTURE TENSE.

1st per. sing. I can or may buy, Chumpa
    la hinlashke.
1st " " I can or may sell, Kanchi la
    hinlashke.
2d " " You can or may buy, Ish
    chumba hinlashke.
" " You can or may sell, Ish Kan-
    cha hinlashke.
3d " " He or she can or may buy.
    Chumpa hinlashke.
" " He or she can or may sell.

FUTURE TENSE—2ND FORM REMOTE.

1st per sing., If I shall or will buy, Chumpa li hokmut.
" " If I shall or will sell, Kanchi li hokmut.
2nd " " If you shall or will buy, Ish chumpa hokmut.
" " If you shall or will sell, Ish kanchi hokmut.
3rd " " If he or she shall or will buy, Chumpa hokmut.
" " If he or she shall or will sell, Kanchi hokmut.
" " If they shall or will buy, Chumpoh okla hokmut.
" " If they shall or will sell, Kanchih okla hokmut.
1st per plu., If we shall buy, E chumpa hokmut.
" " If we shall sell, E kanchi hokmut.
" " If we all shall buy, Eho chumpa hokmut.
" " If we all shall sell, Eho kanchi hokmut.
2nd " " If you all shall buy, Hush chumpa hokmut.
" " If you all shall sell, Hush kanchi hokmut.
3rd " " If they all shall buy, Oklat chumpa hokmut.
" " If they all shall sell, Oklat kanchi hokmut.

FUTURE PERFECT TENSE—IMMEDIATE,

1st per sing., If I shall have bought, Chumpa la hinla tukmut.
" " If I shall have sold, Kanchi la hinla tukmut.
2nd " " If you shall have bought, Ish chumpa hinla tukmut.
" " If you shall have sold, Ish kancha hinla tukmut.
3rd " " If he or she shall have bought, Chumpa hinla tukmut.
" " If he or she shall have sold, Kancha hinla tukmut.
" dual, If they shall have bought, Chumpoh okla hinla tukmut.
" " If they shall have sold, Kanchih okla hinla tukmut.
1st " plu., If we shall have bought, E chumpa hinla tukmut.
" " If we shall have sold, E kancha hinla tukmut.
" " If we all shall have bought, Eho chumpa hinla tukmut.
" " If we all shall have sold, Eho kancha hinla tukmut.
2nd " " If you all shall have bought, hush chumpa hinla tukmut.
" " If you all shall have sold, Hush kancha hinla tukmut.
3rd " " If they all shall have bought, Oklat chumpa hinla tukmut.

PAST TENSE, 2ND FORM—REMOTE.

1st per sing., If I can or may buy, Chumpa la hinla tokmut.
" " If I were about to buy, Chumpa la chin tokmut.

" " If I should h ve bought, Chumpa la he tokmut.

IMPERATIVE MOOD, PRESENT TENSE.

1st per sing., Let me buy, Ak chumpa.
" " Let me sell, Ak kanchi.
2nd " " Buy, Chumpa.
" " Sell, Kanchi.
3rd " " Let him buy, Ik chumpa.
" dual, Let them buy, Chumput ikokla.
1st " plu., Let us buy, Ke chumpa.
" " Let us all buy, Keho chumpa.
2nd " " Buy you, Ho chumpa.
3rd " " Let them buy, Oklat ik chumpa.

FUTURE TENSE,

Not definite as to time, and is used as the future indicative; not to express bare futurity of action, but a purpose.

1st per sing., Let me buy; I will buy, Chumpa lashke.
" " Let me sell, I will sell. Kanchi lashke, etc.

A verb transitive with prefix personal pronouns in the indicative mood, present tense.

1st per sing., I see him, her, it or them, Pisa li.
" " I see you, Chi pisa li.
" " I see you, (plural), Huchi pisa li.
2nd " " You see him, her, it or them, Ish pisa.
" " You see us, Ish pi pisa.
" " You see them, etc., Okla ish pisa.
3rd " " He or she sees me, sa pusa.
" " He or she sees you, Chi pisa.
" " He or she sees him, her or it, Pisa.
" " He or she sees us, Pi pisa.
" " He or she sees us all, hupi pisa.
" " He or she sees you, (plural), Huchi pisa.
" " He or she sees them, Pisa or okla pisa.
3rd " dual, They see me, Sa pisut okla.
" " They see you, Chi pisut okla.
" " They see him, her or it, Pisut okla.
" " They see us, Pi pisut okla.
" " They see us all, Hupi pisut okla.
" " They see you (plu.) Huchi pisut okla.
" " They see them, Okla pisut okla.
1st " plu. We see you E chi pisa.
" " We see him, her or it, E pisa.
" " We see you, (plu.), E huchi pisa.
" " We see them, Okla e pisa.
" " We all see him, he, it or them, Eho pisa.
2d. " " You see me, Hussa pisa.
" " You see him, her or it, Husb pisa.
" " You see us, Hush pi pisa.
" " You see them, Okla hush pisa.
3d. " " They see me, Oklat sa pisa, sa pisa.
" " They see you, Chi pisa.

Kancha hinlashke.

3d " dual They can or may buy, chumput okla hinlashke.

" " They can or may sell, Kanchit okla hinlashke.

1st " plu We can or may buy, E chumpa hinlashke.

" " We can or may sell, E kancha hinlashke.

" " We all can or may buy, Eho chumpa hinlashke.

" " We all can or may sell, Ehŏ kancha hinlashke.

2d " " You can or may buy, Hush chumpa hinlashke.

" " You can or may sell, Hush kancha hinlashke.

3d " " They can or may buy, Oklat chumpa hinlashke.

" " They can or may sell, Oklat kancha hinlashke.

SUBJUNCTIVE MOOD, PRESENT TENSE—INDEFINITE.

1st per. sing. When I buy, Chumpa li mut.

" " When I sell, Kanchi li mut.

2d " " When you buy, Ish chumpa mut.

" " When you sell, Ish kanchi mut.

3d " " When he or she buys, Chumpa mut.

3d " duol When they buy, Chumput okla mut.

" " When they sell, Kanchit okla mut.

1st " plu When we buy, E chumpa mut.

" " When we sell, E kanchi mut.

" " When we all buy, Eho chumpa mut.

" " When we all sell, Eho kanchi mut.

2d " " When you buy, Hush chumpa mut.

" " When you sell, Hush kanchi mut.

3d " " When they buy, oklat chumpa mut.

SECOND FORM, IMPLYING A FUTURE CONTINGENCY.

1st per. sing. When I buy, if I buy, chumpa, likmut.

" " When I sell if I sell, kanchi likmut.

2d " " When you buy, if you buy, Ish chumpakmut.

" " When you sell, if you sell, Ish kanchikmut.

3d " " When he or she buys, if he or she buy, Chumpakmut.

" " When he or she sells, if he sell, Kanchikmut.

2d " dual When they buy, Champut oklakmut

1st " plu. When we buy, etc., E chumpakmut.

" " When we sell, etc., E kanchikmut.

" " When we all buy, etc., Eho chumpakmut.

" " When we all sell, etc, Eho kanchikmut.

2d " " When you buy, etc., Hush chanpakmut.

3d " " When they buy, etc., Oklat chumpakmut.

PAST TENSE—IMMEDIATE.

1st per. sing. If I bought, if had bought, Chumpa li tukmut.

" " If I sold, if I had sold, Kanchi li tukmut.

2d " " If you bought, if you had bought, Ish chumpatukmut.

" " If you sold, if you had sold, Ish kanchi tukmut.

3d " " If he or she bought, etc., Chumpa tukmut.

" dual If they bought, etc., Chumput okla tukmut.

" dual, If they sold, etc., Kanchih okla tukmut.

1st " plu., If we bought, etc., Echumpa tukmut.

" " If we sold, etc., E kanchi tukmut.

" " If we all bought, etc., Eho chumpa tukmut.

" " If we all sold, etc', Eho kanchi tukmut.

2nd " " you bought, etc., Hush chumpa tukmut.

" " If you sold, etc., Hush kanchi tukmut.

3rd " " If they bought, etc., Oklat chumpa tukmut.

PAST TENSE—REMOTE.

1st per sing., If I had bought, Chumpa li tokmut.

" " If I had sold, Kanchi li tokmut.

By changing tukmut to tokmut all the numbers can be conjugated and translated as above.

FUTURE TENSE—IMMEDIATE.

1st per sing., If I shall or will buy, Chumpa la chikmut.

" " If I shall or will sell, Kanchi la chikmut.

2nd " " If you shall or will buy, Ish chumpa chikmut.

" " If you shall or will sell, Ish kancha chikmut.

3rd " " If he or she shall or will buy, Chumpa chikmut.

" " If he or she shall or will sell, Kancha chimut.

" dual, If they shall or will buy, Chumput okla chikmut.

1st " plu., If we shall or will buy, E chumpa chimut.

" " If we shall or will sell, E kancha chimut.

" " If we all shall or will buy, Eho chumpa chikmut.

" " If we all shall or will sell, Eho kancha chikmut.

2nd " " If you all shall or will buy, Hush chumpa chikmut.

" " If you all shall or will sell, Hush kancha chikmut.

3rd " " If they all shall or will buy, Oklat chumpa chikmut.

" " If they all shall or will sell, Oklat kancha chikmut.

" " They see him, her or it, pisa.
" " They see us, pi pisa.
" " They see us all, Hupi pisa.
" " They see you all, Huchi pisa.
" " They see them, Oklat pisa-pisa.

A verb transitive with prefix possessive pronouns, in the indicative mood, present tense:

1st per. sing. I see him her or it for you, Chin pisa li.
" " I see him, her or it for him or her, In pisa li.
" " I see him her or it for us, Pin pisa li.
" " I see him, her or it for us all, Hupin pisa li.
" " I see him, her or it for you, (plu.), Huchin pisa li.
" " I see him, her or it for them, Okla in pisa li, in pisali.

2d " " You see him her or it for me, Is san pisa.
" " You see him, her or it for him or her, Ish in pisa.
" " You see him, her or it for us, Ish pin pisa.
" " You see him, her or it for us all, Ish hupin pisa.
" " You see him, her or it for them, Okla ish in pisa.

3d " " He or she sees him, her or it for me, An pisa.
" " He or she sees him, her or it for you, Chin pisa.
" " He or she sees him, her or it for him or her, In pisa.
" " He or she sees him her or it for us, Pin pisa.
" " He or she sees he him, her or it for us all, Hupin pisa.
" " He or she sees him, her or it for you.
" " He or she sees him, her or it for them, Okla in pisa.

1st " plu. We see him, her, or it for you, E chin pisa.
" " We see him, her, or it for him or her, Il in pisa,
" " We see him, her, or it for you, E huchin pisa.
" " We see him, her or it for them, Okla il in pisa.
" " We all see him, her or it for them; Iloh in pisa.

2d " plu. You see him, her or it for me, Hus san pisa.
" " You see him, her or it for him or her, Hush in pisa.
" " You see him, her or it for us, Hush pin pisa.
" " You see him, her, or it for us all, Hush hupin pisa.
" " You see him, her or it for them, Okla hush in pisa.

3d " " They see him, her or it for me, Oklat an pisa.
" " They see him, her or it for you, Chin pisa.
" " They see him, her or it for him or her, In pisa.
" " They see him, her or it for us, Pin pisa.
" " They see him, her or it for all, Hupin pisa.
" " They see him, her or it for you, Huchin pisa.
" " They see him, her or it for them, Okla in pisa.

SENTENCES TO ILLUSTRATE THE USE OF TRANSITIVE VERBS.

I see a man, Hattak o pisa li.
I sell a horse, Issuba ho kanchi li.
You sell a horse, Issuba ho ish kanchi.
You see a man, Hattak o ish pisa.
You see the man, Hattak a ish pisa.
You sell the horse, Issuba ha ish kanchi.
A man sells the horse, Hattak osh issuba ha kanchi
The man sells a horse, Hattak ot-issuba ho kanchi.
A man buys the cow, Hattak osh wak a chumpa.
The man sells a cow, Hattak wak o kanchi.
They buy the horse, Issuba ha chumpa.

NOUNS WITH ADJECTIVES AND VERBS.

Issuba achukma, a good horse.
Tanampo achukma fehna, a very good gun.
Ulla nakni achukma ho, a good boy who (is.)
You buy a bay horse, Issuba homma yo ish chumpa.
He walks in the path of peace, Hina hanta ya a nowa.
A good man is coming, hattak ahukma yosh minti.

THE PARTICLES,

These are the most difficult words in the language to arrange, understand, and define; a literal translation of them is not attempted. They are sometimes used when there is no corresponding word in English. They are generally used, and may be translated, as articles, pronouns, conjunctions and prepositions.

1st Articles, A, an, the. Second relatives, who, which, whom, that. Indefinite pronouns, some, some one, any, anyone. Double pronouns, he, who, she who, they who.

The following will exhibit some of the articles:

The Ak. hak, yak, amo; hamo, yamo: ash, hash, yash, ato, hato, yato, atok, hatok, yatok, atuk; hatuk, yatuk, okut, hokut, yokut. okuto, hokuto, yokuto, ot, hut, yut, uto, huto, yuto, ano, huno, yano, oka, hoka, yoka, okuno, hokuno, yokuno, a, ha, ya, ano, hano, yano, kak' kamo, kumo, kut, kuto, mak, mut, muto, ahamo, chash.

The particles, oke, hoke, yoke, are used after verbs. The particle shke, (pronounced skay), is suffixed to verbs, and to other words where the verb to be in English is understood.

NOTE.—The pronouns in Choctaw have no Third Person.